THE
TWILIGHT
ZONE

Rod Serling's

THE TWILIGHT ZONE

ADAPTED BY WALTER B. GIBSON

ILLUSTRATED BY EARL E. MAYAN

GROSSET & DUNLAP   Publishers   NEW YORK

LIBRARY OF CONGRESS CATALOG CARD NO. 63-18982

MANUFACTURED IN THE UNITED STATES OF AMERICA

FOREWORD

HERE IS A PARADE OF STRANGE, UNCANNY STORIES, all newly written and original in treatment. To give them authenticity, they have been based in varying degree upon well-recorded incidents or experiences in which many persons have sincerely and implicitly believed; particularly those who participate in weird events. As a result, these tales combine the elements of actuality and fantasy, putting them in that bourne where they so rightfully belong — The Twilight Zone.

A few classic cases have been told with stress on their original details, but with due effort to capture the moods of the individuals involved and to add the dramatic quality needed for their full appreciation. Mere narrative is often insufficient to portray the emotional reactions of those who are confronted by the unknown, or who find themselves boxed in that borderland of existence where it becomes impossible to distinguish the real from the unreal. Only by living those experiences with them — as you most certainly will in these pages — can it become possible to recognize what they really underwent.

Other traditions of ghostland have been developed in these stories with special emphasis on modern settings where they could very well occur. Incidents of similar nature have been incorporated to give them stronger impact; and every story has been carried to a plausible culmination, which is a far cry from the legendary tales that often disintegrated more rapidly and thoroughly than the evanescent phantoms who formed their principal characters. In short, the recognized factors found in cases of the uncanny have been treated as they could — or even might! — occur in everyday life, assuming that ghostly conditions do exist.

There is a singular fascination in these stories of the grotesque and unexplainable that combine the true with the incredible. This interest began in ancient times, as witness a famous story, by the Roman author Pliny, which involved the ghost of an old man complete with clanking chains. It became a dominant factor in the life of the Middle Ages, when warlocks and witches presumably roamed at will. It has reached a new peak through the efforts of modern psychic investigators to gain new insight on such subjects. All indications are that this field will expand in times to come.

This may seem surprising in that it forms a link between the superstition of the past and the scientific progress of the future. But what is our modern learning other than a series of forays into the unknown, which grows to vaster and unbelievable proportions the farther we advance into that uncharted realm!

The ancient alchemists talked of transmuting lead to gold, only to be ridiculed by the chemists of a later day. Yet those first students of natural philosophy, as science was then called, would have derided any prophet who might have correctly predicted the wonders of nuclear physics that lay only a few hundred years ahead.

As for ghosts, there were skeptics a hundred years ago who laughed at stories of haunted rooms in the castles and manor houses of a century before. But if those same scoffers could have been projected to the present, they would have had their wits scared out of them if they had walked into a modern living room and seen a television set in full operation.

There is, of course, the question: where can we find solid ground for all this ghost stuff? The answer, already indicated, is: in the authenticity of the original accounts themselves. It does not matter whether a reported occurrence was magnified or distorted. That goes on in our newspapers every day, yet we still accept the things we read as facts. Day after day, people who swear in courtrooms that they will "tell the whole truth and nothing but the truth," come up with statements so conflicting that only one can be right while the other must be wrong. Yet each person's testimony, if honestly given, is to some degree acceptable in the eyes of the law.

So it goes with psychic phenomena. All we need to know is whether a person who saw a ghost or heard ghostly sounds was sincere in his report. Then we know that, right or wrong, it was a phase of human experience. What it proves or disproves is not the immediate point. Something happened; that at least is established. Other persons believed — or disbelieved — what they heard; and out of that came some final conclusion, whether true or false. Still something happened, like the time an apple dropped from a tree and hit Sir Isaac Newton on the head. After wondering why the apple fell down instead of up, Sir Isaac propounded the Law of Gravitation. If instead, he had laid down a line of fine logic proving that neither he, the apple, nor the tree had ever existed, historians still would agree on one thing: somebody was hit on the head by something.

So it is with persons who claim they have seen ghosts. Somebody was hit by something; not on the head but *in* the head. Such is the impact of a full-fledged ghostly experience, the sort of "shocker" that turns a doubter into a believer. While such adventures may not be too happy in real — or unreal — life, one thing is certain. It is fun to read about them, as you will find out when you delve into the pages that follow.

CONTENTS

THE GHOST
OF
TICONDEROGA

THE GHOST
OF
TICONDEROGA

Donald Campbell, Laird of Inverawe, halted his horse on the steep hillside as he studied the scene below. At the bottom of the rugged roadway lay the green slope of a glen, where a silvery stream cascaded from thick woods to join the muddy river that wound its way through the well-tilled valley. Beyond the glen rose another hillside. Like the one on which Inverawe paused, it was studded with huge, odd-shaped stones and patched with clumps of purple heather.

Through the gap above the glen, Inverawe could see mountains rising like gigantic steps to the twin peaks of Ben Cruachan, which towered like mighty sentinels against the cloudy sky. Off in the distance, the struggling afternoon sunlight caught the blue glint of a deep-set loch, a narrow lake of the Scottish Highlands.

All that was beyond Inverawe's domain. He was master only of this winding valley, with its glen and skirting hillsides; and at that, his rights were scarcely more than a landowner's. But his heart lay far beyond, off amid those misty, ever-beckoning Highlands, where past and future blended in a timeless present and the wild freedom of Scotland ever seemed to dwell.

How often Inverawe would view that scene again was a question. For this was the summer of 1755, and war with France threatened the United Kingdom of England and Scotland. Already, reports of wilderness fighting in the outposts of America were causing war clouds to thicken over Europe; and Inverawe, as an officer of the Royal Highlanders, probably would be called for active duty. So it was with a pang of regret that he wrenched his gaze from the distant mountains, whose clouds seemed somehow ominous, and resumed his ride down to the glen. Then, as he raised his eyes in a parting glance, he caught sight of movement much closer by.

A ragged, furtive figure was dodging down the hillside, stopping at one rock, then another, as though to hide himself from something above, for he was continually looking back up toward the ridge. As Inverawe reined in his horse to watch, the man continued his frantic tactics, never realizing that he was being observed from below, until he was almost at the road. Then the fugitive stopped in sheer fright at sight of the horseman blocking his path. He seemed about to dive for futile shelter in the heather; then desperation evidently gave him sudden decision. Stumbling forward, he raised his quivering hands in frantic appeal.

4

"Help me!" the man gasped. "Save me, before they overtake me! My life is at stake!"

"Who are you?" Inverawe parried. "An escaped prisoner? Or an outlaw?"

"Neither. It all grew from an argument in a tavern. There was a brawl and I killed a man. But it was in fair fray. I swear it, on my honor as a MacNiven!"

"A fair fight, you say?" rejoined Inverawe. "Then why not give yourself up to the law?"

"Because blood avengers are on my track," MacNiven insisted hoarsely. "They would kill me on sight! That I do not doubt."

Nor did Inverawe doubt it.

He could tell that MacNiven had been in a fight. The fellow's face was bruised and his clothes were blood-stained from wounds more severe than scratches from the brambles that had torn them. Tavern brawls were frequent in the surrounding villages, and the participants became vengeful if any of their friends were hurt. For nearly ten years, all Scotland had been seething with hotheads and malcontents, following the final effort of Charles Edward, the Stuart Pretender, to regain the British throne then occupied by George II.

Inverawe himself had been engaged in that struggle, but on the side of King George. He had fought at Culloden against some of the Highland clans whose names he respected. And afterward, he had secretly sheltered and protected some of those very rebels, rather than have them fall prey to the vengeful English. So for the moment, MacNiven's pleas were reaching sympathetic ears.

"You must save me!" MacNiven pleaded. "I'm giving myself up to you. You can't let them kill me like a dog."

Inverawe weighed the plea; then agreed:

"I can hide you for a few days, long enough to make sure that you will be given a fair trial."

"But there can be no fair trial hereabouts—"

"In that case, I shall send you safely on your way."

"You will swear to that?"

"Aye, on the word of an Inverawe, which never yet has been known to fail friend or foe."

Inverawe's promise braced MacNiven, who ·realized that he had met the laird of this locality. Inverawe, close to middle age and a man of commanding appearance, was the sort whose word would stand. But now, MacNiven's fearful glances up the hillside told that he expected pursuers to appear upon the brow at any moment. Again, he pleaded:

"You must hide me quickly, Inverawe. But where?"

"Down in yon glen," returned Inverawe. "Hurry there, while I watch for pursuers and divert them if need be."

"But they will scour the glen and find me there—"

"Not where I intend to hide you. Get down there and wait."

MacNiven bounded full speed down the road. Inverawe waited until he had almost reached the glen. Then, since no pursuers had appeared, the laird rode down and joined the fugitive. Inverawe tethered his horse and guided MacNiven on foot up the slope beside the tumbling stream. A great hush lay beneath the overhanging fir boughs, which cut off the sunlight and produced a weird gloom that added to MacNiven's terror, but Inverawe was too occupied to notice it. Near a high rock, he indicated a tiny rivulet that came down a steep embankment and ordered:

"Follow me up beside this burn; and stay close."

MacNiven clambered close behind his guide and it was well he did, for above the bank, Inverawe turned sharply and was swallowed by a thicket of evergreens. MacNiven pressed through and found Inverawe waiting beside a low, overhanging ledge.

"Under there," the laird said, "you will find a safe hiding place. By dusk, I shall be back with food for you. So in you go."

MacNiven stooped to look beneath the ledge.

"Why, it's no larger than a fox hole!" he exclaimed. "How can a body hide in there?"

"Two bodies did," returned Inverawe. "One was William Wallace and the other Robert Bruce. That was four hundred years ago, and the secret of this hiding place has been handed down from one Laird of Inverawe to the next, ever since. So until now, I alone knew of its existence."

"But if others should find it, they would turn this fox hole into a fox trap," protested MacNiven. "I am no Wallace — nor a Bruce —"

"That I know," interposed Inverawe, a ring of sarcasm in his tone. "They were brave Scots; perhaps there are no longer any like them. But my ancestors gave refuge to those who needed it, and they, in their turn, kept the secret. I offer you safety, on those same terms."

As MacNiven still hesitated, Inverawe stooped beneath the ledge and slid feet first into a narrow hole that slanted down between the rocks. He was swallowed bodily from view, until his voice came hollowly from the depths:

"Follow me down here!"

Encouraged, MacNiven followed and found Inverawe in a high-roofed cave that arched beneath the steep slope of the glen. From there, Inverawe led MacNiven to an inner cavern, where a pool of clear water trickled down into the rocks.

"All the spring water you need," the laird told the fugitive. "I shall bring food later, as I promised."

Inverawe squeezed his stocky bulk up out through the fox hole and started down to the path. As he looked back, he saw MacNiven's wan, nervous face peering from beneath the ledge; but he darted quickly from sight as both men heard distant shouts and the muffled barking of dogs, indicating that pursuers were approaching the glen. They had gone by, however, when Inverawe reached his horse, which was patiently waiting for him. So he mounted and rode on around the next hill to his mansion, which stood surrounded by outlying farm buildings.

There, Inverawe found a villager named Drummond awaiting him.

Twitching his cap between his hands, Drummond announced: "We're tracking down a murderer, Laird, so while the rest went on ahead, I waited here to tell you. Your cousin, Ian Campbell—well, Laird, you see it was like this—"

Inverawe smiled knowingly. His cousin Ian was several years younger than he, but the two were as close as brothers. Ian, bold, dashing, quick to accept any challenge, was just the sort who would be leading the hunt for a murderer. Inverawe could understand why the villagers were so close on MacNiven's trail, if Ian had roused them.

"You mean you have a message for me from my cousin Ian?"

"Aye, in a way, yet not exactly so." Drummond halted, twisting his cap worriedly. "My message is *about* your cousin. It was Ian who was murdered, and in cold blood, sir! Since the slayer headed this way, we thought you should be on the watch for him —"

Drummond broke off. The color had left Inverawe's face and his body swayed as from a sudden shock. Drummond, knowing nothing of Inverawe's meeting with MacNiven, attributed the laird's stunned silence solely to the news of Ian's death. Excusing himself, the villager hastened off to rejoin the search party, leaving Inverawe alone outside his front door.

Long minutes passed; then Inverawe, like a man in a trance, entered the house and made his way numbly to the kitchen. The servants, like the members of the family, who had already heard the news, discreetly stayed away, feeling that the laird would want to be alone with his grief. So Inverawe did, but he had a duty first. In the kitchen, he cut slabs of cold mutton and thick slices of cheese, which he wrapped with flat, round buns called scones. That done, Inverawe stabled his horse and taking a lantern along with the bundle of food, walked back through the gathering dusk to the already darkened glen.

There, he lighted the lantern and made his way to the cave, where he called to MacNiven. The fugitive recognized the laird's voice and came to the mouth of the cave to receive the bundle of food. The darkness of the cave was not sitting well with MacNiven, whose voice came in almost a whimper:

"You can't leave me alone here — it's fearful —"

"As it should be," Inverawe replied coldly, "for a man with blood on his hands. I promised you shelter — nothing more."

"But how will I know when the way is clear?"

"Tomorrow I shall bring more food and tell you if the search has ended. Then you would do well to go your way before I regret my promise."

Grimly, Inverawe made his way from the glen, extinguishing the lantern as he emerged into the moonlight. From behind him, the whisper of the wind-swept firs, the ripple of the burn, sounded like strange, taunting voices. On the way back to the mansion, he had a feeling that he was being followed; and at intervals, he swung quickly about, wondering if MacNiven, the murderer, had become suspicious and bold enough to stalk him from the cave.

But only the weaving trees, the hulking contours of the hills, eerie shapes in themselves, were visible in the moonlight. Soon the white walls of the farm buildings loomed like welcoming specters; then the stone mansion itself, with darkened windows. Inverawe entered and went straight to his own room; there, propped in bed, he tried to sleep, but the events of the afternoon disturbed him.

7

The meeting with MacNiven, the oath that Inverawe had so unwittingly taken, the fact that his own cousin, Ian, was the slayer's victim, all carried a touch of fate that stirred his Highland imagination. Half aloud, Inverawe muttered, "I wonder if the like of this has happened before!" Then, to put the question to the test, he lighted a pair of candles on the table beside him and chose a book from the shelf above. The volume contained the prophecies of Coinneach Odhar, a famous Highland seer of the century before, many of whose predictions had been fulfilled during the years between.

As Inverawe delved through the musty pages, an odd thing first annoyed him, then puzzled him. It was the repeated wavering of the candle flames. It couldn't be due to a draft from the hallway, for the door was tightly shut. The window was open, but not a breath of air was stirring outside, as Inverawe could tell from the tree leaves, which were as motionless as if frozen by the silvery moonlight. Yet the flickering continued, and with it, Inverawe felt a weird, chilling sensation that caught the tempo of his heartbeats. Then, as he tried to shake off the feeling and return to his book, a shadow slowly stretched across the page.

Inverawe looked up, and the icy throbs faded as his heart warmed with sudden joy. Beside the bed stood his cousin, Ian Campbell, studying him with a fixed, solemn gaze. Ian, here — and still alive! Welcoming words sprang from Inverawe's lips, only to fade as quickly. In the flickery light, Ian's face was as waxen as the candles themselves, except for streaks of blood that came from his clotted blond hair, down his cheeks and chin to the open neck of his torn jacket. There, Inverawe saw great knife gashes across Ian's throat and chest. Any one of them would have been sufficient to have caused his death, for his jacket, too, was all gory.

Ian's lips barely moved as he spoke in a hollow tone:

"Shield not the murderer, Inverawe! Blood must be shed for blood!"

As Inverawe blinked in disbelief, Ian's image faded. This could be no dream, for Inverawe was wide awake. And now all he saw were the white walls of the room, the closed door, and the open window with the trees beyond; everything exactly as it had been before. Strained, shaken, he snuffed out the candles and tried to go to sleep.

With morning, Inverawe was morose. His family said nothing about Ian's death; and he, in turn, kept silence. The hunt was on again for Mac-Niven, who had last been seen heading over the hill and was thought to be boxed in this area. Inverawe rode out on his horse and ran into Drummond with a group of uniformed fencibles from a neighboring village.

"Take care if you meet up with MacNiven, Laird! With blood already on his hands, he will not stop at another murder. He is a desperate man — and dangerous!" Drummond warned.

Desperate, MacNiven might be, but more fearful than dangerous. Cannily, Inverawe inquired:

"This tavern fight between Ian and MacNiven. Was it a fair one?"

"Aye, it might be said so," Drummond admitted grudgingly. "But only because Ian was quick to turn about before MacNiven could dirk him in the back, as he would have, gladly. MacNiven won because he had the longer knife, though he fought fair when Ian forced him to it. But we'll not hold that in MacNiven's favor, once we find him. He'll die like the dog he is!"

They were closing in upon the glen, to scour it as MacNiven had feared and as Inverawe had anticipated. Later in the day, Inverawe joined the searchers there, carrying a knapsack with him. He knew that they would never find the secret cave, and when they had finally gone, Inverawe climbed to the cave and quietly called MacNiven, who came cautiously from the fox hole.

"Here's food again," announced Inverawe, "But I can shield you no longer. They have searched the glen, so you now are free to escape as best you can."

"But what if they are still close by?"

"That will be your concern. I shall come here again tomorrow. If you are gone by then, good riddance. If not, you will have overstayed your time and you must take the consequences."

Inverawe left the glen and returned home, satisfied that he had done his duty both toward his unwelcome guest, MacNiven, and the uninvited ghost of his cousin Ian. At dinner, the laird was more his usual self. His family — which included a son not quite of age — was relieved by the way he had taken Ian's death. But as the evening went by, Inverawe began to brood anew.

Had he done right to grant further refuge to MacNiven? Or should he have obeyed the order of Ian's ghost? Torn between his oath and his duty, Inverawe decided that tomorrow might hold the answer. He went to bed, but before snuffing out the candles, he reached for the book of prophecies again, wondering how much it had influenced him. As he glanced through the pages, the candles flickered as before, and a shadow crept across the opened volume.

Inverawe looked up slowly. Again, he saw the figure of his cousin Ian, and from those slow-moving lips came the same accusation:

"Shield not the murderer, Inverawe! Blood must be shed for blood!"

"But I have talked with MacNiven today," Inverawe whispered. "He is no longer under my protection. Yet you still demand that blood must be shed for blood!"

Inverawe's own words echoed from the surrounding walls, as though Ian had repeated, *"Blood must be shed for blood!"* But that could not be, for again the ghost was gone and Inverawe was blinking in the candlelight, the book between his tight-clenched hands.

In the morning, Inverawe had breakfast with his family. Then, quietly, determinedly, he set out for the glen. Today, he carried no slices of mutton, no slabs of cheese, no scones. Beneath his tunic, he took a dirk, the longest in his collection of trophies from the battlefields where he had fought. Oath or no oath, if he found MacNiven there still, he intended to bury that weapon in the cringing murderer's flesh, the vengeance Ian wanted.

But the cave was empty. The slayer had gone — and so had Inverawe's troubles. Back home again, the laird listened quietly while his family spoke of Ian's funeral, to be held in the kirk beyond the hills on the following day. That night, Inverawe was ready for sleep. He felt that with MacNiven gone, Ian's ghost surely must be satisfied. Then, to satisfy his own whim, Inverawe decided to finish reading a passage from the prophecies of Coinneach Odhar, the Highland seer. He turned to a page and read:

"On one occasion, the seer was passing Millburn, where he noticed the old mill, a very primitive building, thatched with divots. Speaking to the mill, he said: 'The day will come when thy wheel shall be turned for three successive days by water red with human blood, for on the banks of thy pond, a fierce battle shall be fought at which much blood shall be spilt.' This prophecy is waiting to be fulfilled."

Inverawe paused in his reading and exclaimed aloud:

"But it has been fulfilled since this book was written! I know that mill, for it is close by Culloden, where the Duke of Cumberland scattered the Pretender's army. Aye, much blood was spilt there — much blood —"

Inverawe's words trailed as the candles flickered and a shadow fell across the page. Inverawe looked up to see the ghost of Ian Campbell, its face as pale, its body as gory as before. From the ghostly lips came a croak:

"Aye, much blood shall be spilt! Now, there can be no other way. I told you, Inverawe, shield not the murderer. Blood must flow for blood."

"But I am not shielding him," protested Inverawe. "He has gone his way, at my order."

"With blood still on his hands," came the stern answer. *"Blood that must someday be avenged. I warned you twice, but you did not heed me. Now, it is with your own blood that you must pay. Once more we shall meet, Inverawe: then you shall pay."*

"But where —"

"We shall meet again at Ticonderoga. Remember, Inverawe. Ticonderoga. . . ."

The word trailed away even as the figure vanished, and Inverawe, not knowing whether to be dismayed or relieved, found himself repeating the strange name uttered by his cousin's ghost:

"Ticonderoga — Ticonderoga."

With morning, Inverawe and his family journeyed to the village where the body of Ian Campbell lay in state, a tragic victim to the murderer Mac-Niven, who somehow had escaped from the very midst of the avenging clans. Inverawe, though steeled to the sight of death, felt misgivings when he viewed his cousin's body. Ian's face, though recognizable, was chalk white; his hair was still matted from his head wounds, while his cheeks showed faint blood streaks. Even the gashes from the murderer's dirk were visible above the victim's collar line. Surely, then, it *must* have been the ghost of Ian Campbell who had three times appeared in Inverawe's bedroom, to utter an ominous prophecy that could be summed in a single word: Ticonderoga.

After the funeral, Inverawe found time to ask Drummond and others who had witnessed the fatal fray if they had ever heard Ian speak that name. They shook their heads. Once back home, the laird kept repeating "Ticon-

10

deroga" in frequent undertones, until he noticed that his family and friends were studying him with worried glances. Then, one day, in a sudden fervor, he told his story to those he trusted most: his wife, his oldest son, one faithful servant whom he had known since boyhood; and a neighboring laird who had known Ian Campbell well.

All agreed that Inverawe had acted according to his proper lights. As for Ian's ghost, they hinted that it might have been the product of Inverawe's shock at hearing of his cousin's death, plus his own strained imagination. But they did not hint too strongly, for like Inverawe, they had the Highland tradition in their blood. A ghost—real or unreal—could not appear thrice without a definite mission. Gradually, though, they discounted the ghostly message because no one had ever heard of a place called Ticonderoga and probably no one ever would. They said as much, hoping Inverawe would brood no longer.

But Inverawe brooded all the more. During the autumn, he rose among the hills, stopping to view the distant mountain mists above the fir-speared glen that now seemed so ominous. During the long winter nights, he sat silently before the crackling fire. With the approach of springtime, those who knew his secret wondered what would happen when he roamed the old familiar terrain and reawakened those tragic memories of the year before.

Then came good fortune, at least for Inverawe. The war with France flamed into actuality. Inverawe's regiment, the Forty-second, was called to the colors. The Laird of Inverawe left his native heath and, as Major Donald Campbell, embarked for America with his troops, landing in New York in June. From there, the regiment was sent to Albany, New York, where British forces were being assembled for the proposed invasion of French Canada.

Frustration followed, for all except Inverawe. While the French and Indians were attacking settlements, faint-hearted British commanders kept calling for reinforcements, fearing they were too few to fight back, though they actually outnumbered the foe. Two years passed, with homesick Highlanders yearning either for action or return to their homeland.

Inverawe wanted action, but even without it, he preferred America to Scotland. He knew that a return to the Highlands would strike him with remorse as deadly as the dirk MacNiven had used to murder Ian. Beneath the laird's grim exterior was a deep-felt sentiment toward the cousin whose death he had failed to avenge. Still through his mind throbbed those ghostly words: *"Inverawe, we shall meet at Ticonderoga. Blood must be shed for blood."*

Reports of Indian massacres, treachery on the part of both French and British, the terrors and sufferings of helpless American settlers, all left Inverawe cold. He was ready to face any hardship or torture, rather than be reminded of an oath that had bound his hands when they should have delivered the vengeance that blood-ties demanded.

One man alone understood. That was Inverawe's son, who had joined the regiment in America as a junior officer. Often, when they chatted with officers in Albany and tales of massacres were related, Inverawe would come out of his reverie and listen intently to the names of the places that they mentioned. There was Oswego, which meant "the pouring out of waters" and Oneonta, "the stony place." There were others like Nowadaga, "where mud

turtles dwelt" or Canajoharie, "the bowl that washes itself," which referred
to a pothole in a river gorge.

All those names and many more had the lilt of the name which was
constantly in Inverawe's mind, but which he never heard: Ticonderoga. Nor
did he mention it, though often his face turned grim when he lapsed into
a reflective mood.

At last, in the summer of 1758, the expedition was ready for the invasion of Canada. An army of twenty thousand, the largest in the history of
America, was assembling under General Abercrombie. The Highlanders were
ordered to Fort Edward, near the upper end of Lake George. The officers
held a dinner at the Tontine Coffee House in Albany; and along with talk
of Scotland, there was mention of Indian names.

That combination roused Inverawe's memories to the bursting point.
"Have any of you heard of a place called Ticonderoga?" he asked suddenly.

The name was new to all the Scottish officers. All shook their heads.

"For two years now," declared Inverawe, "I have been expecting to
reach Ticonderoga, but no one seems to know anything about it. So I con-
cluded that it might be on our route to Canada."

"You'll find no Ticonderoga that way, Major," Colonel Grant, the commanding officer of the regiment, told him. "We start from Fort Edward;
thence to Lake George, so named in honor of our king, God save him. From
there, boats will take us thirty miles northward to the foot of the lake. There,
the French have fortified the stream leading from Lake George into Lake
Champlain."

"Do you know the name of the French fort, Colonel?"

"It is called Fort Carillon," returned Grant. "They have named it that,
according to our scouts, because it is close by a waterfall and the sound is
like a chime."

"And beyond Fort Carillon?" inquired Inverawe. "What then?"

"Beyond that, we shall reach Lake Champlain itself, a long but straight
route to the Richelieu River, which we shall follow into the heart of Canada."

"And still no Ticonderoga."

Inverawe's vague, faraway tone brought a narrowed gaze from Colonel
Grant. The other officers sensed something strange and listened intently when
Grant demanded:

"Where did you hear that name, Ticonderoga, Major? And from whom?"

Inverawe, studying the faces at the tables about him, felt an overwhelming urge to tell them all.

"I heard it in Scotland, from the ghost of a man who had never left
the Highlands!" he announced.

The flickering candles on the walls, the rough-hewn beams and darkened panels added to the drama as Inverawe launched into the tale that
explained his moodiness of the past two years. He told how he had met
MacNiven, the vow that he had given the murderer, the accusation uttered
by his cousin's ghost, and the prophecy of a future meeting at Ticonderoga.

The older officers sat silent when Inverawe finished. The younger ones
were half amused, expecting the story to turn into a joke; but when they
glanced at Inverawe's son, he gave them a warning gesture. Colonel Grant

caught the sign and eased the situation. With due solemnity, he raised his glass.

"A toast to Ticonderoga," he proposed, "if there is such a place. If not, let us drink to ourselves and success to our cause."

The next day, the Highlanders marched to Fort Edward. From there, they continued to Lake George and joined the army that was embarking in hundreds of large, flat-bottomed rowboats, some with supply rafts in tow. The army included red-coated English grenadiers, Colonial militia in varied uniforms, and green-clad rangers, who formed the advance guard and scouted the paths and landing places along the lake's thirty-mile shore.

While the Highlanders were being assigned to their boats, Colonel Grant was called to a meeting of General Abercrombie's staff. With him, the colonel took a young lieutenant to make any necessary notes. The orders concerned the disposition of the various troops when they reached the lower end of Lake George, but since that depended upon the positions held by the French, detailed descriptions were given of the terrain toward Lake Champlain.

Among the reporting scouts was an Indian of the friendly Mohawk tribe, who delivered a harangue that was translated, sentence for sentence, by a ranger who served as interpreter.

"The enemy has moved out from their fort," the ranger interpreted, "which is close to the place where the waters meet. They are expecting more men from Canada, so unless we attack them soon we can never drive them from their place between the lakes."

During the Indian's speech, Colonel Grant twice caught a word that was familiar. As the interpreter was leaving, Grant asked him:

"Can you repeat exactly what the Indian told you?"

"Why, yes. He said that the enemy has moved out—"

"No, no. I mean can you repeat it in the Indian's own tongue?"

The ranger reflected; then went into the language that the Indian had used. As he finished, Grant commented:

"Twice you used the word, Ticonderoga. What does it mean?"

"Either 'where the waters meet' or 'between the lakes,' which is about the same thing," explained the ranger. "That's what the Indians call the place where the French built Fort Carillon. Ticonderoga."

Colonel Grant turned to the young lieutenant beside him.

"Say naught of this to Major Campbell," the colonel warned. "Nor, for that matter, to anyone. After the story that the major told in Albany, it might shake their confidence. Even the boldest men become superstitious on the eve of battle."

That afternoon, the Highland regiment embarked as part of the vast flotilla that stretched half the length of the thirty-mile lake. Inverawe, looking from the bow of a whaleboat, was fascinated by the scene ahead. The long, narrow surface of Lake George had the glint of a Scottish loch, nestled amid woods and mountains. It impressed the other Scots the same way, but only Inverawe suffered pangs of regret when his thoughts harkened back to his native Highlands.

Others, watching Inverawe, guessed what was in his mind, but none made mention of it, least of all Colonel Grant. When the regiment encamped that night on a point that jutted from the west shore, Inverawe sat alone, still wrapped in thought, while the others chatted or sang songs of their homeland. Cannily, Colonel Grant did not even approach Inverawe, feeling that a chance remark or even a glance might bring up the name, Ticonderoga. If so, the colonel was sure that his own face might give some inkling of what he had learned.

With morning, a mist lay over the lake. It lifted gradually as the boats plied the smooth blue water, and new scenes of magnificence were revealed. In the distance, Inverawe saw rising mountains, some with craggy heights reminding him of the twin peaks of Ben Cruachan, a grim reminder of the very view that he had hoped to escape. Sad memories of his cousin Ian loomed stronger than ever, until, as the boat neared the end of the lake, the sound of gunfire turned his mind to action.

Upon landing, the Scots learned that the British advance force had driven back the French in a spirited skirmish, though not without serious losses of their own. That night, outposts were placed in the woods, and the next day the British advanced in greater numbers, forcing the French back to their earthworks on the slope leading up to Fort Carillon.

On the third day, General Abercrombie decided to drive the French from those defenses, so that he could besiege Fort Carillon and prevent Montcalm, the French commander, from receiving reinforcements. So instead of waiting to bring up cannon from rafts on Lake George, Abercrombie ordered a direct assault by the English Grenadiers and the Royal Americans, with Grant's Highlanders being held in reserve.

This did not please the Scottish regiment. Some of these dark-kilted veterans had belonged to the Forty-second when it had been known as the Black Watch and famed for its fighting qualities. So Colonel Grant conferred with various officers, advising them how to control their men if they became impatient. But he did not summon Major Campbell to any of these meetings. Of all the officers, Inverawe had been closest to his military duties, making such advice unnecessary.

The assault on the French earthworks resulted in disaster. The English regulars and Colonial militia encountered barricades of felled trees with sharp-pointed branches just short of the French trenches. While struggling with those obstacles, they were mowed down by French cannon and musket fire. Sight of such carnage would have restrained any reserves other than the Highlanders. Instead, it goaded them to action.

Without waiting for orders, they surged forward and their officers were unable to restrain them, for a very good reason. In the first wave that started up the slope was the commanding figure of Inverawe, going along with his men. Too late did Colonel Grant realize that discretion was not the greater part of the valor that inspired Major Campbell.

The barricades meant nothing to the charging Highlanders. As they reached the spiked abatis, they flung away their guns and hacked their way with claymores, huge two-edged swords with double-handed hilts. Some reached the French trenches, but they were too few to capture them, because by then, most of their companions had fallen under a hail of devastating fire.

Among those was Inverawe. His officer's uniform had made him the

14

chief target of Montcalm's marksmen. Close to the barricade, the brave major sprawled, with bullets in his legs and body. Despite his agony, he rolled to the shelter of a tiny hummock, where he looked ahead and saw the wave of Highlanders reach its crest and then subside under the pall of bluish smoke from the merciless French guns.

Inverawe gestured back to the rest, telling them to take to shelter, as he had. They obeyed, almost to a man, waiting to join the next wave of their fellow-attackers, not realizing that Inverawe himself would never arise for the assault. But Inverawe was thinking of his men alone; and when his eyes scanned the slope about him, he was amazed to see one figure standing close by, gazing down impassively, his whole form, with folded arms, half-veiled by the curling gunsmoke.

Propped on one elbow, Inverawe slapped his other hand against the turf as he gasped:

"Drop down, man — or you'll be a dead one —"

Then he broke off—for the man standing there was already dead. Though Inverawe's eyes were smarting from smoke and his gaze had dimmed from loss of blood, he knew that face. Chalk white, even to its lips, it was the ghostly face of Ian Campbell.

"*We meet again, Inverawe.*" There was no accusation in those words, though their tone was as solemn as a knell. "*We meet, as I promised — at Ticonderoga.*"

From Inverawe's parched lips came the gasp: "Ticonderoga!"

"*Aye,*" the ghost responded. "*You have paid the price for shielding a murderer. Blood has been shed for blood.*"

A sound interrupted. It was the drone of bagpipes, followed by shrill notes spurring the main body of the regiment to its next charge. Inverawe looked down the slope and saw the kilted figures of the Black Watch driving upward, the pipers among them, with men rising all along the way to join the new assault upon the impregnable French positions!

The shrill of the pipes was drowned by the roar of guns, accompanied by spurts of flame along the entire rim of the French defenses. Inverawe looked up into the thickening smoke that now was billowing down the slope and saw Ian's figure still standing there, dimming as in a mist. As bullets sang through the phantom form, hidden lips issued the parting words:

"*Farewell, Inverawe!*"

Next, Highlanders were charging up through that swirl, spreading the smoke where Ian's form had been, showing only vacancy there. Bullets now were taking toll, for Inverawe could see the attackers falling, two or more at a time, as they met the close-range fire from the French earthworks.

Further charges followed, all with disastrous results. In between were lulls, while the French reloaded and conserved their ammunition for coming assaults. During these respites, men crawled up the slope, gathered in their wounded comrades and carried them back to safety below. Then those same rescuers joined the next wave of attackers, only to be mowed down. There were four hours of this, until General Abercrombie finally ordered a retreat; but he was less stubborn than the attacking Highlanders. The command had to be issued three times, before they finally withdrew from the slope where slaughter reigned.

Among those carried to the boats was Inverawe. There Colonel Grant found him, suffering from mortal wounds. Before Grant could speak, Inverawe understood what lay behind the colonel's saddened gaze. A glint showed in Inverawe's eyes, as he declared:

"*This* is Ticonderoga. You must have learned it somehow, Colonel. That is why you were avoiding me."

"It is," Colonel Grant admitted. "But how did you find out?"

"Because I saw him once again, the ghost of my murdered cousin Ian. He told me we would meet at Ticonderoga — and we did."

More than three hundred members of the Highland regiment were slain in that battle, Inverawe's own son among them. Several days later, Inverawe himself died of his wounds, fulfilling the ghostly prediction. On the very verge of death, he was heard to mutter: "Blood shall be shed for blood."

Such was the story of the prophetic ghost, seen thrice in Scotland; then, for the last time, three years later, at Ticonderoga. So it has come down through the years, as attested by Inverawe's family and friends. At the time he described the ghostly visitations that occurred at his home in Scotland, and mentioned that odd word, Ticonderoga, the French had not even begun to build Fort Carillon at the place which only the Indians knew by its native name.

As for Inverawe's final meeting with the ghost on the battlefield itself, that account was recorded by James Grant, lieutenant-colonel commanding the Forty-second Highland Regiment, who had heard it from the dying man's own lips.

But that was not all.

On the very day that the battle was fought at Ticonderoga in the backwoods of America, a distinguished Danish physician, Sir William Hart, was strolling with an English friend around the Castle of Inveraray, in Scotland. Against a sullen, clouded sky, they saw a strange mirage of fighting men in Highland uniforms, engaged in a fierce battle. The doctor and his friend called to a Scottish servant, who stared in wonder at the gigantic images in the sky, many of whose faces he identified and called by name, groaning as he saw them fall.

That same amazing vision was reported by a young Scottish lady and her sister, who were crossing the new bridge over the Aray River on their way to Inveraray, when they chanced to look up at the sky. They, too, recognized many friends among the Highlanders, including Inverawe and his son, both whom fell as the astonished women watched the fantastic scene unroll itself.

Other persons also reported that strange sight in the sky. Added up, the accounts included a surprisingly large number of identified dead. Weeks later, bulletins arrived from America, confirming the tragedy of Ticonderoga almost to the final detail.

Perhaps the massed minds of the dying victims projected their agonized message to their Scottish homeland to prepare their kinfolk for the shock that was to come. Whatever the answer, if you have your doubts, don't mention them in the Scottish Highlands. There are people there who still believe in the ghost of Ticonderoga and the vision over Inveraray. What is more, they are likely to convince *you*.

BACK THERE

BACK THERE

The heavy April shower turned into a torrential downpour as the cab pulled up beside a red brick house on a quiet Washington side street. The driver studied the white double doorway with the dull bronze plaque beside it.

"Guess this is it, mister," said the cabby. "I can see the sign, even though I can't read it. You'll get soaked, though, if you try to make it in this rain."

Peter Corrigan thrust the fare into the cabby's hand.

"I'll chance it," Corrigan said. "Just wait until I make sure it's the right place. If it isn't, I'll hop back into the cab and we can try again."

Hatless, Corrigan pulled his coat up over his head and grabbed his suitcase as he left the cab. He dashed across the sidewalk and up the step to the shelter of the tiny portico above the double door. Wiping the rain from his eyes, he read the bronze plaque. It said:

POTOMAC CLUB

Founded

1858

Corrigan gave the cab a wave of dismissal and pounded the big brass knocker. No one answered; and now the cab was gone, while the terrific rain kept pelting in at a sharp angle, soaking Corrigan. Then, just as he was looking about for better shelter, the door was opened by a solemn, stoop-shouldered attendant in a faded blue uniform jacket with a dull, gold-braided collar.

"I'm sorry, but I didn't hear your knock, sir," the attendant apologized. "I was busy elsewhere. You must be Mr. Corrigan."

Then, as Corrigan nodded, the man added:

"I had no idea it had begun to rain so hard. Why, you're drenched, sir! Let me provide you with some other clothes while I have yours dried and pressed."

Crablike, he ushered Corrigan up a short flight of marble steps. They crossed a tiled foyer and as Corrigan looked back, he noted that the front door was out of sight below the curving stairs, so it was not surprising that the attendant had been unaware that it was raining.

Corrigan felt as though he had stepped into another world, here in the silence of the huge, high-ceilinged foyer of the Potomac Club, where even footfalls were hushed. Or rather, it could be a forgotten world, for Corrigan felt engulfed in a timeless atmosphere. Everything was old, from the antique light brackets that cast a dull glow on the carved, oak-paneled walls to the gilt-framed portraits that adorned them.

Even the pictured faces belonged to the past, as was evident from their stern expressions and their old-fashioned costumes. Yet they were like a gallery of living men as the attendant conducted Corrigan past them, each surveying the dripping newcomer with an air of disapproval. As Corrigan was ushered through a cloakroom, he looked back and had the uncanny feeling that he caught parting glances from the last portraits in the line.

The young man shuddered off a sudden chill. Whether it was induced by those painted eyes, or the dampness of his rain-soaked clothes, he wasn't sure. Then he was in a little dressing room where the solemn attendant opened a large wardrobe cabinet stocked with old-fashioned suits.

"I'm sure you will find your size, sir," the attendant told Corrigan, "if you don't mind wearing one of these old costumes. We keep them for official receptions, honoring the founders of the club. So you won't feel out of place—"

A voice interrupted, calling through from the cloakroom:

"William, you're needed in the lounge!"

Bowing, the attendant told Corrigan, "I'll be right back, sir."

Corrigan tried on a light blue suit with long-tailed coat and broad lapels. He rather liked the ruffled shirt front and shoestring necktie that formed part of the costume. As he combed his hair and studied the result in a full-length mirror, Corrigan grinned. This was certainly an excellent way of acclimating himself to these old-time surroundings.

A brilliant young astrophysicist, Corrigan recently had been accepted for membership in the Potomac Club, which especially welcomed men of scientific achievement. His sponsors were here, awaiting his arrival from New York on this first visit to the club. Corrigan was still chuckling at their probable reaction to his present getup, when William returned.

In the soft light of the dressing room, the attendant's face seemed suddenly youthful. Momentarily, his shoulders were erect and his uniform lost its faded look. Somehow, Corrigan remembered his face from somewhere, as though he had been an old friend. Then he decided that it must have been the sincerity of William's welcome; the nod of approval that the attendant now gave. For as William picked up Corrigan's suit with his left hand and draped it over his right arm, the attendant slumped back into his stoop-shouldered, wrinkle-faced self.

William conducted Corrigan out through the foyer, where the portraits now seemed less austere. From their expressions, they approved Corrigan in his present garb, and he still could not shake off the uncanny sensation that those were living eyes surveying him from the surrounding walls. At least, he was beginning to feel that he belonged to the Potomac Club, though the grip was uncomfortably tight.

William's voice broke Corrigan's reverie. With a sweep of his left hand, the attendant gestured Corrigan through a doorway, saying:

"Your friends are waiting for you in the Monument Room, sir."

Three men looked up from their table as Corrigan arrived. They were Roy Millard, noted researcher in the field of parapsychology; Louis Whittaker, the famous biochemist; and Zachary Jackson, dean of American historians. Millard and Whittaker were middle-aged professors, who took their work seriously and showed it. They stared at Corrigan in slight annoyance, until Dr. Jackson, elderly and with twinkling eyes, chuckled from deep in his gray-white beard and commented:

"We wondered when you would get here, Mr. Corrigan. From the theories Millard here has been expounding, we expected you to come whirring in from the future in a time machine. Instead, you have stepped from out of the past." He gestured to an old portrait that hung above the great stone fireplace. "Why, you look just like Bushrod Chichester, who founded the Potomac Club."

Smilingly, Corrigan explained that his cab had encountered a cloudburst coming in from the Washington airport and that William had supplied him with this temporary wardrobe to replace his own. That seemed to satisfy Professor Millard, who promptly returned to his pet theme.

"In your work, Mr. Corrigan," declared Millard, "you talk about breaking the sound barrier. I am trying to break the time barrier. It can only be done through a study of momentary relativity."

"And what," put in Whittaker, "is momentary relativity?"

"You should know," returned Millard. "You once took some time exposures so that a plant appeared to grow visibly, though it actually required a few months. You also made slow-motion shots of falling rose petals that barely seemed to drift downward. What if you put both on one synchronized film?"

"It would look as though the plant bloomed while the petals fell," replied Whittaker, "or the other way about, if you prefer."

"Let's consider people instead of plants," suggested Jackson. "According to your theory, Millard, our moments of comprehension contract and expand, so that sometimes things move so fast that they cause a mental blur, while at other times, they are painfully slow, as in a dream state."

"Exactly," nodded Millard. "That is momentary relativity."

"And you believe," persisted Jackson, "that people can project themselves into another time era, physically as well as mentally?"

"I do. When they reach a state of complete physical and mental inertia, induced perhaps by surrounding conditions, they break the time barrier, precipitating themselves into another sphere from which they may—or may not—return."

This was striking home to Corrigan, who already felt himself a misfit. From the moment he walked into the Potomac Club, he had seemed to be playing a part in an old-time drama that grew stronger as it progressed. Right now, he was engaged in a scientific discussion with an ultra-modern group, yet feeling as well as looking as though he belonged back in some earlier time. With something of a mental wrench, Corrigan snapped himself into the present.

"Suppose you went back in time to the day before the stock market's greatest crash, October 28, 1929," he said to Millard. "With your knowledge of what was due to happen, couldn't you have sold out before the prices fell?"

"Of course I could have," returned Millard, "and a lot of people did. That was probably the very thing that caused the crash."

"Do you mean to tell me that they acted on the advice of someone who had come from the future and therefore could tip them off?"

"They might have. I have checked that very case. There is documentary evidence to show that a large number of investors took the advice of an astrologer whose yearly horoscopes, printed in January, 1929, predicted the Wall Street crash almost to the exact date, saying that it would be caused by unfavorable planetary conditions, and advising people to sell before that time."

"So the stock market crashed because of a faker who pretended to know the future."

"Not one who pretended to know. One who really did know."

"And you think that the astrologer gained his information from a person who was projected back in time and told him?"

"How else could he have learned it? I don't believe in astrology, Mr. Corrigan, any more than you do. No one can predict the future. So the only way to find out about it is from someone who has actually experienced it."

"But the past is fixed," Corrigan argued. "The mere act of projecting a person into it would change it, and it can't be changed because it *is* fixed. That spikes your theory, Professor Millard. All logic is against it."

"We are beyond the bounds of logic," retorted Millard. "Take your own case, Mr. Corrigan. As an astrophysicist, you are planning to project human beings to the moon and other planets. That was once regarded as impossible and therefore illogical."

Millard swung next to Whittaker.

"As a biochemist," continued Millard, "you are constantly confronted by the illogical, such as forms of plant life, chemical elements, or even animals that have developed unaccountably. And in your studies, Jackson"—Millard turned to the elderly historian—"you must know of many cases where persons disappeared so strangely that they might have been swallowed by time, rather than space."

"There have been such cases," acknowledged Jackson, "so I can accept your theory, dependent upon more tangible proof or evidence."

"But tell me, Dr. Jackson," persisted Corrigan. "Wouldn't this projection of the individual change history as we know it?"

"Not necessarily," returned Jackson. "A projected person could become part of the historic incident in question. He might thereby help to shape it, but he certainly could not change it. I have my own theories on that score."

Jackson glanced over the top of his glasses at Millard and Whittaker, who were beginning a private debate. Jackson took Corrigan by the arm and suggested:

"Come, let me show you around the club as a new member, while I express some of my own opinions."

They stopped first by the fireplace, where the low crackle of burning logs and the wavering gray smoke seemed to blend with the elderly historian's reminiscent tone.

"That portrait of our founder, Bushrod Chichester, was placed here the day the club opened in 1858," Dr. Jackson began. "So were these other paintings"—he indicated two framed canvases on opposite walls, each representing a sylvan scene from ancient Greece—"and this crystal chandelier."

Jackson pointed toward the ceiling fixture, which glittered in the reflection of electric bulbs that had replaced its old-time gas jets.

"They came from Pendleton's gambling establishment on Pennsylvania Avenue," explained Jackson. "He died the year this club was founded. Many of the tables and chairs were bought at auction from Pendleton's Palace of Fortune. I often fancy that I can hear the click of the roulette wheel, or the call of the faro dealers."

Corrigan almost heard them himself, only to identify the click as the snap of a burning log and the calls as the voices of Millard and Whittaker.

Next, Jackson took Corrigan into the lounge, where the elderly historian pointed out antiques from old Washington residences, exquisite objects of Oriental art that Commodore Perry had brought back from Japan, and souvenirs President Buchanan had collected just before the Civil War. As Dr. Jackson summed it:

"Everything in the Potomac Club is exactly as it was a century or more ago. It grips you with that spirit and sometimes, when I leave, I feel about to step out into the past. That is why I go along, to some extent, with Millard's theory."

"I should go along with it, too," Corrigan chuckled, glancing down at his attire, "considering I am dressed for the part."

As they reached the foyer, Dr. Jackson indicated the portrait gallery.

"These men were our founders," he declared. "See how their eyes grip you with the spirit of their time! Those eyes viewed stirring scenes of the Civil War. They were eyes that saw Lincoln; some even witnessed his assassination. They draw you back, wanting to tell you more. If we could only meet those men and ask them—"

"Excuse me, sir," interposed Corrigan. "There goes William. I must ask him if my suit is ready."

"Do that." Dr. Jackson nodded. "I will be back with the others."

William was near the marble steps when Corrigan overtook him. The tiled floor of the foyer was damp, but Corrigan didn't notice it. That mental slip resulted in a physical slip as well. Corrigan's feet shot out from under him, carrying him down the steps. He caught at the wooden rail, twisted himself half about, and luckily broke his fall; but it wasn't enough to avoid a stunning thump as the back of his head hit the post at the bottom of the stair.

Corrigan caught a fleeting glimpse of William's wrinkled face looking down at him in horror. That sight was obliterated by a galaxy of shooting stars that instantly blacked out. Then, gradually, Corrigan came back to consciousness once more and opened his eyes to see William again.

"You had a bad spill, sir," said William, as Corrigan rubbed the back of his head. "I couldn't catch you. How do you feel now?"

24

Corrigan wasn't entirely sure. For one thing, William looked younger at this close range. His face was smooth; his uniform and its gold braid were brighter. He was stronger, too, for with his left arm, he brought Corrigan to his feet and steadied him there.

"I guess I'm all right," decided Corrigan, as he tried to review past events. "I wonder—is it still raining?"

"Raining?" repeated William. "No, sir, it isn't raining."

"It's probably stopped by now," agreed Corrigan. "I think I'll take a little walk. Some fresh air will help me."

Corrigan went slowly down the steps, guided by William's supporting arm. The attendant moved ahead to open the door inward with his left hand, half-obscuring his figure as he did. Corrigan nodded a thank-you and stepped out into the sultry April afternoon.

William was right. The rain had stopped. An open carriage was standing at the curb. From the box, a uniformed coachman tipped his high hat. Still feeling unsteady, Corrigan decided to ride instead of walk. He climbed into the rear seat and settled back.

"So you have these hacks in Washington now, just like Central Park," he remarked.

"Central Park?" queried the coachman. "Where is that?"

"In New York."

"Oh." The driver nodded. "Well, whatever you have in New York, we have here in Washington."

"Everything except subways."

"Subways?" Puzzled, the coachman shook his head; then queried: "Where would you like to go, sir? To Willard's?"

The name struck a familiar note with Corrigan.

"Yes. Make it Willard's."

The coachman clucked to his horse and leaned back as the carriage started. In a confidential tone, he stated:

"You know how bad these side streets are, sir. Wouldn't it be better if I took the Avenue, even though it is a little longer?"

"The Avenue will be all right."

Eyes half-closed, Corrigan thought back, wondering if all this was part of his initiation as a new member of the Potomac Club. Perhaps William had been instructed to give him the old-fashioned costume. That talk about time travel, Jackson's remarks on the ancient atmosphere of the club rooms, this antique carriage waiting out front, all seemed too pat. Corrigan decided to draw out the coachman.

"Tell me," asked Corrigan. "When did the rain stop?"

"The rain? We haven't had any today, sir. It's been muggy, as you can see"—the coachman flicked his whip toward the dull, leaden sky—"but nary a drop of rain."

Corrigan looked at the narrow, red-brick sidewalk and saw that it was entirely dry. So, for that matter, was the unpaved street along which they bumped. To his amazement, Corrigan saw some pigs crossing in front of the carriage, grunting moodily because they could find no mud in which to wallow. Even more surprising, the coachman pulled up the horse to let a flock of honking geese waddle by in search of water.

"You can see how dry it is," observed the coachman. "We had a little rain early in the week, but it didn't last."

"And when did the cherry blossoms come out this spring?"

"Cherry blossoms?" The coachman was really puzzled. "I never heard of them blooming here in Washington."

That, Corrigan thought, was carrying it too far, though he had been almost ready to believe he had really stepped into the past when he left the Potomac Club. Then, as the carriage swung into Pennsylvania Avenue, he was suddenly and totally convinced.

This was unquestionably Washington, but completely different from the city as Corrigan had last seen it. The Capitol building loomed a few blocks to the southeast, but its dome was very new and glittery, while the immediate surroundings were strangely barren of other buildings. Yet here, where Pennsylvania Avenue should have been practically an open park, there were rows of buildings on both sides, with carriages and wagons hitched in front of them.

Not an automobile nor even a trolley car was in sight; only horse-drawn vehicles, like a scene from an old photograph. As Corrigan's carriage turned into traffic and rattled along the cobbles away from the Capitol, Corrigan studied the building fronts. He saw tall, striped barber poles, some red and white, others more patriotic, in red, white, and blue. A huge wooden watch face hung above a jewelry store; an even larger wooden musket represented a gunsmith; while life-sized wooden Indians peered from the doorways of tobacco shops.

On opposite corners at the right stood two large but squatty hotels. One bore the sign: THE NATIONAL. The other, THE METROPOLITAN, was smaller, but impressive because of its marble front. But when the carriage had joggled a few blocks farther, Corrigan was shocked by the contrast on the left. There a dilapidated row of buildings gave way to a conglomeration of clumsy wooden sheds flanked by tumbledown shacks with hog pens in the offing.

"The Center Market," the coachman said. "A busy spot, all during the war. We call it the Marsh Market because of the marsh around it."

The man evidently referred to the marshy ground that ran clear back to a muddy ditch that looked like an old canal. Then the scene changed for the better. Set back from the Avenue, in a neatly landscaped area, stood a group of reddish stone buildings with odd-shaped towers that Corrigan recognized as the Smithsonian Institution, which he had often visited while engaged in his scientific research.

But it was different from the Smithsonian that Corrigan remembered—not from the past, but from the future. Different, too, was the scene straight up the Avenue, where Corrigan saw a bulky structure of red brick. Puzzled, he asked:

"Isn't that where the White House should be?"

"It's there," the coachman assured him. "But it's around the corner of the Treasury Building. You're looking at the red barn that Old Buck built on the grounds while he was still President."

Corrigan's gaze drifted to the left; his eyes narrowed as he viewed a square-shaped ruin that stood more than a hundred feet high.

"And what is that? An old abandoned chimneystack?"

"Why, that's the Washington Monument, sir," the coachman proclaimed proudly. "They've been fifteen years and more, getting it that high. So it should take them that much longer to finish it."

Now Corrigan's mind was in focus. The incredible had happened, but it was beginning to make sense. This must be Washington during the last days of the Civil War, for as Corrigan studied the passers-by, he saw many soldiers in bright blue uniforms, but among them, others in ragged, faded gray. Those were Confederates who had either deserted their cause or had surrendered and had been given their parole. That was why they were so friendly with the blue-clad Union troops.

Corrigan was beginning to enjoy his ride when the carriage wheeled in front of another large, rambling hotel and the coachman announced:

"Here we are at Willard's, sir."

For the first time, Corrigan thought of money. He thrust his hand into the pocket of his borrowed coat and, to his surprise, brought out a wad of paper currency. He found an odd-looking bill that at least bore the familiar figure "5," so he peeled it off and handed it to the coachman. More confident now, Corrigan stalked into what he thought would be the familiar surroundings of the Willard Hotel, which he knew as well as the Smithsonian Institution or the Capitol itself.

Only he didn't know this Willard Hotel. The famous old hostelry of the Civil War period was an absolute contrast to its modern counterpart of a century later.

The thickly carpeted lobby spread out everywhere, terminating at one end in a vast dining room already thronged with patrons who were ordering huge dinners, though it was scarcely more than late afternoon. Gentlemen in clothes like Corrigan's—he looked to make sure he was still wearing them —were bowing to hoop-skirted ladies as they descended the sweeping staircase. High-ranking Union officers were strolling by in stately style, and Corrigan stepped aside to watch the grand parade.

Corrigan's elbow nudged a stack of thin newspapers that were resting on a newsstand. He saw the title *Washington Evening Star* and purchased it with some large copper coins that he found in his pocket. About to scan the headlines, Corrigan paused first to note the paper's date:

FRIDAY, APRIL 14, 1865.

Corrigan stood stunned. This day was destined to be the saddest in the annals of America, for on the evening of this fateful Friday, the assassination of President Lincoln was to shock the nation and the world. If ever there was a chance to change the course of history, that chance was Corrigan's right now!

Frantically, Corrigan thumbed through the *Star* to find the theatrical news. He came across the announcement that President and Mrs. Lincoln and General Grant had taken a box at Ford's Theater to witness the final appearance of Miss Laura Keene in *Our American Cousin,* that night.

That was enough for Corrigan. He started out into the gathering dusk with just one thought, to get to the theater and do all he could to prevent the coming crime. A hack was standing handy, and Corrigan told the driver to take him to Ford's Theater at once. There was no need to give the address: Tenth Street between E and F. The hack driver knew it.

27

Arriving at the theater, Corrigan sprang across the planking that bridged the deep gutter between street and sidewalk. He rushed into the lobby and found the box-office closed. After he had rapped repeatedly at its shuttered window, the blind finally slid up and a dull-faced youth peered through the grating.

"Take your time," the youth said. "We're just opening up, and the rush hasn't even started. What price seat do you want?"

"I want to see the manager."

"He won't be here until after dinner. All I can do is sell you a ticket. They run twenty-five, fifty, and seventy-five cents."

In his pocket, Corrigan found some paper scrip, small fractional currency of less than a dollar, which was used extensively during the Civil War. He made up the right amount and pushed it through the window:

"Here is seventy-five cents."

Corrigan received his ticket and thrust it in the breast pocket of his coat. Then, sharply, he insisted:

"I still want to see the manager."

"Maybe you'll find him in the refreshment bar next door," the young man suggested. "If not, go around backstage and ask for Mr. Ford."

In the establishment next door, Corrigan asked for Mr. Ford, to meet with the return query: "Which Mr. Ford?" When Corrigan retorted, "Any Mr. Ford," he was told that no Fords were about. A few patrons of the place showed undue interest in Corrigan's inquiry, so rather than become involved with them, he left abruptly. Around the block, he found a dingy alley and walked through it past a stable, where a brownish horse lifted its nose and whinnied a greeting. At the stage door, Corrigan pounded emphatically until a stocky man in overalls appeared and demanded to know what he wanted.

"I want to see Mr. Ford, the manager."

"About what?"

"About the President coming here to the theater tonight. He is in danger. Someone wants to kill him and he must be warned."

"You won't find the manager around here."

"Suppose I see for myself."

As Corrigan pushed by, the stocky man made a hard, wide swing with his fist. Expecting it, Corrigan parried and countered with a short, telling jab. Staggered, the stocky man howled for help, and immediately three other men came running in response. While Corrigan tangled with them, the stocky man deserted his pals and ran from the alley. He returned with two men in blue frock coats and round straw hats, who grabbed Corrigan from each side, clamped handcuffs on him, and dragged him to a waiting wagon.

There, Corrigan learned that he was in the coils of the Metropolitan Police. All the way to their headquarters, Corrigan kept berating them: "Let me go, you fools! Don't you know that the President is in danger? That's what I was trying to tell them at the theater!"

28

"Then tell it to the sergeant," one of the officers retorted. "He'll listen."

The sergeant did listen.

"While you idiots are holding me," argued Corrigan as he faced the desk at headquarters, "President Lincoln will be shot tonight during the performance by a man named Booth."

"Isn't there a play actor named Wilkes Booth?" quizzed the sergeant.

"That's the one," rejoined Corrigan. "John Wilkes Booth."

The sergeant picked up a playbill that was lying on the desk and smiled indulgently.

"Ford's Theater was handing these out today," he said. "But there's nothing here about Booth. He isn't even in the show."

"But he'll be hanging around the theater, waiting his chance!" Corrigan insisted.

The sergeant turned to the two patrolmen.

"Did you see anyone hanging around Ford's Theater?"

"Only this fellow." One patrolman indicated Corrigan. "We were called in to get rid of him by a stagehand named Ned Spangler."

"Spangler!" The name rang a bell to Corrigan. "He's one of them!"

"One of whom?" demanded the sergeant.

"The plotters who are out to kill the President!"

The sergeant gestured to the cell room and ordered:

"Put this man away. He's either drunk or crazy."

Behind the bars, Corrigan waxed even more indignant, shouting loud enough for the sergeant to hear him:

"Drunk or crazy, you say! You'll find out differently! I tell you, I know, I *know* that tonight Wilkes Booth plans to assassinate President Lincoln. Don't ask me why or how I know. I just *know* — and I intend to prevent it, even if I have to break down these bars!"

From the desk, the sergeant glowered in the direction of Corrigan's cell. Then, glancing about at his men, he demanded:

"One of you find a way to calm that fool down!"

A young patrolman responded: "I know a way, Sergeant."

"And what would that be, Frescott?"

"To listen to him. Maybe he is talking sense."

"Have you gone daft, too, Frescott?"

"Hardly, Sergeant. I just know that he sounds positive about what he says. A man who talks that way may know something."

Corrigan quieted as he heard that, thus adding weight to Frescott's words. But the sergeant was still unconvinced.

"What would you have me do?" he demanded. "Send all the reserve patrolmen to Ford's Theater on the word of some demented fool?"

"It wouldn't hurt," rejoined Patrolman Frescott, "to put a guard on the President's box."

"But the President already has a guard, a regular man assigned from this department. If he wants more, he can call for them. Who are we to tell the President what to do? Besides, he has the whole army at his disposal, if he needs it. Don't forget, General Grant will be at the theater with him."

The sergeant let those words sink in; then added:

"I'm telling you, Frescott, unless you use more judgment in sizing up these situations, you won't go far in this department!"

That might have settled it but for Corrigan, who renewed the clatter from his cell door, hoping to stir Frescott to further action. A frown on his roundish face, Frescott began a new protest, only to be interrupted by a well-dressed man who strode into the patrol room, glanced toward Corrigan's cell, and turned to the desk.

"Sergeant," the newcomer asked, "is that the man who created the disturbance at Ford's?"

"Yes. He says his name is Corrigan. What about him?"

"I want you to release him in my custody."

"And who might you be?"

The visitor drew a calling card from his pocket and handed it to the sergeant, who read slowly:

" 'Bartram J. Wellington, M.D.' So you're a doctor —"

"A specialist in mental ailments. The government has assigned me to cases like this. We've picked up dozens of persons who have been talking about assassinations and other plots. It has reached the proportions of an epidemic."

"That wouldn't surprise me. What do you do with these cases?"

"We examine them, to find the cause of their dementia, if we can. Sympathetic treatment, proper rest, a full consideration of their stories will often bring about a cure. There's nothing criminal in their actions."

"There is when they assault someone, Dr. Wellington. Like the way this Corrigan was pitching into Spangler."

"Spangler? Who is he, Sergeant?"

"Ned Spangler, a stagehand up at Ford's," the sergeant explained. "He was the one who made the complaint."

"I'm told they all pitched into Corrigan. That's why the case was reported to our department." Wellington strolled over to Corrigan's cell, and studied him with a friendly smile. Then, swinging about, he added: "I think I can handle him, Sergeant, if he's willing to come with me."

"How about it, Corrigan?"

From his cell, Corrigan agreed. "I'm willing."

As a turnkey was unlocking Corrigan's cell, a patrolman arrived and handed a note to the sergeant. Corrigan approached the desk and said:

"Let me tell you one thing, Sergeant. The President is in more danger than you suppose. General Grant will *not* be there with him tonight—"

The sergeant gave Corrigan a quick, sharp stare.

"What makes you say that?"

"I happen to know — well, that is — I just guessed—"

"And you guessed right. This message says that General Grant is leaving by train for Philadelphia and won't be at the theater tonight."

Real suspicion was gleaming in the sergeant's eyes now, which was exactly the opposite of what Corrigan wanted. It would be best to go along with Dr. Wellington, an intelligent man who seemed ready to listen. It was Wellington himself who swayed the balance. A sympathetic smile upon his broad, handsome face, he remarked quietly:

"You see how quickly a man in this condition grasps for every straw? Believe me, Sergeant, it is the business of our medical department to find out where such people come from and how they learn the things they do. We always manage to sift the facts. I'll have Corrigan's story soon enough."

Corrigan was willing to bet that Wellington wouldn't, but he did not say so. It was better to play along with this keen-mannered physician. The sergeant waved dismissal, and Corrigan walked out with his new friend. From behind him, Corrigan heard the earnest voice of Patrolman Frescott:

"I still think there is something to that plot, Sergeant."

"You'd better get back on duty, Frescott, or quit your job for keeps."

"And what if I should quit right now?"

"Before you've finished making tonight's rounds, when we're as short-handed as we are? It will be the Blue Jug for you, if you try that trick!"

The voices dwindled as Corrigan and Wellington reached the outside air. It was still muggy, with a slight touch of chill. But Wellington disregarded it.

"It's only a short walk to the National Hotel," he said. "That's where I'm stopping, and we'll find it easier to talk there."

"But President Lincoln is in grave danger—"

Corrigan caught himself rather than start an excited tirade that would cause Wellington, too, to class him as demented. Quietly, Corrigan asked:

"What time is it, doctor?"

Wellington consulted a large gold watch.

"Just half-past six."

"Then the play won't start for another two hours," declared Corrigan, much relieved. "That allows us plenty of time."

To Wellington's apparent surprise, Corrigan dropped the subject entirely and took an interest in the passing throng as they continued on to the National Hotel. Once there, Wellington conducted Corrigan through a lobby almost as lavish as the Willard's and up the stairs to a distant room on the second floor. There, they sat down together, and the physician made out a simple report, listing Corrigan's full name, age, residence, and occupation. On the verge of saying "astrophysicist," Corrigan quickly changed it to "scientist."

"A scientist," repeated Wellington. "Are you acquainted over at the Smithsonian?"

"Not with any of the present personnel," Corrigan answered quickly.

"What gave you the idea that the President would be assassinated?" Dr. Wellington asked next.

"I just happen to know," began Corrigan. "Well, call it a premonition. After all, you should understand such things. You are a psychiatrist—"

"A what?"

Corrigan was quick to correct himself, realizing that he had used a term not yet known to the English language. "I meant to say," he declared, "that you, too, are a scientist. Perhaps it wasn't a premonition. Maybe I just heard too much talk."

"Then why didn't you say that before?" Wellington eyed Corrigan closely. "What started you off on this? Did you have an accident?"

"Well, no. Not exactly."

Instinctively, Corrigan pressed his hand to the back of his head. Wellington promptly stepped over, turned up the gaslight, and took a close look. He pressed the bruised spot gently, and Corrigan winced.

"A bad contusion," declared Wellington professionally. "When did this happen — and how?"

"About an hour ago," replied Corrigan. "I slipped on some steps and hit the back of my head."

"That could account for your delusions." Wellington stepped over and closed the window, to cut off the blaring music of a parading band. "You need rest and quiet. First, let me attend to that bruise."

From a drawer, Wellington brought out a large handkerchief and soaked it with a liquid that smelled like witch hazel. He bandaged Corrigan's head with the handkerchief; then produced a wine bottle and a glass.

"A little sherry will help you," said Wellington. "That blow may have given you a slight concussion, enough to cause a mental lapse."

"But I don't ordinarily drink wine—"

"Call it a doctor's prescription then. Perhaps it will enable you to relax and remember some point you have forgotten."

Corrigan liked that suggestion. As he sipped the wine, he began thinking of ways to win Wellington's full cooperation.

"If you could reach someone close to the President," suggested Corrigan, "I'm sure I could recall more details of the plot, enough to forestall it completely. But there is no time to lose."

"That I understand," agreed Wellington, "so lie back and rest, while I send a messenger direct to the surgeon general's office. That should gain us an immediate hearing."

Corrigan closed his eyes. He heard the slight thump of the closing door; then a prolonged, scratching sound, as of a key turning slowly in the lock. He opened his eyes and tried to rise, but his arms and legs seemed chained. He finally managed to start forward, only to slump as he reached the door, which was locked from the outside as he had feared. His mind was alert, but his body was paralyzed. Thinking it might be due to the stuff on the handkerchief, he managed to pull away the bandage.

It was dark now, but in the glow of city lights from the window, Corrigan noted the initials J.W.B. on the corner of the handkerchief. Even his vocal cords seemed paralyzed as he gasped:

"Bartram J. Wellington. . . . B–J—W. . . . B–J—" Corrigan's breath came with a hard gasp. "J—W" Another gasp – "J—W–B. . . . J—W–B." His mind, still alert, turned those initials into a name: "John Wilkes Booth!"

Horror riveted Corrigan as he realized how he had been duped by the arch-fiend of the conspiracy. Booth must have been among the group in the bar on Tenth Street. From Spangler, Booth had learned how Corrigan had tried to barge in through the stage door. Actor that he was, Booth had played the part of a physician in order to remove Corrigan — the man who knew too much — from the police cell where his shouts might eventually have brought him an intelligent hearing.

With that realization, Corrigan's head swam. He collapsed into unconsciousness which persisted until a dull, slow pounding gradually aroused him. It came from the door, where a voice was calling, "Is anybody in there?" Corrigan found his own voice and responded, "Yes." A key rattled, the door opened, and a man entered, almost stumbling over Corrigan. The man found the gas jet and turned it up. In the glow, Corrigan stared at the blue-coated, straw-hatted figure of Patrolman Frescott.

The glitter of Corrigan's eyes, white and wide with dilated pupils, told Frescott more than Corrigan himself realized.

"Knockout drops!" exclaimed the patrolman. "That's what Booth gave you. I should have suspected it."

Pulled to his feet, Corrigan mumbled: "What time is it?"

"Ten o'clock," Frescott replied. "Nobody would listen to me, Corrigan. I had to find you to learn what you know."

"I know this. We must get to Ford's Theater right away!"

Corrigan still moved numbly as Frescott rushed him down to the lobby and out to the street. Among the waiting carriages, Corrigan saw the one that had brought him from the Potomac Club. He managed to wave, and the carriage wheeled over. Frescott pushed Corrigan into the seat and told the coachman:

"Ford's Theater — and hurry!"

As they sped post-haste along the Avenue, Frescott told Corrigan all that had happened during those intervening hours.

"While I made my rounds," stated Frescott, "I had a friend check things for me. He brought me word that there is no Dr. Wellington and no mental department. But he also said that my description of the man fitted the actor, John Wilkes Booth. When I learned that Booth was staying at the National Hotel, I finally quit my rounds and went there. I made the manager give me a key to Booth's room, and there I found you. So what can we do right now?"

"A lot," rejoined Corrigan, moving his arms and legs to find out if they were working again. "At the theater, we must go right to the President's box and backtrack from there. Even if we cause a commotion, it will spoil Booth's game. He will panic, because he was really afraid of going to Ford's until he heard at headquarters that General Grant would not be there."

"But where did you learn so much about this plot, Corrigan?"

"I'll explain that later. Even if nobody is willing to believe me, I won't care. If only we can get to that theater in time!"

Along Pennsylvania Avenue, soldiers and other passers-by were rushing out to stop the dashing horse and rattling carriage, thinking it was a runaway. While the coachman slapped the reins and lashed his whip, Frescott kept lifting himself up from his seat, showing his blue police uniform and waving people back with his straw hat, letting them know that this was an emergency. Corrigan clung tightly to the carriage rail, as they rounded the final corner.

Arriving at the theater, Frescott sprang out, and Corrigan managed to follow. But they never reached the lobby. As they were crossing the planking, frantic people came surging from the theater shrieking:

"They've shot the President! They've shot the President!"

"It was Wilkes Booth who did it!" shouted Corrigan, fighting to get through the crowd. "By now, he's on his horse, heading down through Maryland."

A man grabbed the lapels of Corrigan's coat, shoved him back toward the carriage, and snarled:

"Yes, it was Booth who did it. But how would you know that? You were out here, not in the theater."

"And if you knew that Booth would ride for Maryland," another man demanded, "why didn't you go and head him off?"

"I'll tell you why he didn't," the first man asserted. "He's in cahoots with Booth, that's why! He wants to put us on a false trail."

"String him up," came another shout, "for the traitor that he is!"

Lynch law was taking over. A growing mob began to drag Corrigan to the nearest lamppost. Aleady weak, he was beaten into submission, his protests were being smothered, when Patrolman Frescott charged the throng, breaking it up with his nightstick. Frescott thrust Corrigan bodily into the carriage, and shouted to the driver:

"Get him away from here and keep going!"

Then the horse was springing forward, with Frescott beating off a couple of men who tried to board the carriage. Dazed, Corrigan sprawled back in the seat and heard the howls of the mob dwindle in the distance. Then there was only the rapid clop-clop of the horse's hoofs as they swung around a corner into a secluded, dimly lighted street.

"Here we are, sir."

The coachman had brought Corrigan back, not to the National Hotel, but to their first starting point, the Potomac Club. In the flicker of a gaslit street lamp, Corrigan made out the white doors and the portico above. He eased to the curb, pulled all the bills from his pocket and gratefully thrust them into the coachman's appreciative hand.

The horse and carriage had clopped from sight by the time the door opened to Corrigan's knock. It was William who bowed him in, and the attendant's face was wrinkled in a puzzled frown.

"I wondered where you had gone, Mr. Corrigan," said William. "Your suit is ready, and they are waiting for you to join them at dinner in the grill."

"Dinner? At this hour?"

"I know it's only six o'clock, sir, but they said you might be planning to go out on an evening plane, so they decided to have dinner early."

It was Corrigan's turn to be puzzled. As he changed back to his own clothes, he realized that he had experienced an entire evening's adventure during his journey into the past; yet he had arrived back in the present within an hour or so of his original starting time!

Definitely, Corrigan was now willing to go along with Millard's theory of breaking the time barrier. With a pang of regret, he also agreed with Jackson. If you were projected into the past, you might help shape history, but you couldn't change it.

As he approached the dinner table in the grill room, Corrigan wondered whether to tell of his experience. His fellow club members probably wouldn't

believe his story; even worse, they might think that he was making up a yarn
to ridicule them. Indeed, Corrigan was beginning to doubt the whole thing
himself. So he decided to keep silent.

Professor Whittaker had left, and another man was with the group,
talking earnestly to Millard. Dr. Jackson waved Corrigan to a chair, then
gestured toward the newcomer.

"Let me introduce another of our members, Mr. Corrigan. This is Mr.
Ray Frescott."

Blankly, Corrigan found himself shaking hands with a man whose face
was the image of the Washington patrolman who had shoved Corrigan into
a carriage a century ago. It was obvious, however, that this twentieth century
Frescott did not recognize Corrigan.

"Mr. Frescott was starting to tell an unusual story," declared Dr. Jackson. "I know that you will want to hear it, Mr. Corrigan."

"It's about my great-grandfather," related Frescott. "He was a patrolman with the Washington police the evening President Lincoln was assassinated. Somehow, he sensed that it might happen, and he tried to warn people,
but nobody would listen, not even the police superintendent, who was in
the theater audience at the time.

"Finally, he found some crackpot who seemed to know about Booth's
plot, and brought him to the theater to prove his point. But they got there
just too late. Afterward, some sergeant wanted to fire my great-grandfather
because he had gone off his beat. But by then, he was the biggest hero on
the force. He later became a police chief, a councilman, and finally a building
constructor. He joined the Potomac Club, and some of our family have been
members ever since."

"And what happened to the other man?" queried Corrigan. "The crackpot whom your great-grandfather brought to the theater with him?"

"The crowd tried to mob him, thinking he was in the plot with Booth,"
rejoined Frescott, "but my great-grandfather sent him off in a carriage, and
nobody ever heard from him again."

The waiter arrived with the dinner menu, and the talk turned to the
subject of a bridge game that was to follow. Corrigan said nothing about
time travel. He was wondering if that bump on the head had jarred his mind
into a discordance of past, present, and future. As the evening progressed,
and his head no longer throbbed, he began to feel sure that this had been
the case.

William was still at the door when Corrigan left for the airport. While
Corrigan waited for a cab which the doorman had summoned, he remarked:

"By the way, William, you didn't have a great-grandfather who worked
here at the Potomac Club — or did you?"

"No, sir. Not a great-grandfather," responded William. "A great-grand-
uncle. His name was William, too, and he fought in the Union Army. He
was badly wounded in the right arm at Gettysburg, so he took a job as
doorman here. Several people have asked me if there was another William
working here long ago. I don't just know why, except—" the doorman looked
up and gave one of his wrinkled smiles — "well, when you get to know this
club, sir, you will realize how it grips you. Some people might say that it's

filled with ghosts, but I don't think so. To me, it is just a place where time stands still."

The cab was arriving on the well-lighted street where Corrigan now was looking in vain for the gaslit lamppost that had been the coachman's beacon when the carriage arrived back from the theater. William flagged the cab, and as Corrigan was getting in, the doorman handed him a bit of cardboard.

"This was in the pocket of that old-time suit you were wearing," said William. "So I suppose it must be yours. Good night, Mr. Corrigan."

Soon the cab was speeding along a smooth street into the blaze of lights that represented downtown Washington. They passed the now completed Washington Monument, which was illuminated to its full height; and off beyond, Corrigan saw the stately pillars of the magnificent Lincoln Memorial. Then, as the cab reached the bridge leading to the airport, Corrigan studied the printed cardboard strip that William had handed him.

Deliberately, he tore the strip in half; then again, again, and again. Near the middle of the bridge, Corrigan tossed the pieces from the cab window. Caught by the night breeze, they fluttered over the rail and down to the broad bosom of the Potomac River.

Those scattered scraps were all that remained of a unique collector's item — the only unused ticket to Ford's Theater on its closing night of April 14, 1865.

THE
GHOST-TOWN
GHOST

THE GHOST-TOWN GHOST

Topaz City, Nevada, was practically a ghost town when Jim Gilbert arrived there around the time of the big gold strike down Death Valley way. The rush had begun to fabulous new towns like Goldfield and Rhyolite, where fortunes were being made overnight and millions of dollars were squandered every day. Even the railroads were racing each other to lay tracks into that bonanza land and build ornate stations to receive them.

Hence Topaz City, a carry-over from the big bust that had followed the silver boom some thirty to forty years before, was becoming more and more deserted. Some of the old silver mines were still being worked in a small way, so there were enough jobs in town to keep a few stores open, but otherwise things were more than quiet. They were all but dead.

That was why Jim Gilbert liked it. A man in his early thirties, he was something Topaz City had never seen before. He was an artist and a rather good one. Complete with brushes, palette, canvases, easel, and smock, he rented one of the many empty, weather-beaten stores on the town's main and only street, turned it into a studio and went right to work. The only thing Jim lacked was the artist's trademark of the early 1900's, a beard. That was superfluous in Topaz City, where beards were a common thing, though they were of the bushy type, not the artistic Van Dyke cut. So Jim decided to remain clean-shaven, a novelty around these parts.

As an artist, Jim fortunately did not have to depend upon the local trade. His paintings, which really captured the spirit of the West, had a ready-made market in New York. He had problems, though, in finding models in Topaz City, as well as a variety of scenery, without going too far afield. The man who finally solved those problems was Bert Tolliver, a local character who was termed "a card" in the parlance of the period. That, at least, was the opinion of Bert's fellow townsmen. In the opinion of Jim Gilbert, Bert Tolliver was the most unappreciated man he had ever met.

Though Bert was less than ten years older than Jim, he looked double the artist's age. The reason was that Bert Tolliver had grown up with Topaz City, starting from early boyhood, becoming as rugged as the lusty town itself during its palmy days and eventually as weather-beaten, though by no means as decadent. For Bert Tolliver still had the sparkling spirit and the twinkle in the eye that all the rest of Topaz City lacked, yet badly needed.

Now only about forty, Bert was practically an old man bcause he had never known any youth. From a messenger boy at the age of six, he had become a printer's devil at ten and a blacksmith's apprentice at fourteen. He had driven twenty-mule teams across the desert, dealt faro in a gambling house, served as turnkey in the county jail, played the piano in the town's only saloon, and ridden shotgun on a stagecoach. He had even become the driver of the mail itself; but that was one week before it quit.

Such was the tragedy of Bert Tolliver. He had always been dependent upon circumstances, with no hope of any escape. He had given far more than he should have for payments received, but had never gained an added reward. Sober, honest, and reliable, he had been taken at face value, nothing more. He was like the silver on which the town depended for its very existence, yet belittled because it was not gold.

Between jobs, Bert had gone on trips with prospectors, but never with a chance of sharing in their discovery. Always, he had been hired as a guide, a cook, or a mule driver. Often, he had gone on the promise of wages that were never paid. Yet Bert had held no grudges; instead, he had been proud of his adventures, even when they had proven misadventures, and he had kept up his spirits by reciting them in detail. As a result, his fellow townsmen had classed him as a blowhard.

During the decline of Topaz City, Bert Tolliver had become broke, and worse. His services were often demanded by canny creditors who knew that he was so honest that he would work cheap to pay off his debts. So when Jim Gilbert paid him cash for whatever he did, Bert simply outdid himself. He introduced Jim to ranchers and mine owners who let the artist paint pictures on their property, and he talked cowhands and miners into acting as models in those settings.

They made a striking contrast, these two men: Jim Gilbert, the slender, youthful artist from the East, with his thin, clean-shaven face, always serious in expression; and Bert Tolliver, heavy of build, yet light of step, whose beard, though the bushiest and darkest in town, was still not heavy enough to hide the ruddiness and broad grin of his ever-smiling features.

Perhaps it was due to those very extremes that they got along so well; at any rate, Jim Gilbert recognized it and put up a proposition that to Bert Tolliver was the opportunity of a lifetime.

"How would you like it, Bert," said Jim, "if I grubstaked the two of us and we went partners in an all-out hunt for gold?"

"You mean head down toward Death Valley and join the gold rush?" exclaimed Bert. "Why, you're taking the words right out of my mouth!"

"Not a chance on that," rejoined Jim. "That boom may go bust any day, and when it does, everybody will twenty-three skidoo right out of there. I was up in the Klondike painting pictures of the gold rush in Ninety-eight, so I've seen all of that I want. No, I have something a whole lot better."

"Like what?"

"Like this."

Jim made sure that the studio door was locked. Then, from a portfolio, he brought out a map and spread it on a large table that it completely covered. Bert studied the details of the map, which included contours, elevations, tiny streams, and other features.

"Say!" exclaimed Bert. "Those are the Skeleton Mountains that lie way south of here; and this is the best map of them I've ever seen."

"Better than that," Jim added, "those special marks show portions of the range that have already been prospected for gold or searched for treasure, at the time this map was made."

"Fine! That should cut three years' work down to one."

"You mean that the Skeleton range is that big?"

"It is big, Jim, and rough. Say, how did you get this map?"

"It was made up from some old maps that my uncle pieced together and enlarged. That was Uncle Ben, my mother's brother, the man who brought me up to be an artist, and sent me to Paris to study. My dad, whose name was Harvey Gilbert, made a lot of money during the silver boom up in Virginia City. He brought my mother and myself back to New York. Then my mother died there. So Dad left me with Uncle Ben and went West again to manage his silver mines. He sent back money at intervals, but finally he sold out his shares, and we didn't hear from him after that. I went to the Klondike, hoping I would run into Dad up there, but no luck. Then later, Uncle Ben heard from someone that Dad had died, but he didn't learn just when or where."

Bert Tolliver nodded sympathetically. He had heard many such stories before. Without them, there would be no West. People came there to find fortune, to forget sorrow, to regain losses, or to seek adventure. Some were born to it, as Bert himself was, and the tough part was that you could get trapped right here in places like Topaz City and never manage to take advantage of the wonderful opportunities all around you.

All that went through Bert's mind as he shrewdly told Jim:

"We've got to play this smart, pardner. You've picked the greatest time ever to go prowling around the Skeleton Mountains. Most everybody else has headed for Goldfield and Rhyolite, so we won't have any competition, provided we keep our traps shut."

"You mean we won't tell anybody where we are going?"

"Absolutely not. Mum is strictly the word. Why, if any of these stay-at-home galoots even guessed where we were bound, they'd flock down to the Skeleton Mountains like a plague of seven-year locusts!"

"Then there is gold in the Skeleton Range?"

"For certain. First, the Spaniards started mining there, three or four times, maybe. Then the Mexicans did the same, but always the Indians closed them out and never left any survivors. Some made markers along the trail, and later some of the old mines were rediscovered. But whenever anyone went back and tried to find them, they never could."

"And why not?"

Bert hesitated. Finally he put a cautious query of his own:

"Do you believe in ghosts, Jim?"

"Well," Jim replied, "I've never seen one."

"And if you did see one, would you be afeared of it?"

"Not necessarily. Are you trying to tell me that those mountains are full of Spanish and Mexican — or even Indian ghosts?"

"Worse than that. It was later that the ghosts began to haunt those canyons. A couple of prospectors would stumble upon an old mine and start to work it. Then others would see them doing it and would murder them then and there. Next, the killers would turn on each other until only one was left. He'd be scared to trust anybody with his secret and even worse scared to go back to the mountains alone. Then he'd finally die, leaving a map that was about half wrong. Somebody would pick it up and go down to the Skeleton Mountains and then the killing would begin all over."

"And which are the ghosts, the original victims or the killers who got theirs later?"

"The ghosts," declared Bert seriously, "would be mostly those of persons who had a rightful claim. Like prospectors who found the old mine workings entirely on their own, not just by having somebody show them the way there, or by working from a map. When a man makes a gold strike, it grips him, like it was a thing of life or death. He'd give his life to keep his secret, and he'd come back from death to stop anyone from stealing it."

This was one of those rare instances when Jim Gilbert really wanted to smile, but he managed to keep his habitual straight face as he asked:

"You know of actual cases like that, Bert?"

"Sure," Bert returned. "The Deacon's mine, for one. They figured the Deacon was working it, because other prospectors kept seeing him down around the Skeleton Range. Besides, he was always showing up in different towns, bringing gold with him. Never enough to cause too much stir in any one place, but it must have added up considerable."

"And did they try to track this Deacon?"

"They really dogged him, but he shook them off. He was a loner from the start, so whatever he found was his, with nobody to tell about it. He made friends with oldtimers around Topaz City and other places; and they cashed some of his gold for him, but he never told them where it came from."

"Has the Deacon's ghost been seen down in the Skeletons?"

"Some folks say, yes. But it could only be within the past ten or fifteen years, 'cause before that, the Deacon was still around hisself."

"Did you ever see his ghost, Bert?"

"No, never. But I'd know it if I did, for I saw the Deacon up here in Topaz City, when he was still alive. Solemn-looking bloke, kind of along in years, though you couldn't be sure of that. Maybe he just looked old on account of the black trousers and black shirt he always wore. He had big black boots, too, and a black Stetson, one of those real wide kind, so you could never get a look under the brim to see if he had gray hair. Those eyes of his would bore at you, like they were asking why you were messing in his business. It wasn't smart to bother the Deacon then, any more than it would be smart to pick a quarrel with his ghost right now."

"So you really think his ghost is around the mine he found?"

"His ghost might be around anywhere. I never heard of a ghost being pinned down to one spot, 'cept when it had gotten into some sort of trouble there and maybe had a grudge to settle. The Deacon never was in any trouble that I heard about. But if you don't believe in ghosts, I'm not trying to convince you. Why should I scare you away from the Skeleton Mountains, considering that map you've got?"

"You haven't scared me, Bert, but you have convinced me."

"Convinced you of what, Jim?"

"That the Deacon's mine is real and that we can't let anybody know we are going to look for it. We must make them think we're heading some place else."

"Like to Goldfield or Rhyolite, to join the gold rush?"

"That's our ticket, Bert. Let's shake on it."

They shook on it and began planning their campaign then and there. Within a few days, Jim Gilbert was casually telling people how he had gone to the Klondike and made paintings of the gold rush there, even doing a little prospecting on the side. Now, he was getting the urge to head down Death Valley way and do the same. He had thought the rush would soon be over, but now he felt it was just beginning, so it would be wise to get in on it.

Bert Tolliver was spreading a totally different yarn. For once, he was purposely living up to his reputation as the town braggart. He was telling the Topaz City folks how he had talked Jim Gilbert into a big deal. They were going to join the gold rush and Jim would paint while Bert panned. That way, they were bound to make some money, and anyway, Bert could not lose, because Jim was putting up the grubstake.

From then on, they put on an act that was ludicrous and therefore all the more real. Jim, the perfect example of an Eastern tenderfoot, began buying any and all supplies that his partner suggested. Bert, the town show-off, couldn't resist swaggering around Topaz City and flashing his limitless bankroll in the stores where his credit had been nil, a week before.

Storekeepers and clerks hopped from shelf to shelf, saying, "What else, Mr. Tolliver?" and "Yes, we have it, Bert, old boy." Paying cash was such a novelty for Bert that it was easy indeed for local merchants to load him with supplies, particularly when Jim, the money man, put the O.K. on every purchase.

Bert, however, was doubly smart as he played the big shot in his own home town. While paying full price for goods with Jim's money, he suggested that the local merchants should forget what he already owed them. So they began tearing up Bert's old tabs, hoping to get further patronage from him, with the result that he was actually buying goods at wholesale.

Privately, Bert made full accounting to Jim, the partner that everybody thought he was taking for a sucker. The two of them had many laughs behind the closed shutters of the artist's studio that they were turning into a supply center. They had bought many times as much as they would need for their trip to gold rush territory, where they could buy more as needed; but Jim argued that the prices would be higher than in Topaz City, so the more they bought the better.

Under cover of all that, they were really stocking up for a three-months stay or longer in Skeleton Valley, their secret destination. Meanwhile, everyone was wondering how the would-be prospectors hoped to carry all their surplus goods. Jim and Bert solved that problem by buying four of the strongest horses available, along with a wagon that was the biggest Topaz City had seen since the almost forgotten days of the famous prairie schooners.

All the town assembled to see the two partners off and have a laugh at their expense. Judge Gomez and Doc Hinckley, both regarded as keen wits, were there to exchange pleasantries. The judge gazed askance at the big wagon and fired the opening remark:

"Why, Bert, old boy, you'll never get to Goldfield with that rig. You'll be driving through so much alkali dust, you'll need a twenty-mule team. So if you'd like to make a trade, say one horse for two mules, with a little cash thrown in —"

"Sorry, Judge," interposed Bert, "but I've thought all that out. I used to drive a mail coach, so I know the roads right good. Instead of going straight to Goldfield, I'm going to take the Southern Trail almost to the border, then go southwest over the Apache cutoff and come northwest by the old Silver Trail. That ought to do it."

"It sure ought," the judge agreed seriously. "But since you'll be a little out of your way, why don't you go right around by the northwest to start. There's a nice trail called the Oregon Trail —"

The rest was drowned in the guffaws of the crowd, which enjoyed Bert's pained expression. If there was anything they liked in Topaz City, it was to see Bert Tolliver "tooken," as they phrased it. The laughter finally subsided so that the townfolk could listen to Doc Hinckley bait Jim Gilbert, who was loading some fancy saddles into the back of the wagon.

"Lookee, young fellow," drawled Doc, "you won't be needing saddles with those drayhorses of yours. Your problem is that your wagon is likely to break down. If you'd like to swap those saddles for a couple of extra wagon wheels, I can accommodate you. The wheels are odd sizes, but that won't matter, since you'll be driving in a circle anyway."

Again there was a roar of laughter, but Jim played it seriously.

He beckoned to Bert, and they went back into the studio, then came out rolling a pair of wagon wheels which they hoisted into the wagon.

"Sorry, Doc," commented Bert. "We'd already bought a couple of spares. Both of them the same size, too."

That turned the laugh on Doc, but he came right back:

"And where do you expect to use those saddles — and why?"

"Where?" Jim replied. "All along the trail. And why? Because I'll be painting Western scenes, every time we stop. I'll need Bert to pose in a saddle as a cowboy, along with anybody else we meet up with on the way."

"There used to be Indians in these parts," reminded Doc. "Don't you intend to include them in your paintings?"

"I sure do." Jim gestured to Bert, who opened the last box that he was loading on the wagon. From it, they took out some Indian costumes and displayed them. "That's why," added Jim, "we decided to take these along."

Again the laugh was on Doc, and Bert added a dry comment:

"If you'd like to come along, Doc, we'll let you play Indian. All you will have to do is set still on a horse and pretend you're Sitting Bull."

With that, the partners clambered aboard the wagon. Bert Tolliver cracked his whip, and they rolled out of town with all the flare of the old days, when Bert had driven the mail coach along that very same Southern Trail.

"Nice going, Jim," complimented Bert, as they clattered along, "the way you kidded Doc when he mentioned the saddles. He's the only person who might suspect that we have been planning to hide this wagon somewhere and take to the saddle instead."

"Won't he still think that, even after what I told him?"

"He will think about it, sure. But he won't be likely to talk to anybody about it. That's all that counts where we are concerned."

Jim began to worry as they rolled along. He wondered, too, how far they would get, since they had started late in the day. But Bert had included everything in his calculations. After they had driven a couple of hours, he turned off on a narrow road to the east, which followed a muddy stream that he identified as the Copper River. When the road doubled back toward the main trail, Bert swung the wagon into a grove of cottonwood trees.

"I'll unhitch the horses and let them drink," declared Bert. "You set up your easel and start to paint. But keep your eye on the trail we just left. If anybody comes along, either way, we'll go back on the trail and continue south, so we will be accounted for, later. But if nobody shows up, we'll keep on down this river road."

Nobody did show up. Bert built a small fire and cooked dinner along toward dusk, then came over to Jim with a cup of coffee.

"You've painted enough now," declared Bert. "Here's mud in your eye, fresh from the Copper River. It adds something to the coffee."

After dinner, they harnessed up and drove all night along the river trail, under a clear, moonlit sky. Toward dawn, they stopped in another grove of trees, waited there all day and drove again by night. They continued that policy night after night, their wagon gliding like a phantom under the silvery moon, along level back roads that Bert had followed often during his some- what checkered career.

During their trek, they veered from east to southeast, south and finally southwest, following a route that reminded Jim Gilbert of an Indian's drawn bow and causing him to wonder if Bert Tolliver really knew where he was bound. But one fine dawn, as the horses labored up a smooth but steady rise, they came to the top of a hump where Bert pointed ahead with his whip and announced:

"There, partner, is where we're bound. Those are the Skeleton Moun- tains."

They were well named. White, gaunt, with great crags furrowed by centuries of wind and rain, the entire range had the appearance of a long, sprawled skeleton; not of some human giant, but of an antediluvian monster that might have been stranded on the bed of a vast receding sea. To Jim, the sight was weird even in daylight, but to Bert, it was like coming home. He clucked the horses over the open ground, picking a course between mesquite trees and giant saguaro cactus plants. Even though the horses were tired, Jim thought they would reach the mountains within an hour; but it took more than half the day, for distance was deceptive in this arid atmosphere. As they approached, the contours of the mountains changed at intervals, due to new angles of view. Bert pointed out some of the more familiar peaks that Jim recognized from the map: Gray Dome, a mighty mass of granite; Crystal Point, glittering with quartz; Black Beauty, a rounded summit composed of basalt; and other formations that showed the reddish tinge of rhyolite and the green stripes of serpentine.

As the wagon reached the base of the range, the mountains loomed more formidably than ever. They became a frowning wall, towering to inaccessible heights, with no apparent way to pierce the mighty barrier.

"If there is gold anywhere," declared Jim, in an awed tone, "these mountains should have it. But how do we get in to get at it?"

"Getting in is easy," Bert assured, "for anybody that has been here as often as I have. But getting at the gold is another matter. You've got to find it first, and nobody has done that since the Deacon was around here."

Jim decided that the subject of the old Deacon could wait. Right now, he was more interested in how they were to penetrate these mountain fastnesses. Bert soon showed him how. He drove along beside the mountains for another mile, and finally an opening showed in the towering rocks.

"This is Skull Portal," stated Bert, pointing through to a low dome shaped roughly like a death's head. "It's where the Indians used to trap the miners, before they found other ways of coming in or out. But since there's no Indians around any more, we'll use this way. It's easiest."

It was easy indeed. The ground was like a broad, level roadway as it wound in through the mountain furrows. It narrowed, though, as they turned the horses into a side canyon, where great crags seemed almost to meet, a thousand feet above, and the side walls were streaked like bony fingers reaching down to clutch the intruders.

"The Giant's Cleft," Bert said. "Kind of gets you, the first time in; but you'll soon forget it. There's so much else that's worse."

From the cleft, the road widened and took them into a side passage that curved into a dead end.

"We'll leave the wagon here," stated Bert, "where nobody is apt to find it, though it won't matter if they do. From here, we go by pack horse up to Hidden Valley and make our headquarters there."

The route proved a tricky one from the start. They loaded the four horses and led them up a rough incline that Jim thought was another dead end. But Bert knew differently. They reached a low, arched opening in the form of a natural tunnel and went through to another valley. More turns brought them to a hidden cleft between two weather-hewn pillars that Bert termed The Twins. Always, their course was upward, until they found an opening that brought them into a natural bowl, surrounded by a low rim of rock. There, Jim gaped in utter astonishment.

The bowl formed a small, fertile valley, with plenty of grass for grazing, as well as grapevines, berry bushes, and even fruit trees. Near a low but steep cliff was an old hut with a crude fence extending from its corner to the rocky wall, where water oozed down in tiny rivulets that joined into a small stream.

"We can corral the horses over beside the cabin," declared Bert, "and then get busy and patch it up. We can even plant some vegetables. I brought seeds along, figuring we'd be here long enough."

"But how can this valley be so fertile," queried Jim, "when the mountains themselves are practically a desert?"

"Only they aren't a desert," returned Bert. "There's enough rain, hereabouts, but it comes all at once. The mountains have been gullied, so it sweeps right through them, except in a few places like this valley, where the water gets impounded. Lots of prospectors worked out of here."

"You mean like the Deacon?"

"No, the Deacon was a loner, like I told you. He kept watching everybody else. I guess nobody will ever know where he made his base."

In the weeks that followed, Jim Gilbert came to know the Skeleton Mountains well, and he was impressed by their more fearful aspects. Bert Tolliver insisted that eyes were always watching in these parts, and Jim was inclined to believe it despite himself. Both were to learn why and how the Skeleton Mountains had taken so much human toll, regardless of outright murder or avenging ghosts, though it seemed almost as though the latter were to blame. Soon, however, they began to wonder if some protective power also functioned.

While hunting for lost mines, they frequently crossed the markings of so-called treasure trails. These included crude drawings of arrows, snakes, and horses, all indicating the direction in which mines or treasure would be found. Other symbols meant to go back or follow a bend or look for special landmarks. But Bert sniffed at all such signs.

"If you owned a mine," Bert said to Jim, "or had treasure hid somewhere, would you go putting up markers telling everybody where to look?"

"No, I wouldn't," conceded Jim, "but why do you take so much interest in them, if they don't lead you anywhere?"

"Because maybe they were put there to lead you the wrong way," returned Bert cannily, "or maybe lead you into trouble. There's one that you are supposed to follow" — he indicated a pointed knife blade painted on a rock — "and maybe when you get where it takes you, it will cut your heart out."

"Let's follow it," suggested Jim with a grin, "and find out."

They were on horseback for this particular trip, and they soon came to a domed rock that bulged a few hundred feet above. High on the rock was a painted circle with lines extended from it like the rays of a rising sun.

"That means there should be a mine shaft straight down below," declared Bert in a scoffing tone. "Why don't you climb up and look down?"

"No, thanks," rejoined Jim, "but I think I'll do a painting of it."

Jim unlimbered easel and canvas from beside his saddle, set them up, and went to work. Bert, having nothing else to do, decided he would scale the rock, if only to prove that the sun symbol was wrong. When Bert finally reached a jutting rock just below the crag, Jim called up to him:

"Stay there, and I'll include you in the picture."

Jim sketched Bert's figure; then waved that he was finished. But as Bert started to resume his climb, Jim saw a slight motion in the rock above. He sprang to his feet, shouting:

"Bert! Look out — it's a rock slide!"

Quick as a cat, Bert reversed his course and squirmed beneath the jutting

48

rock just as a mass of cracking stone tumbled down over it, raising a huge pile of dust as it swept down the face of the cliff.

The avalanche carried the jutting rock with it, and Jim expected to see Bert's broken body at the base of the cliff when the dust cleared.

Instead, a call caused Jim to look up, and there was Bert perched in a crevice where he had wedged himself, letting the slide ride out beyond him. Soon, Bert made his way down to the base and declared:

"See what I mean, Jim? It was a booby trap, fixed so some fool like myself would go up and jar it loose. Thanks, Jim, for warning me." Bert looked at Jim's painting and added: "Say, that's great! You had actually put me in it, when the thing happened!"

Bert stopped, then shifted his gaze from canvas to cliff and back again. "Funny thing," he said. "The top of the cliff looks like a face in your painting, but the cliff itself doesn't. Kind of like the old Deacon, with the dome as his hat."

"I did get a face into it," admitted Jim, stepping back and scanning the canvas with half-closed eyes, "but it was accidental. I've noticed this in my paintings, though; if something odd shows up in them, it is generally traceable in the original scene."

"Then why doesn't the Deacon's face show on the cliff now?"

"Because it isn't the same as it was." Jim was studying the cliff as he spoke. "The face was formed by the loose rock that broke away and nearly took you with it. Maybe the Deacon was looking out for you, Bert."

"Or for you more than me, Jim. You were smart enough not to go up there at all. I only hope he wasn't looking out for his mine, too."

"What do you mean by that, Bert?"

"Well, if it's at the foot of the cliff, it's covered so deep with loose rock that we would need a hundred men to clear it by the end of summer. But I don't think the mine is down there. Like I said, some of those signs are put there to trap you; and that goes in this case."

"Only the Deacon helped us out of it. Let's hope he stays on our side, next time we're in trouble."

Jim Gilbert made other paintings of key scenes while he and Bert Tolliver continued their exploration of the Skeleton Mountains, concentrating on the unmarked portions of Jim's map. Whether they went on horseback or on foot depended upon the distance to be covered, as well as the type of terrain.

They were already into their second month when Bert suggested a hike over the brow of Hidden Valley to explore the vicinity of Crystal Point, which was an open area on the map. Jim took along brushes and canvas; and while Bert was probing the bed of a dry stream for traces of gold, Jim did a painting of Crystal Peak with low, blackish clouds gathering off beyond. He had finished when Bert came lumbering up from the stream, shaking his head and muttering that he'd had no luck. Then, glancing at Jim's canvas, Bert exclaimed: "I'm doggoned if you haven't done it again!"

"Done what, Bert?"

"Put the old Deacon into a picture. There he is, black hat and all, sort of a profile, as you call it, made out of the edges of those clouds. I wonder if they really look like that."

Jim noted the resemblance that he had inadvertently worked into the cloudscape, but he shook his head. "They can't be the same now," he said, "because the clouds have kept on gathering since I finished the picture."

"I'll say they have!" exclaimed Bert, looking at the sky. "Those are storm clouds, and we'd better skedaddle back to the valley by the quickest way." He took a look at the map and traced it with his finger. "That would be through Ledge Canyon. Let's go!"

As they jogged toward the canyon, Bert had more to say.

"Believe me, Jim," he insisted, "this is another warning from the Deacon. He's on our side — or his ghost is — because when a storm hits these mountains, you're really in for it. But in the canyon, we'll be protected from the wind and rain."

Bert was right. The steep walls and narrow gap at the canyon top provided shelter when the storm broke. They paused there, on a slight slope well down the canyon, and Bert pointed up to a streak of rock that showed white in the thickening darkness.

"That's the ledge they named this canyon after. Looks kind of ghostly up there, don't it? For my money, this is the spookiest place in these mountains —"

Bert was interrupted by a distant moan that grew suddenly into an echoing howl. With it, the chill of a ghostly breeze swept through the canyon. Bert shoved Jim up the rough face of the cliff and shouted above the fearful echoes:

"Keep climbing, and don't stop until you reach the ledge!"

They were some twenty feet up from the canyon floor, when a whitish shape appeared at the upper end and swelled to a fantastic size as it approached with a deafening roar. Momentarily, Jim thought that he was viewing a gigantic ghost until he recognized it as the crest of a mighty flood tide. The heavens had opened with a deluge, and all the water from the cloudburst was funneling down this canyon in an increasing wave!

By the time the flood arrived in full, Bert had climbed another twenty feet to the ledge and was leaning down with extended hand. He grabbed the canvas that Jim still carried even though it had impeded him. Then Bert hauled Jim himself up to the safety of the narrow projection. By now, loose chunks of rock were dropping from the canyon walls into the torrent that would have battered Jim and Bert into eternity, had they let it catch up with them. Now the rain was coming through the canyon in a devastating sheet, with wind strong enough to whip them from their precarious perch.

But Bert, by then, had found a gap at the inner wall of the ledge. He dragged Jim into its shelter, and they were both amazed to find that it opened into a snug cave. Bert used a flashlight to study the walls.

"This cave has been hand hewn!" exclaimed Bert. *"This* is where the Deacon must have ducked whenever he was seen around Ledge Canyon. Everybody thought he'd skinned out the other end ahead of them; but all the while, he was living up here behind a ledge that nobody ever climbed to take a look at."

"We wouldn't have either," agreed Jim, "if you hadn't heard those flood waters coming and known what they were."

"Yeah, and we wouldn't have even come this way if the Deacon's ghost hadn't warned us by cramming itself into another of your pictures."

"You really believe that, Bert?"

"I sure do, considering that we've wound up high and dry in the Deacon's own hideaway. Why, we wouldn't have even made it if we hadn't stumbled onto footholds that he must have hacked in the rock, so neat like that I'd never noticed them before. That's why our climb was so easy."

Jim couldn't dispute that argument, so he didn't try. Soon the roaring waters had run their course, so Jim and Bert came from the cave and made their way down from the ledge, finding that the footholds were the very sort that Bert claimed. An hour later, they were back in Hidden Valley, which had escaped much of the storm, and they found the horses unharmed.

They had brought supplies for a good three months, which was fortunate, as they still were searching for the Deacon's mine when that period was nearly ended. Bert had planted corn and other vegetables, much to Jim's amusement. But now they had been harvested and were proving a welcome change from a canned and dried food diet.

Bert finally suggested an expedition beyond Gray Dome and into the southern portion of the range. They took all four horses, riding two and using the other pair as pack horses; but at times, the going became so rough that they divided the packs among the horses and led them all.

Their gold-hunting technique was simple, but tedious. They worked their way down what Bert termed a likely-looking mountain stream, panning for gold all the way. As more streams joined the original one, the task became bigger and when they reached the valley two thousand feet below, they were dealing with a small river. But Bert insisted that they keep at it and finally, when they were working in a shoal of sand, their pans came up with a few gold flakes. Jim became enthusiastic, only to be curbed by Bert.

"Not enough," declared Bert. "Now we've got to work upriver and find out which stream these flakes washed down from."

In working back up, they gave special care to little pools and rocky pockets where small streams joined the large one. They were well up to the headwaters and running out of supplies as well as patience, when their pans showed better results and Bert was sure they had found the real gold-bearing tributary. His confidence increased as they continued up it.

"I'll keep panning," Bert told Jim, "while you start painting. Most galoots that make a gold strike never can describe the place just right or even remember what it looks like when they go to find it again. They get kind of over-excited, I reckon. So while I'm getting warm, you keep cool and get that picture done. Then we'll know where we are, for sure."

Oddly, Jim himself was nervous. He stalked about, unable to find the right spot. He had the feeling that eyes were watching him from the rocks above. As a result, he kept glancing over his shoulder every time he was about to paint. He finally settled for a view that showed a high rock at the right and a lesser slope at the left, with Bert working upstream in between. When he finished the painting, Jim called to Bert, who couldn't hear him above the rushing water. So Jim took the canvas down to show it to Bert, who let out a "Yippee!" just as Jim arrived.

"We've got it, Jim!" shouted Bert. "It's panning out like I hoped. There's gold close by and plenty of it. Now, if we only knew which way to look —"

Bert stopped, more interested in Jim's painting than in the gleaming find that he himself had made. "The Deacon!" he said in an awed tone. "You've got him in the picture again. See how his face shows on that big rock, looking down across the gulch?"

Jim saw it, too, and was pleased, for this was one picture that they could check by the original scene. They did so and found that Jim's brush had captured an actual rock formation that resembled a staring face. The hollows that represented eyes were fixed on the slope opposite, so Bert decided to explore that sector first.

"If it's good enough for the Deacon," he declared, "it's sure good enough for me."

Directly up the slope, Bert found traces of a dry gully down which the gold could have washed. He followed the gully up to some chunky rocks which looked as though they had been cemented in place. Bert started hacking away with a pickaxe and told Jim to get another; but before Jim could get one, there was a crash and Bert disappeared in the dust of flying rock and the splintering of wooden timbers beneath. Jim rushed to the mouth of the shaft and heard Bert's voice come up from a dozen feet below:

"Don't bother about that pickaxe. Bring a lantern instead!"

Soon, Jim joined Bert in the shaft and found him brushing himself off, with no serious hurts. Here, the shaft began a gradual descent beneath the slope. They followed to the end, where the lantern's glow showed chunks of yellow-streaked quartz projecting from the wall. Bert hammered off some pieces and studied them closely.

"Gold, all right," he declared. "This must be the Deacon's diggings, but it goes back to the Spanish days. If we don't find other shafts or tunnels around here, we can sink some ourselves. We've struck it rich, Jim."

By daylight, the samples impressed Bert even more. That night, the partners sat around their campfire happily discussing the future. Jim went to sleep soon after they turned in, but he awoke at fitful intervals and always, he saw Bert moving about, sometimes tending the horses; at others, stalking to or from the mine shaft to make sure it was still there.

At breakfast, Bert looked haggard and worried, scarcely listening to Jim's suggestion that they should go back to Hidden Valley and bring down all their remaining supplies to make this their new and permanent base. Then, suddenly, Bert halted Jim's discourse with an abrupt objection:

"Listen, Jim. We've got to go our separate ways, right now, today. We're still pardners, you understand, but I want you to go and put in our claim while I stay here and work the mine. When you come back, bring a crew with you. Then we'll really be in business, understand?"

"Sure, Bert, sure. But why can't we work together?"

"Because we've got too big a secret for just the pair of us. You know what's happened in these mountains. Pardners turn on one another, and that's the end of it. Each wants what the other has got. He wants all for hisself, the whole kit and caboodle. That's the way it goes."

"But that couldn't happen with us. Look how we've gotten along."

"Sure, it's all for fun, pard, as long as you're just hoping for a strike. But when you've hit it — or even think you're going to hit it — you begin playing for keeps. That's human nature."

"You might just call it inhuman nature, Bert."

"Why not? It's all one and the same. You get a crazy idea and you stick to it, like a mule that won't budge, or a bronco that wants to buck. Critters show it and give theirselves away; but humans nurse it like a grudge."

"There couldn't be a grudge between us, Bert!"

"Couldn't there? Hah!" Bert brought a wad of tobacco from his pocket and bit off a chaw. "I've had grudges against everybody in Topaz City — and with good reason, the way they've treated me. Now that I'm rich, I'd like to take it out on those galoots.

"So last night, I began saying to myself, 'How is this Jim Gilbert any different from those mavericks?' and then I answered, 'Bert, you varmint, he grubstaked you and took you as a pardner.' Then, I said, 'Sure, he took me 'cause he couldn't get nobody else he could trust. That's how everybody else has always treated Bert Tolliver.' And do you know what that made me think?"

"No," snapped Jim, a bit angrily, "but I'd like to know."

"It made me think that here was the first chance I ever had to cross up a guy before he could turn around and do me dirt. Believe me, you and I are real pals, Jim, because if we weren't, I would have done you in last night. I was tempted that much. Maybe if it grows on me, I won't be able to hold off."

"And from the way you're talking, Bert, that might go for me. You're beginning to get my dander up. So what's our next move?"

"Just this. You saddle up one of the hosses — the strongest one is Lubec, so take him — and go down to the foot of the mountain. Ride due west across the desert, and straight ahead, you'll see the lower end of another range, the Ragged Mountains, they are called. Keep going, and you'll come to the town of Monad. That's the county seat, where you register our claim."

"How far is it across the desert, Bert?"

"Three days' ride at most, with water holes along the way. Just keep straight for the lower end of the mountains, and you can't miss. But whatever you do, don't turn northward."

"Why not?" Jim asked.

"Because that's where you will see mirages. Nice blue lakes and green woods. Sometimes even towns. The mountains look so far away, while the mirages look so close, they fool you. But it's twice as far up the desert as it is across. People who head north are never heard from again."

Jim saddled Lubec, packed a bag of sample ore from the mine, hung his canvases on his saddle, and filled his canteen.

"I'll take three days' supply of food," Jim told Bert. "That will leave you enough to stay here and work the mine until I get back."

A few hours later, Jim Gilbert was riding across the desert, finding it easy going with a good horse like Lubec, though rather monotonous. Giant saguaros dominated the scene, with occasional traces of a roadway among them. The water holes, however, proved dry at this season. When Jim finally made camp at one, he found barely enough water for Lubec to drink his fill.

The second day proved worse, but Jim kept steadily on his course and felt sure that he and his sturdy horse could stave off the ravages of thirst long enough to complete their crossing of the desert. At noon, they reached another water hole, but found it totally dry. Jim dismounted and took the horse along by the bridle, while they both studied the situation. Then, patting Lubec, Jim said, "We'll have to try the next place, old fellow."

With that, Jim gripped the pommel of the saddle and raised one foot to a stirrup. It was then that Lubec gave a whinny and began to rear. At the same instant, Jim heard a warning rattle from the ground. He wheeled about, drew his revolver, and blazed away at a snake that was starting to strike at the horse. The shots made short work of the rattler; but when Jim turned to mount his horse, Lubec was gone.

Utterly terrified by the rattlesnake, the horse had galloped off into the desert, leaving only a trail of dust among the saguaros and the other cactus clumps. Worse, he had carried Jim's saddle, pack, and water canteen with him. Left with only his gun, Jim stared hopelessly for a few moments; then started on the run, hoping to overtake the horse.

The course led northward, and as Jim kept up his pace, the dust cloud dwindled. But there was no sign of the horse beyond it. Instead of slackening speed, Lubec had kept on outdistancing Jim to such a degree that now the desert had swallowed the horse without a trace. Jim paused, mopped his sweating forehead, and then began calling for Lubec. But his voice choked in his dry throat.

Desperately, Jim plodded onward, managing to call at intervals, but finding the cause increasingly hopeless. Finally, when ready to drop in his tracks, he looked up at the sun and judged that he had wasted at least three hours in his hopeless quest. No sign of his horse; and now there was no turning back, for even if he found the faint trail again, it would bring him only to a dry water hole at the halfway point of a journey he knew he could never make on foot.

In that moment of utter despair, Jim Gilbert had one grim solace, his revolver. It still had bullets in it and when the time came that he could trek no farther, nor stand the anguish of his already tormenting thirst, he could at least cut the agony short. A bullet through his brain would do it, and Jim had heard it recommended as the only procedure for a plight like this.

He tried to struggle on, only to settle hopelessly in the sand that seemed thicker, hotter than ever, its clutch that of a living monster. Then, as he swallowed hard and tried to call again for Lubec, a quiet voice interposed:

"Well, it looks like you've gone and lost yourself out here."

Jim turned and blinked up at the speaker, wondering where he could have come from. He saw a solemn, weather-dried face beneath a wide hat brim and decided that the man must be an old-time prospector. He certainly knew his way about the desert, for like Jim, the stranger was on foot, yet showed no signs of physical exhaustion.

"Yes, I've lost myself," gulped Jim, "and I've lost my horse, too. I don't know which way to go — on ahead, or back to the trail."

"Go on ahead, until you find a water hole."

"But I may not find one — and if I do, it may be dry — and anyway, I'll be lost that much worse — and still without my horse —"

"No, no. You'll find your horse waiting for you, son."

Jim blinked. He could still see the man's face, floating there, but the rest of his figure seemed all blacked out, due to the effect of the sun on Jim's eyes. The man's expression, like his tone, was sympathetic, but Jim could not quite make sense from what he said.

"You mean — if I find a water hole — I'll find —"

"You'll find your horse. You're new to the desert, son, or you would know that a horse will go for a water hole whenever he needs it. Some of them are right smart at finding water, too."

"They've got horse sense." Jim managed to grin despite his predicament. Then, glumly, he added: "Only I don't have it. I wouldn't be here if I did. So without my horse to guide me I can't find the water hole where you say my horse is."

"I know this desert pretty well," the solemn man rejoined. "Maybe I can steer you there. Come along, son."

He reached out a hand as if to help Jim to his feet, but by then, Jim was up and struggling forward. He managed to keep side by side with his older companion, who maintained a slow but even pace, pointing with his hand whenever he wanted Jim to turn in another direction. To Jim, it seemed that they were zigzagging all over the desert, but the sun was lower now and Jim's brain at least was clearer. He could see the oldtimer's full figure now, a black outline against the desert's white.

And then, as Jim was meeting the stranger's steadying gaze and noting the fixed but sympathetic smile upon his lips, the man spoke in his same even tone:

"Look straight ahead of you, son."

A horse's neigh greeted Jim as he obeyed. There was Lubec, at what looked like a water hole. As Jim urged himself on, the horse pawed at the ground, dipped its head, and took a drink. Arriving there, Jim found a muddy ooze that had satisfied Lubec and that the horse seemed willing to share. But Jim settled for a drink out of his canteen, which was still hanging from the saddle.

Then, remembering the stranger who had guided him here, Jim turned. "Sorry, friend," he said apologetically. "I should have offered you a swig first. How about one now?"

Jim proffered the canteen, but the man shook his head.

"I'll be heading along," he said. "I haven't far to go. Tomorrow, you head that way — to the north."

Jim looked in the direction indicated, and the prospect was indeed inviting. In the midst of the desert, he could see the sheen of blue water, glistening from far away. He studied it for several minutes, telling himself that it could only be a mirage. Then, suddenly it faded. Jim turned again to the stranger, only to find him gone. Momentarily, Jim wondered if he had been a mirage, too. Then Jim laughed at his own folly.

While he had been gawking toward the north, his benefactor had left, as he had been about to do. In the deepening shadows now thrown by the surrounding cactus plants, it would be as hard to trace a walking person as Jim had found it to track his running horse, a few hours earlier.

That night, Jim tethered Lubec, then rolled himself into a blanket, for the desert night was growing cold. After an hour of looking up at the clear stars, he drifted into a comfortable sleep. When he awakened after what seemed several hours, he found himself staring into the starlight again; but his view was partially obscured and when Jim saw why, a chill gripped him.

Looming above him was a figure, swaying slightly as though ready to deliver a downward gunshot or a knife thrust. The shape seemed ghostly at first; then Jim's mind jumped back to the stranger who had guided him here. He could almost picture those eyes boring down at him, with a smile, no longer sympathetic, but cryptic. No wonder the stranger hadn't far to go; he had simply eased from sight among the saguaros and bided his time for murder until now.

But why? As Jim lay there, the perfect victim, keeping motionless only to prolong these last few moments, he suddenly had the answer. He felt a light touch on his neck that could have been a ghostly breeze emanating from a phantom figure; but reason told him that it must be the probing glide of human fingertips. Bare hands were locating Jim's throat, so as to strangle him and leave him here, apparently a victim of thirst beside a dried-out water hole. No bullets, no knife wounds, just the inevitable death that came to those who strayed from the trail and headed north.

Now the indefinable touch was gone, and through Jim's frantic mind ran another thought: Bert Tolliver! All that talk of breaking up, of the need for one to establish the claim, while the other worked the mine, was simply a clever means to an evil end. Questions galore flocked through Jim's harassed brain:

Had Bert sent him out into the desert where the smiling stranger waited? Were the two in cahoots, hoping to get rid of Jim? Had Bert warned against heading north, figuring that Jim would go against his advice? Had Bert started an argument, with that very scheme in mind? Could this killer, whose strangling hands were ready now, be Bert himself? Could Bert have come along and overtaken Jim on the trail? If so, how did the stranger figure?

One bigger question shouted down all the others. Jim seemed to scream it to himself aloud: "What am I doing lying here? What am I doing —"

He should be doing anything but lying there, a helpless victim. Unfortunately, Jim's gun was in his saddlebag with his holster, but he still had hands of his own, and they could strangle, too. That thought brought action. With a sideward roll away from the figure who crouched above him, Jim struggled to get free of the blanket and attack on his own.

It was like getting out of a strait-jacket. Before Jim managed to work free of that troublesome blanket, he could have been shot or knifed a dozen times. But all that while, the threatening figure remained immobile, a few yards away. By the time Jim managed to get to his feet, he saw that it was neither ghost nor human. It was a horse, his horse.

Lubec had slipped his noose during the night and had wanted company. He had strolled over and gone to sleep standing up with his nose dipped almost to Jim's chest. Viewed upward from below, the horse's head and neck had looked exactly like a human form in the starlight. The touch that Jim had mistaken for a ghostly breeze or the approach of strangling fingers had merely been Lubec's friendly nuzzles.

Relieved, Jim patted the horse, tethered him again and went back to sleep. Soon, dawn was streaking the sky and Jim arose and made ready for an early start. He saddled Lubec and laughingly told the horse:

"Did you hear what the oldtimer said? Go north! He was a mirage himself, the way he tried to lure me on. I'm going to go by what Bert told me, because Bert is okay. So today, we will go back to that trail and follow it, the way Bert told us —"

Jim was turning the horse southward while he spoke; but now, he paused as he noticed something odd in Lubec's gait. Jim sprang from the saddle and studied the horse's hoofs. Jim's sudden fear was right; Lubec had lamed one forefoot, either during his mad gallop or while pawing at the water hole. It didn't matter which. What did matter was that the horse could not go on, at least not any faster than Jim himself.

The oldtimer's parting words rang through Jim's brain like the clear chime of a bell:

"Tomorrow, you head that way — to the north."

That was the only way. Already, Jim had figured that it would be suicide to return alone and on foot to the waterless cross-trail. With Lubec badly lamed, the result would be the same. Having come this far north already, the only hope was to go on, trusting in the stranger's advice. Jim took the bridle and clucked:

"Come on, Lubec."

They went on, northward, all that day, under the burning sun, plodding through sand that was growing deeper, taxing Jim more than it had the day before. Jim gave Lubec his head, hoping that the horse might find another water hole, but with no result. Lubec preferred to let Jim lead him.

By dusk, they were both exhausted. How many miles they had come, Jim didn't know, except they were too few. But as Jim stood there, ready to make camp in the gathering desert twilight, a voice spoke from beside him:

"Tomorrow, son, keep heading north."

It was the same stranger, with the same smile. Jim saw him plainly, clearly now; the long face beneath the wide-brimmed black Stetson; below, black shirt, black trousers, black boots, all silhouetted against the dimming sky. Then darkness deepened; again, the figure was gone.

Another dawn; another trek. Jim, leading his patient horse along, kept staring dead ahead, as in a dream. He saw a blue lake, green woods, vistas of towering cities beyond. Jim kept asking the plodding horse, "Do you see them, too, Lubec?" and the answer kept coming, "Yes — yes — yes —" in the form of steady nods, the result of the horse's slow, painful gait.

But always, each alluring scene was gone when Jim blinked and looked again. At last, there was only one thing that he could see, floating there ahead of him — the face of the smiling stranger. Then the man's full figure formed itself again, all in black, gesturing forward as he said:

"Keep heading to the north!"

"Tomorrow," panted Jim. "We head north, Lubec and I, tomorrow —"

"Today, son. Right now. Head north now."

Jim was sagging to the sand, with Lubec ready to settle beside him. But he came to his feet now, tugging at the bridle, repeating, "Head north — now," as they wobbled on together, horse and man. Then Jim's disjoined thoughts began to express themselves in panted phrases:

"Look ahead, Lubec — mirages, that's all — all we will see. Lakes — woods — cities — you never get to them. They all — go away — and all you see is the horizon. A thin black line, Lubec — and you never get to it either. One long line — straight across — no, two lines, now —"

Laughing crazily, Jim tugged at the bridle, steadying himself, thanks to the horse. Then, stumbling on, he kept saying:

"Two lines now — a high one and a low one. You take the high line — I'll take the low line. They're spreading more now; one higher, one lower. We'll get to one horizon — the low one, the near one — even if we never reach the high one, the far one —"

It seemed a crazy, meaningless struggle, but Jim kept it up, for he and Lubec were no longer alone. Beside them was the stranger from the desert, back again, his words a monotone tuned to the ringing in Jim's ears:

"Keep — on — go-ing . . . Keep — on — go-ing . . . Keep — on, son. Keep — on —"

The ringing drowned the words, and when Jim looked toward the man, he saw only a black blur beside him. But when he stared ahead, he could still see that close horizon, a broad black streak now, straight across the desert and right in front of him. It glistened in the sunlight, so it would have to be a mirage; but it was close, so close that Jim was sure that he could reach it. Then he was actually there, gasping gratefully as he sank to the ground, closing his eyes against the blinding sun and still clutching Lubec's bridle as the horse stood patiently with lowered head.

A weird wail came from the distance, shrilling lounder, closer, each time it was repeated. With it, Jim was conscious of a roaring sound. He opened his eyes and looked along the line that he had mistaken for a horizon. Now he saw what it was, a railroad track, its steel rails stretching straight across the desert. The shriek was from the whistle of a locomotive that was thundering in Jim's direction, its black smoke clouding the desert sky.

As Jim came to his feet and waved his arms, the engine chugged to a halt. The crew of the work train jumped to the ground and helped Jim into the caboose. They gave Lubec a pail of water and led the horse up an improvised planking into an open box car. The locomotive started, and the train was under way again.

While they were rolling toward the town of Monad, Jim learned the surprising facts behind his lucky rescue. He had stumbled upon a new branch line that had been pushed across the desert to reach the thriving gold fields. The work had been done within the past few months, while Jim and Bert had been exploring the Skeleton Mountains. Hence Bert's advice against heading northward had been sound, so far as he had known.

Now Jim's concern was for the solemn stranger who had guided him to safety in the very middle of the desert, where other persons previously had perished from thirst and exhaustion. But none of the train crew had seen anyone answering to the description that Bert gave. From their smiles, it was plain that they doubted such a man existed.

After a few days' rest in Monad, Jim hired a crew of mine workers. They crossed the desert on a train, unloaded horses, mules, and equipment; then trekked down to the claim that Jim had registered. There, Bert had uncovered another old mine shaft, and soon they were bringing out loads of pay ore.

When the mine was on an organized basis, the partners put a superintendent in charge and made a trip to Topaz City to close out their business there. Stacks of mail had accumulated, and while Jim was going through the letters, Bert entered the studio and stared at a canvas resting on an easel. Bert's tone carried a note of awe as he asked:

"When did you paint that, Jim?"

"Over in Monad," replied Jim, "while I was taking a rest. I didn't finish it there, but I've been adding bits from memory every now and then. From the way you're looking at it, I'd say it reminded you of someone."

"It sure does. Why, it's the old Deacon, to the dot!"

The full-length portrait showed a solemn man with a faint smile on his weather-beaten face. His hair was completely hidden by the broad brim of his black Stetson. Black trousers, black boots, black shirt open at the top, completed his attire, forming a sharp outline against the desert background, which Jim had also painted. Understanding dawned in Bert's gaze as he queried:

"You mean this was the oldtimer — the stranger you told me about — the man who met you out there and told you to keep heading north?"

"That's right, Bert."

"I should have known it. You must have had the Deacon on your mind, the way his face showed in those mountain scenes you painted. You were sure to see him some day and you did, when you needed him most out there on the desert. Seems to me he must have been with you all along, Jim, looking out for you."

"I know he was," declared Jim solemnly. "He wanted us to find that mine, and he wanted me to live so I could keep my share."

Jim picked up a letter from the table. "This came from my Aunt Ethel," he said. "She enclosed a picture from a lot of family photographs. The only one she could find of my father, and she is sure it was taken not long before he died. Here it is."

Jim handed the photo to Bert, who studied it in amazement. It was the face of the painting, the face of the man Bert had known as the Deacon, the same man Jim had met on the desert. "I should have known it then," Jim said softly. "He said, 'Keep heading north — son.' And when he said 'son' there was something in his voice that made me think he meant it. And now" — there was a choke in Jim's own voice — "now I know he really did!"

JUDGMENT
NIGHT

JUDGMENT NIGHT

Silent, stealthy, sinister, the sea fog wrapped its all-pervading swirls about the slowly moving ship, blanketing it in an utter hush. At moments, those misty coils opened into rifts, allowing glimpses of the gliding vessel, had there been eyes to see it. Then the creeping ship was blanketed again, as if feeling its way through eternity.

For the grip of the fog was not only nebulous; it was timeless. Rather than a solid motorship of steel and substance, the craft could have been a figment of the fog itself. True, this was wartime, when caution often forced a skipper to adopt a ghostly style of navigation in dangerous waters. But for all that, this still could be a ship that never was and never would be, considering how the reluctant fog allowed so little to be seen of it.

A lone ship, going on and on to nowhere.

So it seemed to the tall, light-complexioned man who stood by the mist-dampened rail, running his long fingers through his blond hair, as he muttered low, slow words. Just as the ship was groping its way through the interminable, so was this man trying to draw some recollection from the past that would orient him to the present and enable him to gauge the future.

Although only in his thirties, he had a worried air that was accentuated by the lines in his face and forehead. Though he looked like a seafaring man, he was definitely unfamiliar with everything around him. His colorless eyes were puzzled as they studied the open deck beyond a short row of cabins. He had trouble reading the name on the lifeboat hanging from its davits. Only the subdued throb of the ship's diesels struck a responsive chord in this man's nature; and that, too, was vague.

He was repeating a name, now, timing it to those pulsating motor beats: "Curtis Lanser — Curtis Lanser — Curtis Lanser —" The name was his; he knew it must be, for it was one thought that had come through to his groping mind. But it was only half right, like the peculiar *thrum-thrum* of the motor, which he recognized because it reminded him of a more familiar sound that he was unable to place.

"Curtis Lanser —"

The name would do, because it would have to do. He could read that other name, now, the one on the lifeboat. So he was Curtis Lanser, on board the *Queen of Glasgow,* a plodding freighter working its way through the fog. A ship of about five thousand tons, one day out of Liverpool, bound for New York. All that sprang to Lanser's mind in a sudden, automatic way; and with it, a short laugh came from his set lips.

Lanser was alone, very much alone, in one sense, here on a strange ship, groping for a glimmer of something that he knew must lie ahead. But he wasn't so badly off; certainly no worse off than the *Queen of Glasgow.* She was alone, too, and in a really serious plight, for she was separated from her convoy. Lanser recognized that from the ship's reduced speed; the total lack of warning whistles from the enshrouding fog or from the *Queen of Glasgow* herself.

Lanser's first laugh had been guttural in tone and nervous. Now, he laughed more lightly and with self-assurance. He was finding his bearings well enough to chart a course; better, perhaps, than this ship could. She had fog to deal with; he had only people. So far, Lanser had been avoiding his fellow passengers, rather than have them find out something about him. That much he recognized; now, he reasoned that if he did not know his own secret, he certainly could not betray it.

Perhaps, on the contrary, he might learn something from those people that would enable him to grope his way back to the self that he had somehow lost. Those other people would be Lanser's convoy; by meeting them, he might return to sanity, just as the *City of Glasgow* was striving to find the other ships that she had lost and thereby regain her safety.

"I am Curtis Lanser." The words came crisply to Lanser's lips. "I am a passenger on the *Queen of Glasgow,* bound for New York. My cabin is" — he fumbled in the pocket of his jacket, brought out a key and looked at it — "Number Twenty-eight. If there are any questions that you would like to ask —"

Lanser paused abruptly as a door opened, throwing a shaft of light onto the deck. A uniformed steward emerged and closed the door quickly to conform to blackout regulations. The steward turned, saw Lanser looking at him, and made a slight bow.

"They will be finished serving dinner soon," the steward said. "You had best go in, sir, if you want to eat."

The steward continued along the deck, and Lanser went inside. He had scored a triumph without speaking a single word. Previously, he would have turned quickly to the rail to avoid a meeting with the steward or anyone else; vaguely, he could recall having done that up to this stage of the voyage. Now he had regained the nerve he had somehow lost. But he still was puzzled as to who he really was, why he was here on this ship, and most of all, what was the ominous thing that lay ahead, the secret that gnawed at his mind as relentlessly as the ship's steady throb.

The ship's bell rang the time, and the sound had a familiar note that added to Lanser's new confidence. He recognized the companionway and went through to the ship's modest dining salon, a small room with a makeshift bar at one end and half a dozen tables at the other. There were passengers sitting at the tables, talking in low, strained tones. Most of them had finished dinner, and perhaps it was the smoke from their cigars and cigarettes that gave the room a hazy appearance that reminded Lanser of the fog.

Like a figure from a dream, a man arose and shuffled across Lanser's path. From an indistinct blur, the man's face became a long, slightly drooping countenance with high-bridged nose and somewhat baldish forehead. He was probably in his late forties and his manner was friendly as he asked:

"You are Curtis Lanser, aren't you?"

"Yes." In the crisp tone that he had used on deck, Lanser added, "I am Curtis Lanser."

"I'm Jerry Potter," returned the baldish man. "We looked for you at dinner. We saw your name on the purser's list, you know, and we were wondering what you looked like."

He was ushering Lanser over to a table where some other passengers were seated, and Lanser accepted the chair that Potter offered. Introductions were in order, so Potter made them. There was Potter's wife, an attractive woman for her age, but with a forced, coy smile that marked her as a former show girl, still trying to play the part. Next, there was Major Devereux, broad and beefy of face, with his back and shoulders set at ramrod stiffness in the jacket of his British uniform. Brusquely, the major introduced Mrs. Devereux, a gaunt, tired, gray-haired woman who did not smile at all.

Finally, there was Barbara Stanley, a girl just out of her teens, who was doing her best to hide a nervousness that the others masked in more accomplished smiles. Like her hair, Barbara's eyes were a deep brown, and they showed a hopeful sparkle when she met Lanser's gaze. The girl seemed on the point of asking some question; then she repressed her anxiety with a quick, almost apologetic smile.

A steward was at Lanser's elbow, asking politely, "Will you have dinner, sir?" Lanser's response, "No thank you," brought another query: "Would you like dessert then?" To that, Lanser's tone became a bit petulant: "No, no, I've told you I don't want any dessert —"

Lanser stopped abruptly and eyed the steward in a puzzled manner. Somehow the man and the situation, were very familiar.

"We've been through all this before," declared Lanser, pursing his lips in a level smile. "It is your turn now, so ask me, will I have some coffee? Then I can say, 'Yes,' meaning that I would like some coffee."

"I was just going to ask you that," said the steward hastily. "Your coffee will be coming right away, sir."

To Lanser, all this was like an echo from the past. The other persons at the table failed to realize how serious Lasser was, so they smiled politely at what they thought was his idea of a joke. That broke the ice and gave Barbara the chance to ask: "Are you heading home, Mr. Lanser—or away from home?"

That was the very question that Lanser had been asking himself, out there in the fog. All this vague uncertainty, the blending of the familiar with the strange, could only end when he learned where he was really going, and why. Home! The word jarred Lanser into a mental whirl, but he sensed that the girl was studying him, wondering why he didn't answer. That meant that the others must be wondering, too. In his dilemma, Lanser heard his own lips mechanically voice what he suddenly knew was the truth.

64

"I am going away from home."

Barbara's eyes were studying Lanser closely. Could she be guessing at the secret which Lanser was still hoping to uncover? Did she know who he was and his reason for being here? Or was that pure sympathy that Lanser saw in those dark, meditative eyes?

While Lanser pondered such questions, tuning them to the *thrum* of the ship's motors, his problem was shelved when Mrs. Devereux commented:

"We are going away from home, too. The major is heading up a military mission in Washington."

"That's where I'm bound for," Potter told Lanser. "Washington. I'm with the War Production Board. Mrs. Potter is going on to Chicago; that's home for her. We've all become pretty well acquainted so far" — Potter included the other passengers with a gesture — "except for you, Mr. Lanser. So, naturally, we've been wondering about you."

Lanser responded with a stiff bow.

"I suppose I should feel complimented."

"Yes, you should," rejoined Potter. "I'm good at sizing people up when I see them — that's part of my work, you know — and I would say that you are a language professor, say from Oxford or some other English university?"

Potter's shot in the dark was helpful. It stirred some of Lanser's recollections back to happier times before World War II, in which he felt that he must somehow be involved, yet in a puzzling way that he could not fathom.

"Yes, I did teach languages," he answered slowly, "but not at Oxford."

"Then where," asked Potter, "did you teach?"

"In Frankfurt, Germany."

"Frankfurt, Germany!" echoed Mrs. Potter, her tone tinged with horror. "But — but what languages did you teach there?"

"English, for one."

"Oh!" Mrs. Potter's sigh expressed the relief that Lanser was sure the others shared. "You were an exchange professor there?"

"Yes, it could have been called that."

The steward was returning with the coffee; and Lanser's thoughts, eased by his faint recollection of the past, became troubled again, in terms of the inescapable present. The steward's face, developing from a hazy outline, became so solidly fixed in Lanser's mind that it crowded his memory as well.

"I've seen you before," declared Lanser. "But where?"

"I wouldn't know, sir," rejoined the steward, "unless you have traveled on this line before. Only we don't get the same passengers often."

From the shabby, neglected condition of the so-called dining saloon, it was a wonder that the *Queen of Glasgow* ever carried passengers at all. But this was wartime, and people had to take what accommodations they could get in order to reach an appointed destination. Not only did Lanser recognize that fact; he knew that it applied in his case as much as with the others.

Besides, the steward's statement belied itself. His face was not the only one that Lanser found familiar. Those of the persons seated at this table came into that same category. Lanser was sure that he had seen them all before; not just once, but often. And where else could he have seen them all, except on this plodding freighter lost in the Atlantic fog?

Eyes half shut, Lanser heard a buzz of voices:

"Here comes Captain Willoughby —"

An image sprang to Lanser's mind. When he opened his eyes, he saw the living replica. A grizzled sea dog in his sixties, with narrowed, coal-black eyes beneath bushy gray brows, a loose-fitting uniform that billowed appreciably as he eased his broad bulk into the chair at the head of the table; all that was Captain Willoughby, exactly as Lanser knew he would be. His rumbling voice was also part of Lanser's preconceived impression.

"Sorry I couldn't make it for dinner," the captain said. "We have a miserable fog out there, so I had sandwiches sent up to the bridge." He turned to the steward. "I have time for coffee now."

It was Major Devereux who queried in a casual tone:

"Any chance of sighting the rest of the convoy, Captain?"

"Not in this fog. In fact, there is no use to try. I've decided that we should go it on our own."

Lanser, listening with slightly tilted head, half closed his eyes as he commented: "Yes, I would say that you are doing exactly that."

Willoughby gave Lanser a sharp look, then turned to the others. "I don't believe that I have met this gentleman," he said.

"Allow me," put in Potter, "to introduce our hitherto missing passenger, Curtis Lanser. Or perhaps I should say, Professor Curtis Lanser."

Willoughby acknowledged the introduction with a bow.

"A keen ear you have, Mr. Lanser, to notice the gradual speed-up of the motors. You have had nautical experience?"

"Yes, particularly where motors are concerned."

Again, Lanser was reverting to an earlier time, which was coming more clearly now; but he was unable to bridge the void between those days and the present. A few more inklings and perhaps he would have it. Each statement that sprang to his lips so spontaneously was in itself a vital clue.

Now the other passengers were noticing the increased throbbing of the motors. Mrs. Devereux tried to cover her nervousness with a quick query:

"Wouldn't it be better to be with the convoy, Captain? What if a whole wolf pack should converge on us while we were all alone?"

Captain Willoughby tried to brush off the question, but Lanser answered it.

"No wolf packs would converge on a single ship, Mrs. Devereux." Lanser's tone was precise. "The principle of the submarine pack is based on the convoy attack."

The rest stared at Lanser, and Captain Willoughby's narrowed eyes were sharpest of all. Then he stated calmly:

"This gentleman is quite correct. Our chief danger would lie in the possibility of a single submarine picking up our trail."

"That is good to know," said Major Devereux. "We certainly should stand a better chance against just one submarine than against twenty."

"Still, it only takes one torpedo," argued Potter. "It's like a stab in the back, being attacked by a submarine. I'd rather have them come after us with a pocket battleship. At least that's something you can see!"

"You will see the submarine," Lanser assured him, "because it will surface. They won't waste torpedoes on a freighter like this when they can shell us and sink us from a range of a thousand meters."

If ever a face turned suddenly grim, it was Captain Willoughby's. The old sea dog gave Lanser a steady look and said bluntly:

"You talk like a U-boat commander, Mr. Lanser."

Lanser set down his cup so forcibly that he broke it, saucer and all, spilling the little coffee that was left. The steward instantly gathered the broken pieces and spread a napkin on the tablecloth. The talkative Mr. Potter promptly rallied to Lanser's cause.

"Mr. Lanser knows Germany and its people," Potter explained to Captain Willoughby. "He is an Oxford professor who taught at Heidelberg —"

"No, no!" interrupted Mrs. Potter. "He didn't say Heidelberg. He said —"

"I heard what Mr. Lanser said," snapped Potter, "and I knew him for an Oxford professor the moment that I saw him. The important thing is that he taught *English,* wherever he was in Germany."

Lanser ran his fingers through his hair again, his eyes taking on a distant stare. Perhaps he did look like a professor, but somehow he knew he wasn't. He was still groping for his real identity, just as the ship was laboring along its course, searching for safety.

The faces about him; Lanser could recall seeing them so many times before. He had heard the same worried voices; he could even repeat their words before they were uttered. The steward was bringing a fresh cup of coffee, as he had so often done before. The motors were running at top speed, and soon they would reach the breaking point. With those throbs came a distant echo like something from another world — Lanser's world.

Now Lanser had left the captain's table and was with Potter, who was introducing him to other passengers, all of whom seemed familiar. But oddly enough, he could still hear the conversation of the persons he had just left, like a dream within a dream.

"This Lanser," Major Devereux was saying, "I had him pegged for a Hun the moment he walked in. An Englishman teaching German! My word, he's more like a German trying to talk English."

"Then why," asked Mrs. Devereux, "should he be traveling on this ship?"

"I know why!" exclaimed Mrs. Potter. "He is a spy!"

Laughter followed, and Potter turned around to see what it was all about. He decided that it was unimportant, as everyone seemed to be congratulating Mrs. Potter for some bright saying. Then Captain Willoughby closed the subject.

"I doubt that we could have a spy on board, Mrs. Potter," he told her. "All our passengers have been well screened. However, I shall talk to Mr. Lanser later."

That brought an inward smile from Lanser. So the captain would talk to him later. Word for word, Lanser knew exactly what would be said, for somehow, he had experienced all this before. With that thought, his elation faded. Then, as from a distance, he heard the soft voice that he had awaited. It came from the captain's table, saying:

"I am sure we do not have a spy among us, Captain Willoughby. Good night, all."

It was the voice of Barbara Stanley. It struck the first chord of human sympathy that Lanser had so far felt, here on this ship where all were against him, yet where he knew that he must stay and fulfill some mission that he couldn't comprehend.

Lanser turned away from Potter, who now was talking to a bartender whose face Lanser felt he had seen a thousand times before. He passed tables where he saw passengers whose names, faces, even their gestures, were more familiar to him than his own. He went through the familiar companionway and the door to the deck. He was out there again, at his place beside the rail. Beyond was the fog, through which the *Queen of Glasgow* no longer glided, but literally lurched under the full speed of its overtaxed motors. The ship was seeking an opening in that impenetrable curtain to the world without; and Lanser, in his turn, was seeking a rift that would enable him to glimpse the world within.

It came with the opening of that same door. Time and again, Lanser had seen a steward come through that door, close it quickly and then go by, announcing that dinner was still being served. It was like a cue for Lanser to go through the same routine all over. But now, instead of the steward, it was Barbara Stanley who came out. As she drew her jacket tightly about her, Lanser called softly: "Miss Stanley!"

The girl turned as she heard his voice. She must have recognized Lanser despite the darkness by the rail, for she came directly there and rested her arm alongside his. Then, with a slight shudder, she exclaimed:

"I feel a chill — like a ghostly chill! It must be the fog, it's so — so weird. A fog carries a chill, doesn't it?"

"It does," replied Lanser. "Let me ask you one question, Miss Stanley. We have met before, haven't we?"

"Why, no. We couldn't have met; not until we came on board."

"You will forgive me then, but I seemed to remember you so well. Like all the others," he added.

"The others?"

"Yes. Everyone down in the dining saloon. I've seen them over and over" — Lanser thrust his fingers through his hair, pressing his head hard — "because always, I am back with them, going over the same things as before."

"I know that feeling," said Barbara sympathetically. "It grips me every now and then, but only momentarily. Does it seem that way right now?"

"No, not right now." Lanser's voice rose to an excited pitch. "This is different. This" — he paused, lacking words, as the fog suddenly cleared from about them — "this is like the rift in the mist, the moments you see clearly, only to have it close in again. You understand, don't you?"

"I think so. Tell me all you remember, from the very beginning, when you first came on board this ship."

"That's the odd part. I can't remember when or how I came on board. It was as if I suddenly woke up and found myself here on deck, standing by this rail. The door opened, a steward came out, and I went down to the dining saloon —"

"Yes, we saw you come to the table tonight."

"But I mean night after night. It happens over and over — and over. Always the same way — leaving me wondering, groping to find out about myself."

"At least you know your name. You are Curtis Lanser, once a professor in Frankfurt, Germany, where you taught English."

"Not quite. I was just Kurt Lanser, then. A schoolteacher, who taught English along with other subjects. You see, I was born in Frankfurt, and I was educated there. I did well in school, so I became a teacher."

"But you said something about being an exchange professor."

"That was Mr. Potter's idea, and I just went along with it. In a way, I was exchanged. From Frankfurt, I was sent to Hamburg, where I taught English to members of the German Navy. When war threatened, I became a —"

Lanser paused, his eyes closing, his face clouding. Barbara spoke softly, but earnestly:

"Don't try to remember everything right now. Perhaps if you could get some sleep —"

"Sleep won't help me." Lanser's voice was strained, and his words echoed the chill of the fog. "I feel as if this were a nightmare. I can tell that there is disaster out there" — he swept his hand into the thinning fog — "disaster and doom. We are being stalked. There is a U-boat out there. I know it — I *know* it!"

As he spoke, Lanser sensed that Barbara's hand had rested on his arm, the only human touch he had felt since the start of this odd but too familiar episode. Now that touch, like the girl's voice, was gone. Lanser swung about to face, not Barbara, but a ship's officer.

"The captain's compliments," the officer said. "He would like you to come with me to his quarters. Just for a short talk."

Lanser went along without argument, again aware of exactly what would happen. When they reached the captain's cabin, they found Captain Willoughby awaiting them there. He gestured Lanser to a chair and motioned for the officer to stay.

"This is Mr. Danbury, my First Officer," Captain Willoughby introduced him. "Would you mind answering a few questions, Mr. Lanser?"

"Anything you may ask, Captain."

"First of all, would you please show us your passport?"

Lanser's hand was already on its way to his inside pocket, where he went through the act of fumbling for what he knew would not be there. Then, as though he had rehearsed the words, Lanser replied:

"I am afraid I don't have my wallet. It must be down in my cabin."

"We can check on that later," Willoughby decided. "Meanwhile, isn't there something you would like to tell us?"

"I can't tell you much," Lanser confessed, "because I don't remember much. I can't recall how I came on board this ship. I only remember odd, disjointed things, as though they have happened many times before."

"At the table. Mr. Lanser, you seemed to have a good working knowledge of German submarines. Does that stir your memory?"

"I wish it could," rejoined Lanser, sincerity in his tone, "but it just doesn't. I must have been repeating things I heard somewhere."

"Just now, on deck," Danbury put in, "I heard you say that we were being stalked, that there was a U-boat out there in the fog."

"Did I say that?" Lanser's surprise was genuine. "Yes, I may have said it. After all, there are likely to be subs in these waters."

"We mentioned them at the table," Captain Willoughby told Danbury. "It may have worried Mr. Lanser, as it did the other passengers. Perhaps we had better postpone our talk, Mr. Lanser. You probably need some sleep. Mr. Danbury will see you to your cabin. Good night, sir."

This time, Lanser did not dispute the question of sleep. He went along with Danbury and when they reached the cabin, Lanser began to rummage in his luggage, muttering about his passport. Again, he knew somehow that the passport wouldn't, couldn't be there. In the midst of it, he pulled out a cap and deliberately tossed it on the bunk, where Danbury promptly picked it up and looked at it.

"Why, this is a German naval officer's cap!" explained Danbury. He turned it in his hands, studying the insignia. "A U-boat commander's cap, in fact! Where — how did you happen to pick up this?"

"Pick it up," said Lanser slowly. "I guess that's what I did. I must have just happened to pick it up."

"You mean, as sort of a war souvenir?"

"Why, yes. There's really no other way I could have gotten it."

It didn't occur to Danbury that Lanser was fighting down his own doubts, striving to ward off some stark, pitiless truth that was clutching him with unseen tentacles, more potent than the grip of the fog outside. But Danbury was beginning to feel genuinely sorry for Lanser now. He classed Lanser as a man who had been through some terrible ordeal, for Danbury had seen many such cases among the survivors of torpedoed ships. He knew how even the hint of some new danger could jar their minds into fanciful channels.

"I'll have a look at your passport tomorrow, Mr. Lanser," said Danbury. "Just a matter of routine, you know, since we don't have it listed. As for this" — he tossed the German navy cap on the bunk — "let's hope we pick up a lot more souvenirs like it, floating somewhere on the briny."

Danbury bowed out and when the door had closed behind him, Lanser picked up the discarded cap. He turned back the inner band and read the words he saw there, inked clearly against the leather:

Kurt Lanser — *Kapitan Leutnant* — *Kriegsmarino*.

Now, a hideous discordance swept through Lanser's brain. The cap dropped from his nerveless fingers. He stepped from the cabin and walked mechanically along passages and through companionways, his footsteps timed to the *thrumm-thrumm* of the motors. Even the ship's bells seemed off key as Lanser heard them chime the time. He reached the dining saloon, which he found deserted now except for the bartender, who voiced a greeting and pushed across the bottle that Lanser indicated.

Lanser poured himself a drink and asked:

"Where are all the other passengers?"

"They've turned in," replied the bartender. "It's after midnight, but I'm keeping open late. If — well, maybe people won't be able to sleep tonight. They might want to come in, you know — as you did, sir."

Lanser wasn't listening. He was studying the clock above the bar, noting the time as ten minutes after twelve. Slowly, he muttered:

"Until one fifteen. Just one hour and five minutes to go."

The bartender stared, puzzled. Lanser finished his drink and helped himself to another. He was thinking back to the cabin, trying to focus his mind on the cap that he had found there and what it really meant. Again, he spoke in a low mutter:

"Kurt Lanser — *Kapitan* —"

Another glance at the clock. How many, how often, Lanser did not notice. Time itself was all that mattered, and it was moving rapidly. It was later that Lanser stated:

"Ten minutes to one. Less than half an hour to go. Those motors, there is something wrong with them. They sound labored."

"They always sound like that," returned the bartender. "They always sound that way on this tub."

Lanser kept listening as time ticked by. First Officer Danbury paused at the bar and called through the door to the galley:

"A pot of coffee for the bridge! I'll wait for it here."

"Five minutes past one," Lanser muttered. "Only ten minutes —" He stopped abruptly, swung about to Danbury.

"Those motors are stopping!" Lanser stormed. "Why?"

"Just a routine checkup," returned Danbury. "We thought —"

"You didn't think! It would be *unthinkable* to stop them now, leaving the ship adrift in sub-infested waters, where we are absolutely defenseless. Those motors have broken down!"

"They will be repaired," Danbury said soothingly. "The fog is lifting, and we will be under way again very soon."

"The fog is lifting!" echoed Lanser. "That makes it worse! We won't be getting under way — ever. We'll drift until one fifteen —"

"That's what he's been saying all along," the barkeeper confided to Danbury. "One fifteen, like something is due to happen then."

"Yes, at one fifteen." Lanser was proclaiming it to Danbury now. "Don't you know that a U-boat has been stalking us for hours and gaining on us ever since our motors slackened speed? Don't you know that the commander of that sub can tell what those sounds mean, just as I did?"

"Calm yourself, Mr. Lanser," chided Danbury. "Practically all our passengers are imagining such things. You're suffering from nerves."

"I'm suffering from knowledge. I know that the U-boat is already surfacing off our port bow. We will be attacked, and we won't be able to run away unless you get those motors started and give them full speed ahead."

"That would be impossible at this moment, Mr. Lanser."

"Then you must warn the passengers. Get them to the lifeboats."

"Suppose we just wait ten minutes," suggested Danbury. "Once your deadline is past, you will realize how foolish your fears were."

Those minutes were ticking rapidly. Lanser wanted to act, but seemed glued to his chair. Everything about him seemed unreal; but as for what was due to happen, Lanser had never been more sure of anything in all his life.

In all his life!

Could this be his life, this strange existence in which he could not act on his own? Why did he have to depend on Danbury and others to act for him? Why did he have to listen to their parrot phrases, when he already knew the stupid things that they would say? While Lanser was debating those questions, the time for action came. The clock showed one fifteen.

Like a justification of Lanser's warning, there came an approaching screech, growing louder, louder, louder and ending with a huge explosion. The whole ship shuddered under the impact. An enemy gunner had scored a direct shell-hit on the drifting *Queen of Glasgow!*

Momentarily, Danbury was frozen with disbelief. Then he was racing to the deck, followed by the steward from behind the bar and the chef from the galley. Lanser's own limbs were now unleashed, and he was dashing along with them. As they reached the outside air, another shell came whining through the thinning fog, shivering the freighter with another crashing blast.

Passengers were surging frantically from their cabins, and Lanser recognized the faces that he had come to know so well. There was Devereux, caught in a daze of grim uncertainty; Potter, so excited that he was momentarily paralyzed; their wives, both utterly terrified. Other passengers formed a frantic throng, while the deck was bathed in the glare of a searchlight from the U-boat, a gray bulk barely distinguishable in the mist.

A stab of flame from the distant deck gun told that another devastating missile was on its way from the thousand-yard range that Lanser had predicted. The shell hit below the water line, and the *Queen of Glasgow* reeled like a stricken creature. The confused passengers were flocking back to their cabins, thinking to find safety there, while Lanser raised his voice to a bellow:

"Get to the lifeboats! It is your only chance. Don't go back into those cabins!"

Nobody heeded the shout. Lanser himself felt powerless to act, yet at the same time immune to the further danger of which he was so oddly aware. Hardly had the group scurried for their ill-chosen refuge, before a whining shell smashed the freighter's superstructure into a shapeless mass.

Not all the victims were trapped or slain in those cabins. Miraculously, a few came stumbling from the twisted ruins. Among them, Lanser saw Barbara Stanley, and he rushed forward, shouting, pointing her toward a lifeboat, the very one he had first noticed when he found himself on board the *Queen of Glasgow*.

Barbara did not see Lanser, and his warning was drowned by the burst of another shell that found the bridge and shattered it, showering chunks of metal all around. But the girl escaped unscathed, for hands were already drawing her into the partly lowered boat, which was dipping beneath the rail as the steel shower rained above.

Lanser could see the U-boat plainly now, for he had reached the bow of the sinking freighter and was shaking his fist defiantly in the glare of the searchlight. Another shell hit the *Queen of Glasgow,* again below decks. The commander of the sub had enjoyed his brutal fun and now was making short work of the freighter. Hurriedly, Lanser dashed back along the rail and waved frantically to the boat in which Barbara had gone, warning it to get away before the merciless U-boat captain shelled it, too.

Fortunately, the fog was closing in again, and the lifeboat was enveloped in its timely curtain. So was the U-boat, but Lanser was still defiant. On an odd impulse, he threaded his way through debris-strewn passages and into his own cabin, Number 28, which he found intact. On the bunk, where he had dropped it, was the cap belonging to the German naval officer, whose name, by some queer quirk, was so like with Lanser's own.

As Lanser picked up the cap, a final, jarring crash shook the old *Queen of Glasgow*. The ship literally seemed to fall apart, for the whole side of the cabin opened and a wall of water closed in on Lanser like a green sea monster. Next he was tasting, swallowing the salt water that choked him, filled his lungs, and completely engulfed him. He lashed out with his arms, trying to break free as a drumming sound beat through his brain, dulling all his recent recollections.

Then the whole watery nightmare faded, and the cabin returned to normal. The drumming sound was simply someone knocking at the door, and Lanser stepped over to answer it. He pulled on the German navy cap, ready to face Danbury or anybody else. The cabin, oddly, had shrunk to a smaller size, but Lanser did not notice that until he opened the door.

Instead of Danbury, he saw a sailor in a German naval uniform, who saluted and addressed Lanser as *"Herr Kapitan."* The man followed with a rapid report in German:

"Word from Lieutenant Mueller, sir. We have closed in on the enemy freighter and are ready to surface as you ordered."

Lanser glanced at his wrist watch. He blinked as he saw gold braid on the sleeve and realized that he was wearing an officer's uniform instead of a plain jacket. The time, too, was puzzling. It was only one o'clock, yet Lanser was positive that not so long ago he had seen a clock — a highly accurate one, as he recalled — that registered one fifteen.

In a musing tone, Lanser muttered:

"One o'clock. Fifteen minutes to go."

That cleared Lanser's mind of the crazy, confused dream that had disturbed the brief doze he was having when Mueller's message arrived. As Captain Lanser, he joined Lieutenant Mueller, a broad-faced, quiet man who was older than Lanser but lacked the decisive manner that had raised Lanser to commander of the U-boat. Together, they ascended the conning tower as the submarine surfaced.

There, Mueller indicated the outline of an old freighter drifting beneath the moonlight, its rusty hull silver-tinted by the reflected swirls of the surrounding, fading fog.

"The Queen of Glasgow, five thousand tons," recited Mueller. "She is the ship we tracked after she lost her convoy. You were right, Captain, she was overtaxing those motors and had to lay to, as you said she would. We are at the range you specified, one thousand meters."

Lanser looked toward the deck gun and saw that its crew was ready He checked his watch; saw its second hand sweeping through the final minute before one fifteen. Lanser raised his hand, ready to point to the men who were handling the searchlight. Then Lanser said to Mueller:

"A few well-placed shells and all will be over for that ship."

"Why not fire a warning shell first, Captain?" suggested Mueller. "And then wait for a brief interval?"

"A warning shell? Why? And wait — for what?"

"There are passengers on that ship, with women among them."

"Passengers have no right on board; women least of all."

"But they are human beings, like ourselves. So are the crew —"

"And therefore they must take their chances, as we do."

"Not when there is no necessity for it," pleaded Mueller. "We could still give them time to take to their boats."

"While their radio man sends out their position and gives ours with it, as well? Sentiment has begun to soften your brain, Mueller."

Lanser's glare had turned his colorless eyes as cold and hard as ice. He glanced at his wrist watch, saw the last few seconds sweep away. At precisely one fifteen, Lanser pointed his finger, and the searchlight's beam cut a swath through the night, focused squarely on the drifting *Queen of Glasgow*. At Lanser's order: "Fire!" The deck gun boomed and the first shell was on its way to a direct hit.

From then on, the freighter received an efficient, perfectly timed bombardment that rapidly sent her down by the bow. Little figures ran helter-skelter about the doomed ship's deck, disappearing amid the collapsing superstructure — except for one man who paused briefly near the sinking bow, shook his fist into the searchlight's glare, then ran for shelter. As the freighter finally slid down into the sea, Lanser ordered the searchlight to sweep the surface, and he called for the gun crew to be ready.

"They were launching a lifeboat on the starboard side," Lanser told Mueller. "If we sight it, we can spare a shell to sink it."

"You mean that you intend to add more murder?"

"I mean that I intend to complete our mission."

Lanser followed the roving searchlight through his binoculars, but the fog banks were rolling in again, even covering the spot where the *City of Glasgow* had gone down. Lanser spoke to Mueller:

"Come below. We must submerge and continue on our way."

In the ward room of the U-boat, Lanser jotted down the details of the kill and listened happily to the steady rhythm of the submerged sub's motors. He signed his report and turned to Mueller with a harsh laugh.

"Too bad I have no more space on my report, Lieutenant," Lanser said. "I could have added that you are an old woman."

"Because I didn't think it right to murder people without warning?"

"That, Lieutenant, is a question of international law."

"Perhaps it is governed by a higher law, Captain. There could be a special kind of hell waiting for us. Maybe we will have to suffer the same agony that those trapped and drowning victims did, before they finally died."

"I agree. That can happen to any of us — once."

"I don't mean just once. I mean over and over, throughout eternity."

"You talk like a foolish mystic, Lieutenant."

"We might go on trying to warn them forever, yet never be able to save them."

Lanser laughed. "I will take my chances. Go get some sleep, Mueller. I think you need it."

Lanser rose, giving Mueller a whack between the shoulders. At that moment, the whole wardroom quivered, and a muffled blast, reminiscent of the shellfire, came to their ears. Angrily, Lanser snarled:

"A depth bomb! Destroyers from the convoy. That radio man must have given our position, despite us. You see, now, Mueller, why our business is murder, as you call it, and not mercy! Where is that higher law now?"

There were more jarring bursts. The depth bombs were hitting closer. Lanser submerged the U-boat deeper, using every trick he knew to escape the impending doom, but to no avail. One violent explosion made the sub's plates quiver, extinguishing her lights and disabling her motors. Another blast, still closer, and the hull of the U-boat gave way. In upon Lanser poured that same green deluge that had inundated the cabin on the *Queen of Glasgow*. Lanser was choking, drowning as he had before, dying that same hopeless, overwhelming death.

And then:

Green water thinned to soupy fog. Instead of total saturation, Lanser felt only dampness on the ship's rail from which he raised his hand and ran his long fingers through his blond hair. He was trying to orient himself to this timeless, oft-repeated scene, as he spoke the name that was only half-familar, but best suited for these new surroundings. Curtis Lanser — the name of a passenger on the *Queen of Glasgow,* for that was the name Lanser saw on a lifeboat that was hanging from its davits. A door opened and a steward appeared. He spoke to Lanser:

"They will be finished serving dinner soon —"

Yes, Lanser had gone through this so often before; but he was still groping, wondering how he fitted into it. Somehow, it seemed endless, part of a mental treadmill so hideously unreal that it might be the only reality that he had ever known or ever would know, perhaps forever and forever.

Yet time was moving on. Time, in terms of mortal reckoning — Minutes, hours, years. Some twenty of those years had passed, and a giant liner was cleaving its way through fog-bound waters, throating a deep, warning whistle to other shipping in the area. It was the same portion of the Atlantic Ocean where a freighter called the *Queen of Glasgow* had wandered from its convoy during wartime, to be trailed to its doom by a lurking U-boat.

No need for convoys now. How different, the swift glide of this mighty ship, blaring its path through the misty shroud, compared to the throbbing, hopeless flight of the wayward freighter! That was so apparent to the woman who stood by the rail near the liner's bow, looking off into the swirling fog.

Time had been kind to Barbara Stanley. The strained, taut expression on her face was not the mark of age. It was due to her recollection of a fearful night in these same waters, when from the safety of a lifeboat, she had watched a sinking freighter carry her dead and dying friends to the ocean's depths. Tonight, almost against her will, she had come from her cabin to the deck of the liner, lured by her remembrance of that other fog-locked night.

Now, as Barbara gazed, the misty curtain parted. Off in the swirl, she saw the dreaded sight that had etched itself in her memory. There, as real as on that fatal night, was the battered hulk of the *Queen of Glasgow*, her bow nosing beneath the ocean's surface for the last long dive. And on the phantom freighter's deck, his hands waving a frantic gesture for the lifeboat to get away, was the man whose name Barbara now whispered:

"Curtis Lanser."

The liner's lookout did not see that ghost ship from the past, even though it belonged to the present — and to the future. But Barbara's glimpse through the misty curtain of time was promptly verified. As she turned from the liner's rail, she saw a muffled man standing there beside her, his eyes fixed on the closing fog. In a hushed tone, Barbara asked:

"You saw — that ship — out there?"

"Yes," came the solemn reply. "She was the *Queen of Glasgow*."

"And you saw the man who waved that warning from the rail?"

"Yes. Kurt Lanser, the commander of the U-boat that shelled her."

In all those intervening years, Barbara Stanley had half-believed that there must be such an answer. Incredible though it might seem, it was the only way to account for Lanser's presence on the freighter and all the facts that he had known. Now, as Barbara studied the broad face of the solemn man beside her, she was suddenly inspired to ask:

"But how do you know all this — about Kurt Lanser?"

"Because I was his second in command. My name is Hans Mueller, and as we watched from the conning tower, I somehow knew what Lanser's fate would be. Within an hour, our U-boat was sunk by depth bombs from a British destroyer. Kurt Lanser believed that he would perish like his victims, only once. But time and again, I have stood at the rail of a ship like this and watched him go down with the *Queen of Glasgow*."

"The ghost of an unhappy man," Barbara spoke in a sad whisper, "trapped forever on the ghost of an unfortunate ship." She was staring hard into the thickening fog, picturing the strange sight that had been unveiled there. "Yes, Kurt Lanser was alone that night, as he was tonight."

The fog had closed in again, but Barbara was still gazing into its impenetrable folds, as she spoke again to the man beside her:

"But tell me, Mr. Mueller, if your submarine was depth-bombed, how could there have been any survivors? How do you happen to be here?"

There was no reply. Barbara turned and stared with wide, amazed eyes. No one was standing there beside her. She was alone, under the fog-blurred lights that showed the broad, open stretch of the liner's sweeping deck.

As in a dream, Barbara Stanley went back to her cabin.

THE CURSE OF SEVEN TOWERS

THE CURSE OF SEVEN TOWERS

Against the late afternoon sky, the frowning battlements and tall turrets of Seven Towers presented a strange, fanciful picture of a giant's castle wrested from its storybook setting and transplanted to modern times. High above the ancient stronghold jet planes were leaving long, snakish trails behind them, catching the gold and crimson rays of the sunset, like streaks from a master painter's brush. Through the deer park in the darkening foreground, past the shadowy outlines of boxed hedges and stately yew trees, the lights of approaching cars were following the curved driveways leading to the massive greystone pile.

Surrounding these mighty bastions was a water-filled moat, which gave the impression that the castle was floating on the surface of a dark, sylvan pool. At the very center of the huge, sprawling structure was a mammoth gateway. From it extended a drawbridge, like a giant's tongue thrust from a yawning mouth. Above, the great iron grating of a raised portcullis resembled tremendous teeth, ready to champ down upon unwelcome visitors who tried to enter the inner court beyond.

But this evening, all visitors were welcome. In contrast to forgotten men-at-arms who had once ridden their warhorses through the fortified castle, the present arrivals drove their cars — convertibles, compacts, station wagons into the gaping maw of the great stone castle. There, they parked in the very spaces where steeds carrying bound and helpless prisoners had formerly been tethered. Like those medieval captives, some of the newcomers were a bit bewildered as they unlimbered themselves from their cars.

To find themselves suddenly planted half a dozen centuries back was something of a shock to those who first experienced it. But to others, those who had visited Seven Towers before, this was just the beginning of the fun. They, too, had been dumfounded on their first trip here; now they relished seeing others in a like plight.

Paul Corley, regarded as a prankster by his London cronies, was one of the regular visitors, who liked to prod newcomers with pointed quips. His roundish moonface totally solemn, Corley approached a rugged, square-jawed Australian named Gordon Woodrow and announced seriously:

"You were lucky, Woodrow, that you didn't hit a deer coming through the park. In the old days, they cut your ears off and branded you twice over for a trifling offense like that."

Helene Loland, a striking, vivacious blonde, overheard Corley's remark as she was alighting from her chauffeured limousine.

"Don't believe anything Paul tells you, Mr. Woodrow," said Helene. "We are all lucky to be invited to Seven Towers for these old-time revels."

"And you are the luckiest of all, Helene," retorted Corley. "If the old original Sieur Dubois hadn't built his gateway wide enough for his horsemen to ride two abreast, that hired hack of yours would have lost all four fenders coming through the gate."

Gordon Woodrow, his lips firmed in restrained impatience, waited until Corley had finished. Then Woodrow put a quick query;

"You say revels, Miss Loland. I thought we were invited here to engage in a ghost hunt, or am I misinformed?"

Both Helene and Corley gave quick, hushing gestures. "Never use that term," Corley said in an undertone. "You don't hunt ghosts in Seven Towers. They hunt you. In fact, don't mention ghosts until the subject is duly introduced. Somebody might hear you up there!"

From Corley's sepulchral tone, Woodrow thought he meant the towering heights above and some spectral beings that might dwell therein, particularly as Corley made an upward gesture as he spoke. Then, as Woodrow scanned the central tower, his gaze came downward and he saw what Corley meant.

On an iron-railed balcony just above the courtyard, a slender man with a gaunt, pale face was studying the arrivals. There, the earlier lords of the castle had taken their stance in olden days, to appraise the booty that their raiding henchmen had brought home. This was the modern version of that line of feudal barons, the Honorable James Boyce, present master of Seven Towers and the direct descendant of the original Sieur Dubois.

Instead of wearing an expression of malevolent contempt, as suited his ancestral bearing, Boyce was greeting everyone with a truly disarming smile that marked him as the hunted type, rather than a hunter. The lips that showed disdain were Gordon Woodrow's, as the burly Australian contrasted the massive bulk of Seven Towers with the insignificant build of its owner.

"He reminds me of a dried walnut kernel," commented Woodrow, "rattling about in an oversized shell."

"That's our Jimmy Boy," Corley chuckled. "I couldn't have pegged him better myself."

The last of the two dozen guests had arrived; now a few of the cars were leaving, among them Helene's hired limousine, which was going back to London.

Servants clad in faded, ancient livery carried the luggage past a guard-room, where a watchman pressed the switch of an electric motor that lowered the portcullis by modern cable, cutting off the outside world.

"Our cars are parked safely for the night," said Corley, in his same sepulchral tone. "Just as we will be later, let us hope."

James Boyce had come down from the outside balcony to welcome his guests as they entered the great hall. After that formality, they were conducted to their assigned apartments, with servants as guides. They passed through chambers hung with heavy ancient tapestries, along a hallway flanked by suits of burnished armor, up grand stairways and spiral staircases to corridors that turned and angled through the labryinthic floors above.

Though it was still daylight, the slanted rays of the setting sun were dimmed by narrow windows and stained glass panes, bringing early gloom to the interior of the castle. Despite her familiarity with these scenes, Helene was gripped anew by their weird spell. That was due partly to the effect of the surroundings on Helene's companion, Cynthia Gifford, a dark-eyed brunette, who had come along on the trip from London. Cynthia, who was playing lead roles in television productions of early English dramas, had been very eager to visit Seven Towers; but so far, the effect upon her had been more than overwhelming. It was chilling.

"I actually froze when I passed those suits of armor," Cynthia confided. "They seemed so icy. I was sure that monsters were crouching inside them."

"Except," corrected Helene, "you can't crouch inside a suit of armor."

"Perhaps I can't," returned Cynthia, "but that doesn't mean a monster couldn't." Cynthia broke off with a sharp gasp and pointed wildly at the servant who accompanied them, as he went into a crouch of his own. But he was only stooping to unlock a door. Promptly, he opened it and bowed Helene into a high-ceilinged room with massive furniture dominated by a large four-poster bed, all vaguely visible by the fading light from a deep-set window in the wall beyond.

"This is my regular room," announced Helene, "and I like it. I come here for a rest cure, in case you don't know. It is quieting, comforting, and far away from the city. I sleep better here than anywhere else."

The liveried servant was turning on electric lamps, and although they were too few to illuminate the room brightly, they gave it a cozy effect.

"That's why I brought you here, Cynthia," continued Helene in her volatile but emphatic way. "I felt it would soothe your jangled nerves. Your room is around the corner in the next corridor. You will like it."

Helene waved to the servant, who conducted Cynthia out into the corridor and around the corner. Helene called a last reminder:

"Leave the light on in your room, Cynthia. I always do, so I can find my way back. These corridors become really, really dark later."

Soon Cynthia found herself in a room that was very similar to Helene's, but a little smaller, which meant that it was better lighted. This pleased Cynthia all the more. She changed to a dinner gown, left the room, and closed the door behind her. She reached the corner of the corridor, then guided herself by the dim light from Helene's door, which was open. Helene was also dressed for dinner, and they went downstairs together.

All the other guests were gathered there, and they were ushered into the great banquet hall, which occupied the entire ground floor space beneath the Tudor tower. Some fifty feet square, the banquet hall was more than two stories in height, allowing for a balcony where minstrels and musicians put on a continuous show, paced by a jester in medieval cap and bells.

The dinner itself was lavish, but quite modern, except for a few special delicacies and rare wines that were served in the Dubois tradition. The party sat at a T-shaped table with James Boyce at the head, facing the musicians' balcony. On Boyce's right was an elderly but keen-faced man, whose manner was remarkably alert. He was Cyril Morcroft, former Cambridge professor and a noted historian, whose works had gained acclaim in literary circles.

Seated on Boyce's left was Gordon Woodrow, who also rated as a special guest of honor. Apparently, the Australian had formed a better opinion of his host, for the two conversed quite amiably, a fact that Corley noted and mentioned — in due undertone — to Helene, who was next to him at the long table. There was something else, however, that impressed them more. Seen side by side, there was a certain resemblance between Boyce and Woodrow; but like their general physique, it was largely in the Australian's favor.

Of the two, Boyce was unquestionably the younger, but he looked older than Woodrow. Boyce, though handsome, was too jaded for a man in his early thirties. Perhaps his years as a confirmed bachelor and an incorrigible playboy had taken their toll. His face was becoming paunchy, his hair thin and balding. His eyes were dull and reflective, brightening only when something of special interest snapped him from his moodiness.

In contrast to Boyce's flabby features and sickly pallor, Woodrow had a firm, sharp-chiseled profile and tawny complexion that marked him as a rugged outdoor man. Only the strong furrows of his high forehead and the gray streaks in his dark hair placed him in his mid-forties, for he still showed all the vigor of youth. As the dinner progressed, Woodrow became all the more dynamic, while Boyce, by contrast, seemed to droop.

After the final course, the guests were served coffee from antique pots, and cordials from musty bottles. While they sat and sipped, the servants and entertainers all departed. The time was ripe for after-dinner speeches, and, rather painfully, James Boyce rose to the occasion.

"Many of you," Boyce began slowly "may wonder how I can afford to keep up Seven Towers in such lavish style. The truth of the matter is, I can't. Except for a few workers who keep the grounds in shape and a few old retainers who refuse to leave, all the rest, minstrels as well as servants, were either hired or volunteered for this occasion.

"Then why do I stay here? Why don't I let the castle go to rack and ruin? Because" — Boyce's tone went hollow — "as the last lineal descendant of the original Sieur Dubois, I am under a curse, which might follow me wherever I go, or might even draw me back to Seven Towers."

As Boyce paused, lighted torches set in wall brackets began to flicker, casting grotesque shadows across the banquet table. The torches had been lighted to provide an old-time atmosphere, as well as to supplement the inadequate electric illumination. Now, running short of oil, they had begun to waver. Only the guests, however, were perturbed. Boyce gave no notice.

"Seven Towers is said to be haunted," Boyce continued, "like many other baronial mansions. Perhaps the ghosts exist only in the imagination of those who think they see them; certainly, they have never been known to harm anyone directly. But they do carry a baleful influence. When they appear in full force, it is a prediction of disaster indeed, immediate doom for the Master of Seven Towers, who right now happens to be myself.

"For this reason I have arranged to turn Seven Towers over to the

League for Preservation of Historic Sites. In the future, if the ghosts do stalk someone to his doom, it will not be myself, but the Director of the L.P.H.S., who happens to be my old and esteemed friend on my right, Professor Cyril Morcroft."

The elderly historian acknowledged the favor with a dry smile, while a buzz of interest throbbed through the guests. Boyce then turned to introduce Gordon Woodrow.

"All this will be of particular interest to the honored guest on my left," Boyce said. "He came especially from Australia to visit English castles and steep himself in their traditions. When he learned that I gave occasional house parties here at Seven Towers, he arranged for an invitation through the Midlands Estate and Home Financiers, Limited.

"Since they happen to hold the mortgage on Seven Towers, I was induced, so to speak, to hold another party, which, I must frankly acknowledge, is being given at their expense. This is, therefore, a farewell event; but as always, I would like everyone to report tomorrow anything unusual that they may notice tonight."

As Boyce sat down, Morcroft put in a dry comment:

"What Mr. Boyce means is that all of you are guinea pigs. Guests new to the scene here may prove more responsive to unknown influences than those already acclimated to these surroundings. Anything you may note may prove significant to those who have delved into the traditions of this castle."

"Speaking strictly as a guinea pig," asserted Woodrow, in a strong, challenging tone, "I am Australian bred, and I have a kick like a full-sized kangaroo. Bring along your ghosts, and I'll plant them right back in their proper haunts."

Woodrow's expressed contempt for ghosts gave bravado to the other guests. As they left the banquet hall, several of them peppered Boyce with questions, which he brushed away in a defensive manner.

"I can't go into details," Boyce insisted. "I might influence your minds. Talk to Professor Morcroft in the library. He knows more about Seven Towers than I do. Now, if you will excuse me, I would like to turn in early. This has been a very trying day."

Most of the guests followed Cyril Morcroft into the library, a room with nooks and alcoves that were literally walled with rare volumes pertaining to British heraldry, lineage, and family tradition. There, the professor gave a scholarly dissertation on Seven Towers, telling how it was originally a Saxon fortress that was taken over by the Normans. They, in turn, had added on a huge corner tower which they styled the Keep. At least two more towers were added within the century that followed.

The Tudor Tower, Morcroft believed, had been the seventh and last; but long before that, the original Saxon Tower had been rebuilt. Two other towers had figured in the Wars of the Roses, when much of the castle had been demolished. Since the building of the Tudor Tower, the castle had been greatly expanded, and many windows had replaced the narrow wall-slits once used by archers. But Morcroft continually smiled off all references to the castle ghosts.

"Tomorrow," he promised, "we can talk about them. Ghosts are much better discussed in the daylight. Seven Towers is steeped in tradition, and tradition breeds legends. That is all that I can say right now."

"And all I can say right now," Helene told Cynthia, "is that I'm tired."

"You mean tired of all this ghost talk."

"Just plain tired. I'm going up to my room and get some sleep."

"A good idea," agreed Cynthia. "I'll come along."

Cynthia didn't add that she wanted to avoid that long trip alone. Some of the other guests evidently felt the same way, for they started upstairs in a group.

The tapestried chambers were dim now; and their walls seemed peopled with lurking figures. In the sparse electric lighting of the long hall, suits of armor seemed to sway like living forms as they reflected the shadows of the passing guests. Life-sized portraits, gazing down from their frames, became real faces in the uncertain light. As they parted from the others at a stairway, Cynthia whispered to Helene:

"I'm scared to look back. Wait a moment. Listen!"

From behind them, came the repeated whisper: "Listen."

"Just an echo," said Helene with a smile. "But you are right, Cynthia. In this place, it is not good to look back. That's the trouble with Jimmy Boy. His mind is so lost in the past that he is afraid of the future."

By then, they were at Helene's room, where the open door still threw a welcoming shaft of light into the corridor.

"I'll light you on to the corner," said Helene. "Remember, don't look back. You'll be all right when you reach your own room."

After Cynthia turned the corner, Helene closed her door. Now Cynthia was in a dilemma that she hadn't anticipated. She had left the lights on in her own room, but she had neglected to leave the door open, as Helene had. Cynthia was groping along a totally darkened passage, feeling as though solid, pressing blackness had closed in behind her. Frantically she tried to find her door, but couldn't. Almost hysterical, she wanted to scream for help, but a sudden recollection froze her lips.

That whispered word: *"Listen!"* Perhaps it had been a mocking reality, not just her own echo. Should she cry out now, she might raise answering shrieks from some eldritch denizen of these unhallowed halls!

Chilled to a standstill, Cynthia could almost feel the clutch of invisible hands. She was ready to dash headlong down the passage into deeper blackness, if only to escape the smothering pall that seemed to choke her.

Then, as Cynthia swayed under the overwhelming spell of her self-induced terror, she saw something that made her give one faint gasp of hope.

As from afar, a spot of light appeared at the deep end of the passage. Gradually, it spread into a luminous orb that assumed an oval shape, the upper edges growing hazier as it enlarged. By then, Cynthia realized that it was coming closer and taking on a human form, for the glow revealed the head and shoulders of an elderly man, his flowing hair and large white beard producing the surrounding haze.

The venerable figure was slow and stately in its approach, and Cynthia saw that the bearded man was wearing an ancient tunic with an embroidered coat-of-arms. It resembled the uniforms worn by the servants in the banquet hall, but it was more elegant. That, coupled with the bearded man's dignified poise, made Cynthia decide that he must be the castle caretaker.

In the radiance that now suffused the passage, she saw the door of her room right beside her. As she found the knob and pressed it, she turned to speak to the bearded man, who at that moment was passing by.

"Thank you for bringing the light," began Cynthia. "I never could have found my room without it."

Cynthia cut herself short. Viewing the man's face at close range in the upward spreading light, she saw that, far from being kindly, his features were cold and cruel. His eyes, staring straight ahead, formed deep hollows below his shaggy hair; while his profile, etched sharply through the glowing beard, was as firmly fixed as his gaze. It struck Cynthia that he was so intent upon some purpose that he had failed utterly to notice her and that even now, he did not hear her words of gratitude.

As she watched the figure continue along the passage, Cynthia was numbly concious of a chilling gust that followed in his wake.

She had opened the door of her room, and she glanced in that direction, thinking that the breeze might have come from there. When she looked along the passage again, the bearded man had gone, though how he had reached the turn so quickly, Cynthia could not understand. Nor did she try; instead, she stepped into her room, closed the door and bolted it, hoping to block out those imaginary terrors that had swept her.

The room with its massive furniture and solid walls was a fortress against fear, a miniature stronghold within the great castle itself. Cynthia stepped to the deep-set window and took a long breath of fresh air. She wondered, though, how a breeze could have come from there, for the night was very still. Too tired to wonder long, she dismissed the matter, turned out the lights, and went to bed.

Whatever the mission or the station of the bearded man who had passed by Cynthia's room, he was making extended rounds tonight. Two other guests, Janice Petersham and Della Weldon, were coming to a stair top, when they sensed a passing breeze. Janice suddenly exclaimed: "Look there!"

Della looked, in time to see a bearded figure turning into what appeared to be a lighted passage. He was gone a moment later, and when they reached the turn, there was no sign of him. What puzzled Janice and Della still more, the light had gone out, too. But since their rooms were on the next floor, they didn't bother to look farther. Instead, they continued up the stairs.

Downstairs, most of the guests had dispersed, leaving only Cyril Morcroft and Gordon Woodrow in the alcoved library. There, the Cambridge professor was spreading old records and ancient diagrams over a large table. All these pertained to Seven Towers and other Midland castles, a subject that the visiting Australian found intensely interesting.

"You can't always trust these old documents," warned Morcroft. "Descriptions of one castle sometimes refer to another. Plans of barbicans or sally ports may never have been carried to completion. Often, they were even falsified, to mislead neighboring barons in the feudal days."

"From what you say," observed Woodrow, "I take it that the lords of Seven Towers were as bad a lot as any of them."

"They were worse," returned Morcroft. "They were like savages."

"That sounds a bit exaggerated," said Woodrow, "considering some of the savages I have met, such as the head hunters in North Borneo."

"Some of the early Saxons were as brutal as any head hunters."

"But the Dubois family were Normans, weren't they?"

"Originally, yes, but they married Saxons, blending a strain of refined cruelty with utterly barbaric natures. They thought nothing of exterminating a rival faction, even by sheer treachery. That is why grim legends have grown about Seven Towers. Let me show you an example."

Morcroft went to a shelf and began looking through some vellum-bound volumes. The stillness was deep, when Woodrow asked suddenly:

"What was that?"

Morcroft raised his head from a book, but heard nothing.

"It sounds like the clank of armor," declared Woodrow. "The slow tramp of men-at-arms. Come over this way and perhaps you can hear it."

Morcroft joined Woodrow near the library door. Both remained completely silent for a few moments. Then Morcroft nodded.

"I hear it now," he said. "Let's look into this."

Stealthily, the two men moved into the great hall, only to have the sound fade. Half a dozen doorways led from the hall, so the clanking could have gone in almost any direction. Woodrow, as alert as though tracking prey in the wilds of Borneo, beckoned Morcroft into a little anteroom.

"This should make a good sound box," whispered Woodrow. "If we hear it again, we can probably locate it."

They did hear it and they located it, a slow *clink-clank* from a passageway that led past the banquet hall. The sound was ominous enough to frighten off most persons, but not this pair of ghost hunters. They hurried to the passage, followed it to the end, and stopped short. Here it ran into a cross passage; and Woodrow, listening intently, heard a faint *click-click* coming from a closed door on the right.

"In there, Morcroft."

Together, they flung open the door and burst into a lighted room as two other men swung about to meet them. This pair was armed, but not with swords. Their improvised weapons were billiard cues. This happened to be the billiard room, and the invaders had interrupted Paul Corley in the midst of a game with a friend named Jeff Aubrey.

"What is this, Corley?" demanded Morcroft. "Another of your jokes?"

"It strikes me that *you* are the joker," retorted Corley, "smashing in on us in such an unseemly fashion."

Woodrow softened the situation by telling how he and Morcroft had been trailing the clanking sound only to be misled by the clicks of the billiard balls. Morcroft still thought that Corley had been spoofing them, even though Jeff Aubrey vouched for the fact that he and Corley had been playing billiards and nothing more. Then Corley himself came up with an idea.

"If you chaps have really picked up a ghostly trail," he declared, "why waste time here? Let's all of us get on with the hunt!"

A few minutes later, they were fanning out from the great hall, listening for the elusive *clanks*. Woodrow heard the sound again and called to the others. They converged, of all places, in the armory hall. There, Corley walked along the flanking rows, lifting the visor of each helmet, to make sure there was no one inside.

The suits of armor were empty; but Corley established one fact. The clang of each helmet, as he closed it, was exactly like the sound of the phantom marchers. That was proven, when the ghostly footbeats came again from a more distant passage. This time, they all heard it; and the four men took up the chase, hoping to block off the unseen procession.

Somewhere they miscalculated, for when they met again, outside the guardroom, they heard the clang from the direction of the banquet hall. They doubled back, and Aubrey reached a tapestried chamber just in time to hear the footfalls dwindling down the passage beyond. He called to the others, and Corley hurried around by another route, coming beneath a stairway just as the tramp of clanging marchers ascended the steps above his head.

Corley shouted the news to Woodrow, who relayed the word to Morcroft. The professor took a short cut to a spiral staircase leading up through the servants' wing and came back to meet the approaching footfalls. But before he reached them, he heard them change direction in the darkness. From their passage, the spectral troop ascended another stairway, and their muffled clangor faded somewhere on the floor above.

When the four men arrived breathless back in the library, the full nature of the chase dawned on Corley and his friend Aubrey. They began to wonder what they would have done if they had run head on into the phantom marchers. Morcroft put their minds at ease on that score. He explained that no one had ever seen the marching ghosts, though many people, over the years, had heard their rhythmic tramp.

To prove that, Morcroft produced a floor plan of the castle, studded with colored dots that gave the exact places and dates of such reports. Woodrow, in particular, was keenly interested in the chart; but after studying it briefly, he gave a disappointed shrug and said: "Most of the places where we heard the sounds tonight are already marked on the chart."

"But not in their correct order," Morcroft reminded him. "Until now, they have been reported singly, hit-or-miss. By checking back on our own movements tonight, we can trace the entire course of the mysterious march."

"In that case," decided Corley, "we've done our stint. What say we call it a night, Jeff, and let these chaps carry on?"

The two left the library, but Morcroft and Woodrow continued their survey for the next hour or more. Finally the library lights blinked off, and soon after, Seven Towers became totally dark, something like a crouching monster, beneath the sable canopy of the starlit sky.

All was silent during the succeeding hours until the soft light of dawn pervaded the scene. The song of the lark came from the meadow, tuned to the call of the thrush from the woods. Stately swans settled on the wide portion of the moat beneath the Norman Keep and glided serenely along the water's glassy surface. Even the deer nosed from the sheltering forest to nibble the tender grass of the lawn.

Viewed at that hour, the castle was at its best. The sunlight was not strong enough to reveal the tumbledown segments of the battlements, nor the rusted chains of the drawbridge which itself was in need of repair. Nor did the modern additions to Seven Towers show their lack of paint. Indeed, it was difficult to tell the old from the new, except for the deep-set windows, one of which marked the room in which Helene Loland slept.

There, the quiet that lay over Seven Towers seemed to pervade the room itself. Ordinarily, Helene could sleep until noon in such hushed surroundings; but today she was awakened suddenly by an odd clatter that developed into sharp hammering and heavy pounding. As Helene started to spring from her bed, she was momentarily startled by threatening figures in the half-light. Then she gave a laugh of relief.

Those looming shapes receded into their proper perspective as Helene blinked and rubbed her eyes. They were simply the ornate chairs, tables, and other bulky furnishings that gave all these old rooms a somewhat haunted look. But that didn't explain the racket that had awakened Helene and was now continuing outside her door.

Obviously, a crew of carpenters was at work, for Helene could hear the clatter of dropped boards, the rasp of saws cutting lengths of wood, with hammers keeping up a noisy obbligato as the boards were nailed in place. At each pause in sawing or when a sharp stroke of a hammer told that a final nail had been driven home, voices rose in raucous laughter.

"There's another for Old Beardie!" came a rough, thick tone. "Make haste, now — we need five more of these!"

A saw sped its pace to a swift whine. A splintering sound told that another board had been cut. In confirmation, a voice announced:

"Aye, and here is another. That makes number nine."

Hammers and saws were both at work now, rapidly finishing their task which, from the sounds, indicated that they were constructing a crude flight of steps.

"There's ten — and eleven — and twelve —"

Hands pressed to her throbbing temples, Helene wondered whether it was the late party, the early awakening, or just this incessant sawing and hammering that was giving her a splitting headache. Then, as voices broke into loud, jeering laughter, with the chorus, "There's thirteen for Old Beardie!" Helene could stand it no longer. She sprang from the old-fashioned bed, found her dressing gown, and wrapped it about her as she picked a zigzag course among the furniture until she reached the door. There, she drew back the ancient chain-bolt and looked into the hallway, ready to voice her indignation at the disturbance.

To Helene's astonishment, the carpenters were gone, and had taken their tools and work with them. Where Helene had expected to see some sort of a ladder standing thirteen steps high, there was only the dim, empty passageway, without a sign of anyone in either direction. The floor, at least, should have shown traces of sawdust; but there was none there.

Still puzzled, Helene went back to bed, but her sleep was fitful. In brief dreams, she seemed to hear echoes of that same sawing, hammering, and shouting, until she finally awoke and saw that it was broad daylight. The twitter of birds had become incessant from the high branches of the trees, and Helene's wrist watch showed the time as half past ten.

She dressed and went downstairs. She passed through the great banquet hall, which was singularly subdued in contrast to last night, and came into the cozy yet roomy breakfast room. Beneath a Gothic window with stained glass shields of the Boyce forebears, a dozen guests were helping themselves to kippers, kidneys, eggs, and muffins from a buffet table.

Cynthia was in the group, and she exchanged smiles with Helene as they passed. Armed with a breakfast tray, Helene sat down at a circular table set in a large curved window. There, James Boyce was chatting with Cyril Morcroft and Gordon Woodrow as they looked out across the moat to the rolling lawns and distant trees.

Boyce had shaken off his morbid mood of the night before. In the sunlight, his face showed a ruddy gleam, and his smile was genuine. Perhaps his relief over the coming disposal of Seven Towers was making him forget the past. Boyce seemed ready for a joke when Paul Corley joined the group.

"Well, shall we all start lying now about things that happened to us last night?" he asked. "Or shall we wait until the rest of the crowd come shrieking down from upstairs, with ghosts snapping at their heels?"

"Let's tell our own adventures first," suggested Helene, "so we will be conditioned for something really gruesome. Then we can go rouse the others and find out how many are dead in their beds."

"There's nothing really weird about Seven Towers," Boyce said, as though anxious to convince himself. "My ancestors thought they saw ghosts because they spent long winter evenings beside the flickering firelight, with nothing better than a feeble candle flame to hunt for imaginary creatures in the shadows."

"But what about people hearing things?" demanded Helene. "How do you explain that?"

"All the more easily," returned Boyce, with a broadening smile. "In the dark, all sorts of trifling sounds are magnified."

"I don't mean in the dark. I mean in the daylight, early this morning."

"When you were half asleep and probably dreaming."

"When I was as wide awake as I am now." Helene was emphatic. "I've always had the same room here at Seven Towers, and the first time, it gave me a bit of the creeps, but I soon got over that. Today, however —" Helene stopped and turned to Corley. "You weren't staging one of your hoaxes, were you, Paul?"

Corley shook his head, and Helene went on:

"No, it couldn't have been a hoax, nor a ghost." She faced Boyce again and added: "It was your carpenters I heard. But *why* so early in the morning?"

Despite the glow of the sunlight, Boyce's face was draining white. His voice shook: "What carpenters?"

"Why, don't you have carpenters regularly repair the castle?"

"I haven't had one here for the past two weeks."

"Then they must have come on their own," claimed Helene. "They were sawing and hammering outside my door, building steps, of all things. I even heard them counting them; there were thirteen in all" — Helene gave a nod of recollection — "and they were making them for someone called Old Beardie!"

Boyce's face was sheet-white now, the sunlight accentuating its utter pallor. His coffee cup rattled in its saucer as he lowered both to the table. Helene saw the effect that the name "Old Beardie" had produced, and she wished she hadn't uttered it. What made it worse, Cynthia arrived at that unfortunate moment and happened to overhear her friend's words.

"Old Beardie!" echoed Cynthia. "What a quaint name! Why, it sounds like the caretaker, or whoever he was I met outside my room last night. He had a white beard and long hair —"

Boyce's hollow tone came in sudden interruption:

"This bearded man came from the far end of the passage?"

"That's right," Cynthia agreed, "and I saw him very clearly. I even noticed his odd old uniform, there in the light."

"But there is no light in that passage."

Boyce's slow words carried a note of utter despair, like the toll of a death knell. Cynthia's recollections became a stark horror.

"But I saw him so clearly — he must have been carrying a light — but no, he wasn't — the glow just moved along with *him!*" Cynthia choked, panicky, then blurted: "I must have been seeing a ghost!"

"A ghost!" The double echo came from Janice Petersham and Della Weldon, who were just now joining the group. Then Della exclaimed, "Why, we saw that bearded man, too!"

Without a word, the master of Seven Towers turned and stalked quickly through the banquet hall. The rest sat in stunned silence, until they heard the slam of a door. Then Morcroft exclaimed: "We must stop him!"

Some of the group hurried after Boyce, while others found a way out through an old sally port leading to a rustic bridge that crossed a corner of the moat. But before they could overtake Boyce, his red convertible roared out beneath the raised portcullis and across the old drawbridge. Crouched like a racing driver, Boyce sped the car shrieking around the turns, until its red streak was swallowed by the green mass of the deer park.

On the lawn, the guests congregated about Cyril Morcroft, asking if he knew where Boyce had gone and why he had left so hurriedly.

"He has probably gone to Yarwick," stated Morcroft, "to see his solicitor and make sure that the castle deed has been transferred."

"From the way he was driving," observed Corley, "he'll be lucky to get that far. You'd have thought the devil was after him."

"Perhaps he was," returned Morcroft dryly. "In the lore of Seven Towers, there is not much choice between the devil and Old Beardie."

That brought startled looks from Cynthia and the others who had seen the glowing, bearded figure of the night before. Morcroft suggested that they adjourn to the castle library, where he would explain the situation fully. So, a quarter of an hour later, all were assembled in the alcoved room.

"Until now," asserted Morcroft, "I was not free to discuss the curse of Seven Towers. My purpose here was to track down old superstitions and debunk them. But now that the ghosts have actually walked, and certain portents have been manifested, explanations are in order.

"The curse dates back to the fifteenth century, toward the end of the

Wars of the Roses. Sir Reginald Dubois, who had been rebuilding Seven Towers, openly favored the House of York but secretly sided with the House of Lancaster. Among the Lancastrians who knew this was Sir Cedric Shapley, who had once been engaged in a bitter feud with Sir Reginald Dubois.

"After a battle that went against the Lancaster forces, it was said that Sir Cedric and the remnants of his bodyguard fled for refuge to Seven Towers, trusting that Sir Reginald would hide them if the Yorkists searched the castle. Later, Sir Reginald claimed they had never arrived there and that they must have been ambushed on the way. The fact that stands is that Sir Cedric and his followers never were seen again."

"And what," put in Woodrow, "did Sir Cedric's friends do about it?"

"They did nothing, because they could prove nothing. But as time went by, suspicion centered on Sir Reginald, due to reports of armored feet tramping through the halls of Seven Towers, presumably the ghosts of Shapley's men!"

"Did Sir Reginald Dubois ever hear those footsteps himself?"

"Definitely, yes." Morcroft thumbed the pages of a heavy-bound volume, "and so did his descendants, in the years that followed, along with other persons, like ourselves last night. But Sir Reginald may well have had a guilty conscience, for he was driven mad by those phantom footbeats. His enemies had sworn that they would capture and hang 'Old Beardie,' as they contemptuously called Sir Reginald. They never did, but when he was on his deathbed, new sounds were heard about the castle. Those of carpenters preparing the thirteen steps of a gallows for Old Beardie."

Helene Loland stared aghast at the professor.

"According to tradition," continued Morcroft, "Sir Reginald, dying, passed on a guilty secret to the heir who succeeded him. Since then, the grim secret has been handed down to each new master of the castle. Whenever one is about to die, the ghost of Old Beardie himself stalks these halls; and the sound of carpenters building his gallows is heard as a threat of doom."

"And what has been done," asked Woodrow, "to end this family curse?"

"Some persons have given up their inheritance to escape it," declared Morcroft. "One branch of the family changed its name to Boyce, as we know, but that was little help. The first Boyce who claimed Seven Towers as his rightful property was given the secret, and found that he had inherited the curse as well. Since then, it has been passed along in the customary way."

"What if something happened to the owner of the castle before he had a chance to pass along the secret?" Paul Corley asked.

"The curse itself has taken care of that," explained Morcroft. "Whoever owns Seven Towers has one advantage — or should I say disadvantage? He knows in advance when his time is up, so he can plan accordingly. The ghost of Old Beardie and the phantom carpenters who build their invisible scaffold see that he receives due notice."

"And Jimmy Boy received his notice this morning!" observed Corley. "From the way he was driving, he's likely to miss that sharp turn at the Yarwick River bridge. If he does, he will never pass the secret along."

"He wants it to die with him," declared Morcroft calmly. "So far as records show, he is the last of the Boyce line. That is why he planned to nationalize the castle and avoid the curse. But it has overtaken him."

Gordon Woodrow gave a disdainful grunt that showed how little he believed in superstition or tradition. In a gruff tone, he demanded:

"Just what is tangible about this curse? How is the castle itself supposed to figure in the strange riddle?"

"There is supposed to be a secret chamber," explained Morcroft, "which holds the full answer. But I have studied all the records of the castle's reconstruction and additions over a period of five hundred years, and I can find no clue nor reference to its existence, other than hearsay."

"But if it does exist, Jim Boyce must know about it."

"Yes, but he would be sworn not to tell anyone except a proper heir."

"Have people ever tried to find the hidden room?"

"Yes. About a century ago, a group of guests went through the castle while the master was away. They hung a towel from each window they came to, intending to check them later, from outside. Any window without a towel might have represented the secret room."

"But they didn't find it?"

"No. The owner of the castle came back while they were still hanging out towels, and ordered them all to leave."

Slowly, Woodrow drew his hand along his rugged chin and gave a knowing nod to the other guests.

"Do you know," he said, with a slight laugh, "that is not a bad idea. If Jimmy Boy, as you call him, is so afraid of the family curse, why not relieve him of his worry? We can work the towel trick ourselves, before he gets back from Yarwick. Maybe we'll find the secret chamber."

The plan swept the group like wildfire. By now, all the rest of the guests had come downstairs, so there were two dozen willing workers. Woodrow formed them into squads, which he assigned to different sections of the castle. In the empty guardroom, Corley found keys with tags bearing the names of the doors they unlocked. These were sorted and distributed among the proper squads. Some of the keys unlocked linen closets, where sheets and pillow slips were available along with towels.

This was truly an all-out effort to crack the riddle of the Seven Towers, but it proved to be a formidable task indeed. There were actually a few hundred rooms in the vast expanses of the castle, counting all the side nooks and dead-end hallways. These, in turn, had from one to a dozen windows each, depending on their size. So the squads had a long way to go.

Woodrow decided to go to the top of the Norman Keep himself, hanging towels from the archers' slits along the way. Helene brought along a reserve supply, and when they emerged through a trap door to the open roof and its surrounding parapet, Woodrow decided to take some pictures with a camera he carried. While he was thus engaged, Morcroft joined them, smiling as though the climb meant nothing. The professor was surprisingly agile.

The parapet around the tower was topped by stone posts, or merlons, with narrow intervening spaces called crenelles, through which ancient archers had shot arrows from their cross-bows. As Woodrow leaned against one of the merlons to focus his camera on the distant landscape, part of the stone post gave way. Helene cried out a warning as the rangy Australian caught himself. Then, daringly, Woodrow leaned across the widened embrasure to watch the falling chunk splash into the moat, far below.

"It must be deep, that moat," remarked Woodrow casually. "Muddy, too, with quite a current."

"It comes from the river," explained Morcroft. "The old records tell how they cut a special channel to supply it."

"Yes, I can see its course, now —"

Woodrow was leaning against another merlon to look down. Morcroft tugged him back and just in time, as another loose stone went plunging to the muddy depths.

"Thanks," said Woodrow, as though having his life saved was a regular occurrence. "I must say, there is a fine view from here."

"Since this is the highest tower," returned Morcroft, "it should give us a fine view. You might find it still finer, looking up from the moat."

"A good touch, Professor," chuckled Woodrow, "but don't worry about me. I've walked ledges a thousand feet up, and I'm as sure-footed as a cat. Well, I can't waste time taking pictures now. I must go down and see how the search is getting along." He paused and then suggested: "Why don't you two stay up here and watch for that red car of Boyce's?"

Morcroft and Helene decided that would be a good idea. To Helene, the next hour proved fascinating indeed, for Morcroft was steeped in the history of this region. The professor pointed out the remnants of forests where outlaws had roamed; he traced the course of a river through a distant battlefield and indicated a hill where ancient Druids had held their pagan rituals. So engrossed was Helene that neither she nor Morcroft noted the approach of Boyce's car until they saw it tearing in through the entrance to the deer park.

Frantically, Helene raced down the tower stairs, Morcroft following. As she flew through the gloomy corridors of the floors below, she forgot that these were ghostly haunts, as she shouted for everyone to hang out the last towels in a hurry, as Boyce was coming back. Helene reached the front lawn before Boyce's car arrived, and looking up, she saw an intriguing sight.

Towels, sheets, and curtains were dangling from every window, not only from the castle front, but from the side walls as well, as far as Helene could see. Wherever battlements rose above the inner court, the telltale markers showed there, too. Woodrow's squads had done a thorough job, and even now, some of the guests were surging from the castle gates to take an admiring look at their handiwork.

One person who did not admire the sight was James Boyce. His car came streaking through from the deer park and shrieked to a halt before it reached the drawbridge. Boyce sprang out, his face red with rage. To him, those cloths were hostile banners that flouted his authority.

Boyce waved to a few gardeners who so far had paid no attention to the goings on within the castle. He shouted for them to get upstairs and snatch the telltale markers from the windows. Next, he summoned the few servants who were in their quarters and ordered them to do the same. While the flaunting banners gradually disappeared, Boyce came storming from his castle to berate the somewhat sheepish guests now clustered on the lawn.

Helene noted that Woodrow was not among them. It wouldn't have mattered, because Boyce promptly singled out Corley as the ringleader.

"This is one joke of yours that has gone too far!" Boyce fairly screamed. "I never should have invited you here. Now, you can get out — and stay out — and take this whole motley mob of ingrates with you!"

"Righto, Jimmy Boy," returned Corley blandly. He turned to the silent guests. "We'd better all get out, before the high constable shows up and tags our cars for parking in the castle courtyard."

As one car after another left, Boyce stood with folded arms and watched them go. The only man who remained was Cyril Morcroft, who gestured for both Helene Loland and her friend Cynthia Gifford to stay.

"Too bad this had to happen," Morcroft said soberly. "But when James Boyce gets over his anger, he will be looking for someone who can help settle the ghost question — which you two can. You, for one" — he spoke directly to Cynthia — "saw Old Beardie. And you" — he turned to Helene — "heard the phantom carpenters."

"And I," a man's voice said from close beside them, "helped track the tramping ghosts. Don't you think I should be welcome, too?"

It was Gordon Woodrow, more poised than ever. His smile was broad and hard, showing that he was ready to challenge anyone who might object. Now that Corley had taken the blame for flaunting the towels from the castle windows, Boyce had no reason to suspect Woodrow had been the instigator. After glancing up at the castle, where by now at least half the improvised banners had been withdrawn from the windows, Boyce returned to the few persons who remained.

"Now," he said, "I am at least with people I can trust. Let's go inside and talk this over."

They went into the library, where the whole mad caper had begun, and Helene felt hypocritical indeed. She was beginning to wonder just who could be trusted. In that mood, she told Boyce:

"Look, Jimmy, since the rest have left, Cynthia and I are going, too, as soon as we can order a car to take us up to London."

"I have to call my solicitor's office in Yarwick," declared Boyce, "so I'll have him order a car from there."

Boyce went to telephone. While he was gone, Helene turned to Woodrow with an accusing glare and demanded:

"Where were you while everyone was being ordered to get out?"

"Making the rounds," responded Woodrow calmly, "taking pictures of the castle from every angle." He brought some rolls of film from his pocket and handed them to Morcroft. "Have these developed," continued Woodrow, "and add them to the archives of Seven Towers. They will definitely prove what I am sure I saw while I was taking the pictures."

"And what did you see?" asked Morcroft eagerly.

"A towel hanging from *every* window. I studied each section of the castle carefully as I took the pictures. None of the windows can possibly belong to a secret chamber."

"Good," Morcroft nodded. "That should help soothe Boyce's worries.

But I wouldn't talk to him about the curse until he is in a calmer mood."

Helene decided to go along with Morcroft's policy, since he seemed sincerely interested in Boyce's welfare. As the afternoon progressed, Boyce became impatient, wondering why his solicitor had not come from Yarwick, bringing the final papers from the finance corporation. Helene, too, was piqued because the hired car did not arrive. Woodrow, as composed and self-assured as ever, talked Boyce into a game of billiards. Helene and Cynthia sat by and watched the match until Boyce's petulance reached the breaking point.

"I'm going to talk to the servants," he decided, "and have them prepare dinner. We can't wait all night for my solicitor to show up, but until he does, we won't know when your car will get here, either."

After Boyce left, Woodrow put his cue in the rack and suggested:

"How about the three of us going up to the top of the Norman Keep to see the sunset? I can take some good color photos with the camera—"

"Not me," interposed Cynthia, with a shudder. "It's beginning to grow dark, and I don't want to run into Old Beardie again."

"Let's go into the library and talk to Professor Morcroft," said Helene.

Woodrow hooked the camera strap over his shoulder and started off alone in the direction of the great tower. The route he followed was the very one the girls had taken to their rooms, the night before. Woodrow passed Helene's door, where she had heard the phantom carpenters building their invisible scaffold. He came to the spot where Cynthia had seen Old Beardie walk by, and continued on to the far end of the passage, where the glowing ghost had first appeared. There, in the gathering dimness, Woodrow took the stairs to the higher floor where Morcroft had tracked the tramping footbeats of the unseen men-at-arms.

Then, instead of continuing on to the Norman Keep, Woodrow paused beneath an arched opening that connected two sections of the castle. All about was solid masonry of closely fitted stones. Woodrow inserted a flash bulb in his camera and shot a closeup of the archway. He followed that with another from a different angle. Next, he began tapping the wall and running his fingers among the crevices as though hoping to discover something.

As Woodrow crouched in the thickening gloom, his keen ear, trained to detect stealthy sounds in the jungle, caught a slight stir from the passage alongside him. He whipped about and saw a white face in the shadows, its lips spread in a grim, challenging grin. Woodrow laughed gruffly.

"Hello," he said. "I rather expected you to show up here."

This was no ghost. It was James Boyce. His sickly smile was forced, but he managed to back it with a show of indignation.

"*You* put them up to that window trick," he said accusingly. "It wasn't like Paul Corley to take the blame without an argument, so I finally figured he was covering for somebody. Except for Morcroft, you were the only man who stayed around and tried to bluff me. You, with that cool way of yours and that camera you carry. Now, tell me — what are you trying to find?"

"The secret chamber," returned Woodrow bluntly. "It hasn't any window, so it must be deep in the castle walls themselves. All the ghostly manifestations stemmed from here, so this must be the place."

Boyce's short laugh sounded hollow beneath the archway.

"Suppose I told you that the castle has no secret chamber?"

"I wouldn't believe you, Boyce," Woodrow replied calmly. "I would start to take this castle apart, stone by stone, beginning with this archway."

"A good idea, Woodrow," Boyce remarked sarcastically. "Why not talk with the Midland finance group before they turn the castle over to the Preservation League?"

"I did. And they have turned over the castle to me instead. That's why your solicitor has failed to show up with the final papers."

Boyce's eyes narrowed to slits as he groped for words.

"You can't — no, they can't allow it. No one has a right to betray a secret belonging only to the descendants of Sieur Dubois—"

"No one will betray it," rejoined Woodrow coolly. "I simply used part of the millions I made from Borneo rubber plantations to buy out the Mid-lands Estate and Home Financiers, and reclaim my family inheritance."

"*Your* family inheritance?"

"Yes. The Boyces aren't the only descendants of Sieur Dubois who changed their name, you know. One branch adopted the name of Wood, the literal translation of the French word *bois*. One member of that group married into a family named Rowe and the name became Wood-Rowe. When a later generation migrated to Australia, where hyphenated names are not as popular as here in England, it was simplified to Woodrow."

"Then you are actually my distant cousin — a claimant to Seven Towers."

"More than that, *Cousin* Jim," interposed Woodrow sharply. "I have records to prove that a generation back, this castle should have gone to a member of the Woodrow family; not to the Boyce who later left it to you. *I* am the real master of Seven Towers."

His eyes still narrowed and his forced smile tense, Boyce realized that Woodrow could be telling him the truth.

"So you see," sneered Woodrow, "it is I who should be giving you the answer to the riddle of Seven Towers and the true story of the family curse; not the other way about. But rather than have you thrown out as a usurper, I am willing to let you fulfill the pledge you must have made when you were told the castle's secret; namely, to pass it along to the rightful descendant of Sieur Dubois."

Boyce's whitened lips went tight, as though in absolute refusal.

"It's either now or later, Cousin Jim," Woodrow said. "If you don't tell me the secret, I won't be sworn to keep it when I do uncover it."

"All right, Cousin Gordon," Boyce retorted suddenly. "You win. But you're asking for it, you know — something that will really shock you —"

"I'm used to shockers, Cousin Jim. I've met up with head hunters, remember? And I've given them rough punishment in return."

"Don't forget there is a curse that goes with this family secret."

"And that curse will become mine instead of yours," chuckled Woodrow. "I'm helping you get out from under, Cousin Jim."

"Very well, then," said Boyce. "Do you have a flashlight?"

Woodrow produced one and turned it on. Boyce gestured for him to focus it on the side wall of the arch. Then, in the glow, Boyce probed the crevices with his fingertips, finding the spaces between two special stones. They were linked by some hidden mechanism that required double pressure, for a muffled click came from within the masonry. Boyce paused, brought out a flashlight, and said:

"Now, you try it, Woodrow — I mean Cousin Gordon."

Woodrow copied Boyce's probe and was rewarded by the same click. Boyce told him tensely: "Now press steadily, against the stonework itself."

Woodrow pressed. An upright segment of the solid wall swung downward, inward, showing jagged edges where the stonework had fitted to exactitude. Five feet in height and three in width, it formed a thick slab hinged at the bottom and governed by a hidden counterweight below. It finally reached the horizontal, held there by the pressure of Woodrow's outstretched hand. The end of the slab settled upon a broad stone step that marked the bottom of a steep stairway hewn in the castle wall itself.

"I was sure this would be it," affirmed Woodrow, in a satisfied tone. "This is where the old Saxon Tower meets the Norman Keep. The walls here must be doubly thick."

He stooped to go through the opening, where the lowered slab was like a drawbridge to the steps beyond. Then he drew back, smiling.

"After you, Cousin Jim," Woodrow invited.

In the glare of the flashlight, Boyce's return smile was bitter, as though recognizing Woodrow's mistrust. Obligingly, Boyce crossed the five-foot bridge, stamping it to assure Woodrow that it was solid and secure. Woodrow followed and squeezed himself alongside of Boyce.

"Go up one step," urged Boyce, "and watch over my shoulder. You will see how simply it operates from this side."

Woodrow moved upward, and Boyce followed far enough to relieve the hinged slab of his weight. Slowly, the stone barrier rose of its own accord, far enough for Boyce to bring his hands beneath it and push it at arm's length into its original upright position in the wall. There was a click as it jammed there, but there was a wide space at the upper edge, here on the inside of the wall.

"You simply work your fingers in there," stated Boyce, in a subdued tone, "and pull down. That lowers it again. It can't go wrong."

Woodrow nodded and gave an upward wave of his flashlight. "All right. Now, let's go —"

He stopped short. His words, spoken in a normal tone, sounded like a shout in these stony confines. He reduced his voice to a mere whisper, the way Boyce had. "Let's go on up. I want to see that secret chamber."

Boyce turned his own flashlight upward and pressed on past Woodrow, who followed closely. The stairway came to an abrupt end beneath a stone ceiling that represented another slab. This one was different from the one below. Instead of being hinged, it simply slid horizontally, like a sliding drawer. Its mechanism was smooth, however, for it glided noiselessly into the wall, revealing a blackened gap above.

"This slab works only from beneath," stated Boyce in his strained whisper. "When closed, its ends are directly below the upright walls, so there is no way to open it from above. Prepare yourself for the worst."

There was a quiver in Boyce's whisper that Woodrow realized was inspired by sheer, stark dread. Boyce continued up the steps, beckoning Woodrow along. Then, the two cousins were standing side by side, playing their flashlights upon a grisly scene.

Sprawled about a squarish, stone-walled room were whitened figures partly clad in armor, like yeomen who had been making ready for a last assault upon a foe. Scattered about were helmets and gauntlets which they had not yet put on; hence the heads and hands of the fighting men were fully in view, nearly a dozen in all.

Those heads were grinning skulls. The hands were bony skeleton fingers, some dangling in the hilts of rusted swords that lay blunted and broken on the stone floor beside their hapless owners. One figure alone was clad in complete armor, but the visor of its helmet was partly lifted and hollow eye-sockets glared like blackened orbs from the whitened skull within. It was to that figure that Boyce gestured first.

"Sir Cedric Shapley." Boyce's whisper was full of horror. "And his loyal men-at-arms. Our mutual ancestor, Sir Reginald Dubois, hid them here so they would not be found if their enemies searched the castle. He slid the stone slab shut from beneath; then conveniently forgot to return and open it."

Coldly, Woodrow studied the sprawled figures. Their broken, blunted swords indicated that they had tried to pry open the thick slab that imprisoned them, before death overtook them. Probably they had already been weakened from starvation when lack of air had resulted in their suffocation, for they had died while rallying to their leader's call in a last effort to mount guard.

"The ghosts of these men," continued Boyce in a hushed tone, "are the marchers who have tramped through the castle ever since. They must have made a last vow to avenge themselves in death after they had failed in life, for they drove Sir Reginald to madness and doom. He could imprison their bodies, but not their spirits."

Woodrow gave a side glance and saw that Boyce's eyes were nearly shut, his face whiter than ever. Calmly, Woodrow focused his camera on the gruesome death scene of centuries ago and took a flash picture. Then he asked:

"How often have you come up here, Cousin Jim?"

"Only once before," returned Boyce, "when the secret was revealed to me. Once was enough, but I promised to pass it along when the appointed time arrived. That I have done just now."

"But you would have preferred to have the secret die with you?"

"Absolutely, and it would have, if you hadn't insisted on my revealing it to you. Remember, the portent of doom has declared itself again. Old Beardie walked last night; the invisible carpenters built their gallows this morning."

"And you actually believe in all that nonsense?"

"Yes. What else can explain the strange things that happen?"

"Imagination. It is easy for people to think they hear and see things in an old castle. As for these" — Woodrow gestured to the armed skeletons — "Sir Reginald Dubois was smart to get rid of his enemies in a quiet, inexpensive way that nobody would guess. He just happened to go crazy and tell his secret later. So ever since, his gullible heirs have taken it seriously.

"Now that I'm taking over," he went on, "I'll have this rubbish cleared out, and I'll turn Seven Towers into a real showplace, with its haunted chamber as a top attraction. So come along, Cousin Jim, or I may get absent-minded and slide the slab shut, leaving you up here with Sir Cedric and his merry, merry men."

Woodrow was already starting down the stone stairs. In a panic, Boyce scrambled after him, only to have Woodrow snap a flash picture squarely in his face, recording all the terror that was etched there. While Boyce blinked and rubbed his eyes, Woodrow jeered:

"Slide the slab shut yourself, then, if you don't trust me."

Boyce obeyed, then hurried down to join Woodrow, who was already reaching for the finger space at the top of the hinged block at the bottom of the steps. He found it below shoulder level so he went down one step and was about to go another, when Boyce called in a hoarse whisper:

"Woodrow! Don't go another step!"

"What do you mean?" snapped Woodrow. "Are you threatening me?"

"I'm warning you! Don't take another step."

"*I* own this castle now," Woodrow said angrily. "And I'll —"

Suddenly Woodrow was clawing wildly in mid-air, seeking a finger hold in the crevice opposite. But his fingertips could not sustain the weight of his burly body which one step more had plunged downward into a sheer void.

From the depths of the sixty-foot shaft came back a trailing cry that was broken once, then again, and finally silenced as Woodrow's falling, thrashing form hit projecting stones along the way. A spinning streak of light accompanied him; his flashlight. Then — a distant splash from the bottom of the pit and the glow was swallowed with it.

From one step above the brink, Boyce pointed his own light downward. He saw the swirl of an ugly, murky current where the channel from the river flowed beneath the castle and on out to the moat. When no head bobbed above the surface, Boyce knew that those eddies had swept the victim along. Even worse than the fearful drop were the jutting rocks that Sir Reginald Dubois or one of his unkindly forebears had left there for the discomfort of any meddler who sought the secret chamber and blundered down the open shaft instead. They studded the route like the pins of a giant board game, making it impossible to miss.

Boyce had intended to show the death-shaft to Woodrow on their way out, but the new owner of Seven Towers had not waited long enough to learn that added secret of the castle. Now, Boyce numbly opened the stone block across from the steps and emerged into the archway, where he closed the tight-fitting wall behind him. When he reached the ground floor of the castle, he found it deserted, so he went outdoors. There, the solicitor had arrived from Yarwick and so had the car that was to take Helene and Cynthia back to London. But the two girls were still there, looking up at the high tower of the Norman Keep which was sharply etched against the fading sunset.

They were calling good-bye to Gordon Woodrow, but they were receiving no answer. That brought a worried head-shake from Cyril Morcroft, who was standing by. Morcroft turned and spoke to Boyce as he approached:

"Woodrow told the girls that he was going to the tower," explained

Morcroft, "to take some pictures of the sunset. But when he was up there earlier, he insisted upon leaning against those loose, wobbly merlons. If he tried that foolhardy stunt again, chances are we shall find him in the moat. And I think we should start looking right now."

Boyce gave immediate agreement. "I'll summon the servants," he said.

They found Woodrow's body a few hours later, under the glare of automobile headlights and powerful electric lanterns. It was near the outlet of the moat, where the strong current had carried it. From the bruises on his head and the twisted condition of his limbs, it was assumed that he had struck some of the outer bastions of the huge tower during his long fall.

At the coroner's inquest held in Yarwick, the verdict was death by misadventure. Testimony given by Helene, Cynthia, and Morcroft was substantiated by the recovery of Woodrow's camera with his body. Examination of the film showed that four pictures had been taken. The water had ruined the negatives so they were no more than a blur, but it seemed obvious that Woodrow had been taking photos of the sunset, when he must have leaned too heavily on a merlon.

Nobody asked James Boyce where he had been while Woodrow was up on the tower. For Boyce was a big loser by Woodrow's death. It turned out that Woodrow had bought Seven Towers at a higher price than the League for Preservation of Historic Sites had offered. Because of Woodrow's death, the sale was nullified and the League acquired the castle at the original figure.

Visitors to Seven Towers now will find that it is a national museum, with Cyril Morcroft as its resident curator. He knows everything about the castle's history and can trace the genealogy of its owners from the original Sieur Dubois on down. Morcroft is convinced that James Boyce escaped the curse of Seven Towers, because he was never the true master of the castle. That title belonged to Gordon Woodrow, both by right of heritage and purchase, at the time when Old Beardie last walked and the phantom carpenters built their invisible scaffold. So it was Woodrow's death that those weird happenings had presaged.

Now that Seven Towers has passed from its hereditary line, the curse must have been lifted, for Old Beardie has made no new appearance nor have the unseen carpenters rendered another audition. But on occasional nights, whn all is very quiet, the tramp of phantom men-at-arms can still be heard. Always, Morcroft listens, for — as he likes to relate — he once tracked those ghostly marchers back to their starting point, hoping he might discover a secret chamber.

But now, Morcroft has given up that quest. Among his prized possessions is a set of photographs taken by Woodrow only a few hours before he met his doom. Those pictures show every window of Seven Towers flaunting towel, pillowcase, or some equivalent emblem, accounting for every room in the castle.

So, whatever doubts may surround the legends of Seven Towers, Cyril Morcroft is definitely positive on two points: One, that Gordon Woodrow fell to his death from the parapet of the Norman Keep; the other, that the castle has no secret chamber.

THE TIGER GOD

THE TIGER GOD

This is the story of the Tiger God as Harold Graylock told it. The story must be true, for Graylock not only witnessed many of the things he told about; he was in at the kill and could produce sworn affidavits. As for the other portions of the strange tale, they fitted the pattern like the missing pieces of a jigsaw puzzle.

It began at the great British Empire Exhibition held at Wembley in London, in 1924. There Graylock saw some fine displays of historic diamonds from India, and he also watched a clever show put on by a troupe of Hindu magicians. So he went to India to see if he could buy rare diamonds for the American market and also to look for even better magicians, figuring that they would be a sensation throughout the United States.

In big cities of India, Graylock met with double disappointment. He saw little that was worth while in diamonds and was told that he would have to deal with native princes who had hoards of such gems. As for the street corner magicians, or *jadoo wallahs* as they were called, they were far inferior to the troupe that had gone to Wembley.

Graylock heard talk of remarkable *yogis* who lived in Himalayan caves and floated in mid-air when the mood seized them, but they were hard to find. He also learned of an in-between group called *fakirs,* more clever than the jadoo wallahs and more worldly than the yogis. But they worked only for the privileged classes, not for the street corner trade. They were pampered in the palaces of the princes, where gates were hard to crash.

Then Graylock learned of the Rajah of Bildapore, the kindly ruler of a tiny domain that occupied only about a dozen square miles. Most of it, however, was an actual diamond mine, so the rajah had an abundance of such gems. His palace also was always open to mendicants and holy men who made pilgrimages to Benares and other sacred places, while troops of fakirs often stopped there.

So Graylock took a train for Bildapore, which was no more than a flag-stop on a branch line. Dressed in tropical white suit and pith helmet, he arrived at the palace and was ushered into the presence of the Rajah of Bildapore, a handsome, bearded man of middle age, whose vigor belied his years. A hunter and sportsman, he rated as the best rifle shot in that part of India, though he had to travel outside his limited domain to get at wild game.

Even when receiving visitors, the rajah wore a simple native costume, with only one diamond in his turban and another on a chain around his neck. With him was his daughter, the Princess Halina, whose large, dark eyes smiled a welcome though the lips of her perfect oval face formed an expressionless straight line. Halina wore diamond earrings, but the stones, though perfectly matched, were small, while her bracelets were plain gold bands.

The rajah's secretary, Shalbar, was a man in his early thirties, who wore a conservative English business suit like some underclerk in an obscure government office. However, his military haircut and short-clipped mustache gave him an air of authority and his keen eyes sized up people in one quick glance. Shalbar applied that process to Graylock.

A big, bluff, friendly man of thirty-five, Graylock had a know-it-all manner that could ruffle people. But he was quick to soft-pedal that boisterous mood, showing courtesy and appreciation that won people over because they had misjudged him. To the Rajah of Bildapore, Graylock delivered a speech so well rehearsed that it sounded natural.

"All over the world," Graylock declared, "I have seen diamonds stolen from one set of crown jewels and placed in another. I have seen fine stones cut into smaller ones to satisfy some whim. I have seen diamonds with curses, their brilliance wasted because of the greed that had tarnished them. So I came to Bildapore because here alone, there are diamonds which have been mined, kept and cherished by their rightful owners and their descendants. All that are a real part of your family heritage should stay here. But if you can spare any for true diamond lovers in other countries, I should like to place them as your agent."

"Mr. Graylock," returned the rajah, in a heartfelt tone, "many people have wanted to exploit my diamonds for cold, base profit. To meet someone like yourself — a man who feels as I do — is welcome indeed. This will take thinking, before I can give an answer. If I could make it worth your while to stay here for an extended visit, I should be overjoyed."

"Your Highness," Graylock replied smoothly, "I have been searching for higher things in the field of Oriental magic. I have heard that there are fakirs whose skill far exceeds the disappointing tricks of the jadoo wallahs I have been told that such fakirs often come here, as do other mystics."

The rajah stroked his beard, then turned to Shalbar:

"Send for Kalma, the fakir who performs real jadoo. He said he would undergo *samadhi* whenever we asked. Now we can put him to that test." Then to Graylock, the rajah explained: "Samadhi is a form of suspended animation. Through such power, a fakir like Kalma can remain buried alive for a month or more."

It took several days to locate Kalma. Meanwhile, Graylock saw other mystics at work, if it could be called such. One was Bardu, a thin, scrawny, bearded man who wore only a loin cloth and sat cross-legged in a low alcove at the end of the palace courtyard. Bardu's eyes had a faraway stare, and his lips were always moving very slightly.

"Bardu is an adept," stated the rajah, "who seldom leaves this niche. He subsists on very little food or water and he remains in *padmasana*, the lotus posture in which you now see him. He recites *mantras* or verses. Through mantra yoga, he can attain samadhi, the sublime state that frees the mind from the body."

Graylock felt that Bardu might already have attained samadhi, for the adept paid no attention to the introduction. But Graylock maintained a discreet silence, while the rajah pointed out other mystics who were practicing *hatha yoga,* as he termed it. One was combining the lotus posture with a headstand; another was gripping his ankles with his hands and rocking on his stomach. The rajah had names for such poses and gave the lesser yogis his approval, though Bardu was the only one who rated as an adept in the rajah's estimate.

Graylock also saw *sadhus* and other ascetics who lay on beds of spikes or hung head down over smoldering fires. Some were crawling like inchworms, simply stopping off at the rajah's palace, during their creeping pilgrimage. The Rajah of Bildapore pitied such sadhus more than he approved them.

"Self-torture is not the true path to the light," he declared, "but it does show subjugation of worldly desire, which is the first step to something higher. To their minds, each moment of torture is a precious gem."

That made Graylock think of diamonds, though he carefully avoided mentioning them. One day, however, the rajah brought up the subject himself.

"I am saving my wealth for my people," he said. "The diamonds that I have inherited belong equally to the descendants of the men who minded them and to my other loyal subjects. I am keeping them in a secret repository to which two men alone have access: Myself and my faithful secretary, Shalbar."

That explained why Shalbar had been suspicious of Graylock at the start. But by now, Graylock and Shalbar had become great friends. They had found that both had served in France during World War I, Graylock with the American army and Shalbar with the British. Also, they were both fond of pets, and Graylock became chums with a mongoose named Juju which spent much of its time on Shalbar's shoulder, except when it was chasing cobras and killing them. Juju soon began jumping on Graylock's shoulder, too.

Then came the big day when Kalma the Fakir arrived at the palace with a troupe of assistants. Though attired in simple robe and plain turban, Kalma was tall and imposing, with hypnotic eyes and a gleaming smile. Graylock was disappointed, though, when Kalma began his show with the Basket Trick, in which he pushed a boy down into an oval basket; then squatted in the basket himself, and finally thrust a sword through it to prove that the boy was gone.

"I've seen that before," Graylock told Shalbar. "The boy coils inside the basket, and the fakir takes care not to stab him. It's a very old trick."

"You think so?" queried Shalbar. "Watch what Kalma does next."

The fakir was peering into the basket as though wondering where the boy could have gone. Suddenly, he lifted the basket with one hand, so he could look beneath it and sweep the solid tiling of the courtyard with his other hand. He then slammed down the basket, spread a cloth over it, whipped away the covering — and there was the boy, standing in the basket.

"But how could he pick up the basket?" sputtered Graylock. "With the boy in it, Kalma couldn't possibly have lifted that weight with one hand!"

By then, Kalma was beginning another trick. In a corner of the court-yard where the earth was deep, he set up a little tent formed by three sticks and a cloth. Beneath, he planted a mango seed, which first grew to a sprout, then to a small bush.

"I know that one," said Graylock. "I saw it in Bombay. He poked in a sprout, then a mango branch, from those cloths that are lying all about—"

Graylock stopped abruptly. By now Kalma's assistants were raising longer poles and using all the cloths to cover them. Green branches sprouted from the top of the huge tent, and the cloths scattered like a bursting cocoon, revealing a twelve-foot mango tree. The rajah turned to Graylock and told him:

"You will find that the roots are firmly planted as with all Kalma's trees. But now you will see something still more wonderful — the fabled Rope Trick!"

Kalma took the end of a coil of rope and flung it some thirty feet in air where it remained mysteriously suspended. He shouted for the boy, who came running into the courtyard and climbed the rope like a monkey to the level of the palace roof, which Graylock noted was three stories high. Kalma gave a loud cry and a handclap. The boy vanished instantly, and the rope plopped down to the courtyard, while Graylock stared up at the cloudless blue sky and the brilliant sunlight that showed the weaving leaves of palm trees, nothing more!

That evening, the Rajah of Bildapore insisted that Kalma's mysteries depended upon a subtle force called the *kundalini,* which awakened the *chakras* or psychic centers of the body, and developed hidden powers. These included *laghima,* the ability to reduce weight to nothing; that was how Kalma lifted the basket. Another was *ishita,* the creation by thought alone, which accounted for the mango tree. The Rope Trick, the rajah said, was due either to *prapti,* the power of instantaneous travel, or to *prakamya,* a form of instant realization of whatever a person wanted.

Juju, the mongoose, interrupted the rajah's dissertation by a sudden chatter from Shalbar's shoulder. Everyone looked toward the door and there stood Kalma himself. The fakir bowed to the rajah; then stated in an even tone:

"Tonight, while I was in deep contemplation, I had visions of the very near future. I have come here to reveal them. First I saw a long table — with several men — some in uniform. Beyond were windows — through them I saw a wall — a gate. I heard a voice — calling for the Rajah of Bildapore —"

"The council chamber at Delhi!" exclaimed the rajah. "They must want me there. I shall get ready to leave as soon as official word arrives."

"You cannot go to Delhi," declared Kalma firmly. "Something more important demands your presence here."

"But what could be more important than the council?"

"In my second vision" — Kalma resumed his slow tone — "I saw people running from huts. I heard them cry, 'Bagh Zalum!' And I saw a watchman — lying dead, a pool of blood beside him. I saw the headman of a village, say-ing, 'Bagh Zalum!' — and again the people shouted in terror, 'Bagh Zalum — the Tiger God — save us from him!' Then the vision faded and I saw no more."

For long moments, the Rajah of Bildapore sat grimly silent. Then he declared:

"I have heard of Bagh Zalum, a tyrant among tigers, so bold, so deadly that there is said to be a secret cult that worships him as a Tiger God. This vision of Kalma's can only mean that Bagh Zalum now threatens my domain. Whether he is a killer tiger or an evil spirit, it is my duty to protect my people from him." The rajah turned to Shalbar and told the solemn-faced secretary: "When the summons comes from Delhi, I shall send you in my stead, while I stay here and prepare to deal with Bagh Zalum, the Tiger God."

Graylock was astonished at the way the rajah accepted Kalma's vision as established fact; but when he thought back to the wonders that he himself had seen the fakir perform, he decided that Kalma might be capable of anything. Later, Graylock broached that point to Shalbar, who agreed without the slightest reservation.

"All that the rajah said about Kalma's power is true," asserted Shalbar, "and more besides. His visions never fail, as you will learn."

The next morning, Graylock saw Kalma perform more wonders. The fakir breathed on a stone and it became a live baby chicken. He made more stones come alive, until he had a flock of chicks running about the courtyard. He placed them in a small basket, inverted it — and instead of the chicks, out came a horde of young, hissing snakes, that made for cracks in the tiling before Juju could spring from Shalbar's shoulder and catch them.

The Rajah of Bildapore attributed that to the power of *vashita*, through which inanimate objects could be imbued with life and changed from one form to another. Also, through such power, objects could be moved without touching them.

Kalma proved that by waving his hands toward a huge water jar that immediately wobbled and then jounced itself all about the courtyard. As the great jar rocked past Bardu, who was seated in his niche, Graylock saw the old adept's stare turn into a glare of disapproval. After the jar finally stopped over by the mango tree and Kalma had departed with a bow, Graylock asked the rajah:

"What about an adept like Bardu? Why does he just sit and watch? Why can't he perform miracles far beyond Kalma's?"

"He can," rejoined the rajah. "Through laghima, Bardu could float in mid-air, retaining his lotus posture. That is a common practice among the *mahatmas* in the Himalayas, who also utilize vashita to drive wild animals away from their caves. But a true mahatma reserves these forces for his development or for self-protection; never as a public show. Instead of diverging from the main path by following such branches, the true adept like Bardu continues his upward progress to samadhi, the highest bough of the mystical tree called yoga."

"Then Kalma is one who preferred to develop his lesser forces?"

"Exactly, but he has gone far because he has worked for good instead of gain. Kalma became a fakir to convince skeptics, like you, that powers of yoga do exist. If he worked for gain, the good would be turned to evil, as wine is turned to vinegar." The rajah gave a convulsive shudder. Then: "But do not worry, Kalma would never debase his art by accepting even a rupee for a performance."

That wilted Graylock's hope of taking Kalma back to America and having him perform the genuine Indian Rope Trick in big outdoor stadiums. Instead, Graylock decided to concentrate on the diamond business. That same afternoon, he was amazed when an official telegram arrived from Delhi, fulfilling Kalma's first prophecy. It stated that the Rajah of Bildapore or a "fully accredited representative" was needed at an important conference. That special phrase meant that Shalbar could go instead of the rajah, as Kalma had recommended.

Orders were given to flag the one daily train that passed through Bildapore, and the rajah sent Shalbar to the station in the royal car, a shiny new Model-T Ford touring car, which was also the only automobile in Bildapore. Shalbar, about to leave, shook hands with Graylock, and remarked:

"If you aren't going on that tiger hunt, why don't you take charge of Juju? The little beggar is moping in my room and needs a friend like you. He will perch on your shoulder by day and sleep on your bed by night, so you won't be bothered by cobras. They stay far away from a mongoose."

The royal car drove away, and Graylock went to find the moping mongoose. Juju followed Graylock immediately, and slept on his bed that night. Next morning, they had a late breakfast together, with Juju nibbling biscuits that Graylock offered him. Meanwhile, a loud shouting began in the courtyard, so Graylock went to the window and saw a group of excited natives, bowing, kneeling and appealing to the rajah, while Princess Halina stood silently by. Graylock asked the *chokra,* or houseboy, to interpret what was being said.

"They are from an outlying village," informed the chokra, "near the great game preserve where His Highness often hunts. Last night, they had a tiger scare and they found a watchman dead at the crossroads."

Graylock heard the repeated cry, "Bagh Zalum! Bagh Zalum!" proving that the villagers had already identified the killer as the much-feared Tiger God. Kalma's second vision had thus been fulfilled; and Graylock noticed that the fakir had arrived in the courtyard and was standing beside the rajah, as if eager to take credit for his prophetic skill. Then a group of men came through an archway, all carrying rifles. The villagers changed their cry to "Nayudu! Nayudu!" Graylock turned to the houseboy and asked:

"What is Nayudu? Another killer tiger?"

"No, Sahib Graylock. Nayudu is a tiger killer."

"What sort of double talk is this? A killer tiger — a tiger killer — I see! You mean that Nayudu kills tigers. That makes him a hunter."

"Yes, sahib." The chokra pointed to a big man who was talking to the rajah. "That is Nayudu, the chief *shikari,* or hunter. The villagers love him."

Nayudu soon made arrangements, which the chokra translated:

"The villagers will work as bearers. They will carry supplies far into the jungle and build *machans,* or high platforms in trees from which the shikaris can shoot. They will serve as beaters to drive tigers from the jungle. If elephants are used in the hunt, the villagers will act as *satmans,* men with spears who follow on foot. They are all eager to get rid of Bagh Zalum."

Later, the rajah summoned Graylock and introduced him to a heavy, broad-faced Hindu named Chopra, who was an important *zamindar,* or land owner.

"Chopra will take charge of the palace until Shalbar returns," declared the rajah, "but I would like you to supervise Kalma's living burial, or sam-adhi, and keep a complete record of every detail while I am away."

Graylock agreed with a bow, and he received an appreciative smile not only from the rajah, but from the Princess Halina, who was thus freed of responsibility during her father's absence.

Now Kalma approached the rajah and placed a token in his hand, a flat disk of metal, with a yellowish gem set in its center.

"This is a *kavacha* talisman," the fakir told the rajah. "Its metal is simply iron, because that has long been recognized as the great protector against wild beasts. The stone in the center is topaz, the color of a tiger's eyes. Keep it with you constantly during the hunt, and no tiger can possibly harm you, not even Bagh Zalum."

Soon the rajah was off to the hunt with Nayudu and the shikaris, who included most of the palace guards. For the next few days, all was quiet about the palace itself. Kalma was preparing for his living burial by means of special breathing exercises which were helpful to suspended animation. Messages were received from the rajah, stating that the hunting party had gone well beyond the village where tigers had been reported, but so far had seen no sign of Bagh Zalum. Then, one morning, Shalbar came in by train from Delhi.

Upon learning from Princess Halina that the rajah had left, Shalbar held an immediate conference with Graylock and Chopra. Juju enlivened the pro-ceedings by jumping back and forth from Shalbar to Graylock as though un-certain which master to choose.

"Juju reminds me of the council up in Delhi," observed Shalbar, with a tired smile. "They're jumping every which way at nearly everybody's beck and call. It's getting pretty sticky, though, for tight little states like Bildapore. No matter how nicely they are run, this Nationalism movement is going to squeeze them out. They talk as though it might happen in thirty days, but my bet is, it will take thirty years."

"Take it easy, old man," rejoined Graylock. "Look at me. Here I am in a place I never heard of a month ago, with a mongoose on my shoulder and a fakir waiting to be buried alive while I supervise the job — unless you can stay long enough to take over."

"Sorry, but I can't," declared Shalbar. "I must join the rajah and have him go to Delhi to see the council himself. It is that important."

The chauffeur of the royal Model-T knew the way to the rajah's hunting camp and was sure that they could make it before nightfall. But before the car pulled away, Kalma approached Shalbar and said:

"Since you will not have your mongoose with you" — the fakir gestured to Juju, still on Graylock's shoulder — "I shall provide you with a kavacha talisman as a protection against cobras."

Kalma handed Shalbar a token similar to the rajah's, but with a ruby instead of a topaz as its central gem. The fakir explained that the yellow gem represented a tiger's eyes; a red gem, a cobra's, thus accounting for the special immunity that each type of talisman provided.

Shalbar left, and by nightfall, Princess Halina began to worry about her father. Kalma, who showed up in that silent way of his, again had an answer to the problem.

"I, too, have felt that the kavacha talismans were not enough protection for your father and his secretary," Kalma told Princess Halina. "So I have prepared these."

From his robe, he brought out a clay statuette, beautifully molded and painted to represent a striped tiger. Next, he produced another statuette, this one in the form of a coiled cobra, covered with gilt.

"The tiger image is for the rajah," declared Kalma, "and the cobra image is for Shalbar. But to retain their potency, they must be kept in the safest of all places. That would be the vault where the famed diamonds of Bildapore are stored. You, my princess, are the only one here who knows where it is located."

The princess hesitated. She was about to speak, when Graylock interrupted, but in a courteous manner that brought a grateful look from Halina.

"But the princess does not know," asserted Graylock suavely. "His Highness the rajah told me that only two persons know where the diamonds are kept: the rajah himself and his secretary, Shalbar."

Kalma studied Graylock with sharp, boring eyes, the sort that could ferret out the truth, and Graylock met that gaze with the confidence of a man who has told it. There was momentary annoyance in Kalma's tone as he spoke again to the princess:

"But you do have a place where you can keep the statues safely?"

"Most certainly," replied Halina. "In my own jewel cabinet."

"That should be satisfactory," Kalma decided. "But first, let me add the incantation that will make the charm itself long-lasting."

He brought out a small box, opened it, and took a pinch of powder, which he sprinkled over the tiger image. He plucked a candle from the table, held it so the melted wax dripped to the statuette. The powder ignited with a flare in which the striped figure seemed to writhe as if alive. Then, with another pinch of powder and the same candle flame, Kalma applied the magical treatment to the cobra image, producing a strange effect of twisting coils before the flame died away.

"Let them cool," Kalma told Halina, "then put them away." With a parting bow, he added, "Wherever they are, they will be safe together."

That last statement could have referred to the rajah and his secretary as well as to the images of the tiger and the cobra. As a matter of fact, the Rajah of Bildapore and Shalbar were together at that very moment, in a tent in a jungle clearing, where the hunting party had halted for the night. In the glare from a kerosene lantern, the rajah was going over a sheaf of questionnaires that Shalbar had brought back from Delhi.

"The same old story," said the rajah wearily. "They want reports on how I treat my subjects. Do they have enough food, enough clothing, enough schools? Naturally, they don't have enough of anything, except tigers. Of those they have too many and particularly one too many, a tiger called Bagh Zalum. You should have brought the council down here to help us hunt him."

"They wouldn't have believed there was a Tiger God if I had told them," returned Shalbar. "No, Your Highness. There is only one answer; we must both go to Delhi. The car will be waiting for us at the end of the short jungle trail, if we leave right now. But a few minutes more will be too late as I told the driver he could go at dark. He fears Bagh Zalum."

"Very well." The rajah scrawled a brief note and laid it beside the lantern. "This is for Nayudu, telling him that we have gone to Delhi. I won't need this" — he clanked a metal disk on the table — "Kalma's talisman that protects me against tigers. We won't find them where we are going."

"Nor will I need this." Shalbar tossed his token on the table. "Kalma says it is a talisman to ward off cobras. I won't need it in Delhi —"

Shalbar broke off as the rajah pressed his hands to his chest and straightened upward in a sudden spasm. Anxiously, Shalbar asked:

"What is it, Your Highness? Are you ill?"

"I — I seem to be burning — right here." The rajah writhed slightly as he gasped, "but it is over now." He slumped a little, drew a slow, easy breath and let his hands slide downward. "We must leave now, Shalbar. As you say, we must leave" — his tone became a smooth, persuasive purr — "and go down the jungle path together."

The rajah's eyes had narrowed to straight slits that showed a strange, amber glint in the light. Shalbar's own eyes were wide open in amazement as he saw the rajah's lips spread in a ferocious leer. Then the rajah spoke again, this time in a snarling tone:

"Let us start, Shalbar." The rajah gestured with one hand. "As you say, there is no time to lose. " The rajah stared at his hand as he raised it, closing and opening his fingers in a clawlike manner. Then he looked at his other hand, which he was clenching in the same way. His face showed utter disbelief, becoming sullen, ugly, as he huddled forward in a low crouch, as if to avoid the light. "There is no time —"

Understanding dawned on Shalbar. He knew the truth, fantastic though it was. He sprang forward and boldly pushed the rajah to his hands and knees. Then Shalbar spoke in a sharp, tense whisper:

"Stay here, Your Highness. You can't let anyone see you like this. You understand why, don't you?" Then, as the rajah nodded, Shalbar added in that same tense whisper: "I'll call to you when the way is safe." The secretary gave a low, forced whistle. "When you hear that signal, come from the tent, but not until then. You understand?"

The rajah nodded and looked up helplessly. Shalbar stepped out of the tent and into the gathering dusk. He looked cautiously from right to left; then suddenly straightened and clamped his hands to his chest, exactly as the rajah had. He felt a brief but violent burning sensation. Then he suddenly writhed to the ground and squirmed there, unable to move his hands and arms, which seemed to be bound to his sides.

Shalbar was able to lash about in the grass which now completely covered him, so he did. Not only that, he managed to rear up and look to see if Nayudu or any of the other shikaris were about. Not seeing anyone, Shalbar gave his signal. It was more than a half-whistled whisper. It was a sharp, fierce hiss.

For answer, the rajah gave a low snarl from within the tent. Just then, Shalbar reared higher and saw Nayudu going by. Shalbar hissed again, this time as a warning, but the rajah took it as a signal to come along, so he did. But he paused momentarily to growl at the light, which bothered him. He reached up and gave it a hard, impatient whack with his tightly closed fist, knocking it clear to the corner of the tent.

Fortunately, as the lantern hit the ground, its flame was extinguished. Still crouched, the rajah came from the tent, but instead of being visible — as he would have been against the lighted tent — his low, huddled form was obscured against the darkened backdrop of the jungle. He heard another hissed signal and he followed it, softly, calmly, giving a purred response.

They moved down the jungle path together; Shalbar gliding ahead, the rajah softly creeping behind him. Somewhere between the camp and the waiting car, they slipped into the jungle. Then came a shriek followed by a loud roar, sounds that would have frightened most jungle creatures. The screech was the self-starter of the Model T, the roar, its motor. The driver felt he had waited long enough.

Two glaring orbs burned along the jungle road, the headlights of the jouncing car. Their gleam was reflected by two pairs of eyes — one pair yellow, the other pair red — that were staring boldly from the jungle brush. But the frantic driver was too excited even to notice them. He kept driving straight on back to Bildapore. When he arrived at the palace late that night, the driver of the royal car told how he had taken Shalbar to the rajah's camp.

So everyone was satisfied and pleased that both were safe. In the morning, Kalma, informed of the driver's report, declared simply:

"My talismans and charms are protecting them. Now I can proceed with my samadhi. I shall go into my trance and be buried alive."

At noon, on the brow of a slope a quarter mile from the palace, Kalma was placed in a wooden casket, where he closed his eyes and slackened his breath. Gradually, his body stiffened, and he did not seem to breathe at all. His pulse had ceased to throb when Graylock tested it. The lid was sealed on the casket, which was lowered into a deep pit that Kalma's followers had dug. Those same men filled the pit with loose earth, tramped it down and then pitched their tents on the slope just below the grave to protect Kalma from the unforeseen.

Graylock, remembering what the rajah had told him about adepts fighting off wild animals in Himalayan caves, could well appreciate Kalma's situation. Once the fakir was in samadhi, the complete disunion of flesh and spirit, his body was at the mercy of the elements or any prowling thing, man or beast, that might dig him up. So his followers were keeping constant vigil.

Kalma, who was allowing himself to be buried alive for the next thirty days, impressed Graylock as a greater wonder worker than Bardu, who called himself an adept, but simply squatted in a comfortable alcove, sheltered from rain, wind, and sun in the safety of the palace courtyard. Bardu could call for help or unlimber from his lotus position at any time. Probably the reason he sat so passively and refrained from using mystic powers was because he actually had none.

All Graylock had to do from now on was visit the hillock daily and receive a routine report from Kalma's followers. In case of dire necessity, such as a torrential rain or signs of burrowing insects, Graylock would order the coffin dug up at once. Otherwise, the living exhumation would take place on the appointed date with Graylock and the other witnesses present.

Meanwhile, a messenger arrived from the jungle camp, with a note signed by the rajah saying that he and Shalbar had gone to Delhi. Nayudu assumed that they had taken a train from a nearby junction; and he sent along the jeweled disks, which he had found on the table in the rajah's tent. Halina put them in her cabinet with the tiger and cobra images, which were so much more important. The rajah and his secretary would be protected by those effigies no matter where they went. Kalma had said so; hence, it must be so.

New reports from the tiger country told that neighboring rajahs, as well as British sportsmen, had rushed to join the great hunt. Since the shoot had been instituted by the Rajah of Bildapore, they gave him precedence. In his absence, they accepted Nayudu, his chief shikari, as the leader. Soon, a cordon of beaters and hunters closed in on a quick, soft-moving tiger that answered the description of Bagh Zalum.

One day, they trapped the Tiger God in a jungle valley surrounded by machans high in the trees, each manned by a shikari, with beaters in between. The only way for Bagh Zalum to slip out was by climbing a tree and surprising a hunter on his thatched platform. That was exactly what the cunning tiger did. He moved in on the shikari, who felt so safe in his high roost, and stunned him with a blow from a heavy, padded paw. The tiger came down and continued on his way, while the shikari was found in his machan, still dazed, an hour or so later.

At another point, some shikaris fired at Bagh Zalum while he was scrambling for the jungle. They heard the crackle of underbrush and small trees; then silence. Either the tiger was lying wounded, perhaps dead, in the brush; or he had gone through to cleared land beyond. Dozens of beaters and shikaris scoured the brush. Suddenly a very live and unhurt tiger sprang up in their midst. The striped terror bounded straight into the bed of a dry watercourse and sped away beneath the shelter of its high embankments. Nobody was on guard there, and Bagh Zalum was gone like a striped cyclone before anyone could get a shot at him.

Next, a new hunting party moved in with a herd of trained elephants, each with a *mahout* sitting in a *howdah,* as a canopied shooting platform. The mahouts were skilled shikaris, all craving a shot at the Tiger God. The satmans, or spearmen, who followed them, were an equally tough lot.

Then one mahout was frozen in astonishment when a tiger sprang from the high branches of a tree, squarely into the howdah! Again, a tree-climbing tiger, who batted the man to the ground, the rifle firing upward as he went. That wild shot made the elephant still wilder; with a scream, the great beast went plowing through the jungle. Everyone let him go, knowing that the tiger would be even more frightened and would jump right in among the satmans.

But this tiger didn't. He crouched low in the howdah and rode along on the charging elephant with all the importance of a royal dignitary, right on through the surrounding horde. The other mahouts caught up with the exhausted elephant a few hours later, but by then, the tiger had abandoned his canopied perch and had gone his way.

Once the Tiger God — for by now, all the hunters knew that he must be such — came face to face with Nayudu, the master shikari himself. Like a flash, Nayudu aimed point blank at Bagh Zalum, who was crouched snarling on an embankment only thirty feet away. Nayudu's moment of hesitation was only to make sure of the kill with his first shot, for he knew that a wounded tiger would only attack more savagely.

But in that fleeting instant, there was a stir in the brush almost at Nayudu's feet, and up rose a hooded cobra, ready to strike at the aiming hunter. Instinctively, Nayudu spun around and aimed at the snake instead, only to hear a mighty roar, as the tiger, profiting from the split-second diversion, came springing from its embankment.

Nayudu dropped low, and his shot at the cobra went wide. Rolling about, he fired from a prone position at the quarter-ton mass of flying stripes that had hurtled only a few feet above his head. But the crackle of the brush sounded ahead of Nayudu's rifle flash, and he knew that he had missed. When he came to his feet, the hooded snake had also slithered off into the jungle. It was as if tiger and cobra had gone their way together, though that, of course, was utterly impossible.

During the next two weeks, these stories and more came into Bildapore, causing great consternation there, for the hunt, after carrying far off into the great game preserve, had reversed itself and was now coming closer to the tiny native state. Chopra, the landowner who was acting in the rajah's absence, sent out reserves to meet the Tiger God's advance, but most of them scattered in terror and took refuge with other hunting parties. Chopra returned to the palace and held a grim consultation with Princess Halina and Graylock.

"You know how these townsfolk are," complained Chopra. "If you talk about a tiger, they see grass waving and leaves rustling everywhere. They get stripes before their eyes, every time they blink."

Princess Halina gave a relieved sigh and added:

"Then you don't think that Bagh Zalum is really close by?"

"On the contrary, he is very close," returned Chopra. "During the past few nights, the tiger has stolen up on guards outside the palace. He has knocked away their guns and they have had to run for their lives. They have claw marks to prove it, and that is why the guards have been deserting one by one. But when the villagers look for the tiger he has vanished as completely as in the jungle."

"Do you mean to say," said Graylock, "that Bagh Zalum goes back to the jungle by day and returns here at night, slipping through cordons each time?"

"I mean exactly that," declared Chopra, "but I have word from Nayudu that he is bringing hunting parties closer in, so that by tomorrow night, he should be able to waylay Bagh Zalum while the Tiger God is going one way or the other."

That same day, Graylock made his usual trip to Kalma's grave and talked to the fakir's followers. They, too, were aware of the tiger scare and were keeping close to their tents, which were well concealed among the trees and bushes beyond the brow of the hill. They agreed with Graylock that it was best to leave Kalma buried as he was, while they sat tight with loaded guns, ready to ambush Bagh Zalum if he prowled past their post.

All that night, one lone recruit patrolled outside the main gateway of the palace, where other guards had been attacked and had fled. Toward dawn, Graylock was awakened by a wild, piercing cry. He grabbed his revolver and dashed out through the courtyard, where Chopra, coming from another wing of the palace, joined him, carrying a rifle. Outside the gateway, they found the new guard lying in a pool of blood; and farther off, Graylock saw a striped shape diving past the corner of an abandoned hut.

Graylock took after it, blazing away with his revolver and Chopra followed but had no chance to use his rifle. In the uncertain light, it was impossible to trace the fugitive tiger through the brush beyond the hut. The killer was gone; for this time, a killer he was. When Graylock and Chopra returned to the guard, he was delivering his dying gasp: "Bagh Zalum!"

The guard's gun lay a dozen feet away, where he had lost it, while trying to ward off the attack. That the killer was a tiger was evident from claw marks that covered the victim's face and body, tearing deep into his throat. That the tiger must be Bagh Zalum seemed equally evident, for a strictly man-eating tiger would have carried away his human prey. This beast was simply a man-hater; and Graylock could now understand why many natives styled him the Evil One and some had sought to appease Bagh Zalum by forming a secret tiger cult and worshipping him as a living Tiger God.

All this while, Bardu the adept had remained complacently seated in his favorite niche, from which not even the threat of Bagh Zalum could stir him. Unfortunately, Bardu had not witnessed the slaying of the guard, because, like the earlier attacks, it had taken place beyond the outside corner of the gateway. The lesser yogis and assorted sadhus all were gone. They had quickly decided to resume their pilgrimages when they first heard talk of the Tiger God.

On the hillock, Graylock talked with the grave watchers and found they had been alarmed by the gunfire, but had seen no sign of the tiger, which must have gone another way. When Graylock returned to the palace, he found that the last few servants, frightened by the guard's death, were packing and leaving. Princess Halina refused to stop them, saying that it was their privilege. So that afternoon, Chopra drove off in the royal Model-T, hoping to find Nayudu and bring back any hunters that he could spare as palace guards.

By evening, the only living persons in the palace were Graylock himself, Bardu the adept, and the Princess Halina. There were no gates. They had been removed by the peace-loving rajah years before. So Graylock helped himself to a big hunting rifle from the rack in the rajah's gunroom and took up a lone patrol, with Juju on his shoulder, in the moonlight of the big courtyard.

Suddenly, a door opened and Princess Halina beckoned excitedly:

"There's somebody — or something — trying to come over the wall into the little back courtyard, just behind my apartment!"

Graylock started through a passage toward a door to the back court, but Halina led him up a short flight of steps to the right, into her lighted dressing room. There she pointed through a rear window down into the back court with its low outer wall. Graylock heard scratchy, scaly sounds from the gloom. Then Juju, on his shoulder, began a quick chatter. Graylock looked up and saw a huge, mobile mass come bulking over the low wall and spring lightly down into the little court. Quickly, he told Halina:

"Bagh Zalum is with us. We must get away from here — and fast!"

"I must bring my jewels," pleaded Halina. From a cabinet, she brought a dazzling array of diamonds, a trifling part of the Bildapore hoard, and folded them in a large scarf. "But I have other things still more precious. These!"

From the cabinet, she took the striped tiger figurine and that of the coiled cobra, placing one on each side of the table lamp.

"Now for something to put them in —"

Halina choked. She was looking toward the door. There, at the top of the steps, was the great head and shoulders of a huge tiger that could only be Bagh Zalum. Somehow, the beast had unlatched the door from the rear court and now had them cornered. But the tiger's fierce, yellow-eyed glare was not for Princess Halina. It was directed toward Graylock, who quickly brought the rifle to aim while Juju sprang from his other shoulder and darted to a corner, realizing that he, a mongoose, was no match for a tiger.

Nor was Graylock. Before he could fire, the big beast sprang and batted the rifle barrel aside with one huge paw. Graylock, trained in the trench warfare of World War I, reversed the gun and drove the butt end toward the tiger's snarling teeth, but the blow was only a glancing one. The tiger swung its paw at Graylock's head, to bat him away; and as he dodged, the beast tried to knock over the lamp with the same stroke; but it came short of that, too. Instead, the massive paw thudded squarely on the little clay tiger image, crunching it to powder.

Halina screamed as she saw the effigy crumble. Then the tiger's paw came up and caught Graylock beneath the chin, but it felt more like a hard stroke from a fist that jarred his teeth as his head jolted back. Next, Graylock, really dazed, found himself struggling, not with a monstrous beast, but a human antagonist who kept telling him coolly:

"Easy there, Graylock — easy, now. It's all right —"

And it was all right. As Graylock relaxed, he found himself looking into the face of the Rajah of Bildapore. Beyond him stood Halina. Her face very pale, she gave an odd, sad smile as her father turned and asked:

"That tiger image that I just crushed; who gave it to you?"

"Kalma," replied Halina. "He said it would protect you from tigers."

"I see." The rajah picked up the cobra image. "And this?"

"It was for Shalbar, to protect him against cobras."

The word "cobras" suddenly stirred Juju. The mongoose came chattering from its corner and darted down the steps, while the rajah shouted:

"Stop him, Graylock! Quickly!"

Graylock was too late. At the bottom of the steps, the mongoose shot through the now open back door into the little walled court. Juju, too, had heard the scaly, scraping sound that Graylock had noted earlier. Now Juju was springing for the weaving, whitish hood of a giant cobra. Forced to a corner, the snake was trying to rear higher, but the mongoose sprang to its neck, clutched tightly with its claws and was about to give the snake a fatal bite, when the rajah arrived, still carrying the cobra image.

The rajah flung the coiled effigy against the wall, where it smashed to bits. At that instant, the cobra seemed to rear higher, flinging the mongoose upward. Then the weird, white hood was gone, and Juju's chatter suddenly began again — this time in happy recognition as Shalbar stepped from the gloomy corner, fondling the mongoose on his shoulder. Shalbar rubbed his neck and spoke to the rajah:

"Just a few scratches, but no bites. Many thanks, Your Highness, for your timely assistance. At last we can be ourselves again."

"We still have work to do," rejoined the rajah. "Let's hope we are not too late. Better get that rifle, Graylock. We may need it."

The fantastic truth dawned on Graylock as he brought the rifle from the very room where he had struggled with a tiger that he had thought was Bagh Zalum. There was bewitchment in those clay figurines. They had turned the rajah into a tiger and Shalbar into a cobra. Either that, or they had made them appear as such creatures to all other eyes. Yet Kalma, ever artful, had not lied when he said the statuettes gave protection. The rajah, as a tiger, could hold his own against other tigers; Shalbar, as a cobra, could cope with cobras.

The rajah met Graylock at the bottom of the steps and gestured him toward the doorway to the big main courtyard, with the comment:

"Lead the way, Graylock. The princess has told me of your loyalty, and I am highly gratified that you stayed after so many others left. So you are still in charge."

"Our worries should be over," rejoined Graylock, "now that you are back, Your Highness. Chopra is due shortly with a crew of shikaris to handle the real Bagh Zalum if he shows up again —"

Graylock broke off and motioned the others back. Stalking silently across the main courtyard was a tiger, its exact size indefinable in the uncertain moonlight, but its intent very plain. It was moving straight for Bardu, the motionless adept, who was still seated with crossed legs and outspread palms in his familiar padmasana posture. Graylock handed the rifle to the rajah.

"Take this, Your Highness," he whispered. "You are a better tiger hunter than I can ever hope to be."

Graylock drew his revolver as an emergency weapon, but the rajah smiled while raising the rifle to his own shoulder.

"Weapons are unneeded," he said quietly. "I have told you that Bardu has the power of vashita and can stop wild beasts in their tracks. Watch now, and you will see a true mahatma demonstrate his mind power."

The tiger stalked steadily toward Bardu's niche, unaware that other eyes were watching, for it was meeting only the adept's unflinching gaze. Then, with a savage spring, the striped form launched itself squarely upon the seated, defenseless figure of Bardu, intent upon the kill. The power that stopped the ferocious attack was not the adept's skill at controlling wild beasts; it was the power packed in the cartridge of the rajah's rifle. A gun shot clipped the killer in the middle of his spring, rolling him over in the courtyard.

Graylock and Shalbar reached the motionless form ahead of the rajah. They didn't have to worry about whether it was still alive, for this tiger had literally come apart in two portions. This dead killer was no tiger at all. The rajah had shot and killed a man who had been wearing a tiger skin. He was lying face down, and in his outstretched hand was a murderous weapon that he had used to strike down and slash human victims, sometimes fatally, as with the guard last night.

The rajah arrived, realized the truth, and used the rifle butt to roll the dead killer face up in the moonlight. The witnesses stared at one another in new amazement when they saw the features of Kalma, the fakir who was supposedly undergoing a living burial in a state of samadhi, on the hilltop! They were still standing there, dumbfounded, when the royal car rolled in with Chopra at the wheel and a dozen shikaris brimming from its sides.

The rajah ordered Graylock and Shalmar to head the expedition that went into immediate action. Their target was the encampment on the hillside, and they moved in so fast and quietly with the shikaris that they captured and disarmed Kalma's few followers in a matter of minutes. Beneath a bush just behind a tent, Graylock found a small tunnel leading straight into the fakir's empty grave.

Once buried, Kalma had pushed open a loose side of the coffin and had wormed through a foot or so of earth into the secret outlet, which had enabled him to reach the tent and enter the back unseen. He had spent his long days in the comfort of the tent, not in the confines of the coffin, where he intended to return only when the time came for the casket to be dug up.

Aside from faking a living burial and getting credit for a real one, Kalma had been able to rove at night, masquerading as the killer tiger Bagh Zalum, using a pronged hook to deliver wounds that looked as though they had come from tiger claws, while he frightened away the surrounding villagers, as well as the guards and servants from the rajah's palace. Kalma had been the fiendish leader of the secret cult that worshipped *him* as the Tiger God!

As to Kalma's main purpose, the Rajah of Bildapore could easily explain that, in the light of all that had happened. Back at the palace, the rajah analyzed the fakir's methods as well as his motives. Graylock, Chopra, and the Princess Halina listened. Shalbar stood by to confirm the data.

"Kalma must have learned that a summons was due from Delhi," stated the rajah, "so he went out and created a tiger scare, thus making two predictions come true. Once Shalbar and I were off in the jungle, he transformed us with the aid of those images, probably through the affinity of the talismans that we already carried.

"It was a case of actual bewitchment, the sort that has often been reported through the years, but which has been difficult to prove. Now we know that such things can really happen."

"And in this case," put in Halina, "it must have happened when Kalma set fire to the powder on those images."

"Exactly," agreed the rajah, "because I felt a burning here —" He paused, pressing his hands to his chest, while Shalbar promptly added:

"And I saw His Highness change to a tiger. His face began to glare, with yellow eyes and snarling mouth. Then his hands changed to paws, his fingers to claws. That's when I knew I would have to get him into the jungle. So I started from the tent, only to get a burning sensation myself."

"And next," chuckled the rajah, "Shalbar was a cobra, hissing for me to follow him into the jungle. From then on, we beat our way back here together. It was more difficult for me, with all those shikaris thinking I was Bagh Zalum and trying to trap me. Fortunately, I was one tiger who knew as much as any hunter, so I did the things that tigers never do. Shalbar also helped me in his nice cobra fashion."

"Like the time I struck at Nayudu," recalled Shalbar. "You made up for that, Your Highness, when you saved me from my own pet mongoose, Juju."

"I was lucky enough to smash that tiger image," affirmed the rajah. "Then, of course, I realized what the cobra statue meant. While they were intact, we could not regain our human forms. That was why Kalma wanted them preserved."

"So you were still working in from the jungle," declared Graylock, "and being mistaken for Bagh Zalum, while Kalma was acting like a real killer here in Bildapore. No wonder no one could tell how the tiger managed to get back and forth between here and the jungle. But why did Kalma want to drive everyone away from the palace?"

"So he could find the secret hiding place," returned the rajah, "the treasure vault that contains all the fabled Bildapore diamonds that you yourself have said you would like to see."

"Kalma didn't find out that I knew where it was," put in Halina, "because Mr. Graylock told him that only two persons knew where they were kept. He said you, father, were one person and Shalbar was the other."

"And that," Graylock said to the rajah, "was what you told me, Your Highness."

"I told you that only two men knew where they were," corrected the rajah. "I purposely refrained from mentioning Princess Halina. I am glad now that I did. With no one to ask, Kalma had to frighten everyone away from the palace until he found only one spot still guarded. He knew that was where the vault would be; but it forced him to show his hand."

The rajah gestured his own hand across the courtyard to where Bardu the adept was still seated in what seemed an eternal pose.

"That alcove is the entrance to the diamond vault," explained the rajah. "So Shalbar and I decided to let Bardu take up his long, contemplative vigil there. Bardu himself does not know that he is guarding all the wealth of Bildapore."

The rajah walked over and spoke to the old adept, who unlimbered from his lotus posture and stepped from the niche, the first time that Graylock had ever seen him do so. Shalbar stepped forward, stooped and lifted a perfectly fitted slab that was set in the alcove. Below was a stairway, leading down beneath the palace.

"If Kalma had slain Bardu," declared the rajah, "he would have found and robbed this secret vault. Fortunately, we ended his career as Bagh Zalum, the Tiger God. Now I am willing to sell my diamonds to the world."

They went down into the vault, and while Graylock walked about, dazzled at the magnificence of the wonderful diamonds the rajah showed him, His Highness explained the reason for his sudden decision.

"From the way things are in Delhi," declared the rajah, "India will some day be nationalized. They want people to spin cotton, not to hunt tigers. So I intend to share my wealth with my subjects here in Bildapore. They can have the best of spinning wheels, diamond-studded if they want, with enough money to buy a few rifles for tiger hunting, too."

Then, with a final smile, the rajah added: "And you, Mr. Graylock, will be my sole world-wide agent for the disposal of all these diamonds."

Today, you won't find Bildapore on any map of India, for it was one of the earliest native states to be absorbed and forgotten. But you may find Graylock in his little jeweler's shop on New York's East Side. He is a kindly old man, who will gladly show you some matchless diamonds from a place called Bildapore. Also, if you ask him, he will tell you this story, exactly as you have read it here.

THE
AVENGING
GHOST

THE AVENGING GHOST

All that could be seen of Pleasant Farm was a bleak, black ruin as Hank Dawson swung his ancient car along the road that skirted Bald Eagle Mountain. A fine old farmhouse it had been, overly large, perhaps, and rather spraddled out, as Hank remembered it; but well built in good northern New England tradition, with granite foundations and solid stone chimneys. Those were all that now remained.

It was just about four months ago that the fire had occurred, on one of those stormy spring nights when the lightning flashed above the mountain peaks and the thunder came rolling in with the wild winds that swept down through the notches. Then, in the wake of all that fury, a mammoth beacon had flared against the midnight sky, rousing the quiet town of Hilldale and sending its antique fire equipment to a scene where it arrived too late to do any good.

For Pleasant Farm, situated on a fertile shelf part way up the mountain slope, was a difficult place to reach and the water supply had been inadequate to cope with such a holocaust. Fanned by the heavy wind, the flames had carried to the huge barn, so that, too was gone, except for its old foundation.

Both farmhouse and barn had been empty at the time. Pete Ryerly, who owned the place, had been raising cattle with a partner from Boston, Lloyd Proctor, but they had sold out their livestock some time before and were turning the farm into an antique shop. That, too, had gone up in smoke, but Pete Ryerly was still trying to collect insurance, which should please Lloyd Proctor, who had put up all the money. Hank Dawson, as deputy sheriff, heard of all such things.

Today, Hank had also heard from Janet Ryerly, Pete's wife, who was now living in the Stony Brook Cottage down the slope from the burned farm. Her note had said that she wanted to talk to Hank right soon, so toward sundown, he had decided to mosey out Bald Eagle way. Now, the wind was rising as the darkness settled, so instead of driving around in back of the cottage. Hank stopped on the road and walked up a path that formed a shortcut.

124

There were dim lights in the squatty cottage, making it all the more grotesque against the somber sky. Hank could scarcely see the outline of a storage shed behind it, because of shrouding evergreens that loomed from the hillside. Those trees were weaving in the rising wind, each with a motion of its own, turning them into a row of ghostly dancers, black against the sky.

Hank paused and shouted above the wind: "Hi, there — Janet!"

The answer was the deep, savage barking of a dog. That would be Duke, the Great Dane Lloyd Proctor had kept at Pleasant Farm until he went on a trip to buy antiques. Then he had put Duke in a kennel over in New Windsor. A good idea, Janet bringing the big dog back here as a protection.

Hank called again. The door opened, and he saw Janet waving with one hand and gripping Duke's collar with the other. As Hank entered, Duke delivered a few growls which Janet punctuated with the order, "Quiet now!" and the big dog subsided. Janet, a woman in her late twenties, was small, but by no means frail, as her handling of Duke proved. Her face showed the healthy glow of outdoor life and the big brown eyes above her cute stub-nose were quite as expressive as her well-formed lips. These lips were smiling when she said:

"You must be psychic, Hank."

"Psychic?" Hank frowned, puzzled. "What's that?"

"It means you can read thoughts at a distance. Telepathy, they call it. I wanted to ask you to come up here and stay a few hours on the first windy night, but I didn't put that in my note. Then, an hour ago, the wind started up, and who arrives but good old Hank Dawson, the man I wanted to see."

"Come to think of it, I'd just begun to see the wind stir kind of heavy when I decided to swing over here. Tell me, what's the trouble?"

"Since you are psychic, Hank, have you ever seen a ghost?"

"Not for sure, but I don't disallow that some folks may have."

"You may be seeing one tonight. Wait while I make some coffee. If Duke acts up, you'll know the ghost is around. Duke always hears it first."

While the coffee perked, Hank put a log on the fire and began to note a variety of sounds. He heard the wind roar down the chimney; he noted a low moan from a corner, but Janet laughed at that, saying it was just a tree bough scraping the roof. Then Hank brought up a subject that was worrying him.

"Tell me about Lloyd Proctor. How did he become Pete's partner?"

"It's the old story," returned Janet wearily. "Pete tells people his big ideas and finds someone to back them. Things go fine until the money runs out. Then Pete blames them and they blame him. You know how Pete brags and fools people. He promised me a wonderful home if I married him. Now look at it!"

"You mean Pleasant Farm?"

"What else? We couldn't keep it going, until somebody put up money to help. Then it burned out, and we're down to this little cottage."

Janet mused briefly; then felt less critical regarding Pete.

"Maybe Pete's ideas weren't too good," Janet went on. "But his backers weren't so good, either. They all pulled out, except Lloyd Proctor."

"You mean that Proctor was better than the rest?"

"For a while. Lloyd put up all the money to improve the farm and buy the livestock. He gave Pete cash in advance to pay the hired help and meet bills as fast as they came in."

"Then why didn't things work out?"

"Because they went at it too big. Lloyd kept taking long trips out West, buying cattle faster than Pete could sell those we were raising here. So Pete had to take on more men to run the place and buy more equipment. That made the expenses climb still bigger than the returns. So they closed out."

"I see. Now, what about the antique business?"

"They planned that as an in-between business; a stopgap, Pete called it. Lloyd went around buying antiques and shipping them into the farmhouse, until the barn could be made into a shop. Then the fire killed that."

"And where was Pete at that time?"

"Around the farm, planning the change-over, until Lloyd wanted him to go to Florida and take options on a lot of land down there. So Pete was away, too, and I was visiting friends in New York, that stormy night."

"And where are they both right now?"

"Pete is down in Florida, clinching the land deal, while Lloyd is out lining up salesmen in different territories. Lloyd mails in checks, enough to cover expenses here, so I'm just marking time until Pete gets back."

Janet had poured the coffee, and they were sipping it when the wind rose in a wild outburst, rattling the windows until the cottage itself seemed to shake. Then the fierce howl dwindled to a strange, plaintive wail that brought an echoing whine from Duke. As the wind rose again, so did the dog's tone, as though Duke wanted to howl in accompaniment.

From far off in the night came a long, sobbing note. It was more than the wind alone, for Hank Dawson, though well acquainted with the storms of this region, had never heard such a sound before. It was a call so distant that it might have come from another world; a chilling, eldritch wail that left spine-tingling shivers in its wake.

Duke was not only pricking up his ears; his hairs were bristling, his back arching, and he was tense in every muscle. His whimper showed a mingling of fear and challenge. With it, he must have recognized the call, for he came to his feet and stalked toward the door as though drawn there against his will. Then, under some frantic urge, the dog began to paw the door.

Hank Dawson had laid aside his coffee cup and was gripping both arms of his chair. Hank's eyes were as fixed as Duke's, and he strained his ears, hoping to catch a repetition of the distant call. Janet stepped over to the door, took hold of Duke's collar, and turned to Hank.

"That's the sound I spoke about," she said. "I told you that Duke would be the first to hear it. So come along" — there was a grim ring to the girl's tone — "and Duke and I will show you what happens next."

They emerged into the night, where the wind had already reached a half-gale fury, a frequent occurrence during these sudden mountain storms. There was moonlight now, but it was flickery, because of the scudding clouds. Hank could no longer hear the odd sob in the beat and tumult of the wind, but the cry must have reached a supersonic pitch that was still audible to Duke, for the dog tried to tug free and dash around the corner of the cottage.

Janet gave Duke that much leeway, then managed to restrain him a short way past the corner. The dog could still hear the strange call, however, for he was more eager to go than ever. With her free hand, Janet pointed to the white outline of the closed storage shed.

"That's where the call comes from," she shouted, above the tumult of the storm. "That's where Duke always tries to go."

"So why don't you let him?" returned Hank.

"Not yet! You'll see why if you watch the shed door."

They were moving slowly toward the shed, due to Duke's incessant tugs. Then, as though actuated by their approach, the door of the shed swung wide open. Duke reared and his tone became half yelp, half growl, the latter for Janet's benefit, since she alone was holding him back. The dog was frantic now to reach the door where that ghostly manifestation was in progress.

Ghostly it was, in more than one way. Hardly had the door opened, before it started to close again; then hesitated and wavered at the halfway mark. The wind lulled and Hank muttered loud enough for Janet to hear:

"Tricky, the way the wind is acting."

"It isn't just the wind." Janet's tone, though hoarse, was filled with awe. "It always acts the same, Hank, as if it was beckoning you on. And there is something that moves in from the night, something that you can't quite see, yet you can almost feel —"

Hank was sensing it now, very sharply. He was sure that he saw a vaguely human form take shape at the edge of the crazily swaying door, as though to hold it at the halfway mark. Then Hank realized that the outline could have been caused by the shadow of the waving tree boughs that filtered the uncertain moonlight just above the shed. Suddenly, grotesquely, the form became a tall, upright oblong, which Hank took to be simply the open doorway, as represented by the black interior of the shed.

By now, Hank had his flashlight out and was focusing it on the doorway, hoping to spot someone there. But at more than a fifty-foot range, the beam gave only a glimpse of the shed's interior; and before Hank could get closer, the door shut with an emphatic slam, as though someone inside was trying to avoid the light.

Right then, Duke took over. He was literally loping for the shed, and although Janet was hanging on and hobbling his gait, the dog was dragging her with him, as she gasped excitedly to Hank:

"Duke always does this when the door slams — he must see something go inside — because, just now I saw it — myself — like an arm —"

Hank had seen it, too, a shoulder, arm, and hand slicking in through the closing crack of the door, ahead of its sudden slam. That, too, could be an illusion, for the windswept clouds were thickening, changing the moonlight into kaleidoscopic patches of black and gray. But Hank wasn't for holding Duke back; quite the contrary. The deputy sheriff dashed forward, pulling his revolver from his holster as he shouted:

"Let the dog go!"

Janet released Duke, and he launched himself like a canine thunderbolt, reaching the shed in gigantic leaps, passing Hank on the way. Janet, coming up behind them, shouted:

"Watch the door — Hank — watch the door —"

Timed to the words, the door flipped open as of its own accord, and Duke bolted through, only to have the door slam again as though some ghostly hand had pulled it shut. Hank, arriving there, grabbed the handle and yanked hard, only to find that the latch was stuck. A few quick tries and the door came flying open, almost sprawling Hank ahead of it. Hank found his footing and surged angrily into the shed, with Janet now right behind him. With a wave of his gun and a sweep of his flashlight, Hank bawled:

"Whoever you are, stay where you are! Put up your hands and keep them up — in the name of the law!"

That order was wasted. Hank's flashlight, covering the interior of the shed, showed only a storage room a dozen feet square and about eight in height, containing a variety of implements such as a lawn mower, wheelbarrow, garden hose and stacks of boxes filled with household goods, plus an array of old bottles.

There wasn't a space in which even a midget could have hidden; but to the right, Hank saw a wooden partition, with another door in its center. There, Duke was on his hind legs, clawing, whining, half-barking as he tried to get through.

As Hank started in that direction, the door suddenly swung open, coming almost at him. Hank thought momentarily that Duke had pawed it open, for the dog was bounding through and the door was swinging shut behind him. But the outside wind still howled and Hank could feel its draft behind him, so he took it that suction had caused the door's action. At any rate, it didn't slam tight shut. Instead, it jounced partly open and Hank grabbed it on the rebound, wresting it wide, so that he could shoulder through.

Hank stood there with his gun and flashlight, in a narrow, low-roofed extension of the storage room, which was nothing more than a small workshop with a simple bench. Duke was in there with him, and the dog was barking heavily now, apparently as frustrated as Hank at finding no one there. Not only was the workshop as empty as the storage room, it was scarcely large enough to accommodate Hank and Duke together, the way they barged about it.

At the far end, however, there was another door which apparently opened outdoors. Hank tried to open it while Duke barked encouragement, but the door wouldn't budge. By then, Janet arrived, took hold of Duke's collar and quieted him, while Hank was finding out that the door was bolted on the inside.

"You can't open that," Janet told Hank. "The door doesn't even give when you try it, so I think it's nailed shut as well as bolted."

Hank agreed, but Duke reverted to his plaintive whine and kept scratching at the door, finally trying the hinged side and giving some appealing barks.

"No use, Duke," said Hank, inspecting the hinges with his flashlight. "They are fixed to stay." Then, to Janet, Hank added: "Listen to the way that wind rattles the loose boards in this shed."

"But it isn't the wind, Hank!" exclaimed Janet. "It's Duke!"

Janet was right. Duke's probing paw had rattled a loose board beside the door. Hank tried to pry it free with his fingers, then used an old chisel from the workbench. The board snapped inward, bringing three more that formed a door in the wall. But it revealed only a shallow space in the wall.

"I thought you'd found a secret door leading outside," declared Janet. "That would account for the crazy goings on around here. But it's only a tool closet."

The closet's contents consisted of a heavy-headed hammer streaked with rust, a garden spade, a pair of new work-shoes caked with long-dried mud, and a pair of dirt-stained coveralls hanging from a nail. Duke sniffed, gave a few sharp barks, then resumed his whines at the bolted door. Hank asked:

"Whom do these belong to?"

"Probably to one of the men working up at the farm," replied Janet, "or else to Lloyd Proctor. He superintended the fixing up of the cottage."

Hank left the articles in the wall closet and jammed it tightly shut. He led the way out through the front door of the shed, with Janet bringing Duke along. They circled the building and Hank tested the back door from outside, finding it solidly nailed and bolted. Duke tried to help by scratching at the door.

"Now Duke wants to get in," observed Hank. "He's still interested in that tool closet. Judging by this long grass, the back door hasn't been opened in months."

They completed the circuit of the shed, and Hank studied the latch on the front door. He found that it joggled slightly when in place, but not enough to open of itself. Hank asked:

"How did you happen to leave this loose tonight?"

"I didn't," replied Janet. "Every day, I check it before dark. I suppose somebody could sneak up and loosen it, but it has never happened except on windy nights."

"So you think the wind loosened it?"

"I wouldn't know." The wind was rising again as Janet spoke, so strongly that it almost swept them from the shelter of the shed. "What do you want to do?" she added. "Stand around and watch to see what happens?"

"No," Hank bawled back. "Let's go in the house."

Soon they were in front of the fireplace again, where Duke nestled down, nose between paws, and quietly went to sleep while Janet was heating up the coffee.

"You see?" she queried. "Duke knows it won't happen again tonight, even though the wind is getting stronger. He only hears that odd sound a short while after dark, and it always leads him to the shed and on into that little workshop."

Hank stroked his long chin. "How often has it happened?"

"Three times, I think." Janet counted back. "That's right, tonight makes four. The first time, it had me kind of scared, for I'd have sworn there was someone prowling out there. So I took an awfully long time finding out there was nobody around.

"Then, naturally, I laid it to the wind. So the second time, I wasn't scared at all. I was cautious and kept hanging on to Duke; but that was chiefly because I didn't want him to go wild and run away somewhere. So I practically laughed it off, figuring it just had to be the wind, even the opening latch and the suction that opened the inner door.

"But the third time" — Janet shivered and the coffee cup rattled as she filled it — "well, I was just petrified. It was like seeing a movie over again, or having the same bad dream. The way the door kept opening and closing, kind of inviting me in, made me want to run. If it hadn't been for Duke pulling me along. I would have run. That's why I sent that note to you, Hank. I just couldn't stay here alone another windy night."

"So each time," mused Hank, "it was just the same as tonight?"

"Almost exactly," replied Janet, "except for you being in on it and finding that tool closet.'

Hank finished his coffee, then remarked:

"Well, since you're so sure that nothing more will happen, I'll mosey along. But I'll stop by tomorrow and have a look at that shed by daylight."

During the night, the wind abated. Toward noon the next day, Hank Dawson drove up to the Stony Brook Cottage and swung in by the rutted logging road that came around the back shed. Hank was driving a newer car than his own, and with him was a polite, gray-haired man whom he introduced to Janet Ryerly, when she met them outside the cottage.

"This is John Hilliar," stated Hank, "the claim agent for the Interstate Fire Insurance Company. He wants to make an adjustment on the farmhouse insurance. I thought he ought to see some of the furnishings here in the cottage, to get an idea of what the rest was like."

"Very well," agreed Janet. She turned to the claim agent. "You see, Mr. Hilliar, we furnished the cottage from the farmhouse, to make room for the the antiques. You can look over what's in the cottage, as well as the boxes in the shed; but the real value was in the antiques."

"So I understand," said Hilliar. "What can you tell me about the antiques?"

"Very little. Most of them were still crated, just as they came in. Pete didn't want to open them until his partner Lloyd showed up, so they could go over them together. But they were both away when the fire hit."

Hilliar decided that he would have a look in the cottage, anyway. He had two other men in the car, both insurance investigators, and he told them to take pictures of the crates in the storage shed and then go up to Pleasant Farm and shoot a completely new set of photos, showing the ruins as they now stood. Meanwhile, Hilliar and Hank went into the cottage with Janet.

While Hilliar listed the furniture he saw there, Janet recalled and described similar articles that had still been in the farmhouse when it burned. Hank was helpful, too, for he had visited the farmhouse in the old days and was able to attest to some of Janet's descriptions. Then they all went out to the shed and checked the boxes there, which included lamps, pictures, household appliances, winter clothes, and some sets of dishes which Janet greatly prized.

"We planned to live in the cottage," explained Janet, "and turn the farmhouse over to antiques by degrees. But there were so many rooms up there, I would think that we lost three times as much as what we saved by bringing it down here. Wouldn't you, Hank?"

"No," amended Hank. "I would say from four to five times as much."

"We'll call it five," declared Hilliar, in a satisfied tone. "I'm quite sure, Mrs. Ryerly, that we could settle your husband's claim without question, so far as the value of the farmhouse and its furnishings are concerned. But he wants double the amount, because of the antiques."

"And so he should," asserted Janet emphatically. "Pete often told me that he carried much more insurance than he needed, just to allow for improvements and valuables. When the antiques began coming in, he was glad he was so well insured, but he began to worry because he didn't have still more."

"I understand," said Hilliar sympathetically. "We have settled claims like this before. But without an inventory, we at least need some proof."

"Lloyd Proctor is the man to ask for that. He's Pete's partner —"

"I know. That is all properly covered by the insurance policy, which allows for losses regardless of individual ownership. But since the policy is in the name of Peter Ryerly, we must look for proof of loss. How he settles with Lloyd Proctor is his business; not ours."

"Then what should I tell Pete when I hear from him?"

"Tell him to get all the data that he can from Proctor, who most certainly should have kept some list of items that he purchased, as well as the places where he bought them. Then we can check back and make a fair settlement, perhaps even a full one."

Hilliar went back into the cottage to make out his report and Janet accompanied him there, while Hank looked around the storage shed, inside and out, hoping to find some clue to the ghostly visitant of the previous evening. Hilliar had just finished his report when the honk of a horn told that the investigators had returned from their inspection of the farmhouse ruins. So Janet saw all four men off in their car. In parting, Hilliar said politely:

"Thank you for giving us so much of your time, Mrs. Ryerly. I only hope it will prove as profitable as it should. But remember" — the claim agent added this quite pointedly — "we still need that proof!"

Janet nodded as she stood there with Duke, who had behaved quite amiably today, even welcoming the strangers in the manner of an official greeter. Hank noted the dog and chuckled as he reached down beside the wheel and passed a strong leather leash out through the car window.

"Here's a present for Duke," said Hank. "It will help you to control him better at night. But if he hears noises around the shed, give him his head. Let him get there fast. He might even scare up a ghost."

The weather was mild the next few days except for a touch of frost that brought the first tints of color to the northern woodlands. Each day, Janet walked down to the rural delivery box with Duke on his new leash. There wasn't even a postcard from Pete, down in Florida, but one afternoon Janet found an envelope with the postmark of a New England town named Andalusia. In it, she found a check for a hundred dollars, signed by Lloyd Proctor, with a note saying:

"Here's more to cover expenses on the place. Hope it will be enough until business gets better." L.P.

About dusk, Janet was carrying dishes from the shed into the cottage, when she noted that the top branches of the yellowing trees were swaying. Off above the mountain, storm clouds threatened, but Janet decided they were moving the other way. After dark, a few gusts brought anticipative whines from Duke, but the wind had eased when the big dog began to bristle and growl.

"What is it?" asked Janet. "Hank again, coming up the path?"

But there was no shout from Hank; nor did Janet hear the eerie, distant cry that had perturbed Duke on past occasions. But since the big dog heard something, Janet bravely snapped on Duke's new leash and took him out. Instantly, Duke bounded for the corner of the house, then on toward the storage shed. Now he neither whined nor whimpered. He became a snarling fury.

It struck Janet that this was the chance to solve the mysterious doings centered in the shed. But she did not want to blunder into trouble, nor to give Duke his head except at her own command. The new leash worked to perfection as Janet dug both heels into the turf. Duke reared up like a reined horse. His snarl was fierce, his fangs gleaming in the cloud-filtered moonlight. As before, the shed door was swinging open; but tonight, a figure was plainly crouched before it. Duke's snarl became a raucous bark; the figure darted through the doorway, grabbing the door as it went by. Janet released the leash.

"Go!" Janet ordered. "Go, Duke, go!"

The door slammed as Duke sprang; then it bounced open, and Duke shot through with Janet close behind. The door to the little workshop also slammed shut, but Duke pawed it open instantly and went snarling through to the workshop. Janet, arriving with her flashlight, heard a man's frantic shout:

"Get him off me — get him off me — quick!"

Duke's great paws were planted on a man's shoulders, bending him down on the workbench, trying to get at his throat. Janet screamed:

"Down, Duke! Down!"

Somehow, Janet grabbed the flying leash, twisted about with a tremendous wrench and brought Duke with her. She yanked the dog into the outer room, looped the end of the leash to a hook on the wall, and turned to the workshop.

There, slumped by the bench, his coat dangling from his shoulders, was Janet's husband, Pete Ryerly. His face, ordinarily handsome, had grown haggard in the weeks since Janet had last seen him. It was sallow rather than tanned by Florida sunshine. His attempted smile became a nervous grimace.

"Why, Pete!" exclaimed Janet. "You know Duke won't hurt you —"

Interrupting snarls told that Duke didn't agree. Janet ordered, "Quiet, Duke!" and as the dog snarled a last protest, Pete came to his feet.

"Is there anyone else in the cottage, Janet?"

"No. Hank Dawson might be coming up" — Janet noted that the rising wind had died down — "but it's too late for him to be coming now."

"I'll follow you to the cottage then. But keep that beast away from me. He got so vicious that only Lloyd Proctor could handle him. That's why Lloyd had to send him to the kennel before going away."

In the cottage, Janet shut Duke in a bedroom and brought out one of Pete's other suits to replace the clothes that the dog had ripped.

"If you'd come in the front way," Janet told Pete, "you'd have been all right. When Duke heard you out back, he probably mistook you for a prowler."

"You mean there have been prowlers around here?"

"Not really," returned Janet, noting the anxiety in her husband's tone. Then, thinking that mention of ghosts might really shake him, she added: "Hank thought it was just the wind banging the shed door. Anyway, it frightened Duke."

"Frightening that monster would be something," snapped Pete. Then, eyes worried, he queried: "So you've let people go into the shed?"

"Only the insurance men. They've been very considerate. They say they can settle the claim in full, if you furnish satisfactory proof of loss."

"If only Lloyd would send a list of the antiques he bought!" exclaimed Pete. "When did you last hear from him, Janet?"

"Why, just today. He sent a check and a nice note. Here, read it."

Pete read the note; then studied the postmarked envelope.

"I've got it, Janet!" exclaimed Pete. "Tomorrow, mail Lloyd Proctor a registered letter, care of General Delivery in Andalusia. Tell him to mail that list, and tell him why it's needed. I can't write him because I'm supposed to be in Florida. Besides, if I mention the insurance, he will think I'm having trouble collecting it. Coming from you, it will sound like a routine matter."

Pete changed to his other suit; then told Janet:

"I'd like to stay overnight, but I can't let anyone know I'm here. The insurance people would want to talk to me, and I owe some bills around town. If you can clear up this insurance, Janet, everything will be smooth. I have my car out back, so keep Duke inside until I blow the horn, meaning I'm on my way."

It was fully ten minutes before the horn honked, and Janet wondered why he had taken so long to reach his car. But Duke was quiet when Janet released him, so the excitement was over for tonight.

The next day, Janet went to Hilldale by bus and mailed the registered letter to Lloyd Proctor in Andalusia. As she left the post office, she met Hank Dawson and his older daughter, Cynthia. Half-jokingly, Hank asked:

"Any ghosts prowling around the mountain last night?"

"No, just the wind," replied Janet, "and it wasn't strong enough to matter. By the way, I've written Lloyd Proctor for that list."

"Good enough," said Hank. "Let's hope you get it."

Janet did get it. Five days later, a bulky envelope arrived containing typewritten sheets with handwritten notations and the signature of Lloyd Proctor at the bottom. It described dozens of items, with the dates and places of purchase, as well as the prices paid.

Duke began barking while Janet was still studying the list. A minute later, she recognized the rumble of Hank's old car coming in by the back road. She rushed out to meet Hank, waving the list as she shouted:

"Here it is, Hank! Just what the insurance company ordered!"

Hank's long face showed a glum expression that dampened Janet's joy.

"I just heard from Mr. Hilliar," Hank stated. "They've been trying to trace Lloyd Proctor through insurance agencies around the country, and now they've gotten a report on him; and a bad one. He's been gypping real estate men with a phony land scheme. Proctor gets them to put up five hundred to a thousand dollars for a franchise to sell Florida land; then he promises them a list of prospects to go with it. But he just goes his way and never delivers."

"You mean that Lloyd has been doing this with the land he wanted Pete to buy for him?"

"That's right. But Proctor hasn't bought any land. Don't worry about Pete, though. He's in the clear. I think it would be a good idea to go down to Boston and talk with Hilliar about this, particularly now that you have that list. Cynthia is driving me down in her new car, so you can come along with us and stay with her."

"That would be nice," said Janet, "but what about Duke?"

"We'll be going through New Windsor, so we can leave him at the kennel and pick him up on the way back. There's something else you ought to know about, Janet. It has to do with this mental message stuff."

"You mean telepathy?"

"That's it. It seems that Mr. Hilliar got in touch with Proctor's parents outside of Boston. Mrs. Proctor, that's Lloyd's mother, has been having dreams about her son. He keeps coming back and telling her that he's drowning, or something. She's got to be told the truth; that her son Lloyd is still alive. So you are one person who ought to talk to her."

They drove down to Boston the next day and Janet delivered the list to Mr. Hilliar at the insurance office. The claim agent complimented Janet on having obtained the list so promptly, and he found that the signature of Lloyd Proctor tallied with samples that the office already had on file. But he made it painfully plain that a complete checkup would have to be made with all the antique dealers named in the lists. Those recent real estate swindles in which Lloyd Proctor was involved, had placed his name definitely on the black list.

That evening, they visited the Proctor home outside of Boston, where they met Lloyd's father, Hubert Proctor, a kindly, gray-haired gentleman who listened attentively to all that Janet had to say about his son. Janet was glad indeed that she could tell how Lloyd had met his business obligations promptly and to the full. She emphasized that Lloyd had kept on sending checks, even after his partnership with Pete had resulted in failure. All that gladdened Hubert Proctor, but only briefly; for when Janet had finished, he remarked in a worried tone:

"The fact remains that you have not seen my son in the past four months. Indeed, nobody who really knew Lloyd has seen him in all that time. That was when his mother began having these recurrent dreams, in which she sees him drowning and hears his calls for help. My wife has been resting all day, so I think you should meet her now and hear what she has to say."

Mrs. Proctor proved to be a quiet, sad-faced woman, who smiled feebly when her husband told her the nice things Janet had said about Lloyd. Hank Dawson and his daughter Cynthia were also the sort who showed real sympathy, so it took very little coaxing for Mrs. Proctor to tell about her dreams. Her eyes took on a faraway gaze as she related:

"Night after night, I have seen my son, and heard his voice. Always, it begins with a call from the dark. The words, 'Mother — mother —' keep stabbing me here." She pressed her hands to her heart, but her eyes retained that distant gaze. "Then I see his face — Lloyd's face — floating in blackness, looking up toward me, his hands raised, seeking help."

As in a trance, the woman looked upward and raised her hands in the appeal that she had just described. Silence was complete and tense in the little living room where Mr. Proctor and the visitors watched and listened. Then Mrs. Proctor lowered her hands and her head; but her eyes were unchanged as she continued:

"Then, gradually, the blackness becomes a rippling pool. I see Lloyd looking up from it, from the midst of those darkened waters. I hear him saying, 'Mother — mother — there is water all about me —' and I watch his dear face go beneath that blackness. Always, for a moment his hands remain; then they, too, dip beneath the surface, leaving only white ripples that die — die — die — until all is black again."

Mrs. Proctor's voice trailed into a drowning gurgle. Suddenly, she came bolt upright in her chair with an anguished shriek: " Lloyd — Lloyd!" Instantly, Hubert Proctor was at his wife's side, calming her, saying, "Wake up — wake up, my darling — it's all a dream —" and a moment later, Mrs. Proctor was blinking at the people whom she had just met, wondering not only who they were, but if they were actually real.

"That is how it always happens," declared Mr. Proctor solemnly. "All these months, my wife has been living and reliving this experience, hearing our son's voice cry not only for help, but for vengeance. For I truly believe that she can only be reflecting our son's real anguish, when he met with some violent death."

During the hush that followed, Janet heard her own voice asking:

"Did Mrs. Proctor have such dreams before?"

"I had other dreams, beginning years ago." Mrs. Proctor was speaking for herself, and her eyes with dimmed with tears. "Always dreams of my son Lloyd at times when he was away from home. Sometimes he was hurt, and I could hear his cry of pain. Other times, he was happy, shouting in sheer joy. And always" — her voice choked — "always —"

"Always, we heard from Lloyd soon after," put in Mr. Proctor. "Once, he wrote that he had met with an injury; again, that he had won a prize in college. Invariably, his mother's dream was in concert with Lloyd's actual experience. This happened so often through the years that when this dream came, we knew it was significant and its repetition certified that fact.

"Now you can understand why I believe our son is dead. You say that you have heard from him, young lady" — Mr. Proctor was speaking directly to Janet now — "but still, you have not seen him. I wondered why he should cry for vengeance, for Lloyd's nature was never vindicative. But since these reports have come in, slurring his integrity, I believe that in death, he has tried to clear his name as he would in life."

Next day, driving northward, Hank Dawson stopped at New Windsor and picked up Duke. As they drove on through Horseshoe Notch, Hank cast a weather eye at clouds beyond Bald Eagle Summit.

"I'll drop Cynthia at home," decided Hank, "and take you up to your cottage, Janet. If the storm hits, I'll stay until it's over."

Janet was glad to have human company. The darkened cottage was huddled like a lurking creature, while the storage shed was white and ghost-like, beneath the swaying trees that resembled hovering monsters. Hank made sure that the shed door was latched, then led the way to the cottage. Soon they had the lights on, a fire burning, and the coffee perking. Then Hank said solemnly:

"Now all we have to do is wait for the ghost."

"You believe it really is a ghost?" gasped Janet. "An avenging ghost — probably the ghost of Lloyd Proctor?"

"You have heard of crimes being reenacted," declared Hank. "Well, you saw it happen last night, through the reenactment of a dream."

"But if Lloyd was murdered four months ago, how could he have sent checks and notes and the list of antiques? And what about those reports from people who say Lloyd swindled them only recently?"

"Signatures and handwriting can be forged. And it's easy to impersonate a man if you don't try to fool people who know him well. A good guy doesn't turn swindler overnight, but somebody could make it look as if he had. Look, Janet, you went out to that shed three times before I did. Each time you saw something, but you didn't find anybody. Neither did the two of us. But if somebody had been hiding in that shed, wouldn't big Duke have found him?"

"I'm sure Duke would have; and now I can tell you why."

Janet's mind was flashing back to the night when Duke *had* found some-one in the shed — Janet's own husband, Pete. That alone seemed proof that something unseen and intangible — a ghost to all intents — had figured on the other occasions. So far, Janet had held back any mention of Pete's visit because she knew he hadn't wanted it to be known. Now, in the light of things that she had learned, Janet was willing to blurt out the truth. But Hank didn't give her time.

"You don't need to tell me why you're so sure," said Hank. "I know. After what we heard last night, I'm wondering where this trail will lead. But I know where it will begin. Out there in that shed — tonight!"

The wailing wind echoed Hank's sentiment, and Duke's whimper came in turn. Already, Duke was bristling as he had before; his ear was attuned to the high pitch that no human being could hear. The big dog arose and moved slowly toward the door, throating new recognition of that distant, sobbing call.

Hank came to his feet: "Let's go."

They went. Tonight, their approach to the shed was steadier, faster than before, as they watched for the latched door to open of its own accord. They were nearly there when it made its first waver, as though extending an invitation from an invisible occupant. Duke gave his mingled yelp and growl, as he began a forward lope. This time, Hank did not hesitate. Above the furious wind, he shouted, "Let him go!" and as Janet did, Hank added: "Now, come on!"

As they started, the door swung wide. There, plain in the blackened oblong, was a whitish figure, its shape visibly human, but only for a fleeting moment. Then, it was gone, with Duke unleashed and bounding after it. Hank and Janet followed so closely in Duke's wake that they were in time to see the inner door swing wide; and again, they glimpsed that phantom form. Then Duke was following it to the back corner of the tool room, where he raised his big paws shoulder high and planted them against the bolted door.

There, in the full beam of Hank's flashlight, Janet saw the huge hound cornering his prey, as he had the other night. But Duke wasn't barking in fury; he was whining in happy recognition. The man he had cornered was stroking him, petting the dog's head and forelegs; and now, Duke was licking the face that Janet could see so clearly that she shrieked despite herself:

"Lloyd Proctor!"

Then to Janet's amazement, as she watched Lloyd's stroking hand, she could see Duke's big head through it! A moment later the hand had vanished and Lloyd's figure, though still vaguely visible, was dissolving too. Last to vanish was Lloyd's face, a kindly, somewhat handsome face that Janet clearly recognized, despite its deathly pallor. Then that vision, too, had vanished, and Duke was there alone, clawing only the bolted back door and whimpering mournfully as though longing for the touch of a hand that was gone.

Hank, too, had seen enough to be convinced. He stood by while Janet patted Duke, who nestled his head in her arms as though he had lost one friend and found another. Then Hank tried the back door and found it bolted. Janet spoke in a hushed tone:

"I saw him, Hank. As plainly as I see you now. It was Lloyd Proctor — or his ghost."

"I saw it, too," declared Hank, "and I heard you call his name. But I would have known him anyway, after seeing his father the other night. Lloyd was a dead ringer for him." Hank paused; then added grimly; "A *dead* ringer."

There was a lull. The wind was dying as though it had done its work. Then Hank spoke emphatically:

"Lloyd Proctor was murdered, right here, at this very spot. Do you know why I know? I'll show you why." He picked up a handy chisel and pried open the tool closet in the wall beside the door. "Look here!"

A moment later. Hank was staring at an empty space, almost as startled as if he had seen Lloyd's ghost again.

"Where are the things that were in here?" he demanded. "Who took them?"

"I don't know for sure," rejoined Janet in a hollow tone, "but do you want me to guess?"

"Yes. It is very important."

"Pete was here," said Janet, her voice taking on a cold, impersonal tone. "Pete Ryerly — my husband. Duke cornered him here in the shed. That's how I know a human being could be trapped here, but not a ghost. Pete was after something, because when he left the cottage, it was ten minutes at least before

I heard his car leave. I wondered then what he was after; now I'm sure it must have been those tools and clothes we found here. I should have told you all this sooner, Hank."

"And there's something I should have told you, Janet. Remember the day I brought Hilliar up here and he sent those two men to the farmhouse to take pictures there? They weren't insurance investigators, Janet; they were state police detectives. While we were in the cottage, they took those things from the tool closet; and instead of going to the farm, they drove back to Hilldale. There they bought duplicate tools and clothes, which they roughened up to match the originals. They brought the duplicates back and put them in that closet."

"And what did they do with the originals?"

"They sent them to the crime laboratory. I'd sort of figured they might be some kind of evidence; but I was thinking in terms of the fire up at the farmhouse. I suspected arson; not murder. But the lab tests showed that what looked like rust on the hammer was really blood. There were bloodstains on the coveralls, too. There was a peculiar sort of clay on both the spade and the shoes, showing that somebody had been digging somewhere."

"So whoever took those duplicate tools and things wanted to cover up," said Janet. Her voice was sad. "It must have been Pete, for he told me where to write to Lloyd and he seemed so sure I would get a reply. Pete must have picked up my letter, using Lloyd's name; then he answered it himself and sent the list."

"Let's lock up the cottage," suggested Hank. "We'll take Duke down to my house in Hilldale, and you can stay there with Cynthia and me until we've solved this case."

During the ride to Hilldale, they lined up more facts.

"Either Lloyd was staying at the cottage," declared Hank, "or Pete decoyed him there. Anyway, Lloyd must have found Pete in the workshop out in the shed. Pete hit him with that hammer, then took the body somewhere and buried it."

"Somewhere," Janet whispered, "where there is deep black water —"

"When Lloyd was slugged," Hank went on, "he must have called for Duke. Maybe it was Pete who shipped Duke to the kennel, so Lloyd could have thought Duke was still around. Anyway, Duke has been hearing that dying call ever since."

"And always on a windy night —"

"Like the night when it happened. It was windy, last spring, the night the farmhouse burned. Pete wanted it to look as if the flames carried to the barn, so he could collect insurance on that, too."

Hank was silent, thinking, until they pulled up at his home in Hilldale. Then he summarized briefly:

"In my work, I play hunches, then find proof. There's two ways to do it in this case. One is to have those insurance people check Pete's past rather than Lloyd's. The other is to get a good dowser working on that water clue, because Pete couldn't have lugged the body very far. In fact, Lloyd may still have been alive at the time. That would fit with his mother's dreams of drowning."

That same night Hank talked to Hilliar by long distance and told him of the new developments. Within the next week, Hilliar gained the anticipated results. Calls to the antique dealers established that they had made sales on the specified dates to a man purporting to be Lloyd Proctor; but their detailed descriptions fitted Peter Ryerly instead. The same applied to the more recent real estate swindle. Dupes who had named Lloyd as the perpetrator, switched promptly to Pete when shown photos of the two men.

It was plain that Pete had begun to cheat Lloyd early in the game, running up fake expenses on the farm, then buying antiques in his partner's name, selling them secretly and shipping dummy crates to Pleasant Farm. Apparently he had murdered Lloyd to prevent him from finding out too much; then, by posing as the dead man, whose signature he had learned to forge to perfection, Pete had continued to profit while laying a false trail that blackened the name of his unfortunate victim.

Meanwhile, Hank Dawson had found a dowser in New Windsor. The dowser was a man who worked at "water witching" as some people styled it, by using a large forked twig, preferably from a willow tree, to find a source of underground water. He gripped the ends of the forked twig, one in each upturned fist, so that the stem extended straight outward. Then he started from the ruined farmhouse to cover the extensive acreage of Pleasant Farm, which was heavily covered over with long grass and thick weeds.

"I never did take much stock in dowsing," Hank told Janet, as they followed along. "These fellows claim they've got an extra sense that makes the willow stick work for them. But I guess it takes something psychic, as you call it, to see a ghost, too. So who are you and I to talk?"

At times, the water witcher would pause while the stem end of the forked twig wavered downward, indicating water. But always, the symptoms were brief or inadequate, until late in the afternoon when he had reached a level spot a quarter mile from the ruined farmhouse and directly in back of Stony Brook Cottage.

There, the willow really behaved in an uncanny style. Despite the dowser's efforts to control it, the stem dipped steadily, forcibly downward pulling the man's brawny hands and muscular forearms with it. Even the skeptics in the gallery of watchers were impressed, for the dowser's face was contorted from the resistance he put up. But whether he was fighting some unseen force or merely struggling with his own subconscious, the divining rod won out. After it pointed straight downward, the dowser relaxed and panted:

"Dig there — and dig deep."

They dug until dusk settled, and in the course of digging, they struck a clayish soil that corresponded to the caked mud on the shoes and spade found in the tool closet of the shed. So Hank ordered searchlights, and in their glare, the digging was continued. Finally, the ground began to cave in funnel fashion; and loose stones, slipping down through, sent back echoing splashes. Hank told the diggers to work more carefully, and soon they uncovered the mouth of a deep well that had probably gone dry many years before and had been forgotten.

Whatever the case, it was filled with water now, and Hank remarked that it probably would show on the survey map of the farm. That map had been in the farmhouse when it burned; and Janet could understand why. If Pete had dumped Lloyd's body here and then covered up the opening, he wouldn't have wanted the well to be located ever. During the summer, grass and weeds had grown over it, leaving no trace whatever.

But the dowser's willow stick had found it; and more. As the searchers probed deep in the blackened water, they came upon the body that they sought. Janet was too sick at heart to wait while they tried to identify the waterlogged remains of Lloyd Proctor, which they soon did, by a monogrammed ring that they found on one finger.

Like the strange cry that had come with the night wind, the oft-repeated dream of a dying face in blackened waters now had become the proven positive token of an avenging ghost.

Vengeance soon caught up with Peter Ryerly. Once he was branded a wanted murderer, law enforcement officers began closing in on him. Unable to tap the bank account of a victim whose signature he could so cleverly forge, Ryerly was cut off from immediate funds and was forced to resort to petty thefts and stupid robberies to keep ahead of the law.

One night he was spotted driving a stolen car. In the chase that followed, Ryerly took to a side road, hoping to shake off a pursuing police car; but it stayed close on the trail. When Ryerly came to a dead-end sign, he didn't stop. Instead, he crashed the barrier and plunged to his death on the jagged rocks of a deep ravine.

Perhaps he mistook the white warning sign for a pale, unturned face floating in a blackened pool; possibly he thought the wail of the police siren was an eerie call carried by the night wind. Whatever his impressions, Peter Ryerly was most certainly driven to his doom by the avenging ghost of his victim, Lloyd Proctor.

RETURN
FROM
OBLIVION

RETURN FROM OBLIVION

They were a great crew, as Bob Embry remembered them from that last night they spent together. Like Embry himself, each was an integral part of their ship, *King Nine,* a B-25 medium bomber that belonged to the 12th Air Force, USAAF., based in Tunisia. Tomorrow, they were going on a milk run to bomb the southern tip of Italy, as they had done before, during this intensive campaign in the year 1943.

As captain, Embry was giving his crew a pep talk, along the usual lines that always brought a responsive note.

"It's like going fishing, fellows," he declared. "Off Long Island, when the mackerel are running, or maybe the bluefish. Boy, would I like to catch up with a school of blues tomorrow! But you've got to be ready for them. You can lose a lot if your tackle is too light."

Bill Kline, who wore the chevrons of a technical sergeant, spoke up:

"Chief, you make it sound like fishing was real hot stuff."

"It is," assured Embry. "The boats go out, as we do. All there is ahead of you is sea and sky, until you reach your objective."

"You mean like Target Bluefish?"

"Like Target Bluefish. Then over go the lines, just the way we drop bombs from *King Nine.* When your mission is accomplished, you head back."

"But there's a difference, Chief. Those boats are sure to get back."

"Not always. Storms can scatter a fishing fleet, and I've been on boats that were lucky to haul into port. But I've always been lucky, fishing, so I'll be lucky tomorrow. Some day, I'll be taking all of you out on a boat to some of those fishing spots, like The Farms or Seventeen Fathoms —"

Embry's voice trailed; he put his hand to his head. The crew knew that their captain was having one of his recurrent fever turns. Kline, hoping to snap him out of it, supplied a quip:

"And to think, Chief, I lived all my life in the Bronx, but until you told us, I never even heard of anybody fishing off Long Island."

"You never even heard of Long Island," put in Jerry Blake, the co-pilot. "Okay, Bronx cowboy. You and your buddies scram, while I go over flight details with the chief here."

As soon as the rest were gone, Blake proffered some advice:

"You'd better see the medic, Bob, and get some more of those pills that helped before. The boys are all with you. That's why they are so anxious for you to be with them tomorrow."

"Right, Jerry." Embry rose unsteadily. "I'll go see the medic. And some day, Jerry, we'll go fishing together, like I said. There's nothing like fishing to make you forget whatever worries you."

Not that Robert Embry was the sort to worry. He had shown a cool head when he took his pre-flight training at Amarillo. He'd taken multiple engine at Randolph. Then he had gone to England and next to Africa. Now, at the age of twenty-four, he was flying his thirty-eighth mission. But when *King Nine* took off, it would just be another fishing trip for Captain Embry and his crew.

It was a hot, still, North African morning when the bombers started on their mission. Their progress was registered in an R. A. F. operations room, where keen eyes watched careful hands push different-colored markers back and forth across a table that resembled a gigantic chess board. A jargon of reports was coming in, guiding the moves in the grim game. One British officer answered a jangling phone, spoke briefly, and then announced:

"Yanks have an aircraft reporting heavy flak damage over Bari. Last heard from over Romadi and headed for the desert. We have a Mosquito group flying there. Have them keep their eyes open."

"What kind of a ship?" asked a man at the table.

"A B-25 Mitchell," replied the officer. "Designated as *King Nine*." He watched the board man move the appropriate marker. Then, over the phone, he stated: "We'll put out the call in case we hear anything, sir. Of course, if they're heading inland over the desert, the poor devils don't stand much chance."

One man who could have gone along with that opinion was Bob Embry. The captain of the *King Nine* had flown over desert wastes before and had often pictured the devastating heat of those endless sands below. Now Embry was experiencing it as an actuality, a heat so fearful that he thought at first it was his fever rising, only to realize that never, in his most delirious moments, had he been swept by a burning sensation such as this.

Face down, Embry felt that the very sand was stifling him. It wasn't soft, it was coarse and it seemed to grind into his face and hands, even penetrating the cloth of his uniform. Slowly, as in a dream, he arose, feeling the heat of the sand still clinging to his sweaty clothes. As he ran his hand across his face and forehead, he felt more sweat, with the slick of oil. He opened his eyes and saw sheer white sand, nothing more, until a stretch of blackness on a nearby dune offered a welcome relief.

As Embry approached, shading his eyes, the blackness stirred and sighed, ending with a metallic twang. Startled, Embry looked up and saw *King Nine* looming above him, nearly intact, but half-buried in the sand. The blackness was the bomber's shadow; the sigh, the desert wind; the twang, a loose portion of the fuselage that was flapping in the wayward breeze.

In a disjointed way, Embry could recall the difficulties of the return flight: How the wing tank had been hit, how the ship had been losing fuel all the way over, how they had fallen behind and gone off course. Embry was sure that they had bellied in, but suddenly he realized that he was basing that on what he saw. It certainly didn't explain how he had made a belly landing of his own, a few hundred feet clear of the bomber.

Odd, how deep the sand was around *King Nine*. No sandstorm could have piled it there or it would have buried Embry completely. Rather, it seemed the result of long accumulation, over weeks or more, but that was equally implausible. The logical answer was that *King Nine* had dug in hard when making that forced landing. The crew could answer that; but where were they?

"Did I order them to bail out?" Embry asked the question aloud, as though expecting *King Nine* to answer. "No, I didn't. We all rode it in, all of us." He paused; then named the list he knew so well: "Me, Robert Embry, captain. Blake, co-pilot. Kransky, radio op. and waist gunner. Jiminez, navigator. Connors, tail gunner. Kline, upper turret gun. Let's see — who else?"

The words were caught and echoed by the hot desert breeze: "Who else — who else — who else —" until Embry realized feverishly that there was no one else. Worse, even those names he had called were not here to answer, except Embry himself. He was all alone in the great white stillness of the vast Libyan Desert, he and a crippled bomber named *King Nine*.

Perhaps the ship itself could answer the riddle! Prompted by that thought, Embry clambered to the upper turret door and dropped down through. He reached the seats that he and Blake had occupied. Both were empty, so Embry took his seat, studied the control panel, and fingered the instruments, hoping the touch would clear his daze. An officer's cap was hanging on the stick, but it wasn't Embry's. Inside it, he read: "Blake, Gerald S., 1st Lt., USAAF."

Embry turned to the tail of the plane and called "Blake!" The only answer was the whine of the wind through a shattered window, followed by the *clack-clack-clack* of a pair of earphones dangling at the radio operator's seat. Now Embry shouted, "Kransky!" but again there was no answer, so he started a slow walk through the length of the plane, calling for the others: "Jiminez! Conners! Kline!" All to no avail.

At least, Embry saw their parachutes hanging on hooks unused. That confirmed his belief that the plane had bellied in and that he had been thrown clear and probably had been knocked out for hours. But the crew hadn't jumped, they weren't dead in the plane, so they must have left it and started walking. If so, why hadn't they taken him along?

While Embry pondered over that, he thought he caught the faint sound of a distant radio signal. He sprang to the operator's seat, grabbed one earphone and listened, while he flicked the switches and finally snatched up a hand mike. Tensely, but efficiently, Embry announced:

"May Day, May Day, this is *King Nine* calling Firefly. . . . *King Nine* calling Firefly. . . . Pancaked in desert. . . . One hour, thirty minutes from last check point. . . .Bearing two ninety degrees. . . . Area flat and sandy. Low hills to the north. No other distinguishing landmarks. No sign of crew. . . . May Day, May Day. . . . *King Nine* to Firefly. . . . Come in, please."

No response. The radio was dead. Perhaps its feeble crackle had only been in his imagination. But he wasn't imagining his responsibility. He was still captain of this aircraft, and it was his job to see his crew through to safety, if he could only find them first.

Embry clambered from the plane and climbed a sand dune, shielding his eyes from the blinding sun as he surveyed the desolate but irregular horizon. Nobody, nothing was in sight, so Embry started back toward the plane, only to stumble on an object buried in the sand. He picked it up, shook it — a canteen with water inside. It was marked with the name of Sergeant Kline. Embry heard himself laughing aloud, but without a trace of mirth:

"Kline, you stupid idiot! You dropped your canteen here! You crazy Bronx cowboy! You're in the desert! You'll need water!"

The only thing now was to find Kline and the others, whichever way they had gone. Almost aimlessly, Embry started plodding across the dunes, carrying Kline's canteen and talking aloud, in a rambling tone:

"Some crew I've got. Some idiot crew. They run around dropping canteens full of water. So I've got to nursemaid them." As Embry moved along, he raised his voice to a shout: "Hey, crew! Where are you? I'm responsible for you guys — or wouldn't you know? You're giving me some bum action!"

Embry tramped along silently then, through the vast hush of the timeless desert. He wanted to drink from the canteen, but wouldn't. He was saving the water for Kline, who would need it more. That brought Embry's mind back to his immediate mission. Again, he shouted:

"*King Nine* crew! This is your captain, here! Come home to papa. I've got to look after you guys. Where did you all go? Please, fellows, where are you? No more hide and seek. I'm responsible —"

Embry cut off as a metallic clank sounded — different, louder than the flapping from the plane's fuselage, which was far, far behind him now. The sound was ahead, dead ahead, for Embry suddenly stumbled on the cause. It was a flak helmet, hanging on an upright strip of metal, clanking in the wind. On the improvised marker, Embry read the simple, painted wording:

TECH. SGT. WM. F. KLINE

R. I. P.

"Kline, I'm sorry," choked Embry. "You must be the one who didn't survive that crash. Only the crew could have buried you here. Rest in peace, kid."

There came a sound from above, sharper than the desert wind, higher, louder, until it filled the whole sky. Embry stared upward, bewildered by the sight of three streaking planes with swept-back wings, leaving long vapor trails behind them as they sped toward the horizon.

"What kind of planes are those?" Embry asked himself. "I've never seen planes like that before. I've never seen any jets —"

He cut off at the word "jets" and stared in new amazement.

"Jet aircraft!" he repeated. "How can I know about jet aircraft, here in Africa, in 1943? There's no such thing as jet aircraft, not yet. But I know about them, F-106's, F-105's, B-58's. But where are they from? What are they doing here in World War II?"

Embry lowered his gaze again and gasped in astonishment. He was no longer alone, he was surrounded by faces, here at Kline's grave. Faces of men he knew, his lost crew. He was calling their names in the order that he saw them as he turned his head:

"Kransky — Conners — Blake — Jiminez —"

All were studying Embry solemnly, anxiously, like figures from a dream. Then, beyond them, Embry saw another face floating against the background of white sand, a face with a bloody gash across the forehead. Embry screamed a final recognition:

"Kline!"

Embry was on his feet, clutching for the phantom figure. Solid hands grabbed him, and he saw faces around him but no longer recognized them as his crew. Then, suddenly, Embry collapsed, but not on soft sand. Instead, he hit solid planking. When his senses returned, he was delirious.

It was many hours later at the South Shore Hospital on Long Island. The switchboard operator rang the head psychiatrist's office and said: "We have your call from Washington, Dr. Grantland."

Dr. Grantland, an elderly, methodical man, was keenly interested in the detailed report that came direct from the Pentagon. He stepped to an outer office and spoke to a middle-aged man whose tanned face showed deep concern.

"You are Mr. Morton, the friend who brought Robert Embry here?"

"That's right, doctor." Don Morton nodded. "But I've only known Bob for a few months. We met on a fishing boat off Montauk, and we've made trips together ever since. Like most folks who fish, we don't talk much. Coming into shore, though, he always says, 'Blue sky and white sand' — as if it was on his mind."

"He said that today? When you came in on the boat?"

"Yes, but nobody paid any attention. The news was coming over the radio, about them finding a bombing plane in Africa that had been lost in the desert nearly twenty years ago. Then Embry was suddenly shouting, wild-like. We'd just got him quiet when some jets flew over, and that started him off again. He was yelling for friends of his, calling us by their names."

"Can you remember any of those names?"

"Yes. He called me Conners — another fellow was Blake —"

"And Jiminez — and Kransky — and Kline —"

"Yes, all of those. Kline was the last one. By then, Embry wasn't looking at us. He was pointing over the side, as if he saw a face in space."

"You've helped us greatly, Mr. Morton," Dr. Grantland said, "and you've helped your friend Embry even more. None of those names was mentioned in the radio report, but Embry was captain of that B-25, and they were his crew."

"But how could he have gone on that flight with them?"

"He didn't. He was taken down with a fever the night before. They were all lost on the desert, trying to get back, except one, whose grave was found there: Sergeant Kline."

The doctor went in to see Embry, leaving Don Morton outside. The patient had improved and was sitting up, but his voice carried a challenge:

"Don't tell me I wasn't there, doctor. I saw *King Nine*."

"I know that you saw your plane in the desert."

"And there was something else that I found there —"

"I know what you found. Kline's grave."

Embry looked up, his face pleased. He had found someone who would believe him. His strained expression faded as he confided:

"For years, doctor, I've believed I was on that flight — or made believe. I've wanted to think that I was there. Suddenly, I heard that they had found *King Nine*. Then I *was* there — as you say — except I never really did go on that flight. But today, I *did* go back there — I'm sure I did."

"Yes, you went back, in your mind. Now you know what happened and that you were in no way to blame. They did the best they could, just as if you had been in command. You're going to be all right, so get some sleep now."

Embry leaned back, closed his eyes, and spoke earnestly:

"I told the crew I'd take them fishing, some day. That's what I was doing, fishing, when the word came. Fishing and trying to forget that I hadn't been there. Then I *was* there, lying in all that sand, struggling through it, as they did, until I found Kline's grave. Then I saw the faces of the crew, and when Kline's face joined them, I knew they were all gone. I'd have taken it easier if those jets hadn't come over. There were no jets back then, so that snapped me out of it — took me away from the past — too soon —"

Embry's voice trailed dreamily. Dr. Grantland left the room and spoke to Don Morton, who was waiting in the corridor and had heard the conversation.

"Embry has been living a strange guilt for twenty years," the doctor declared, "all due to the uncertainty of what really happened. Now that is over. He will soon go fishing with you again."

A nurse came down the corridor, bringing Embry's fishing clothes, which had been left in the examination room. The doctor gestured to a bench.

"Put the clothes there, nurse," he ordered. "I don't want the patient disturbed. I'm going into his room shortly, to see if he is asleep, so I'll take them in then."

Embry's shoes were on top of the pile and overbalanced it as the nurse placed the clothes on the narrow bench. As she quickly caught the pile, sand trickled from every fold and pocket; and when the nurse tipped the shoes, more sand poured out, adding to the sizable white heap. Dr. Grantland turned to Morton:

"How did you get Embry across the beach? Did you drag him?"

"We didn't come in on the beach," replied Morton in an awed tone. "We went out from the pier and docked there when we came back. From there, we took Bob straight to my car. I wouldn't know where that sand came from."

"Nor would I," said Dr. Grantland. "Good-bye, Mr. Morton."

But from the warmth of their parting handshake and the whiteness of the sand itself, Don Morton somehow knew that both he and Dr. Grantland had one place in mind — the Libyan Desert. For where else could that sand have come from?

THE HOUSE
ON THE SQUARE

THE HOUSE ON THE SQUARE

As a team of ghost hunters, Bruce Barlow and Jeff Shelby were top flight. They had fun and profited from their part-time profession, which began while both were students in an eastern college. During a summer vacation, they visited the old Black Swan Tavern, once an overnight stop for stagecoaches between New York and Montreal.

A new owner had restored the tavern for the modern tourist trade, but no one would stay there, because strange groans were heard at night which were attributed to the ghost of an innkeeper who had been murdered in the place, many years before. But Bruce and Jeff slept there willingly, for a fee, in order to dehaunt the inn.

They finally traced the sounds to the attic, but found only some old boxes, storm windows, and an ancient sign saying: HIGBY'S INN, J. L. HIGBY, PROP., that being the name of the murdered innkeeper. So the ghost hunters pitched their cots, but took care not to disturb any boxes, or the old sign, which was attached to a pole propped against the slanted attic roof.

After a few hours, the groans awakened Bruce and Jeff. Both flicked their flashlights on the same spot and exclaimed: "J. L. Higby!" But they didn't mean the ghost of the murdered innkeeper; they meant the sign that bore his name. Its pole had once extended above the tavern door, so the sign was attached by hinges. These had weakened over the years, and the wind coming through the eaves swayed the sign, producing loud groans that had magnified more weirdly in rooms below than in the attic itself.

That settled the problem of the tavern ghost; and Bruce and Jeff were paid off handsomely for their job. They debunked some more haunts that summer, but they cracked a still bigger riddle the next season. That was when they investigated a decrepit mansion where a mysterious pool of blood appeared at intervals in a corner of the living room, where one man had shot another to death during an argument over a gambling debt.

The ghost hunters were shown the room by a caretaker, who pointed out the exact spot where the strange pool appeared. He had photographs to prove it was no illusion. The pool measured eighteen inches across, and it was always at least a foot away from the corner of the room.

"You never know when you will find it," declared the caretaker. "One bright morning, you walk in and there it is. Always in dry weather."

"What happens the night before?" asked Bruce. "Do people hear strange sounds?"

"Not to my knowledge," replied the caretaker. "All they saw was the blood and that was enough. They walked out real scared."

"We won't walk out," promised Bruce. "No ghost can fool us."

They watched the corner of the room steadily, for one week. It rained on the third and fourth nights, then cleared. The fifth night was uneventful, but on the sixth night, Bruce said to Jeff: "Look there!"

A slow trickle was emerging from beneath the baseboard of the wall, gradually forming a reddish pool. They watched it for the next few hours, taking photographs in progress. It finally lessened, leaving a one-foot space between the wall and the pool. Bruce, studying the track that the trickle had followed, discovered some damp, paper-thin flakes.

"These are fragments of dried leaves," he declared. "They must have blown in through some opening up near the roof and then worked down inside the wall."

"And the rain of a few days ago must have come down through, too," added Jeff, "but the leaves kept absorbing it until they became over-saturated. Then the water began to trickle down and out."

"Let's get a carpenter's level and check this floor," suggested Bruce. "I'll bet we find a depression there, too slight for the eye to detect."

Bruce was right. Tests with the level showed that the floor was a trifle out of true, enough for the pool to form just far enough away from the corner to leave no trace of its source. Also, the ghost hunters took samples of the supposed blood before the pool dried, something that no one had done before. A chemical analysis showed that the ruddy hue was due to decayed vegetable matter, specifically dried leaves.

Summer after summer, the two ghost hunters pursued their intriguing profession, with more and more triumphs to their credit. Some of these proved to be surprisingly simple; almost ludicrously so. There was the case of an old house in New York's Greenwich Village, where the basement and ground floor had been made into a duplex apartment with a huge living room. In it was an old-fashioned chandelier suspended by a long chain from the ceiling. On nights when dinner parties were held, the chandelier was seen to sway, while lighted candles flickered on the table just below.

One local historian linked the wavering lights to an old Dutch legend of more than two centuries before, involving witchcraft; but Bruce and Jeff came up with a more modern solution. They discovered that tremors were produced by trains on a subway line that ran a block away. When a north-bound express attained a certain speed its vibration corresponded to the building's sway, and the ghostly manifestations resulted.

Equally intriguing were the weird lights that danced in the windows of an abandoned country schoolhouse in Vermont. They were attributed to the ghost of a man who had committed suicide there, after trying to set fire to the building. Ghostly manifestations had been reported over the years but had taken on an almost nightly frequency when Bruce and Jeff came to investigate.

The ghost hunters found that the weird flickers were reflections from cars that took a little-used turnoff from a new through highway. Only cars that were using their bright lights could produce them. Other cars went by unnoticed due to a high intervening embankment.

There was an element of danger in some of these investigations, particularly when the two friends were searching old quarries or roaming swamps and woodlands where snakes and wild animals might be encountered. Nor did Bruce and Jeff discount the chance of running up against human opposition, such as poachers, moonshiners, or even escaped convicts.

In addition to cameras, flashlights, compass, and other equipment, Bruce always carried a long, stout cane with a heavy, bulb-shaped head. The stick, which his uncle had brought back from the Orient, was known as a "Penang lawyer" because, in the settlement of Penang, the only way to win an argument was with the use of a heavy cudgel, preferably of that type. Jeff, who was a good pistol shot, always carried a .32 automatic for emergencies.

Bruce's stick came in handy when they investigated a summer cottage which squeamish renters had left because of odd sounds they had heard from a closed bunk room. On opening the door, Bruce and Jeff were swept back by a blackish shape that swooped out with all the force and fury of a tornado. But Bruce was ready for it, swinging the bulbous end of the "Panang lawyer" into the thing, which scattered all apart.

The monstrous form was a swarm of bats that had been hibernating in the bunk room and were responsible for the weird sounds. But for Bruce's timely work with the club end, which he used with mallet-like force, he and Jeff might have been badly clawed and bitten by the winged horde that they had released. Instead, they soon cleared the cottage of the pests and the ghostly rumors as well.

Jeff's turn came one season when they were ghost hunting in an old mill which a prospective buyer wanted to turn into a country tearoom. Along with ghostly groans and moans, slow footsteps were sometimes heard descending the old stairway in one corner of the building. Yet no one had ever seen the spectral figure that belonged with them, and the fact that it was invisible made it all the more uncanny.

It didn't take long to track down the more standard sounds. The groans were due to the creaky condition of the beams and timbers; the moans were echoes from the gushing millrace. But Bruce and Jeff were watching the stairs, which were outlined in the dim light, when the footsteps began descending them in slow, even fashion.

That steady, invisible approach was enough to scare off almost anyone, but Bruce was ready to surge in blindly and start lashing with his cane at the imaginary prowler, when Jeff suddenly ordered:

"Hold it! I'll handle this!"

Then, pressing the switch of his flashlight, Jeff spotted its beam some four steps lower, and blasted point blank with his gun at where the unseen figure's feet should have been. One more footstep came with a halting plop, and Jeff's light was focused upon a very dead ghost in the form of a huge rat.

That was the creature that had produced the inexplicable sounds. Night after night, the rat had come boldly down the stairs, thudding its full weight upon each succeeding step. The corner served as a sound box that magnified the emphatic thumps until they reached the proportions of a cautious human tread, which had been accepted as something ghostly. Jeff's keen sight, plus his still keener insight, had given him an inkling as to the actual cause.

The ghost hunters promptly recommended that a crew of workmen strengthen the building by day, to eliminate the creaks; and that some capable cats should patrol the premises by night, to handle any brother rats who might be taking over for the martyred rodent who had played ghost. The result was that all unexplainable manifestations immediately ceased, and the team of Bruce Barlow and Jeff Shelby was paid off handsomely for their ghost-breaking job.

A marked difference grew between Bruce and Jeff during the years they worked together. To a great degree, it accounted for their increased success. Bruce became constantly bolder and more contemptuous of "ghosts," while Jeff chose a scholarly and analytical approach. As a result, they pleased both types of customers, believers and skeptics. Oddly enough, the careers that Bruce and Jeff chose after graduation from college had much to do with this. Bruce became a physical director and athletic coach at a boys' school, while Jeff continued with postgraduate studies and took his doctor's degree in philosophy.

Each summer they teamed as usual and profitably debunked their regular quota of haunted houses, though they differed in their manner of approach. Bruce was more than ever eager to smash right into a case on a trial-and-error basis, while Jeff insisted on a preliminary survey of a scientific sort. To that, Bruce objected strenuously.

"If I waited for you to analyze all these cases," Bruce told Jeff, "we would never get around to the real explanations of the so-called ghosts. That may account for the few cases where we didn't find an answer."

"Perhaps," observed Jeff in a speculative tone, "some of those cases were not as simple as you suppose."

"You mean you're beginning to *believe* in ghosts?" demanded Bruce. "You're crazy! Anyway, let's not talk about our failures. What we want is more jobs like the one we just finished."

Bruce referred to a "haunted" glen outside of New York City, close to the famous Sleepy Hollow where a headless horseman had once supposedly ridden. A luminous, beckoning figure had been seen below a rustic bridge, and the owner of the glen had installed big automatic searchlights to trap the ghost. But always the apparition vanished at the first blaze of the lights, recording another triumph for superstition over science.

When Bruce and Jeff had taken over, they promptly dismantled the searchlights. Instead, they took their stance at the spot where the ghost usually appeared and at the first bluish flicker, they had photographed it close up with infra-red equipment. The developed prints had shown it to be marsh gas that added a lifelike shimmer to a stump of phosphorescent spunkwood.

The searchlights had defeated their own aim by drowning the trifling glow with an overpowering glare.

Bruce and Jeff had come into New York City and collected a full fee with bonus from the owner of the dehaunted glen. It was early September, and Bruce had a week to go before his vacation ended, so he proposed that they make it profitable.

"A lady up at Sleepy Hollow told me that if we wanted a house that was really haunted," declared Bruce, "we would find one in Redgate Square, right here in Manhattan. She lived in the neighborhood, so she should know."

"All right," agreed Jeff, "Let's go and have a look."

They finally located Redgate Square, set back from a dead-end street near the East River. The fourth house from the left, which bore the number 306, was a misfit in an otherwise well-kept row. Its whole front looked neglected, its brickwork colorless, the white window trimmings dull and grimy. Its front gate was canted at an angle on a wobbly iron picket fence that was badly rusted. A low balcony jutted from its second floor front, giving it a squatty appearance. On the gate was a sign:

FOR SALE OR RENT

A. J. WHITTAKER REAL ESTATE

They checked the address, and Bruce flagged a passing cab with a wave of his Penang lawyer. Ten minutes later, they were talking with Mr. A. J. Whittaker in his real estate office. He was a quiet, elderly man, who gave a dry-faced smile when they told him why they were interested in 306 Redgate Square.

"Ghost hunters, eh?" queried Whittaker. "Well, I'm willing to meet your usual terms, if you will stay a week in that house."

Whittaker dug a big envelope from a bottom drawer and whacked it to get rid of a long accumulation of dust, as he stated:

"A confidential file on Number 306. Often, I've wanted to get rid of it, but I knew some day all this data would be needed."

From the envelope, Whittaker brought out title deeds, leases, floor plans, photographs, letters, and other documents, as he continued:

"One of the early owners was named Howard Glendon, who lived there with his uncle and a very powerful serving man named Crandall. At times the uncle became erratic — I might say violent — and had to be confined in a barred room at the back of the fourth floor. At other times, he was seen glaring from windows, or heard howling about the house. Only Crandall could control him. Later, Glendon sold the house and took his uncle abroad, so he said. But no one actually saw the uncle leave the house."

Whittaker produced an old photograph that showed the second story balcony of 306 Redgate Square. There, a man was glaring from a window above the wrought-iron rail, apparently enraged at the photographer who had snapped that chance shot of him. The man's face showed a demoniac leer, and his lips were distorted in a ferocious snarl. While Bruce studied those demented features, etching their details in his mind, Whittaker stated:

"That is Glendon's uncle in one of his milder moods. Otherwise, they would have had him confined in the top floor back room."

Jeff was becoming restless, but Bruce was intensely interested, Bluntly he asked: "Do you think the uncle died there?"

"He might have," replied Whittaker, "because all the disturbances have originated in that room at the fourth floor back. A family named Rowland moved in after the Glendons left, but they were glad to move out a few months later. They had trouble keeping servants, who were essential in those days."

"And then who moved in?" inquired Bruce.

"Several families." Whittaker gestured to the files. "They are all listed here, and they all had servant problems. Some closed off the fourth floor, letting servants sleep on the third floor, but they kept hearing things being moved above them, which was as bad as living on the top floor.

"Finally, the Ashursts took over. They had five daughters and three servants who had been with the family for years, so were willing to accept the odd situation. One maid, Della, had the back room on the top floor and complained about feeling ill, but she decided to stay it out, because the eldest Ashurst daughter was about to be married. On the evening of the wedding rehearsal, Della came screaming down the stairs, stark mad. They rushed her to a hospital, where she shrieked at any mention of the room where it all happened. Two days later, she died. Nobody has dared to sleep there since."

"Jeff and I won't mind," declared Bruce nonchalantly. "Let's go over to the square right now. The sooner we begin this deal, the better."

Soon they arrived at the house in Redgate Square, ready to invade it, bag and baggage. But for once, Jeff Shelby felt himself a silent and unwilling partner in a ghost hunt entirely engineered by Bruce Barlow.

From the moment the rusty gate groaned on its hinges and the flagstones gave dull echoes underfoot, Jeff felt that he and Bruce were unwanted in these peculiarly gloomy preserves. The overhanging balcony seemed like the raised jaw of a monstrous creature, ready to gobble its hapless prey, for its overhang cut off all view of the neighboring balconies. When the rusted lock of the heavy, dark front door refused to yield to Whittaker's key, Jeff was tempted to turn and dash out through the gate. Only his regard for Bruce restrained him from that cowardly act.

The door finally opened, and they entered a long, low hallway with a gloomy, stiffly furnished reception room on the left. The hallway led into a dining room, finished in oak, which added to the morbid *motif*. Jeff noted a prevailing musty odor and commented:

"Damp in here, isn't it?"

"Damp?" echoed Whittaker. "Why, this house is the driest in the block. Not a trace of mildew on the walls; and these floors" — he stamped loudly along the hall — "why, they haven't a warped board anywhere. Look at the furniture, all in perfect condition."

"Still, it seems so moldy —"

"What does, Jeff?" broke in Bruce. "Your imagination?"

That quieted Jeff, but when they reached the kitchen, he glanced suspiciously at an old-fashioned elevator device in the corner, which had been used as a dumb-waiter to send food and drink upstairs. Bruce noted Jeff's look and flicked a flashlight up the shaft.

"No skeletons here," laughed Bruce, "but we can look in all the closets as we go along."

They went up to the second floor and into the front parlor, which was weird indeed, for the overstuffed chairs and couches were draped with white sheets that gave them a ghostly look despite the strong afternoon sunlight. Jeff stopped at the very window shown in the old photograph and stared out over the balcony rail just as Glendon's uncle once had. Momentarily, Jeff wondered if something in the house could have caused the man's wild look; for Jeff felt a sudden mistrust of everything behind him, including his long-time friend Bruce Barlow and the polite, obliging Mr. Whittaker. Jeff shook off a sudden chill as he wheeled about, only to find that neither of his companions was even looking in his direction.

Bruce had opened a suitcase and was spreading the ghost-hunting equipment on a table he had cleared for that purpose. There were cameras, films, and other photographic equipment; also metal measuring tapes, a ball of cord, and some lead fish weights.

"We measure walls for thickness," Bruce explained to Mr. Whittaker, "and use the cord and weights as a plumb line to see if air shafts, wells, and so on are truly vertical. And here's an old friend" — Bruce brought the carpenter's level from the bag — "that enables us to spot slanted floors." Bruce gave a side glance toward Jeff. "Remember the old house with the pool of blood, Jeff?"

Jeff nodded. Now Bruce was spreading out a nest of small, shallow bowls with a flask of mercury and two pairs of soft-soled shoes.

"We fill the bowls with mercury," Bruce told Whittaker, "and set them at key spots. If anything more solid than a ghost comes prowling by, the tremors of the mercury will indicate it. Then Jeff and I put on the soft-soled shoes and go sneaking up on it. The mercury is good at detecting vibrations, too. That's how we tracked a subway ghost in Greenwich Village. Remember that case, Jeff?"

Jeff remembered and gave a shiver, but it wasn't recollective. It had to do with the atmosphere here in the parlor of the house on the square.

"This place is cold," he complained. "Terribly cold. Can't we start a fire in the fireplace?"

"Certainly," agreed Whittaker, "but I haven't noticed any chill."

"Neither have I," declared Bruce, taking a thermometer from the bag, "and what's more, the temperature hasn't dropped a single degree since we came in here. I checked it downstairs, and it is still the same."

Jeff decided to defer the fire, and they continued their tour of the house. The second floor back was mostly bedrooms, and so was the entire third floor. To Bruce, the third floor seemed less chilly than the second; but the fourth floor proved truly ominous. It was reached by a stairway that went up to a landing in a rear corner of the house; then turned and brought them to the approximate center of the top floor.

At the front were two bedrooms with a lengthwise wall between, giving each a large front window. But the arrangement at the back was quite different. Due to the back stairs, the space for bedrooms was limited, so they were arranged in tandem form. First, there was a squarish room, with no window;

only a transom above the door to admit light and air from the hallway. In the back corner of that outer room was a door leading to the inner room, which was also squarish and had a small window above a rear court.

Each room was identically furnished with a cot, table, and chair, but the inner room, despite its window, was the more ominous, for this was where the ghostly manifestations had presumably driven the occupants to madness and death. Bruce studied the window, noted its heavy frames and some deep holes that went into the woodwork beneath a metal reinforcement.

"These were for the bars originally on the window?" he asked Whittaker.

"Right," returned Whittaker. "The bars were removed after the Glendons sold the house and left."

Bruce thrust his head and shoulders out of the window, which was just large enough to accommodate him. He drew back in and gestured for Jeff to do the same. Jeff did and saw that the wall went straight down to the court, with no chance of reaching any windows on the floors below, as they were off at other angles. Again, Jeff felt the sickening sensation of a menace close behind him; but here it was worse than in the parlor two floors below, because the threat of a fall was actual. Jeff shied back into the room quite suddenly.

Again, the others were too busy to notice Jeff's reaction. Bruce was mapping out the campaign that he and Jeff were to follow, while Whittaker was listening with commending nods.

"We'll start right here in this room at midnight," declared Bruce, "since that seems to be the zero hour. I'll sleep here and let Jeff have the cot in the outer room. I'll get the facts first hand, and Jeff can attest them."

Jeff wondered how good a witness he would be if his present jittery mood continued. But he maintained a discreet silence.

"What about the rest of the house?" asked Whittaker.

"We'll keep tabs on it until midnight," replied Bruce. "Give it what Jeff calls a preliminary survey. I don't think we will have to investigate it further, once we've made short work of the ghost business up here."

"There is no electricity in the house," reminded Whittaker, "and it may take a few days to have it turned on —"

"And by then we won't need it," interposed Bruce, with a confident smile. "Anyway, this ghost business started back in the gaslight era. So they didn't have electricity, either."

Whittaker left, stating that he would have dinner sent in for the ghost hunters from a neighborhood restaurant. Bruce and Jeff made their immediate headquarters in the second floor parlor where they had their equipment, and their first act was to start the fire that Jeff wanted. But even that cheery blaze failed to lessen Jeff's occasional chills. Jeff was glad when Bruce suggested that they make a survey of the house; first, by the fading daylight, later with their powerful flashlights.

When the dinner arrived, they ate it in the somber, oak-furnished dining room; then went up to the parlor again, where, by the firelight, they made notes of all that they had accomplished so far, which in the final analysis, was very little. When they listened for suspicious sounds, all they heard was the occasional spurt of a taxicab out in front of Redgate Square. Then, as midnight neared, Bruce picked up his Penang lawyer from beside the fireplace and said:

"It's nearing the zero hour, Jeff. Let's go."

"Yes, let's go," blurted Jeff, "but not upstairs. Let's go down and out the front door. We can come back for our stuff tomorrow."

Bruce's face clouded angrily in the flicker of the firelight.

"You mean you really want to quit, Jeff?"

"I do. This place has got me, Bruce. It isn't right. No creaks, no noises, none of the usual stuff. Instead, it's filled with some gripping force."

"I've heard you talk that way before, but you always changed your mind before we finished the job."

"Yes, I have sensed things elsewhere," conceded Jeff, "but the force, or whatever it was, seemed to dissipate itself. Here it gathers and becomes stronger. Look, Bruce, some of those places really were haunted to a degree. Otherwise, every house, every swamp, every odd place would be haunted. But you know and I know that it only applied in certain instances. The influence, or whatever it is, isn't strong enough to hurt you if you see it through, as we have. But this house is charged with it, Bruce, charged like a load of mental dynamite. They've made tests in psychic laboratories, proving that thoughts can accumulate like thunderclouds and strike with physical impact!"

"And do you know what I think of those tests?" demanded Bruce, his face showing a weird grin in the firelight. "They are bunk — and more bunk. Speaking of bunks, ours are waiting upstairs. So come on."

They went up to the fourth floor back, sidestepping some mercury bowls and an automatic camera that they had planted on the final stairway, just in case of prowlers. They entered the two back rooms and flashed their lights about them. Bruce closed the hallway door and turned the key from the inside, but he left the transom open.

"If anything comes creeping up here," declared Bruce, "you will be the first to hear it. So pass the word to me in the inner room."

"Nothing will come creeping up," returned Jeff. "The danger is in there, Bruce. Let's move my cot in with yours, so we can meet it together."

"Not a chance, Jeff. I'm sleeping in there alone with the door shut between us. We've got to meet the original conditions."

Bruce flicked his light into the inner room, entered and turned to close the door, only to find that Jeff had followed him.

"Suppose something happens in here?" asked Jeff. "What then?"

"Nothing will happen," retorted Bruce, "because it can't."

"Don't talk that way, Bruce. It doesn't take a ghost to make things happen. Suppose you should hear something, as we have in other places —"

"If I hear anything," put in Bruce, sitting down on the cot, "I'll let you know. With a tap on the wall, like this."

Bruce used the head of his heavy cane to rap the wall at the very spot where Jeff's cot was located on the other side.

"Suppose you should see something," persisted Jeff from the doorway. "How will you signal that?"

"With two taps, like this." Bruce rapped twice with the Penang lawyer. "Only I won't see anything. Let's turn in and get some sleep."

"What if something more happens?" questioned Jeff. "What if this — this influence *is* real —"

"Okay, okay," interposed Bruce indulgently. "In that case, I'll give three raps" — he tapped the wall accordingly — "so close the door and call it a night. By morning, we'll be laughing at this nonsense. Our big worry will be collecting our fee from Whittaker."

Oddly, Jeff felt a lot easier when he closed that connecting door and went to his cot in the outer room. It was as if a tremendous pressure had been lifted from him. But it made him worry more about Bruce, who was not sensitive to psychic impressions. Even this outer room had an oppressive effect upon Jeff, but he felt that he could cope with it.

Jeff placed his flashlight and his automatic on the chair beside his cot, finding it a help to have them there, for he was willing to admit that his fears might be more physical than mental. He listened intently for any stir from the inner room; then he realized that the wall was too thick for him to hear anything less than heavy raps from Bruce's big cane. Finally, in the utter stillness and complete blackness of the outer room, Jeff managed to drop off to sleep.

How many hours passed, Jeff could not tell, but he awakened very suddenly, wondering where he was and how he had gotten there. He was really chilled now, for he was in an ice-cold sweat despite the stuffy warmth of the outer room. As he gradually pieced the facts of the preceding day and recognized his pitch-black surroundings, he realized that he was waiting, waiting, waiting for something he was sure would happen in that stillness.

It came, the sound that jarred him into stark reality:

Knock!

It was sharp, from the wall beside Jeff's head, the signal that Bruce had promised. So Bruce had heard something! Now Jeff was listening for it himself while he lay there unable to move. Something more was due; of that he was certain. Then it came:

Knock — Knock!

The double signal jolted Jeff upright in bed. So Bruce had seen something, there in the inner room! Yet out here, all was still black. Tensely, Jeff swung from the bed, then halted, again sensing that more was due:

Knock! Knock!! Knock!!!

Even as the heavy cane strokes thudded, Jeff was grabbing up his flashlight and his automatic while he headed for the door to the inner room. He found the knob, wrenched the door open and plunged through to the other room where he stopped. He pressed the flashlight button and swept its beam around while he loosened the automatic's safety catch with the thumb of his other hand. Then Jeff gave a short, nervous laugh at his own folly.

There was Bruce, lying comfortably in bed, the Penang lawyer propped against the wall where he had placed it. Already, faint daylight was coming in through the little window high above the courtyard. Possibly Bruce had noticed it and had delivered those knocks to awaken Jeff and tell him that the night's vigil was over. Yet it wasn't like Bruce to have carried it that far. One rap would have been enough, signifying that he had seen something; namely, dawn. Maybe Bruce had only half-awakened, given the raps and gone to sleep again. Anyway, there was nothing to fear. Jeff stepped to the cot and said:

"I guess you were right, Bruce. There was nothing to worry about —"

Jeff caught himself as he saw that Bruce was staring upward. But Bruce wasn't awake, even though his eyes were open. At the glint of those wide, fixed pupils and the white surrounding them, Jeff was horror-stricken, there in the light of early dawn. He pressed his hand to Bruce's forehead; tilted his ear to listen for a heartbeat. The forehead was cold; the heart was still.

Bruce Barlow was dead!

Madly, Jeff Shelby dashed from the inner room, found the key in the outer door and turned it. He raced downstairs, jarring the mercury bowls, snapping the automatic camera as he passed. He reached the front door, unbolted it; then rushed across the square and down the street to an all-night lunchroom, where he put in a frantic call to the nearest hospital.

The ambulance arrived, but to no avail. Brue Barlow was pronounced dead, the cause heart failure. Yet in all the years that Jeff Shelby had known his fellow ghost hunter, Bruce had never shown a single symptom of such a condition. To Jeff, there was only one explanation for Bruce's death. The creeping, haunting, crushing sensation that Jeff had experienced in that house and had managed gradually to shake off, must all have caught up with Bruce at once, with a deadly result.

Only Jeff, who had stout-heartedly gone through so many earlier adventures, could testify to the existence of an unseen terror that seemed to emanate from the very walls of this house of horror, as though they had absorbed some murderous force, only to pour it out on anyone who challenged it!

They closed the old house after the inquest. For years, it remained unoccupied, becoming more and more dilapidated. During those years, Jeff Shelby tried to forget the tragedy that had snuffed the life of his best friend, Bruce Barlow. But often he would awaken in the dead of night, reliving that horrible blackness, again hearing those frantic knocks.

Had Jeff Shelby really heard them? That was the question he asked not only himself but other persons versed in psychic matters. They came to these conclusions:

Possibly Bruce Barlow had heard some weird sound, then had seen a strange shape; and finally had found himself ensnared in an actual death struggle with some unknown force. Bruce had remembered the signals and had given them, but too late. By then, the power had fully materalized from the unreal into the real; following that, it had returned to the unreal, being absorbed into the surrounding walls.

That was a theory that bordered on the supernatural. In contrast, some persons who accepted only the supernormal were inclined to the opinion that Bruce, in his sleep, had experienced a heart attack. It had created illusions in his mind — auditory, visual, and finally a sensation of imminent doom. Desperately, he had flashed the mental impression of those promised knocks to his only contact with the world, his close friend, Jeff Shelby. Already keyed to a high mental pitch, Jeff had caught those telepathic flashes and had believed that the knocks were real; which, in a way, they were, to a sensitized mind like his.

A few years later, this case had another tragic aftermath. Two sailors on shore leave found their way into the neglected old brick house on Redgate Square and looked for a place to sleep. They naturally chose the spot where they thought they would be least likely to be found and rousted out, the remote inner room at the fourth floor back. There, they pulled one cot in with the other and went to sleep.

Next morning, one sailor was found dead in the courtyard, where he had plunged to his doom. The other was picked up on the street, in a complete delirium. Accused of having pitched his companion from the window, he denied the whole thing. Jeff Shelby was called to New York to testify in the accused sailor's behalf, which he did.

In one of his more lucid moments, the surviving sailor was able to tell what had happened to his unfortunate shipmate. Graphically, he said:

"I woke up — and there was something closing in on my matey. I don't know what it was, but he was screaming, 'I hear it — I see it — it's got me!' And then he was breaking away from something, diving for the window, grabbing like he saw bars there — only there weren't any bars — and then he was gone — out through. But there was blackness still there — turning to come at me — so I didn't wait. It got me in the doorway — but I yanked clear of whatever had me — then I ran down the stairs — then outside —"

Hearing that, Jeff Shelby realized that it might have been his own experience, if he, too, had slept in the inner room as he wanted. In Jeff's case, the thing that had snuffed the life of Bruce Barlow had found its human prey and gone its way into the unseen before another victim came along.

DEATH'S
MASQUERADE

DEATH'S MASQUERADE

Nearly everybody in New Orleans knew Miro's in the old, old days. It was a little shop where faces peered from a window beneath an overhanging balcony just off the Rue Royale. Faces, faces — and still more faces! — some of them changing every day, so that the window, which to many people looked exactly the same, actually was always different.

Every year, there came a time when those faces began to disappear from Miro's window until finally none was left. But they could still be seen — all of them! — in the brightly lighted streets and popular meeting places of New Orleans. There, Miro's faces would laugh at you, leer at you, or give you a solemn, cryptic look, according to their mood and that of their maker, Miro.

For Miro made all the masks that he displayed in the window of his little costume shop, where people came to buy or rent costumes for the biggest annual event in New Orleans, the famous Mardi Gras. Miro put in new masks as he made them and took out the old, which was why the window always changed. It became empty around carnival time when the masks kept going out, until on Mardi Gras Day, which marked the climax, there wasn't a face left. They were all being worn by merrymakers called Maskers, who thronged all New Orleans.

Miro knew his customers like any other merchant. He was like the news dealer, who sold people their copy of the *Daily Picayune,* or the laundryman, who saw them once a week, or the barber, who cut their hair once each month. But Miro's customers only came around once a year. That was why he knew them so much better than the other merchants did. He had more time to think about them, and they were never in a hurry when he saw them.

Of course, Miro did some odd business between times. He had his lesser clientele, to whom he sold lottery tickets, good luck charms, and even voodoo powders when there was a call for them. But he was indifferent to such trade, just as Broullard, the confectioner who supplied the great frosted cakes for many Mardi Gras functions, cared nothing for the ragamuffins who came into his store to buy penny buns.

Of course, there was one noteworthy exception in Miro's case. That was Paul Garneau, who stopped at the mask shop nearly every day and always bought some trifle. Paul had studied law, then had given it up because it interfered with his social life. He liked to watch Miro make masks, because they reflected the old man's moods. More than that, when Mardi Gras approached, Paul liked to watch the customers try on their choices and pose for Miro's opinion.

Paul observed that after each customer had gone, the old mask maker made an entry in a little black book. After some coaxing, Miro finally showed the book to Paul, under an oath of strictest secrecy. In it, certain names were followed by a neatly shaped death's head, and in every case, the person had died within the following year. In short, Miro knew when an annual customer was not coming back; and he told Paul why.

"Most of my masks are gay," declared Miro, "because the Mardi Gras itself is gay, and I try to catch its mood. But if I am sad or angry or utterly despondent, that mood goes into the mask I am making. Yet some people seek out those masks."

"You mean people who are in a mood to die?"

"In a way, yes, but not always. It is not until the person puts the mask on that I really know. Then, behind that person, I see a skeleton figure, with bony hands, the Grim Reaper, ready to take toll, which he does. Here, take my black book. Compare it with the obituaries in the *Daily Picayune!*"

Paul did just that and found out that Miro was one hundred per cent right. After that, Paul frequented Miro's steadily when Mardi Gras approached. When Miro approved a costume with a nod that seemed a trifle sad, Paul knew that the wearer would be listed in the black book.

Paul Garneau had an idea. He would make good use of old Miro's strange gift. So Paul began convincing his girl friend, Carlotta Engard, that she had a psychic sense. When they were dining at Dizard's or sipping coffee in the old French Market, Paul would say in a hushed tone:

"That person over there — can't you see Death looming behind him, ready to clutch him with those skeleton hands? My word, that can't be our friend Mr. Tyson, who opened that new jewelry store on St. Charles Avenue. Yes, I believe it is, but don't breathe a word about that skeleton you saw."

Poor Carlotta soon began really seeing such things because she believed them; and the reason for her belief was the accuracy of Paul's predictions, which he so craftily identified as hers, though they were really Miro's. After three or four years of this, Paul Garneau was ready for his grand coup, the winning of the Louisiana Lottery.

The Louisiana Lottery had been outlawed years before; but it still operated under cover, though its $10,000 grand prize was a mere picayune compared to the old days. What was more, no one could win the lottery, because it was fixed. But many tickets were sold by little shopkeepers like Miro, so it didn't take Paul too long to learn that the man behind it was Noel Dizard, whose restaurant was among the best in town.

Of course, Dizard always bought his Mardi Gras costume at Miro's, so Paul was there when the portly, ever-smiling restaurant owner made his annual call. Dizard recognized Paul as one of his customers; in turn, Paul showed Dizard some of Miro's nicest costumes. Rather reluctantly, Dizard chose a stony-faced Aztec mask, and Miro just as hesitatingly put a death's head after it in his little black book.

"I saw Death standing there," Miro told Paul later, "because that was the mood of the mask. But I wasn't too sure that it fitted the face behind it."

"That is because Dizard's smiling face is a mask itself," Paul said. "But I hope you are wrong this time. I like Dizard."

The curious fact was that Paul Garneau did like Noel Dizard, whose restaurant served some very fine dishes. But Paul could not let sentiment interfere with business, so he talked Carlotta into seeing the figure of Death close behind Dizard, every time they dined at the restaurant. Meanwhile, Paul kept buying lottery tickets at Miro's along with good-luck charms that practically guaranteed a winning number.

That Mardi Gras, Paul wore a costume representing the Laughing Cavalier. As such, he dropped into Dizard's for a late snack on the very night when the lottery winner was to be announced. Paul knew the way to Dizard's private office, and when he saw that the way was clear, he strolled in. Dizard had just returned from a grand ball given by a Mardi Gras group, or Krewe, and he was still wearing his Aztec mask and costume. The Laughing Cavalier sat down at the desk and faced the Aztec King. Then, before Dizard could ask his visitor's purpose, Paul laid his cards on the table in the form of a hundred dollars' worth of lottery tickets.

"One of these tickets should win the grand prize," said Paul, his tone deep and hollow from within the mask. "So pay me and save us both trouble."

Dizard's response was a laugh that sounded like a bellow.

"What if everybody asked to be paid one hundred to one?"

"Nobody else will ask. They don't know the lottery is fixed. I'm only asking you to be honest, Dizard, and declare an actual winner. Besides, I see the figure of Death creeping up behind you. I can ward it off, Dizard, by giving you these voodoo powders" — he tossed some packets on the desk — "which were especially prepared by Miro."

Angrily, Dizard brushed away the tickets and the packets and bellowed: "Get out of here!"

"I see Death closing in" — from behind the mask, Paul's tone was ominously persuasive — "I see bony hands at your throat, Dizard —"

Instinctively, Dizard raised one hand to his throat, then reached for a desk drawer with the other. Paul launched himself across the desk.

"Let me help you, Dizard! You are already in Death's clutch! Let me pull those bony hands away —"

A consummate actor, Paul Garneau was pretending that he was fighting off a pair of deadly, clutching hands. But Dizard, also grabbing for the hands that gripped his throat found only Paul's there. Gradually, the struggle ended. Dizard slumped dead.

"Too bad," Paul said in a solemn, musing tone. "I just did not have the strength to cope with Death himself."

In the desk drawer, Paul found the revolver that Dizard had tried to reach. Also, he found $30,000 in cash. Dizard's profit from the lottery. Paul, being honest, took only $10,000 for himself. Then he unlocked the back door of Dizard's office and hurried down a back stairs to a courtyard that led to the Rue Dauphine.

They found Dizard's body an hour later, along with the scattered lottery tickets and voodoo powders. Because of the money left in the desk, it didn't look like a robbery at first; but during the weeks that followed, Detective Henri Blanc, of the New Orleans police, finally eliminated all suspects except a man who had been wearing a Laughing Cavalier costume.

At Miro's, Blanc found that Paul Garneau had purchased such a costume and that he had also bought the lottery tickets and the voodoo powders. Also, Paul had been losing so much money in his favorite gambling houses that it seemed quite likely he had taken cash from Dizard's desk, as there was no other place where he could have gotten it. So, in due process, Paul was arrested, charged with the murder of Dizard, and brought to trial.

As a lawyer, Paul decided to take charge of his own defense. The odds, in local gambling circles, promptly rose to twenty to one against him, as the state was represented by Mark Zeeman, the most capable prosecutor in Louisiana. Using evidence supplied by Detective Blanc, the prosecutor traced every move of the Laughing Cavalier from the time he left Miro's shop until he entered Dizard's office.

Zeeman was a big man, with a broad, heavy, firm-set face which always maintained the same glowering expression, while he boomed away in a domineering tone. He was at his best when he called Paul as a witness and demanded:

"Can you, Paul Garneau, possibly deny that you were the last person to enter that office while Noel Dizard was still alive?"

Paul didn't deny it. Instead, he admitted it, which brought a gasp from the courtroom. Then, calmly, Paul related:

"There was someone already in there with Dizard, when I entered — a weird, grotesque figure of Death, clutching Dizard's throat from behind. I thought the attacker was some crazed Masker, and I tried to wrench him away. Then, suddenly, he was gone and there was Dizard, slumped on the desk. I decided that the killer must have fled by the back door, which was open, so I followed. But by the time I reached the Rue Dauphine, he had vanished. I knew then that Death himself had taken my good friend Dizard, so it was no use to go back."

"A highly imaginative story," sneered Zeeman. "It is just too bad that you cannot furnish witnesses to support such fanciful testimony."

"But I can," Paul assured him. "First, I shall call on Carlotta Engard."

Carlotta took the stand and sincerely avowed that she had often seen a figure of Death hovering over Dizard, as she had with certain other persons who had died quite suddenly. Scoffingly, Zeeman declared that her unsupported testimony would not do. So Paul called his next witness, old Miro. Blandly, the mask maker told how he, too, had seen the Grim Reaper looming above Dizard, as well as other persons. Under cross-examination, Miro produced his little black book. When names were read from it, an awed hush fell over the jury until Zeeman turned to them and stormed:

"All trumped-up evidence! All hearsay — all a trick! That book could have been faked to fit the case. Let's put this to a real test!" He turned to Miro, who was seated placidly in the witness box. "Since you are so good at seeing Death, look around this court and tell us where his figure is hovering now!"

That was an old trick which Paul had expected Zeeman to spring. Paul hoped Miro would respond in a way that would impress the jury, but he only shook his head.

"I judge masks," Miro declared, "because their features are fixed. I cannot judge people, because their features are mobile. Of course, there are a few people whose faces can be termed masks, due to their fixed expressions."

"And do you see any such faces in this courtroom, now?"

"A few, but they are not good examples, except for *your* face."

The judge silenced a ripple of nervous laughter from the courtroom. Paul Garneau leaned forward intently as Mark Zeeman suddenly demanded:

"Then tell us, Miro, do you see a figure of Death behind me?"

Miro studied Zeeman as Paul had often seen him study customers in the costume shop. Then Miro began to nod slowly.

"Since you ask me," he said, "I do. It is coming closer — closer —" Miro turned to Carlotta, who was riveted in her chair. "You see it, too, don't you?" Then, as Carlotta hesitated, almost on the point of nodding, Miro stared at Zeeman and added: "Its fingers are clutching, now!"

Contemptuously, Zeeman turned to the jury, gave them his fixed glower, and raised his hands to his throat. In stentorian tones, he boomed:

"So these witnesses see me in Death's clutch, as Garneau claims he saw Dizard. They want us to believe that Dizard raised his hands like this and struggled against bony fingers that were otherwise invisible. Do you see any hands but mine, gentlemen of the jury? Can you see the bony fingers of Death?"

Zeeman reeled momentarily as he spoke. A gargling cry sounded in his throat. His body came up to its full height, bending back as though drawn by invisible hands. Then the unseen grip apparently relaxed, for Zeeman toppled forward, hitting the front of the jury box and sprawling across it, inert, while the jurors shied away and court attendants came rushing over.

The judge pounded with his gavel and called a recess. It proved to be a long one. Mark Zeeman was dead. And he had gone in the very manner that he had scoffed at as something impossible. He was gone, with Death's invisible clutch upon his throat.

The doctors pronounced it heart failure, and the trial was resumed with one of Zeeman's assistants as prosecutor. But the jury wasn't taking any chances, not after seeing what the figure of Death could do, even though visible only to a psychic few. They acquitted Paul Garneau on the first ballot.

Paul made out nicely because he had bet his bottom dollar that he would be acquitted. He went about with a pose of injured innocence, gambling more extravagantly than ever. Old Miro neglected his trade and began working on a special mask and costume which he said were to be his masterpiece. Then, realizing he was falling behind, he bundled it away and said nothing more. Paul knew about it, for he was keeping close watch on Miro. In his turn, Detective Blanc was keeping watch on Paul. As Blanc put it to his superiors:

"I still think that this man Garneau killed Dizard because he needed money. If he gets in financial straits again, he may try another murder."

But Paul, though he lost much through reckless play, did not run out of money. During his brief prosperity, he had met a new friend, Steve Lucas, who mistook him for a man of substance and lent him cash when he needed it. Now, a year had passed and the Mardi Gras again was due. So were some $10,000 worth of notes that Paul had given Steve.

What made it bad was that Paul had been winning lately and now had the money, or most of it. But to pay off Steve, he would leave himself broke, and Paul couldn't do that. Instead, he became clever indeed. First, he began telling Carlotta that he saw a Death figure hovering over Steve, and soon Carlotta began to believe that she saw it, too, as she had with Dizard. Even though Carlotta wasn't totally convinced, Paul did not worry. This time, things were well set.

At Miro's, Paul found that the old man was still seeing his vision of the Grim Reaper as before, but was not keeping such exact records. That, too, was helpful. This year, Paul bought a very special costume representing a Pirate Chief, but he did not put it on at Miro's. Paul just took it along and told Carlotta and others about it, so everyone knew that, come Mardi Gras, Paul Garneau would be swaggering about as a Pirate Chief, as he had previously swashbuckled as the Laughing Cavalier. Word of this reached Detective Blanc.

Then, toward Mardi Gras Day, when Miro's shop was all but empty, Paul stopped in one evening and confided in the old mask maker.

"I have a friend who wants a special costume," said Paul. "I know you have one put away back there in the shop, and I'm sure he would pay a good price for it. How about accommodating him, Miro?"

Finally Miro agreed and named a price. Paul paid the money.

"My friend is outside," Paul told Miro, "so I'll collect from him and send him in. He doesn't want to be known, so don't give him much attention. And don't mention this to anyone, ever. You understand?"

Miro understood. Paul went out, and his friend came in, a stooped, shambling man whose face was muffled in his upturned coat collar. He went to the darkened back corner of the shop. There he straightened up and became Paul Garneau. He found the special costume and put it on. When he was ready, he reverted to the shambling gait and stopped to ask in a disguised voice that he knew could not be recognized from within the muffling mask:

"How do I look, Mr. Miro?"

Miro gave an appraising glance, then tilted back his head and began a titter that became a cackle, then a laugh. He continued to laugh and laugh, as Paul had never heard him laugh before. That, of course, was the best of omens, for Miro was always saddened when he saw the figure of Death in the offing.

Paul left the shop. A block from Miro's, he phoned Carlotta and told her:

"Steve Lucas is expecting us at his apartment, because I said we would take him to dinner with us. Poor chap, we ought to see that he has a good time before Death takes him. So meet me over there, right away."

This being Carnival time, Steve Lucas was holding open house. As Carlotta walked in, Steve, a smallish man, was standing in the living room, wearing a sad-faced clown costume. He was just greeting Carlotta when a pair of French windows opened from a balcony behind him and the skeleton figure of Death launched into the room.

Never in her wildest fancies had Carlotta seen the Grim Reaper more vividly, nor had he ever shown his power so forcefully. With skeleton hands, the Death figure grabbed Steve by the neck and shook him as a terrier would a rat. Steve's clown mask came off and Carlotta saw his eyes go goggly while his face began to turn blue. Realizing how deadly that clutch of Death could really be, Carlotta turned and raced out the front way, screaming for help. On the threshold she ran into a man in the costume of a Pirate Chief, and she gasped in happy recognition.

"Quickly, Paul!" panted Carlotta. "Steve is in there — but Death is choking him — it may be too late to save him —"

It wasn't quite too late. Steve was still gasping when the Pirate Chief reached the living room and pulled an old-fashioned pistol from his sash. He aimed it at the figure of Death, and to Carlotta's amazement, the Grim Reaper, who should have feared no weapons, did an odd thing. He flung Steve aside and instead of vanishing, drove for the Pirate Chief, trying to wrest the pistol from him.

In the struggle, the gun went off. It was Death who took the bullet, for he sprawled to the floor. In the full light, Carlotta saw that he was not actually a skeleton figure, but that his costume consisted of bright white streaks painted on black velvet to represent ribs and other bones. His skull was a paint job, too, for it came off like a loosened helmet and rolled away, revealing the face beneath.

The man who had masqueraded as Death was Paul Garneau!

Amazed, Carlotta turned to the Pirate Chief, who should have been Paul. He unmasked and revealed himself as Detective Henri Blanc.

The situation really unraveled itself when Steve Lucas recovered sufficiently to talk. He brought out a wallet containing the notes for the cash that Paul Garneau had owed him.

"Paul said to have these ready," Steve related, "so he could pay them off. Instead, he tried to kill me so he could steal them back, and nobody would have been the wiser!"

"And he wore that Death costume," Carlotta exclaimed, "so that this time I would be positive I saw the Grim Reaper take his toll!"

"I knew Garneau was planning something," declared Detective Blanc. "So I kept watching his apartment. I heard him phone Mr. Lucas and arrange to come over. Instead, when I trailed him, he went to Miro's. I figured he planned to pick up a different costume, so I doubled back to his apartment and put on the Pirate Chief outfit, not just to surprise him here, but because he might want it as an alibi if he ducked back to his place. But I never expected to see him in a Death outfit!"

Later Detective Blanc talked to Miro and learned that the old mask maker had designed the Death costume, hoping it would clear his mind of those visions of the Grim Reaper. It hadn't helped, so he had packed the special outfit away. But Paul Garneau had been smart enough to find it; too smart, as it turned out.

"A very odd thing happened," explained Miro. "I half-guessed that the 'friend' Paul sent in for the costume was Paul himself. When he asked me how he looked in his costume, he was wondering if I saw Death in back of him. And I *did* see Death, so close that it could lay its hands on him.

"Ordinarily, that would have put me in a sad mood, and I'd have shown it. Paul knew that and was waiting for my warning nod. But when I saw Death — heh-heh! — I saw Death laying his hands on Death — heh-heh-heh! — a phantom Death gripping the man who was masquerading as Death" — Miro gave a high-pitched cackle — "it was so funny that I laughed — and laughed — Ha-ha-ha-ha-ha-ha-ha-ha-ha —"

THE RIDDLE
OF THE CRYPT

Buried in this
Crypt circa 1700
Commandant
Lesang

THE RIDDLE
OF THE CRYPT

The cabin cruiser *Rover* had just rounded Porpoise Point when Irene Morrow gained her first view of Cliff Island. Her brother Roy pointed it out as it loomed in sight, and Irene exclaimed, "How beautiful! How very, very beautiful!"

It was indeed a splendid sight, a mass of steep gray bluffs rising like the walls and towers of an enchanted palace floating on a clear blue sea. As the cruiser swung eastward of the island, the setting sun gave a scintillating touch to the granite heights, producing a scene straight from the pages of a fairy book.

As the boat sped closer, the island seemed to spread in size, creating another surprising illusion. Then, suddenly, a frowning headland cut off the sunlight and darkened the water with a sullen gloom, broken only by the tufted white of waves that crashed on the cold gray stones below. In a trice, all the sparkle was gone, and the face of the island became rugged and forbidding.

The transition struck Irene as she was repeating the enthusiastic words, forcing her to modify them:

"How very, very beautiful — and yet so weird and ghostly!"

In a sense, the change was fearful. The *Rover* seemed due to crash on the rocks. But Jerry Lane, the youthful skipper, deftly swung to port, almost skirting the spray of the treacherous breakers. Dead ahead, Irene saw a cleft in the rocky wall. It widened, and sunlight streamed through the jagged gap, transforming the moody black cliffs back to their glittering gray.

"We are coming into Middle Harbor," shouted Roy, above the tumult of the waves. "Don't let Jerry scare you. He really knows this channel."

The channel followed a fold between the high crags, and after a medley of sunlight and shadows, the cruiser hummed into a cozy cove where a few dozen speedboats and cruisers were moored alongside some trim sailboats and a motley lot of weather-beaten fishing craft.

From a short pier, a gangplank ran down to a float where arriving craft could pull alongside regardless of the tide, which was heavy along this part of the New England coast. Soon Roy and Irene were ashore with their luggage, which was handled by a lanky man in overalls, whose face was as rugged as the island's cliffs. He carried the bags to a car old enough to mark its owner as one of the early settlers. It bore the crude legend:

J. CUPPY — TAXI

The settlement about the pier was a combination of a fishing and tourist haven, with a post office, some stores, sea food restaurants, and fishing shacks. But the slopes that funneled up from the harbor were studded with cottages of early twentieth century vintage. They were reached by zigzag roadways and paths with rock-hewn steps that served as shortcuts. Then Roy drew Irene back to the outer end of the pier and pointed to a ledge set back beyond the very top of the slope. On that dominant height, Irene could make out the front of a brand-new ranch house, ruddy in the sunlight's glow.

"That, I will have you know," said Roy, "is our humble abode. The most modern habitation on all Cliff Island with the best outlook."

Irene's round, enthusiastic face beamed an appreciative smile. She was starting to say that the place looked wonderful, even from a distance, when Mr. Cuppy put the last bag in the taxi. So they hurried to the ancient car and climbed in while Cuppy took the wheel and asked:

"Where to, Mr. Morrow?"

"To Castle Rock," returned Roy. "We're living in the new ranch house there."

Mr. Cuppy sat as if frozen behind the wheel. Then he slowly turned his thin red neck and gave his two passengers a long, beady look, turkey fashion. Next, he made a move as if to get out and remove the bags. Then, without a word, he looked ahead again, wheezed the old motor into action and headed the car up the hill.

The view was increasingly beautiful all the way up the long zigzag road. Middle Harbor was an ever-changing scene, with occasional glimpses of the ocean through the rocky walls of the channel. Then, at the top, the island became a saucer-shaped plateau, and Irene could see the ocean all around, with an island-studded bay toward the west. There, the sun, going down beyond the mainland, blended crimson, gold and purple in one magnificent splash.

The taxi gained new life down a slight, winding slope. It passed a stretch of barren, rocky ground, veered away from a thick clump of pine trees, and groaned up a slight, curving quarter-mile grade that brought it in back of the ranch house. Instead of using the driveway, Mr. Cuppy stopped on the road, unloaded the bags while his passengers alighted, and said:

"That'll be one dollar."

As Roy handed Cuppy a bill, the taxi man clambered back into the car, saying, "Got to get down to the dock right quick. The *Countess* is coming in." With that he swung the car about and rattled away, as Irene asked:

"And who is the Countess?"

"A boat," replied Roy. "The steamer from the mainland. But she isn't due until nine o'clock tonight. I can't understand what's wrong with Cuppy."

"I can," came a cheery voice behind them. Irene turned and saw a smiling young man with a shock of light hair. "I've been watching from our ivory tower, expecting to see this happen."

"This is Alan Blount," introduced Roy, "who is helping me in my study of marine fossils. Go on, Alan. Why wouldn't Cuppy carry the bags?"

"Because no person living on Cliff Island will set foot on the blighted ground surrounding Castle Rock. That road is the dividing line. You'll see people walk by on the far side, looking at us as if we were saying, 'Shinny on your own side, this side is taboo.' A crazy superstition, that's all."

Irene smiled, recalling many places she had been where odd customs and strange superstitions were common; but they had never worried her. Besides, she didn't want to be bothered by visitors on Cliff Island. She was here on assignment for her company, International Metallurgics Associated. She had traveled through South America for I. M. A., and they had given her the job of translating and condensing all subsidiary reports from Spanish and Portuguese into English, a two-month job at least.

Roy, a professor of biology at a state university, had heard of the wonderful ranch house on Cliff Island and had rented it while making his fossil survey. So Irene had decided to come and do her work there. She liked the place as they entered the back door through a modern kitchen where Roy gestured to two bedrooms on the right and said:

"Those are bachelors' quarters for Alan and myself. You have the left wing, sis. It was planned as a garage, but nobody keeps a car on Cliff Island, or the taxi business would die. So they turned it into a studio with a glass window in place of a front door. Come and see it!"

It instantly became Irene's dream room. From the picture window, she could see the whole harbor, with the limitless ocean beyond, while a casement window at the side gave a view of the pine woods and the stretch of rocks beyond the curving road.

Each morning, Roy and Alan left early, and Irene went to work on her translations, pausing at intervals to look from the front window at a scene as varied as it was beautiful, for the moods of the clouds and the ocean were many. But at times, Irene found herself drifting into a dreamy state, in which the present faded and everything seemed as distant as the boundless sea. Always, she was jolted from such reveries by the sensation of watching eyes and a figure creeping behind her.

Then Irene would snap from the clutch of the unknown, often with an involuntary scream. All about, she would see floating blobs of blackness that would gradually dissolve. After such shocks, Irene felt an urge for human company. The fact that the Islanders regarded this ledge as taboo struck home with numbing force. Irene would rush out to the back road. There she felt safe, though no one was ever around.

Sometimes Irene regained her calm by walking down the road to the pine woods, which was beautifully shaped and exquisitely green, compared to the otherwise drab landscape of the plateau. In bright sunlight, the evergreens were restful. On cloudy days, or under the colorful tints of an early sunset, the grove took on a deeper green that absorbed Irene's worries with it.

The rocks beyond the grove were typical of the island's ruggedness. A hundred feet to the right of the evergreens, several hundred heavy stones were tumbled in a pile at least thirty feet across and half that high. The pile interested Irene, because it was man-made. She passed it late in the afternoons when she cut across to a path that led down among the cottages to the harbor. There she met Roy and Alan when they came in on the *Rover*. Often she stopped at an employment office to try to hire a woman to help with the housework. But when she said "Castle Rock" none was ever available.

Sometimes Irene had a fish or lobster dinner with Roy and Alan at one of the seafood places. Other times, she prepared dinner at the ranch house. Almost always, they went up the hill in Cuppy's taxi — until one afternoon when the whole ocean became a mass of white billows formed by a low-clinging fog that kept creeping up the island's craggy walls. By the time Irene reached the dock, she could just make out the bulk of a coast guard craft that was moored there. From it, a loudspeaker called off names, giving information about boats that were overdue. One announcement came:

"Miss Morrow — Miss Irene Morrow — message from the *Rover*. Fog-bound at Port Clarion — will return to Middle Harbor tomorrow."

Irene ate alone at the pier restaurant and stayed late, hoping that the fog would clear, but it lessened only slightly. She found Cuppy asleep in his cab, wakened him, and they started up the hill, with Cuppy working his way slowly in low gear. Irene decided that this was a good time to get first-hand evidence on the Castle Rock taboo.

"I won't ask you to drive me to my door," she said, "but I would like to know why nobody on Cliff Island will come to Castle Rock."

"Well, the Rock has a curse on it," returned Cuppy. "Some sort of spell that has never worn off from long ago. People have seen strange critters up toward the Rock, the kind that change to giant bats."

"If you mean vampires," retorted Irene, "they are bunk. I have seen vampire bats in South America, but they prey on cattle, that's all."

Just then, a huge, swooping shape came into the glare of the car's bright headlights. Its wings were like mammoth arms as it loomed from the fog. Irene's nerves, which had been getting worse daily, were so raw that she started to scream, but rather than show weakness, she reduced it to an "Eeeek!" An answering "Eeeek!" came from the flitting shape, which was gone instantly, leaving only the whitish swirl of the fog. Irene decided it was an ordinary bat, magnified by the fog to gigantic proportions. As they neared Castle Rock, Cuppy suggested:

"Look, Miss Morrow. I'll back my car so the lights will guide you into the house, so nothing can come at you in the dark —"

"You mean a vampire?" broke in Irene. "Like the one we just saw?"

"I'm not sure what we did see," returned Cuppy. "The worst thing is the yellow eyes that people see up here. They come from that pine woods" — he gestured to an ominous bulk of blackness on his right — "but lookee, lady. If you get in the house and keep all the windows tight shut, nothing can sneak in with you, not even none of the fog. That's all I've got to say."

Cuppy used his bright lights as a path to the house, and Irene followed it. Once she was inside, Cuppy cut his headlights to dim, probably finding they reflected less glare from the fog. He started back down the road, and Irene went into her studio-garage, where she looked toward the pine grove, wondering if she would see those yellow eyes.

Then, suddenly, she did. Tiny, yellow beads, they squinted from the swirl of the fog and hovered as though coming closer. Irene wondered if Cuppy saw them from his creeping car. Then, just as her nerves reached the shrieking point, Irene gave a laugh that was hysterical but glad.

Those yellow eyes were the taillights of Cuppy's car. Their red lenses had gone to pieces years ago, leaving only little bright bulbs, like yellow, beady eyes. Irene realized that when Cuppy swung past the grove, because then, for the first time, his dim headlights showed and the taillights veered at a new angle.

Irene wished that this harrowing night was over; instead, it had just begun. When she opened the front door for air, fog billowed in. When it vanished after she slammed the door, it seemed all the more like a living thing. There was a magnetic force here, that created living phantasms, for when Irene looked from the window, she could see fog-faces form there, then dissipate in ghoulish swirls. She ran about clamping windows and bolting doors, until overwhelmed by mental and physical exhaustion, she collapsed in a big chair in the living room. All the lights were on, but she was still fearful until she fell into a sleep so deep that when she was finally roused from it, she started up, trembling.

All the lights were still on, but their glare was lost in the dazzle of broad daylight. There were no longer fog-faces peering at Irene, but real faces, those of her brother Roy and his assistant, Alan Blount. It was morning, the fog had lifted, and they had come back in the *Ranger.* When Irene told them what had happened, they nodded.

Their own work was so exacting, so limited on board the *Rover,* that Irene's talk of dazed moods and the floating blackness struck them as the result of her daytime intensity and isolation. One night alone had touched off Irene's accumulation of nervous tension. Roy and Alan stayed home that day. At night, they strolled beneath the stars with Irene and pointed out the constellations, which made earthly worries seem small.

The next day, Roy had another idea. He told Irene:

"We've been talking this over, Alan and I. We want you to come with us to Port Clarion, and while we're studying starfish instead of stars, you can go to the library and dig into the history of Cliff Island. There may be something behind this nonsense about Castle Rock, so let's get to the bottom of it."

Port Clarion was much like Middle Harbor but on a larger scale.

There, Irene saw the tubby *Countess,* a little steamer with its two decks sprouting tourists, as she came in from her morning tour of the islands of Fisherman's Bay, which included Cliff Island as the outermost. At the library Irene said that she was visiting Cliff Island — carefully avoiding any mention of which part — and that she was intensely interested in its history. When she joined Roy and Alan for dinner at one of the big pier restaurants, Irene was well briefed on her subject. But she waited until the *Rover* was speeding through the moonlit bay back to Cliff Island, with Jerry Lane at the helm. Then she sat in the cockpit with Roy and Alan while she went into her story.

"Apparently, Cliff Island was settled by the French in the early 1600's," stated Irene, "and they kept it clear up to the year 1715."

"That's not surprising," put in Roy. "The French had many outposts that they managed to keep from the British."

"In this case, they really held them off," Irene informed him. "The cliffs were like a fortress, and French peasants raised crops and cattle on the plateau, but occasionally their fishing was curtailed when the British occupied Middle Harbor. So about the year 1700, a French sea rover was appointed to take charge. He was called the Commandant Lesang, and he sailed into Middle Harbor on a ship called the *Aventure.*

"The first thing that Lesang and his crew did was build a citadel on the high rim of the plateau, right where we are living now. That is why it is called Castle Rock. He used to light beacons on a high point called *Cap Bec,* or Cape Beak, but which is now known as Signal Head."

"I know Signal Head," said Roy. "We'll show it to you when we get there. But go on with the story, sis."

"The arrival of the *Aventure* caused great joy," continued Irene, "but all changed to gloom when Lesang ruled the island like a tyrant. He and his evil crew committed murder, tortured helpless prisoners, and brought terror to the island. Finally, the British attacked, bombarded his citadel, and took over the island. The inhabitants were shipped away, and it was years before the island was settled again."

"And what happened to Commandant Lesang?" asked Roy.

"He disappeared," replied Irene. "Some say he escaped in a boat from one of the other harbors. Another account says that he was killed during the attack on the castle. It is even claimed that he was killed earlier but that his ghost returned and was still in command when the castle was demolished."

"That could be the groundwork for the vampire talk," agreed Roy. "Did you run across any of that stuff in the old archives?"

"Yes. Weird yellow eyes have been seen gleaming through the fog. People have been attacked by a gruesome monster that slashes their throats. Some persons have disappeared like Lesang himself."

"Disappeared completely? Without a trace?"

"In some instances, yes. But bodies have been found floating far out to sea and others have been discovered in the deep pit over which the old castle was built."

"Which is now our cellar," commented Roy grimly. "No wonder the place gives you the shakes. I can't blame people for not wanting to come near it."

"I'm sure I can stick it out now." Irene's tone was determined. "I should have laughed it all off when the yellow eyes turned out to be nothing but a taxi's taillights. However, keep a good grip on yourself while I tell you the most fearful legend of the lot. When the full of the moon arrives, the *Aventure* is sometimes seen sailing into Middle Harbor. Then things really cut loose."

"You mean all those things you've just mentioned?"

"And more. Once the ghost ship has been sighted, Lesang's own ghost is sure to appear. That's one legend that just won't die."

"It's a funny thing," put in Alan. "We've talked with a lot of characters around Middle Harbor, but they've never handed us any of this."

"Because that's the last place where they ever will talk about it," rejoined Irene. "The librarian, Miss Lacey, says that the Islanders are so afraid of its hurting the tourist trade that they've even suppressed all picture postcards dealing with it. Those used to be popular some twenty years ago, and Miss Lacey told me of a shop that was still bootlegging them. So I bought some."

Triumphantly, Irene produced a batch of picture postcards which Roy and Alan studied eagerly in the light of the cockpit. One card showed Castle Rock in its barren state; another, with an artist's conception of Lesang's citadel towering upon it. One card showed the pine woods, which was appropriately termed "The Haunted Grove," while another had the stone pile labeled "Old Norse Ruins." Another card depicted Signal Head, with its ancient beacon in full flare, and there was a closeup of a high ledge titled "Bat Roosts on Cliff Island" with bats hanging there.

"According to a book in the library," stated Irene, "those roosts were cleaned out long ago. Now the Islanders pretend they never heard of them."

"There would, of course, be some specimens remaining," declared Roy in his professorial style. "You saw one the other night, but Cuppy wouldn't admit it."

They were passing the *Countess* now, waddling in from her evening rounds, and ahead lay Cliff Island, more ghostly than ever, though Irene was ready to face its eerie heights with new confidence. Roy pointed out Signal Head, and Irene realized that the old beacon point was quite close to Castle Rock but off at a different angle than the road, which was why she had never noticed it. Then Irene remembered a postcard that she had been saving for the last. She brought it out and said:

"Here is the old *Aventure* herself, sailing into Middle Harbor. They've pasted her over a photo of the island, trying to make it look real ghostly."

They showed the picture of the *Aventure* to Jerry Lane. From her three tall square-rigged masts and high stern, he identified her as a French ship of the early 1700's. But the young skipper added that it looked like a stock picture from some old book and that it certainly was not a ghostly craft coming into the Cliff Island Channel, which was incorrectly shown in the composite photo.

When they finally arrived in Middle Harbor and docked at the float, Jerry ducked down into the cabin, then poked his head up and grinned at Irene.

"I hear you've been needing company up at the house, and I thought maybe I could help out," he said. With that, he brought a brown-and-white spotted cat into sight and handed it, purring, to Irene. "Her name is Ginger, and she came on board in Port Clarion. Maybe she'll be happier at Castle Rock than sailing in the *Rover*."

Irene thanked Jerry profusely and carried the contented cat to Cuppy's cab. Cuppy noticed Ginger, and while they were driving up the cliff road, he remarked:

"You may be needing that cat at your place. She looks like a good ratter."

"This cat," returned Irene, "still has all her nine lives, which is the same number as a baseball team. So she isn't a ratter; she is a batter. I may let her go after some of those bats that are still hanging around their old roosts under the cliffs. Like the one you and I saw in the fog, Mr. Cuppy."

That quip silenced Cuppy. For the next few days, everything was peaceful. Then, one mild evening, while Irene was doing translations in her study, and Roy was playing pinochle with Alan in the living room, a new scare struck. Irene had let Ginger out, and as the cat hadn't returned, Irene picked up a long five-cell flashlight and went out the back door to look for her new pet.

With the powerful beam, Irene spotted Ginger frisking halfway down to the haunted grove. Irene called and turned off the light as the cat came bounding toward her. Ginger's light color made her quite conspicuous in the moonlight that filtered through a film of wispy clouds. Irene was looking straight toward the blackish contour of the pine woods; and something she saw there made her laugh lightly. Then suddenly her throat closed up and she froze all over.

Coming straight from the woods were those yellow eyes! Irene's laugh, inspired by her recollection of Cuppy's taillights, faded as she realized his taxi wasn't anywhere around. The eyes grew larger as Irene stooped to snatch up Ginger. Then they were full upon her, and she was swinging the long flashlight wildly to ward off a clawing, jabbing fury that attacked her savagely from the dark. Half smothered by the monstrous thing, Irene kept clubbing with the flashlight as she raced to the house, screaming for Roy and Alan. They came out the back door just as Irene made a last valiant sweep with her improvised cudgel and stumbled into her brother's arms, still clutching Ginger. Roy and Alan identified the thing from the woods as it soared off.

It was a huge owl, the biggest that either had ever seen.

In the living room, Irene put salve on her scratched neck and wrists while Ginger stalked about gratefully. Then, with a forced laugh, Irene said, "Well, we have taken another chunk out of that vampire legend."

"And it's lucky the owl didn't take a chunk out of Ginger," declared Roy. "Considering that owls fly off with chipmunks, a cat isn't too big for them."

During the rest of that week, Irene found a new formula that helped her work and kept her cheerful. She broke those introspective spells by talking to Ginger. For variety, she took brisk walks across the fields. Soon she had found the perfect goal, Signal Head, which offered the best view of the island.

There was a strange fascination about that jutting point. Often, as she approached it, Irene heard voices calling, "Irene — Irene —" and she smiled as she identified them as the cries of seagulls off the point. By then, she could hear an echoing "Irene! Irene!" and she would look almost straight down to the booming breakers, hundreds of feet below. By craning a bit more, she could see the narrow strip of rocky beach where the reluctant surf shattered, foamed, and retreated after every crash.

As Irene became accustomed to the scene, it became more alluring, magnetically drawing her to the cliff edge that she no longer feared. Then, one day as she was staring downward, the whole world seemed to fade except for that captivating tumult far below. Eyes half closed, Irene felt herself swaying forward, forward, forward, until a voice spoke from behind her:

"You would be safer back here a little way."

Irene spun about with a frightened shriek. She almost lost her footing on the brink, but the man had anticipated that before he spoke. His quick hand caught Irene's arm in an iron grip and with a strong tug, he had her a dozen feet back from the treacherous rim before she gained a glance at his serious, yet kindly face. Irene was amazed to see that the man, despite his remarkable strength and youthful vigor, was really quite elderly. Vaguely, she recalled having seen him down at the dock.

"I am Dr. Felton," the elderly man said. "I am the island physician. This week, they gave me a nice new six-year-old station wagon, the only car on Cliff Island that isn't a taxi."

Irene saw the car as they left Signal Head and started walking back toward Castle Rock. It was parked near where Cuppy always stopped.

"I need a wagon as an ambulance," explained Dr. Felton, "but in your case, it wouldn't have helped. Those rocks are a long fall down."

"I know." Irene nodded. "I shouldn't have been so near the brink. But how did you realize that I was in danger?"

"I've been coming up here every day," returned the physician, "to see a sick farmer at the far end of the island. Each day I have returned at the same time, and I have seen you looking over the cliff. Always, you seemed to be getting closer to the edge. I knew it wouldn't do."

They reached the front door of the ranch house. "Won't you come in?" Irene asked, and when the doctor nodded, she exclaimed happily:

"Why, you're one person who isn't afraid to walk in here!"

"I'm not an Islander," Dr. Felton replied. "I retired a few years ago, and the township appointed me as resident physician here. But I've heard all about Castle Rock" — his gray eyes narrowed but remained as kindly as ever —"or perhaps I haven't heard all about it. You might be able to tell me more."

Irene sat down in a big chair and began to fondle Ginger, who nestled, purring, in her lap. Though willing to talk, she parried: "Like what?"

"Well, those scratches on your neck and wrists, for one thing," said Dr. Felton. "You certainly didn't get them from this amiable pet of yours."

"I got them from an owl," Irene informed him. "A big owl, while I was saving Ginger from it. I saw big yellow eyes, coming at me from the woods—"

"And you had heard of those eyes before. They must have frightened you."

"They did," returned Irene, grateful for the doctor's understanding. "I saw a bat one night, too. I've seen floating blackness by day, and I've watched the fog make faces by night. But I'm over all such things now —"

"Except cliff walking. Other people have felt that urge, too."

"You really mean there is — there is something uncanny here?"

"I mean, don't be frightened, whatever does happen. Have you ever seen a full-rigged ship come in by full moonlight? Like a ghost ship?"

"No, but I've heard of it," admitted Irene, "and I know what it signifies. Doctor, is there anything to this vampire talk involving a Frenchman named Lesang, who lived more than three hundred years ago — and yet —"

"And yet may still live today?" Dr. Felton shook his head slowly. "It's hard to tell where legend ends and fact begins. You're a sensible young lady, so I can tell you this: I have been in many parts of the world, and I have found the same taboos, the same superstitions, the same unexplainable ailments or accidents, so often attributed to the same strange causes, that it may be they have much in common. Here on Cliff Island there have been too many odd deaths."

"I know that," agreed Irene. "I was reading about some of those cases in an old book over at the Port Clarion Library."

"I'm not talking about what was in old books," rejoined Dr. Felton. "I'm talking about what was in the newspapers during recent years. One woman was found dead in the haunted pine grove, very badly clawed. From your own experience, an owl could have been responsible, though I think in her case, the wounds were worse than any owl could inflict.

"On three different occasions, people have walked off cliffs, one from the very brink where you were today. In every case, they were apparently drawn to their doom by some baleful, indefinable influence. People have seen mammoth bats; not just small ones that they imagined were large. Other persons have disappeared entirely from Cliff Island."

It was growing late in the afternoon, and the doctor noted that although Irene was by no means nervous, she was becoming restless. He asked the reason, and when she told him she would have to go to meet her brother and his assistant, Dr. Felton offered her a ride down to the harbor in his wagon. Irene accepted, and when the *Rover* came in, she introduced Roy and Alan to the physician. The result was that they all dined together in an outdoor corner of the pier restaurant, where spray from scudding speedboats occasionally flicked over the rail.

But their conversation, unlike the gay chitchat so common on the pier, concerned very serious matters. Much of the island's mystery, including the vampire angle, became more intriguing, but also more shuddery, the further they discussed it. When Dr. Felton learned that Irene had seen actual vampire bats in South America, he smiled slightly.

"So that was where you heard how vampires dissolve into black specks and fog," said Dr. Felton. "That means those experiences could have been your imagination. Still, I feel that a vampiric influence is at work and that after failing earlier, it resorted to methods unknown to you."

"You mean like luring me to Signal Head, to push me off?"

"Not to push you off. To hold you there, teetering between "Stop" and "Go," to put it in modern terms. The invisible creature — he could be the notorious Lesang — was waiting until dusk, when his powers grow to their full. Then he could materialize into a solid being and kill you, vampire fashion. After that, he would let you fall to the rocks below, as his alibi."

It was Roy who voiced a strenuous objection:

"Come now, doctor! Don't tell us that vampires need alibis!"

"Of course they do," rejoined Dr. Felton, more serious than ever. "How could a monster like Lesang go on living — I should say existing — except through ignorance on our part? In the Middle Ages, simple-minded peasants recognized such creatures for what they really were and proceeded to get rid of them. Today, we make foolish excuses. We blame these happenings on cliff bats, on broken taillights, on owls' eyes, on everything except what they really represent, the baleful influence of a vampire!"

Dr. Felton paused to let that unnerving statement strike home. Then, he turned to Irene and said calmly:

"Since you are already under the vampiric influence, it is waiting to claim you as its next victim. When it strikes, we must be ready."

"And that," said Irene, "means that I am just a guinea pig."

"You are a very wonderful guinea pig, who can lift the curse of three centuries and still remain unharmed, if we take due precautions. Believe me, Miss Morrow" — sincerity shone in Dr. Felton's gray eyes — "if I could make myself the bait for this experiment, I would do so gladly. You know how many lives have been lost already. I can assure you that as many more will be endangered, unless we stop this fiendish creature here and now. You understand?"

"I understand. If this influence is working on me as you say, I should be the one most interested in seeing it settled forever. But must I first see that ship come in?"

"It would be helpful," stated Dr. Felton, with a nod. "Real or imaginary, it would show that you are conditioned to become the vampire's prey."

Roy and Alan stayed close to Castle Rock from that evening on. During the day, one occasionally went out in the *Rover* with Jerry; but the other was always on hand. In the evenings, both were at the ranch house, helping Irene get dinner ready, for she had to stay right there to keep a lookout for the phantom ship that, in her mind, at least, was becoming very real.

At intervals each evening, Irene would stroll out in the brilliant moonlight, sometimes as far as Signal Head. She went alone, rather than risk breaking the spell. Roy and Alan would keep watching Irene from the picture window of her studio, ready to dash out if she ventured too close to the cliff edge, or if any other danger threatened. But always, Irene was duly cautious and soon returned to the house.

Then came the night when the rising moon was at the full. Irene's hopes — or were they fears? — had reached a high point when Jerry Lane arrived in Cuppy's taxi, with word for Roy and Alan.

"The fog warnings are out," informed Jerry. "Thought you ought to know in case you want anything in Port Clarion. The only way to get there is to head out tonight."

"Nobody's going to Port Clarion," rejoined Roy. "Send Cuppy's taxi down the hill and join us in a game of three-handed pinochle."

"Because you're going to stay all night, Jerry," Alan added. "Now that you're here, we'll need you to help watch for vampires. When it's foggy, they are most apt to be around."

Irene shuddered at that recollection. Then she realized that if the fog thickened, she would never see the phantom ship.

"I'm going out to take a last look at the moonlight," Irene told the three men. "Don't worry. I'll be back."

"You'd better be," returned Roy, "and anyway, we'll watch."

The full moon had risen high enough above the hazy horizon to show the harbor clearly and vividly, even to its tiniest boats, though off shore the mist was thickening, playing odd tricks while Irene watched. In the broad path of light that stretched from the moon across the dancing wavelets to the foot of Signal Head, Irene saw a billow of white that puffed like a balloon and floated onward. It was followed by another, then a third; and as those mighty masses moved shoreward they became the great white sails of a full-rigged ship!

It had to be a ship, because Irene could see a darkish line just beneath that rose at one end to a long prow; and at the other, to the high stern that marked it as the old *Aventure*. This could be no illusion, for Irene could make out every detail of the old-square rigger that Lesang and his cutthroat crew had sailed into Middle Harbor three centuries ago!

Irene wanted to rush back to the house and tell the others, but she couldn't take her eyes from the fantastic sight for fear of losing it. On quick inspiration, she walked slowly, steadily — but knowingly — toward the edge of the cliff. That brought Roy and Alan dashing to her rescue, as she knew it would. But before they arrived, the ship with the billowing sails had reached the channel and gone out of sight within its cleft.

"I've seen the *Aventure!*" exclaimed Irene as they drew her back. "Watch for it — you'll see it come from the channel into the harbor!"

But the ship was slow in coming through, and now thick fog, stirred by the wind that could not reach the cleft, was pouring in from the sea. Then, as Irene pointed out the prow and foresail of the *Aventure* nosing from the channel, the fog came with it, enveloping it so completely that only Irene really saw it.

"That was it," said Irene. "I saw enough of it to know."

"We saw enough to believe you, sis," declared Roy. 'Let's go back to the house."

"Ship or no ship," added Alan, "we'll keep close watch tonight."

Half an hour later, Dr. Felton drove up in his station wagon and stopped at the ranch house. He was enthusiastic when Irene told him that she was sure she had sighted the phantom ship; and he was pleased because there were now three men on watch in the house.

"I'm going on over to see my patient," stated the doctor, as he was leaving. "I won't need to stop on the way back. You have everything under control."

After another hour, Irene went to the studio and tried to rest. She kept awakening fitfully, and each time, a glance at the big picture window showed that the moonlight was still clear, though fog was slowly working up over the edges of the cliff. For the dozenth time, she studied the side window and saw that its metal casements were firmly latched. Except for just a touch of fog, everything was as clearly defined as if by daylight, except that the scene was colorless.

The pine boughs were one massive black blot, though Irene could make out the tree trunks beneath them, as straight as penciled lines. To the right the rocky ground was tinted a splendid silver by the moonlight. That applied particularly to the pile of stones forming the misshapen mound, which one legend claimed was the remains of a tower built by roving Vikings on early visits to America.

Either the wisps of fog were causing the effect of motion among the silvered rocks, or Irene was seeing black spots again, for she saw something gliding, snakelike, from the rock pile toward the grove. Then she was study-ing the blackened trees again and under the moonlight's bewitchment, the world about Irene seemed to fade as she was fascinated by the sight of gleam-ing yellow eyes, emerging from that darkness.

They were growing, those eyes, moving upward, hovering above the level of the trees. Then Irene was horrified to see that the eyes belonged to a mammoth creature with outspread arms, batlike in its shape, but human in its action. For instead of flying, it was approaching in a series of long bounds, until it was at the window, filling it.

Then Irene's hands were on the sill and she was staring through the panes, not only eye to eye, but face to face with the monster from the dark. It was a man's face, tawny, shriveled like the shell of a dried coconut, with long, jagged yellow teeth showing from a lipless mouth beneath a snoutlike nose. Its hands were beside its face, scratching at the window panes with fingers that resembled claws, yet which, like the face, were of man-sized proportions.

Frozen by that leering visage, Irene could neither move nor even think. She was like a terrified bird transfixed by a serpent's gaze, for at this close range, the yellow, fiery eyes were more fearful than anything that Irene could have imagined in her worst and wildest dreams. The tightly clamped window was her one guarantee of safety; but as Irene watched, it began to yield.

Those clawish fingers were working like knife points between the sec-tions of the metal frames. First, the long nails, then the thin fingertips, then the leathery hands gained a powerful grip. The lipless mouth leered more viciously as tinkles of breaking glass told that the panes were falling from the yielding metal, which was twisting like mere cardboard.

Now the window was gone, and the ghoulish creature was doubling up, edging its head, arms, and legs in through the gap. More overpowering than that sight was the moldy odor of decay that permeated the room with a stifling pungency, choking Irene as she tried voicelessly to scream. Then the thing was upon her, those claw hands at her neck, the fang-teeth wide, as though to deliver a ferocious bite.

At last, despite the suffocating effect, the touch of those fearful claws loosened Irene's vocal cords. Her scream echoed from the studio walls and was followed by the clatter of an opening door, which projected a shaft of light from the living room. Roy's face appeared there, then Alan's, with Jerry's behind them. They saw the studio bathed in the moonlight from the picture window, with Irene in its midst, struggling with an indefinable mass that identified itself when she tried to twist away.

That was when a gloating face looked up triumphantly, just long enough to deliver a hateful snarl. Savagely, the defiant creature flung Irene from its hideous embrace, squarely at her rescuers. As Roy and Alan caught the girl, the vampire reversed its course, sprang to the window and doubled itself through and outward.

Roy gestured to Jerry to take care of Irene. Then, with drawn revolver, Roy rushed out the front door, while Alan, also armed with a gun, took the back way. They saw the monster plop from the side window, spread its wing-like arms, and take off with long zigzag bounds toward the woods. They blazed away and despite its crazy course, Roy must have clipped it in one flank, for it sprawled to one side, bobbed up again and bounded away at another angle.

But before it reached the grove, a small squad of men with shotguns surged out from beneath the trees. Seeing its course blocked, the bounding creature made for the broken rock pile ahead of the blasting shotguns. Roy and Alan closed in upon the monster there and were joined by the men from the woods, headed by Dr. Felton, who had evidently induced some farmers to set up an ambush for the vampire in the grove. But when they clambered about the rock pile, they could see no sign of the monstrous figure. The evil thing had completely disappeared.

Dr. Felton gave an anxious look, which Roy understood.

"The thing got Irene," he said, "but I am sure she is all right."

"That we had better find out."

Dr. Felton told his men to stand guard over the rock pile, while he went to the house with Roy and Alan. Irene was all right, but very faint, more from fright, however, than from loss of blood. Dr. Felton was pleased to find that her wounds were scratches only; none from the vampire's bite. He treated the wounds, and Irene soon felt well enough to go with the group to the rock pile.

On the way, Roy announced that he had shot the vampire, and Dr. Felton was highly pleased by the news.

"When these creatures take on human form," declared the physician, "they temporarily lose what might be termed their inhuman immunity. In short, in order to become solid and therefore formidable, they also become vulnerable. I am told that it takes some time for them to change from one state to another."

"Then where did Lesang go," demanded Roy, "if he didn't dematerialize?"

"He went down into that rock pile. That's where we saw him last."

"But why would he go into that old Norse ruin?"

"It isn't an old ruin," put in Alan, in answer to Roy's question. "I've talked to fishermen on other islands, and I find that some of their ancestors go way back to Lesang's time. They say it was the peasants on the island who tore the castle down and piled it stone by stone over Lesang's grave. Then they went their way of their own accord, even though the English wanted them to stay."

"So Lesang was buried here," Dr. Felton exclaimed. "You have seen snakes go into stone piles, and rats, too. We have just fought and trapped a creature that can squirm like any snake or rat. Look here!"

Dr. Felton took a long stick, thrust it down at various angles into the rocks and probed about, discovering gaps a foot or more in size.

"This rock pit," he announced, "is honeycombed with passages big enough for that monster to squirm through. We will find him under it."

No one doubted that now. They set a watch over the rock pile, day and night until the fog lifted and heavy highway construction equipment could be brought by ferry from the mainland. Then they began excavating the great stone pile. As the work proceeded, two points became apparent:

These actually were the stones from Lesang's old citadel on Castle Rock, for mortar was visible on many that were underneath. They also found a definite course of narrow but well-propped openings that twisted down through to form a tunneled route that only a rat or an inhuman vampire would have dared to follow. At last the heap was cleared, and they came across a broad, flat stone inscribed with the name, Lavignac. That rang a bell with Alan.

"The fishermen told me about the Lavignacs," he exclaimed. "They were the original family who owned the island over several generations. Lesang claimed that they had given him their title. So he was buried with them."

Beneath the slab, they found the old Lavignac family crypt, with a central burial chamber arched to form a low vault. There they identified the Lavignac family coffins, all broken apart and scattered about, their remains reduced to skeletons. That must have been the work of the usurper, for in the one unbroken coffin of the lot, lay the leathery thing with long sharp teeth and yellow eyes, that could only be Lesang the vampire, its batlike arms folded and claws clenched like fists.

From its glassy stare, Dr. Felton decided that the thing had been caught in the midst of one of its transmutations, unable to leave the near-human form that it had temporarily taken. He found the wound that Alan's bullet had inflicted and the physician pronounced the creature dead. Whether the next full of the moon would revive the vampire, Dr. Felton did not wait to learn.

Late that afternoon, the Morrows were leaving Cliff Island in the *Rover,* bound on a cruise which they hoped would help them forget the recent harrowing events. Alan Blount, who was with them, spoke quietly to Roy Morrow, who turned to Irene and said:

"Look back, sis, at Signal Head."

There, on the Head, smoke was rising. Puzzled, Irene exclaimed, "Why, somebody must have started the old beacon, the one that —"

"That once marked Lesang's arrival," completed Roy, when Irene hesitated. "But in this case, it is marking his departure."

"What do you mean by that, Roy?"

"Only that Dr. Felton, as health officer, has just decided to burn a lot of rubbish and with it, that thing we found in the old crypt."

The smoke billowed high against the afternoon sky, forming a thick black cloud that spread oddly into a weird, batlike form. A higher tuft of smoke was caught by a slight breeze and thinned sufficiently for the bright glare of the golden sun to shine through two momentary openings, giving them the semblance of a huge pair of yellow eyes.

Then the illusion faded, as did the dying smoke itself. All that remained of Lesang, the vampire from the Cliff Island crypt, was a smoldering beacon on Signal Head.

DEAD MAN'S
CHEST

DEAD MAN'S CHEST

If Lew Barton hadn't dreamed of some day owning a castle on the Hudson, he would never have seen the giant skull that was destined to bring him strange adventure.

Lew was working on the tanker *Eastern States* that made steady, plodding trips up the river from New York City to Albany. It was hot on the long, open deck of the Blister Wagon, as the crew appropriately nicknamed the tanker, so they preferred to go below and play cards; all except Lew Barton. He preferred to stay up at the bow and watch the ever-changing panorama from the Palisades on up through the Highlands and beyond.

What intrigued Lew most were the homes and mansions far up on the heights, some of them resembling European castles transplanted to America. Occasionally, Lew would look at some barren knob or towering crag and picture the kind of home that he would like to build there. But the giant skull was no such daydream, though it was partly an illusion dependent on one of the river's moods.

It was a hot Indian summer afternoon when the tanker swung around a bend into the blackness of low, glowering clouds, where a sudden breeze chopped the water into whitecaps. Instantly, the mountains were transformed to brownish monsters that loomed twice their normal size. Then, suddenly, the clouds opened and a great stream of sunlight came through the rift, striking a towering dome and turning it into a vast replica of a human skull!

Every detail was etched in light gray and deep black before Lew's riveted gaze. Foaming waves lapped the skull's jutting jaw. Above that were jagged teeth, a wide grinning row. Two matching blots formed the nose; higher, larger and much wider apart were the black hollows of the eyes. Above that, a great white bulge of rock became a forehead, which was lopped off squarely at the top, giving a flattish effect to what should have been a fully rounded crown.

Then the river squall hit with all its fury, and Lew was racing back along the tanker's deck, swept along by sheets of torrential rain. He arrived below drenched as a water rat, to the amusement of the card-playing crew. But the image of the giant skull was fixed in Lew's mind. He felt as though his sight had pierced a forbidden veil and made him a victim of the Storm King's wrath.

Often, Lew looked for the giant skull again, without result. Going up the Hudson, he seldom saw the same place at the same time and under similar conditions. Changes of season made a great difference. In the summer, the mountains were green, and many lost their rugged look. In the winter, when they were white, the river was often ice-bound, and Lew made no trips at all.

After Lew gave up his job with Eastern Tankers and switched to Wilton Barges, his trips became slower, but that didn't help. As they neared a point which Lew thought might be the one, a squall hit too soon. After they had thrashed through it and the visibility improved, Lew saw rugged cliffs and towering summits, but none of skullish formation or proportions.

Later, Lew began taking cabin cruisers up and down the Hudson and through the Barge Canal that ran across New York State to Lake Erie. In the winter, he took such craft down to Florida and soon decided that he no longer wanted a castle on the Hudson, but would settle for a cabin cruiser instead. But he needed money for overhead, upkeep, taxes, and other items.

Lew still remembered the great white skull, however, and kept on looking for it, but without any luck. By now he knew almost all the landmarks along the Hudson and had inquired into their histories, but nobody had ever heard of a huge death's head that leered downstream just when a storm was about to strike.

One autumn, Lew Barton heard from Craig Gentry, an affable young man with just enough means to loll about continuously in a good used cabin cruiser called the *Willy Nilly,* that went north and south with the birds, often with Craig as skipper and Lew as crew. So Lew stopped at his friend's tiny Manhattan apartment and found it overflowing with stacks of papers that came from half a dozen boxes of assorted sizes. Indicating the mess with a wave, Craig said:

"We're going treasure hunting, Lew. I'll pay expenses and we'll go fifty-fifty on whatever we find over that. It may take us a few years —"

"And whose treasure are we going after?"

"Captain Kidd's. I've gathered data on his entire career. He buried treasure in New England, Long Island, the Bahamas, up the Hudson —"

"Count that out, Craig. I've checked rumors about Kidd hiding treasure up the Hudson. They're either phony or all worked out. So count me out, too."

"I'll count the Hudson out, but not you. I'll tell you why."

Craig proceeded with an exhaustive and scholarly dissertation on the ways and wiles of the notorious Captain William Kidd, referring to documented accounts and even a few exhibits as he proceeded.

"Many pirates liked to kill an unsuspecting follower and bury him with their loot," declared Craig, "so that his ghost would scare off treasure hunters. But Kidd went them all one better, in a really gruesome way. He would kill a man by bashing him on the head with a bucket, a shovel or a cutlass, whichever was handiest. He would then bury the body, but bring back the head."

"The records show that?" asked Lew. "What was the idea?"

"Because ghosts, far from scaring people away, have been known to guide them to scenes of crime. Kidd was quoted as saying, 'It is the head that knows, because it contained the brain that knew.' So he kept the skulls of his victims, on the theory that the body would attract nothing more than a disturbed, unthinking ghost that could furnish no guidance whatever."

"Kidd really was kidding himself with that crackpot notion!"

"On the contrary, Kidd was far ahead of his time," argued Craig. "I have made a deep study of psychic phenomena, particularly poltergeist disturbances, where strange sounds are heard, objects are thrown about and unexplainable violence may bring injury or death to investigators. I find that they are often due to the presence of some elemental, as blundering, earthbound entities are called."

"And how can that help our treasure hunt?"

"Very effectively. The last headless victim that Kidd buried with his treasure was Jed Brock, a boatswain's mate from Kidd's ship, the *Quedagh Merchant*. And here" — triumphantly, Craig opened a square, brass-bound box measuring about a foot in each dimension and brought out an object from within it — "here is the skull of Jed Brock himself. It was brought to Kidd's trial in London, but was not produced as evidence, though it has been preserved ever since."

Lew Barton was staring at the skull as through a fog. He took it, held it at arm's length and studied it through half-closed eyes; then asked:

"You're sure this skull belonged to one of Kidd's men?"

"Absolutely," returned Craig. "See how the top of the head has been lopped off, squaring it behind the forehead? That was from a stroke of Kidd's cutlass."

"I have seen this skull before," affirmed Lew. "We are not ruling out the Hudson Highlands. Instead, we are going there first. I'll tell you why."

In detail, Lew described how he had sighted the giant skull and how ever since, he had tried to identify it with some headland, yet had failed. His account was quite as fanciful as all that Craig had related about Captain Kidd and Jed Brock, the bosun's mate. But Craig not only accepted it; he enthused over it.

"It fits Kidd to the dot!" exclaimed Craig. "His maps were false, his codes faked. He even buried some treasure openly, the part that he was willing for his backers to find as their share and think that it was all he had. Instead of a treasure map, Kidd fixed this skull to look exactly like one that he saw staring down the Hudson. You were lucky enough to spot the same giant skull, Lew."

"Then you think that's where Kidd buried the rest of his loot?"

"Certainly. Right in back of that flat spot that you noted on the cliff top. We'll take Jed's skull with us and look for the treasure in your skull."

"Don't call it my skull," rejoined Lew grimly, "until we find it."

They started on their quest in Craig's cabin cruiser. Lew was able to limit the stretch of river where he had seen the giant skull to a matter of about a dozen miles; but each time they covered it, they were disappointed. The season was right, but none of the hills fitted Lew's description.

"I've been over this a dozen times," declared Lew, "always wishing I could be my own skipper and try it again. Now I have that chance, but no luck!"

"We'll keep right on trying," assured Craig. "The harder it is to find, the smarter it shows Kidd was, making it all the more likely that he buried his treasure there. Lots of his logbooks start with comments on the weather, so that fits with the fact that the skull can only be seen under certain conditions."

For three days, they toiled up and down that stretch of river, trying new angles when rounding different points, until suddenly, during one late afternoon try, Lew pointed over a high ridge that flanked the Hudson and exclaimed:

"Storm clouds! Speed up, Craig!"

Craig gave it full speed ahead. They cut close past the point and shot straight out into the channel just as the high clouds opened above a low, approaching squall, as Lew had seen it once and only once before. Gleaming in the sunlight was the giant skull, its grinning teeth, hollow nose, and blackened eye-sockets forming the face of a thousand-foot bluff, its flattish top spoiling the contour of its otherwise rounded dome. Detail for detail, the mammoth death's head was a replica of the human skull that Craig snatched from its box and held at arm's length for comparison — the skull of Jed Brock, the bosun's mate!

Then the squall blotted out the cliff, and the cruiser was tossed like a cork on huge, churning waves that seemed to gush up from the riverbed itself. Never, even on ocean trips, had the *Willy Nilly* met with such a test. But Craig managed to weather it and dock the craft in the shelter of a little cove, where he and Lew danced in glee after the storm had passd.

Next, they brought out a topographical map and found the towering cliff that had so briefly disclosed its skullish secret. It was called Round Hill, and though it was skirted by a highway halfway up, its overhanging brow was too steep to scale. The best way to reach the top was to go around by a back road called Spruce Lane that led up from White Brook Hollow, then take an old trail that led past some circular pits called the Granite Bowls, and on up beside the brook to High Ridge, directly in back of Round Hill.

They had brought along hiking clothes, so they put them on and went ashore, carrying bags and equipment with them. They walked to an old river tavern midway between a little-used landing with its weather-beaten pier and the railroad tracks that were higher up on the Hudson's bank. They had dinner at the inn and then stayed overnight to make it appear that they were actually hikers, interested only in tramping the local trails.

The next morning was foggy, so there was no chance of going out on the river for another look at the giant skull. Anyway, they were eager to get to their new goal, so they started on their hike, loaded with their equipment, which included the square box containing the precious skull. It took longer than they thought, for it was mid-afternoon when they finally clambered past a little spring that marked the source of White Brook and came to High Ridge. Over that final hump, they continued to the flat ledge that so resembled the lopped-off skull of poor Jed Brock.

The ledge was perfectly smooth and level, forming practically a solid stone foundation. It offered a fine view down the Hudson, but they were too far back now from the brow of the cliff to notice any of the skull formation below But those, in Craig's opinion, did not matter. He was more interested in studying the ridge behind them. But all they found there was rough ground, small jutting rocks and scraggly bushes, a dull ending for a treasure hunt.

With dark, they pitched a pup tent at the rear of the flat ledge and tried to go to sleep, with the box containing Jed's skull between them. Distant lightning flashes and muffled rolls of thunder were ominous in the offing.

"I don't like it here," declared Lew. "We're up where thunderheads gather, right in the Storm King's lap. This may be a rough night before we're through."

"Rougher maybe than you think," added Craig. Then, cryptically: "When you deal with elementals, you are apt to rouse the elements."

"You mean having Jed's skull along might kick up a storm?"

"It did down on the river, didn't it? That squall nearly sunk us."

"Well, yes — but it had to be stormy when we saw the giant skull."

"That's it, Lew. The two are interlocked. You can't get around it."

Lew didn't agree with Craig's notions, which he was beginning to think were quite as crackpot as any ever held by the notorious Captain Kidd. But rather than carry the argument further, Lew compromised by saying:

"Anyway, Craig, we'll stick it out tonight, so we can hunt treasure tomorrow!"

They stuck it out, almost until dawn, when the Storm King struck with wild rage. The lashing wind swept away the pup tent and next, Lew and Craig were clinging to the rocks, wrapped in their blankets and their ponchos, while lightning flashed and split trees within a hundred yards of them and the thunder roared above the fury of the gale. They managed to gain partial shelter from bushes where they propped up the tattered pup tent amid a tremendous downpour.

Then, when their hopes were at their lowest ebb and it seemed that no terror could be worse than the tempest raging about them, the climax came, in the form of a sight that buoyed their hopes, yet imbued them with new fear. From the ridge behind the fringe of the ledge where they were squatted, they saw a clumsy figure crawling upward as though emerging from the ground itself. Craig mistook it for a bear until Lew gasped, "It's human — yet it isn't human!"

Human in shape, yes, for a vivid lightning flash showed it to be a bulky figure clad in the clothes of an old sailor. It was inhuman, though, because in the brilliance of the lightning's flare, they could see right through the hulking figure to the background of the trees beyond the ridge!

Seldom had a ghost revealed itself under such singular circumstances. A ghost in broad daylight would have been startling enough; but in this pitch-black, rain-deluged darkness, the recurring appearance of the thing amid the blinding lightning streaks was beyond all sane belief. With each flicker, it loomed closer from the hump. After each blackout, instead of appearing in luminous form, it was gone, only to be back when the lightning blazed again.

Then, the fateful form reared to its full height, its arms raised in a menacing gesture, as though ready to hurl itself upon the staring men, while the terrific thunder reverberated like a peal of doom. In the glare that streaked the entire sky, the two men saw the most startling, horrifying thing of all.

The ghost of the mountain ridge had no head!

That sight could have caused the most stout-hearted viewer to turn and run, regardless of consequences, which in this case would have meant going over the front edge of the flat-topped ledge and down the bulging bluff to certain doom beside the river below. In fact, both Lew and Craig were coming to their feet, ready to flee, when they saw that macabre, terrifying touch of the missing head. To them, it had the opposite effect of what Captain Kidd had anticipated. Sight of a headless ghost stirred their numbed senses, bringing home the realization that this was the moment they had wanted.

"It's Jed Brock!" shouted Craig. "He's not after us — he is coming for his head!"

"Then let him have it!" Frantically, Lew was tugging at the box clamps. The lid came open and Lew gave the box a tilt. "Here it is!"

Craig caught the skull as it rolled out, held it poised for a breathless moment as the thunder finished a tremendous roll and the lightning flared again, showing the headless horror ready for its final lunge. Then Craig flung the skull with all his might, straight at the weird shape that had now materialized to completely solid form.

What happened then was strangest of all. The skull stopped in mid-air as it hit the grotesque figure; then dropped straight down. At the same instant, the materialized form vanished. The effect was elusive, for the lightning flickered at that moment, but when it flared again, there was no sign of the ghost or the skull. Both were gone, like the sudden, earsplitting thunderclap that came like a monstrous note of their departure!

Lew and Craig stayed huddled while the lightning lessened and the thunder rolled in dwindling fashion down the Hudson. The rain reduced to a drizzle and the entire storm abated, as though its work was done. In the light of the distant flares, they saw no further sign of the vanished ghost. Then dawn was streaking the sky and daylight brought the surety that the two treasure seekers had felt the night before.

Ghost or no ghost, the skull that Craig had flung in sheer, stark desperation could not have gone far. The slope behind the hump was studded with too many bushes, roots, and rocks for the thing to roll on down the path that followed the course of White Brook. Yet when Lew and Craig reached the exact spot where the skull had fallen as though striking something solid, there was no sign at all of the grisly object.

Could Jed's ghost have grabbed it and fled with it? If so, there was no reason why it should have gone far. Thinking in such terms, Lew, looking toward the beginning of the slope, suddenly pointed and exclaimed:

"Look!"

Little rivulets still were trickling from the heavy rain. Some were joining, others were forming pools. But one tiny stream was pouring down beneath a low rock, into a hole from which it did not emerge.

"The skull!" exclaimed Craig. "It rolled down in there!"

Together, Lew and Craig shoved away the rock and found a larger cavity. With a pickaxe and spade that they had brought, they worked frantically, digging through loose earth, prying out imbedded stones. Finally, the pickaxe struck metal, the rusted lid of an iron chest! As they dug around the coffer to release it from the roots that had gripped it over many years, they came across the bones of a human skeleton, all except the skull.

But when they finally managed to haul the heavy chest up from the hole, a loose object dislodged itself from between two stones that had trapped it, and tumbled down into the pit to join the skeleton remains. That rolling object, which for the moment was very like a living thing, was the missing skull of Jed Brock, reunited at last with the body to which it belonged.

For the coffer, when Lew and Craig opened it, proved definitely to be the dead man's chest. The name of Jed Brock, boatswain's mate of the *Quedagh Merchant,* was inscribed within its its lid. Captain Kidd, penurious to the last degree, had used his victim's own chest as a treasure coffer, possibly believing that it would further encourage Jed's headless ghost to haunt the spot. In the chest, Lew and Craig found Spanish dubloons, British sovereigns, French louis d'or and other currency which at the present value of gold were worth thousands of dollars, with added value as rare coins. There were jewels, too, that Kidd had looted from ships in the Indian Ocean; in all, a haul sufficient to guarantee each treasure finder a few new cabin cruisers and perhaps even a castle on the Hudson.

But it was after they had dragged their find down from the mountain and stowed the chest, treasure and all, aboard the *Willy Nilly,* that Lew and Craig began to realize how really lucky they had been. As Craig headed the cruiser out into the river and swung slightly upstream to clear the cove, he gestured toward the towering bulge of Round Hill and asserted:

"I sure called the turn. Kidd saw the mountain that looked like a skull, so he buried his treasure on top after making Jed help him lug it up there."

"If Kidd figured it looked like a skull," retorted Lew., who was studying the mountain, "he really had a wild, fantastic imagination."

"No wilder than yours. You saw the grinning mouth, the nose, the eyes, even the flattened top of the head. You pointed them out to me."

"Yes. But they weren't here when Kidd came up the river. Look."

As Craig looked, Lew continued:

"I know now why I couldn't see the skull except in just the right light and at the proper distance. As it gets close, it loses its effect. There's the mouth — see what it is?"

"Why — why" — Craig was stammering in amazement — "it's the posts of the old pier from riverboat days and the windows of the tavern and the old buildings spreading out from it. They haven't been here more than a hundred and fifty years — and that was long after Kidd's time!"

"Right, and the nose above came later than that," chuckled Lew. "It's formed by the twin tunnels where the railroad tracks go through the hill."

Utterly confounded, Craig looked higher and exclaimed:

"And those eyes — why they are part of the highway that curves around the mountain! They are the parking spaces that were built as overlooks, so tourists can stop and see the river view!"

"And away up above," added Lew, "is that flat place we mistook for a natural ledge. It is ground they leveled off and put in a concrete foundation for a new airplane beacon. That was several years ago, and here is a new map that has it marked as Signal Tower B, but it hasn't been built yet."

"Steamboats — railroads — automobiles — airplanes" — Craig listed them in order — "none of them were ever dreamed of, when Captain Kidd sailed up here with his treasure. What an imagination he had!"

"Maybe he just dreamed of the future," speculated Lew, "as we dreamed of the past. Anyway, Kidd's treasure is our treasure now."

"Thanks to Jed Brock," reminded Craig Gentry. "We started on this hunt with a dead man's skull, remember?"

"Yes," agreed Lew Barton, "and we're coming back with the dead man's chest."

THE THIRTEENTH STORY

14

12

11

10

9

8

13

7

6

5

4

3

2

1

Obituaries

x **Cause of Death**

Of Dolhon & Cha

er, Lady
rshall,
of death of
said the ba

(UPI)—Official determination of the cau
was made yesterday by the coroner, w
to death on a piece

d an autopsy, said that

THE THIRTEENTH STORY

Dolban and Chadley, Importers, were located in the Longview Building, one of those quickie skyscrapers that sprouted up during the Roaring Twenties and managed to survive even after modern glass, chrome, and plastic construction began to dominate the Manhattan skyline. Twenty-odd stories high, the Longview Building stood on a plot of ground the size of a postage stamp in comparison. It was tall, but so thin that each story had only space enough for an office in the front, a display room in the middle and a storage room in back, plus the single shaft of an elevator, which after many years, was converted to the automatic type.

The building was particularly suited to firms like Dolban and Chadley, because it gave them a whole story to themselves, without too high a rental. Homer Dolban, the senior partner, was a little wizened old man, who never smiled nor said much. Luke Chadley, the junior partner, was much younger and not only a glib, forceful talker, but a human dynamo. Like almost everybody else in the Longview Building, they seemed to know their business.

The only problem that Howard Crayle, the owner of the building, ever had with Dolban and Chadley was when they signed their lease. Dolban looked over the fine print and was willing to accept it, but Chadley, in booming, loud-voiced style, took exception to the very first clause, as he exclaimed:

"You've given us the fourteenth story! What about the numbering in this building?" he demanded sharply. "Does it have a thirteenth story?"

"Why, no," admitted Crayle. "It has long been a regular custom to leave out thirteen, when numbering the stories in a building."

"I'm not talking about custom," stormed Chadley. "I'm talking as a customer. This building is twenty stories high, so it must have a thirteenth story."

"Well," conceded Crayle, "technically it does have. But —"

"That's all I want to know," snapped Chadley. "Then this fourteenth story that you are forcing on us is actually the thirteenth story."

"No, no. It really is the fourteenth —"

"Don't tell me! I can count. I don't like the number thirteen whether it is real or disguised." Chadley turned to Dolban. "We won't sign, will we?"

The senior partner agreed that they wouldn't.

"The only other vacant story is the twelfth," declared the building owner, "but you may not want that either, because you see —"

"We'll see if we like it," put in Chadley, "and if we do we'll take it. But don't try to tell me that thirteen isn't an unlucky number. If it wasn't, there wouldn't be so many buildings without a thirteenth story. But one from fourteen still leaves thirteen; that's why we won't take the fourteenth story."

That settled it. Dolban and Chadley looked at the twelfth story, found it the same as the rest, and took it. But Howard Crayle couldn't help wondering why a man as keen-mannered as Luke Chadley should be so superstitious.

There was a very deep and totally unsuspected reason behind it Secretly Chadley was plotting a very dastardly but very clever long-range crime. He intended to do away with his aged partner when the right time came; and Chadley didn't want to worry about any silly jinx that might cause him to make a slip at the crucial moment. Having gotten the notion of the thirteenth story out of his system, he promptly dismissed it from his mind and concentrated on the project that lay ahead: murder.

The way Dolban and Chadley operated was this: Homer Dolban, through long years as an importer, had connections all over the world and made excellent deals. One month, the storeroom would be stocked with Swiss watches; the next month with Australian kangaroo leather, and so on. Chadley, making the rounds of the wholesalers, would often have the goods sold at a fancy profit as soon as the shipments arrived, for Dolban had an uncanny way of importing only the type of merchandise that was both needed and wanted by the trade.

With their profits, Dolban and Chadley bought other merchandise and finally accumulated a million dollars' worth of one very special item — diamonds. Old Dolban kept them in a wall safe in the office. And now, with the lease running out after a few years, he decided that this was the time to sell them and turn the profits into a whole lot more. Dolban preferred to go to California and make sales to jewelers there, while Chadley favored Europe. However, in this case, Dolban, as senior partner, had the entire say; not only that, their private agreement stipulated that only twenty-five percent of the total proceeds were to go to Chadley, as junior partner.

So Dolban, who alone knew the combination of the wall safe, decided to stay until about nine o'clock and then leave the office in time to catch his ten o'clock plane for Los Angeles. Chadley, without breathing a word to his partner, booked passage on a nine o'clock airliner to Europe for the same evening and reserved vacation accommodations at a resort hotel in the Swiss Alps.

Never had Chadley shown any dissatisfaction regarding his arrangement with Dolban. He had let Pop, as he called his partner, have full control. But they had kept their business so closely to themselves that if something happened to one, the other could walk out with all the assets and nobody would be wiser.

Something was to happen to Dolban tonight. To make sure it did, Chadley went up to the office with Pop after they finished a pleasant dinner together at a neighborhood restaurant. They entered the Longview Building and pressed the button for the elevator. It came down dark, as Lubin, the janitor, usually turned off its lights at night and Chadley often did the same. Dolban entered, turned on the light switch and pressed button Number 12.

When they reached their floor, Dolban stepped out first. Chadley, following, did two things. He pressed the top button to send the car up above the twentieth floor. Then he planted a gummed block of hard rubber against the end of the heavy door to the elevator shaft. When it closed, it did not go quite all the way shut.

After they chatted awhile in the office, Chadley said to Dolban:

"Look, Pop. I want to see some friends on Long Island, so why don't I take you in a cab to the airport, right now? We can talk out there until your plane time."

Dolban agreed. He opened the safe, took out the diamonds and put them in a very special brief case. He went out to the elevator, carrying the brief case. Chadley followed. About to press the button for the car, he asked:

"Your ticket, Pop. Are you sure you have it?"

Dolban set the brief case against the wall, found his ticket in his pocket, and nodded. He wasn't watching Chadley, who now pressed the door edge with his fingers, drew the door to the elevator shaft open, and at the same time reclaimed the hard rubber block. He picked up the brief case with his other hand and said:

"Here is the elevator, Pop, and here is your brief case. Somebody must have turned off the light, so step right in and turn it on again."

Dolban reached for the brief case and stepped squarely into the yawning blackness of the shaft. As he suddenly realized that the car wasn't there, the old man wheeled about and grabbed for Chadley, who expected it and knew that if Dolban's fingers gained a grip, it would be a death clutch. But Chadley was prepared for that. He swung the brief case hard against Dolban's face, literally sweeping him back into the shaft, like a figure of straw. That brutal blow was calculated to break any death grip, and with it, Chadley swung full about. He had planned that, too, for all in the same action, he grabbed the big door and gave it a tug that sent it clanging shut.

For one grim, prolonged moment, Chadley shut his eyes to black out not only the scene but all memory of what had happened. He was leaning against the closed door, as he had so often pictured he would be. In closing, it had cut off any sound of Dolban's last scream, as well as any crash from below. So now, to Chadley, it was just something that hadn't happened; at least, not yet. It was time for Chadley to be leaving for his plane to Europe; not for another hour or more would Dolban have been on his way to the airport. Later, people would think that the accident happened at that time.

Coolly, Chadley pressed the button that brought the elevator car down to the twelfth floor. It arrived there, lighted, and Chadley waved back to the office, calling, "Good-bye, Pop!" as though Dolban were still there. Then he went down in the elevator, turned off its light, and went out by the street door as he always did. Next, he was in a cab, telling the driver to take him out to Idlewild and to hurry.

Only the driver didn't hurry. They moved along at a steady, constant pace, while the cabby kept soothing Chadley in a monotone:

"Listen, friend, you never get nowhere, thinking ahead. Don't worry about places before you get there, or you'll be back where you started. Like with me, the time I went through a dead end and plunged into the river. I was in a hurry to get back to town, and do you know what? That's where I thought I was! All that evening I was at a party; then I was home and getting up the next morning to take a shower — and *splash!* I was in the river and it was the night before! That jarred me back to sense and I got the door open and came up. But that could have been the end of me and I'd never have known it until that last moment!"

The driver went on and on, but so did the cab. And suddenly, they were at the airport, with plenty of time for Chadley to make his plane. Then he was clutching Dolban's precious brief case — Chadley's own brief case, now! — while he was letting his other luggage be weighed. From there, Chadley next found himself at the gate, waiting for it to open, while he heard two army fliers talking nearby. One was telling of a harrowing experience.

"Believe me," the flier said, "when that chute wouldn't open, there was just one moment when I wished hard that something would save me. I must have blacked out, for I thought for sure the thing did open. There I was, floating down to the ground; then I was in the truck, going back to base; next I was getting my discharge, which isn't due for a year from now. Then I was in a bathing suit, roaring along in a speedboat — and *bang!* We hit a snag or something. There was a jolt and I was looking up at that chute just as it opened like a big balloon, putting me right back where I was when all that crazy chain of thought began. If I had hit the ground instead, with no chute, it would have been the same sort of shock, only it would have been the end of me!"

The two fliers drifted away, and now Chadley was on the airliner, dozing comfortably as they spanned the Atlantic. Next, he was going through customs in the same way, letting bowing officials see that the brief case contained nothing but papers, because all the diamonds were in a very clever double lining where Dolban had carefully placed them while Chadley had watched him.

Finally, Chadley was checking in at the Swiss resort hotel, where he was given Suite 3B, which he had reserved. Each day, he went out on the veranda, lolling around, having an attendant bring him the New York newspaper as soon as it came in. Always, he was looking at a distant, snow-clad mountain with rocky ledges. One day, two men paused near Chadley's deck chair. One had a limp and leaned heavily on a cane, as he pointed to the distant summit.

"That's where I went off," he said. "From that high ledge. We were on the way down when the rope broke. Just as I went over the brink, I seemed to catch myself. Then everything was all right and we came down the mountain, laughing at my near-accident. We were here in the hotel, I was at the dance that night and a big banquet a week later. Then, all of a sudden, I was overwhelmed by a huge avalanche —"

"That must have been when you hit the snowbank!" exclaimed the other.

"Exactly," the first man said. "You can see it there, a thousand feet below the ledge. I took it at a slant, and that's what saved me. But if I'd hit those rocks instead, my crazy dream would have ended as it did, but permanently!"

The two mountain climbers were gone and the attendant was stopping beside Chadley, saying, "Your New York newspaper, sir!" and Chadley glanced at the front page as he always did. His gaze was riveted by two photos, side by side, Dolban's and his own. With them was the caption:

PARTNERS IN LIFE — PARTNERS IN DEATH

Something seemed to crash Luke Chadley head on. His whole dream sequence ended, in an utter and absolute blackout.

A minute or so later, the attendant came back, found the newspaper flapping in an empty deck chair. He picked it up, carried it into the lobby and handed it to the clerk, who read English and liked American newspapers. The clerk saw the name, Luke Chadley, and exclaimed:

"My word, that's the name of the man who reserved Suite 3B beginning a week ago. No wonder he never came to take it."

"He looks a lot like the man out in the deck chair," commented the attendant, studying Chadley's photo. "What happened to this fellow?"

"He fell down an elevator shaft in New York," replied the clerk, "trying to save the older man you see here. They were partners and when the bodies were found, they were clinging tightly together, each with a hold upon a brief case that contained their whole fortune, a million dollars' worth of very fine diamonds. My, how unlucky they were!"

Those were the very words that Howard Crayle was saying in New York when he discussed the sad fate of two of the best tenants who had ever rented space in the Longview Building. Crayle was talking to Lubin, the janitor, as they studied the elevator and tried to figure why it hadn't been at the twelfth story when Dolban and Chadley thought they were stepping into it.

"My, how unlucky they were!" Crayle exclaimed. "But Chadley had a hunch that something of the sort might happen. He wouldn't take the fourteenth story, because he thought it was the thirteenth."

Lubin's face went puzzled.

"But isn't the fourteenth really the thirteenth story?"

"Not in this building." Crayle pointed to the button panel in the elevator. "See that letter M? It stands for Main Floor, which is really the first story. So count the rest going up: one will be two; two will be three; and so on. Stop when you get to thirteen."

Lubin counted and stopped on the number 12 as he announced:

"Thirteen! Say, but that's only the twelfth — and that was where Dolban and Chadley had their office!"

"You are right," responded Crayle sadly. "Theirs was really the thirteenth story."